PRAISE FOR SARAH A. BAILEY

"*Heathen & Honeysuckle* is a second-chance masterpiece. **An absolute must-read.**"

- *USA Today* Bestselling Author Cali Melle

"*Wicked & Wildflower* is romance at its most breathtaking–emotion-packed and **brimming with delicious tension.** Sarah always creates a world you can get lost in, with characters so real it feels like they're sitting next to you, and *Wicked & Wildflower* is no exception. **Simply unputdownable.**"

- Bailey Hannah, author of *Alive & Wells*

"*Pacific Shores* is anything but fictional. It feels like a home away from home in the form of beautiful friendships, relatable characters, and **emotions that burst off the page**. This series is forever cemented in my soul."

- Emily Tudor, author of *The Road Not Taken*

"A perfect blend of **carefully crafted plot** and **irresistible heat.** Sarah is a master at creating relatable characters that you can't help but fall in love with...Her writing is both passionately sexy and **deeply heartfelt**, and *Wicked & Wildflower* is no exception. **Pure perfection.**"

- Ambar Cordova, author of the *Baker Oaks Series*

wicked &
WILDFLOWER

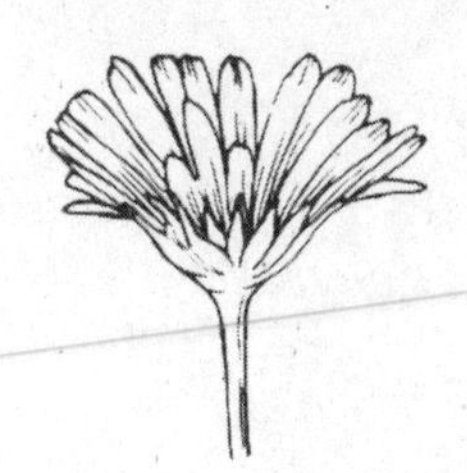

wicked & WILDFLOWER

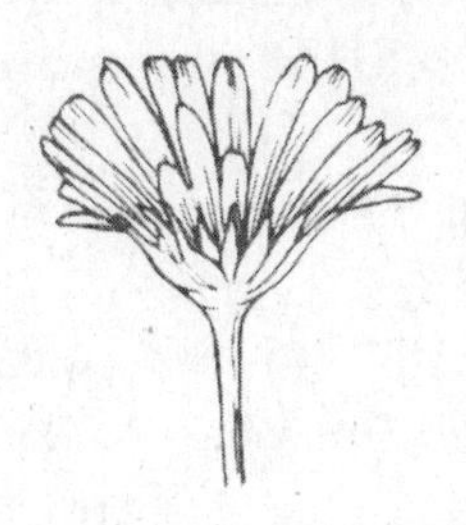

SARAH A. BAILEY

Page & Vine
An Imprint of Meredith Wild LLC

Paperback ISBN: 978-1-964264-18-9

For all the wicked wildflowers out there:
Your worth is invaluable.

And if you still need convincing, turn the page.
Everett is waiting for you.

CONTENT WARNING

Wicked & Wildflower is intended for readers 18+ and includes heavy emotional and explicit content.

Detailed warnings can be found at:
www.sarahabaileyauthor.com

One – Wicked

I'm About To Start Barking

"The blonde at the pool table." I nod toward the end of the bar. "What's she drinking?"

Emilio raises a brow at me. "Vodka soda. Why?"

"Dude, come on." Ryan shakes his head. "She's clearly on a date."

"You're right. She is on a date, and she's *clearly* bored out of her mind." My two friends follow my gaze across the room and watch as the pretty girl bites back a yawn. We catch her subtle eye roll as the man she's with shoots the cue ball toward a pair of stripes at the center but misses tragically, knocking one of her solids into the pocket instead.

He lets out a forced laugh. "I'm a bit rusty, I guess. I used to play all the time in college, though, and I couldn't be beat. Did I mention I went to Cornell?"

Emilio, Ryan, and myself suppress our own groans as we turn back to the bar. The two of them return to their conversation, but my eyes stay on her.

She laughs lightly, feigning interest in the stories of his college years as she misses her next hit. "I'm not very good either."

She's lying.

The way she kicked her hip out and bent her elbow was unnatural. She was forcing herself into a poor position. If I had to guess, I'd say she could play circles around the douchebag, but for some reason, she's dumbing herself down. That tells me they don't know each other well. This is their first date, perhaps even their first time meeting.

Which makes me feel significantly less guilty about the fact that I'm going to steal her away.

I snap my fingers at Emilio. "Can you send her another vodka soda and put it on my tab?"

"No," the bartender says without looking at me.

"Don't be an asshole, Everett," Ryan mutters.

I look back and forth between my two friends. Ryan runs a hand through his rich brown hair, brown eyes stare back at me unamused, while Emilio's dark features are narrowed at me like I'm some kind of pariah. I hold my hands up in surrender. "I'm not an asshole. I'm saving her. She looks miserable."

Ryan scoffs behind his beer. "I'm sure that's what it is. A selfless act that has nothing to do with how hot she is."

I mean, of course it has a *little* to do with how hot she is.

She's fucking stunning.

Shoulder-length blond hair. Red manicured nails are constantly tucking her straight strands behind her ears so she can show off her pretty, pert nose and full pink lips.

The way her dark-washed denim skirt hugs her ample hips is enough to put all the atoms in my body on alert, let alone the mile-long, smooth legs beneath it.

"Jesus, Everett. You're like a panting dog." Ryan laughs at me.

"I'm about to start barking."

"All right, I'm gonna send her over another drink, but only because I can't wait to watch her throw it in your face," Emilio chimes as he turns around and begins pouring.

I let Ryan tell me about his most recent work-related chaos. As the county's deputy sheriff, he's got no shortage of crazy shit to talk about, but I'm only half listening.

I smile to myself as Emilio walks the drink over to the blonde at the pool table. Her eyes light up as she accepts it, and Emilio nods his head toward me. She fights a smile as her pretty cheeks pinken. I raise my glass and nod when her date's head whips around, shooting daggers at me.

He puffs himself up, but that only gets him to about half my size. Balling his hands into fists, he begins to make his way toward me, when she places a hand on his shoulder. She whispers in his ear as his eyes dart back and forth between her and me. Finally, he nods and steps back.

She looks at me, lifting an eyebrow as she assesses me. It's clear she likes what she sees. Whether it's my tattooed arms on display beneath my T-shirt, my beard, or my brown eyes that I've been told more than a few times are quite easy to get lost in, it's clear the way she's staring at me is a stark contrast to how she's been looking at her date. Her steps are slow and calculated as she moves across the bar, a sly smile on her face.

Slipping into the seat next to me, she slides the vodka soda I bought her in front of me. Her hair sways as she sits down, and I can now tell it's naturally a dishwater blond, but she's got platinum highlights that accentuate the dreamy shade of her storm-blue eyes. "Didn't anyone ever tell you it's impolite to hit on another man's date?"

I slide the drink back to her. "I think what you meant to say is 'thank you.'"

She lets out a surprised huff as she shakes her head, and I notice her hiding a smile on her lush, glossy lips as she tucks her hair behind her ear once more, revealing smooth cheeks dusted with freckles. "You're forward." Turning to her side, she faces me head-on. "Was it that obvious?"

"Yes." I lift my beer to my lips. "For future reference, if you've got to fake your pool skills—or anything else, really—in order to accommodate a man, he's probably a waste of your time."

She hums. "And what are your pool skills like?"

I slowly raise one brow at her. "You wanna find out?"

Her eyes lock on mine—kaleidoscope shades of blue—as she slowly extends the glass to her mouth and takes a sip. I can't tell if it's a challenge or an acceptance. She looks down at her lap as she sets her drink on the bar. "It's a blind date. Not my idea." She chuckles to herself. "I'm new in town, and I was pressured to get out of the house, but I'm really not interested in getting to know anyone."

"What are you interested in?" I ask, leaning closer. I can't help it. It's instinct.

She smells like coconuts and something tropical.

Her gaze flickers to me again, taking a short moment to look me up and down before settling on my face. She studies me like I'm a risk, and she can't decide if it's worth taking. "If I'm being honest, a good lay who won't call me afterward."

I can't help the laugh that bursts out. Her face remains completely blank as she studies me. It was the last thing I was expecting to come from her mouth, but I'm not at all disconcerted.

I call over to Emilio, who's standing with his back to the bar, pretending like he isn't listening. "Can you get us two shots of—" I turn to look at her.

She contemplates for a moment before shrugging. "Fireball."

"Fireball?" I scoff.

A salacious smile tilts up her glossy pink lips. "Felt like the night needed a little spice."

Emilio slides the two shots across the bar, and I catch them, handing one to her and grabbing the other for myself. "I have a feeling it's about to get spicier." I raise my glass toward her. "Cheers—" I pause. "I didn't get your name, *cariño*."

She hesitates for a moment, glancing around the bar. Her eyes dart everywhere except her date, who's glaring at us. Finally, her head swivels back to meet my gaze. "Are you about to offer me the good lay I was needing tonight?"

I try and fail to fight my smile. "I didn't plan on being quite so *forward* about it, but yeah. I was definitely gonna try." *Fuck*. She has got me on my toes. Nothing about the way this exchange has gone is how I typically play things, but it's working nonetheless.

I'm normally much more composed. In control. I've got a process that works. Something tells me my game wouldn't work on her at all, that she hardly thinks I'm worth her time, and yet, she's essentially offering me the only thing I'm ever looking for anyway. This woman is throwing me for a loop, and I don't even know her name.

She knocks her shot glass against mine quickly and downs the Fireball, chasing it with her vodka soda. "One more, Emilio," she says through a hiss as she holds a finger up.

My friend looks over at me, eyes wide. I take my shot as he hands her another, and she tosses that one back too. I watch her shiver as the liquor courses through her veins. She squints her eyes as she gets it down before facing me again. "No names."

"What?"

She shoves her empty glasses across the bar, crossing her legs. "No names. Nothing that can tie us together later. You're hot, I need to get laid, and I'm assuming you won't complain about that offer. So, we can fuck, but I don't want to know you."

I hear Ryan cover up a cough next to me. Emilio leaves the bar area entirely, I'm assuming to hide his laughter. I've never had a woman—or a man, for that matter—tell me they had no interest in *knowing my name* before.

She studies my face with that intensity again, devoid of emotion. She's all business. But as I drown in her blue eyes and heat creeps across my flesh at the sight of her smooth skin and soft lips, I decide to go for it.

If I don't take my chance with this woman now, I'm going to spend forever wondering what if. She may look at me like I'm a risk, but I know for sure she's a challenge, one I'll gladly accept.

"Fuck it." She smiles as I kick my barstool behind me and grab her hand. "I've got a place we can go." She jumps out of her seat and begins to follow me before we're stopped short.

"What the fuck?" her date shouts from the other side of the room.

Shit. I forgot about him.

I pause, releasing her hand, but she grips mine harder. I turn around and watch her flash him an apologetic smile. "I'm so sorry, but..." Her shoulders meet her ears as she sucks in a breath. "When you know, you know. Y'know?"

"You're kidding me, right?" he seethes.

I nod toward Emilio, who's watching us like one of his soap operas. "Take all her drinks and put them on my tab." I nod toward her date. "Sorry, man."

She giggles as I haul her off behind the bar and into the back office. Emilio will be on my ass about it later, but I don't care. I enter the keypad on his door and wait for it to click before I push it open. He's got a black leather couch next to the door and his desk across from it. Other than that, the room consists of a standing lamp in the corner, an old-fashioned bar against the window, and a rug in the center of the floor.

"Is this your bar?" she asks.

"No, but the owner owes me a favor." He doesn't, really, but I do change that fucker's oil for free, so he can deal.

She hums as I shut the door behind us, spinning her so she's pressed against it. My chest crushes hers, and I can feel the softness of her full breasts. I place both hands on the door above us, dropping my head so my nose hovers just over hers.

"You sure about this?" I ask.

Her breathing increases at our proximity, her cheeks flush, and she pulls her lip beneath her teeth. Her blue eyes are hooded and hungry, but there is a shyness to them too. The look in them tells me this isn't something she does often, and fuck, if that doesn't turn me on more. It's her attraction to me causing her to be this reckless.

"Let me check."

One hand slowly finds its way beneath my T-shirt. Her skin is cool against mine as her fingers brush my stomach, traveling downward. I keep my hands exactly where they are, afraid I'll do something she doesn't like.

I hiss as she brushes against my cock, hard as steel beneath my jeans. She brings her other hand up my neck, gripping the back of it and pulling me down. I fall into her like gravity. Squeezing my dick, she whispers, "I have to see what I'm working with here."

"Ah, baby," I rasp against her lips. "Let me show you."

Before she can get in another word, my mouth is on hers.

Two – Wicked

Normally, I Can Only Do That To Myself

"Lift your legs for me, *cariño*."

She immediately listens as she hooks her leg around my waist.

"You listen so well," I say into the soft skin of her neck as I nip and pull at her flesh. I feel her tighten around my cock at that. She likes my praise.

She was in control at the bar, played the game well, but it's clear she doesn't do this often. Neither do I. While I've had my fair share of casual hook-ups and one-night stands, I've never done so without learning my partner's name, and rarely without taking them back to my place or theirs.

Watching this fierce and outspoken woman turn timid and pliant in my arms the moment we were behind closed doors was a surprise—albeit, not an unpleasant one. I've always liked taking the lead in the bedroom. Or, well, office in this case.

I drag my lips across her collarbone, she claws at my back, and I fuck her hard against the door. She doesn't hold back the moans that fly from her pretty lips as I hit just the right spot inside her.

The moment the door clicked shut behind me, I kissed her breathless, stealing her words and doubts with my mouth. Then, I did the exact same thing with my cock when I shoved her skirt above her hips, slipped a condom on, and sank inside her slowly. I felt drunk on her, and I didn't have it in me to move us to the couch, or even the desk. I needed her immediately. I needed her against the door.

She didn't seem to have any complaints about it, though. She let me guide her through each movement with trust I'd give her everything she was looking for.

Our position allows me to fuck her rough, and I swear, she's the tightest, wettest pussy I've ever been inside. She fits me like a goddamn glove. She takes every fucking inch, meets me thrust for thrust as I slam her body against the wood.

"Harder," she moans.

Fuck.

"Are you flexible, baby?" I pull away to look at her. Her head is thrown back, a look of pure ecstasy on her face.

She doesn't open her eyes or close her parted lips as she nods lightly. I grasp under her knee and hike her body up, swooping underneath her other leg until both her calves are hanging off my biceps. The movement brings her hips inward and her ass outward, allowing me the freedom to pump faster and fuck deeper.

"Oh my—" She inhales a sharp breath. "Oh, fuck. Yes. Right there."

I'm losing my mind as my pace increases to a reckless rhythm. Electric heat shoots down my back, gathering in my spine. My body is on fire, and I can feel my cock pulsating, readying to spill inside of her. I can feel her wetness coating the inside of her thighs, the warmth of her pussy euphoric, and the way she tightens every time I hit that spot so deep has me going cross-eyed.

She's growing tighter and slicker by the second, her moans becoming so loud I'm sure any patron using the bathroom could hear us at this moment. I'm past caring, though. I continue pumping in her hard and fast, determined to throw us both over the edge and into the freefall of bliss.

"I'm going to—"

"That's it, *cariño*. Come for me. You're taking it so well."

"Fuck!" The word is soft, sweet, and breathless as it falls from her lips on a cry. She becomes impossibly tight, and my mind scatters as the heat inside my spine explodes into white-hot pleasure. Her release floods over me as she screams out in ecstasy.

I remain buried inside her, my face in the crook of her neck as we float down from the high of our orgasms. It feels as if we're both stunned into silence, only our heavy breathing filtering through the room.

I lift my head, and her eyes flutter open. Blue and bright with lust, they soak me in. A soft, glowing flush runs across her cheeks and down to her heaving chest. I'm still holding her against the wall—still inside her—but I feel frozen, unable to pull out or pull back. The moment stretches on for what feels like forever and not even a second at the same time.

She's just...so pretty. Unbelievably so.

I don't know her name, and by the sound of it, she has no intention of ever seeing me again. But I can't help myself as I lean in. Her eyes widen as I press my lips to hers, soft and feather-light, just one final taste of this mysterious, fierce, alluring woman I'll never get to see again.

She accepts my kiss. She gives it back. A soft moan escapes her lips, and I take the opportunity to slip my tongue into her mouth. She clasps her arms around my neck and tightens her grip on me, forcing us closer. I suck her bottom lip beneath my teeth, giving myself the allowance to get swept up in her. I lift her off the door and spin her, bending to set her down on the armrest of the couch.

Slowly, I pull out of her and remove my lips from hers.

She blinks up at me with those big eyes, and the softest, shyest smile forms on her face.

It's that moment I decide I'm going to get her name. Her number. Convince her to see me again because I'm nowhere near done with her. I'm nowhere near done with her lips, with those eyes, with the body I didn't even get to see in full. I need to see her come, see it happen on my tongue, on my fingers. I want to see her beautifully laid out in my bed. I want to know what she likes to drink besides vodka and Fireball, and I want to know how good she really is at pool. I want to know why she's new in town and how long she's staying, why she's here and where she came from.

I begin forming a plan in my head. If there's anything I know about myself, it's that I'm fucking charming. I'll convince her to see me again. I only need to keep her in this bar long enough tonight to do so.

As I step back to remove the condom, her eyes go wide while a soft gasp leaves her mouth. "Oh, my God."

I glance down and realize for the first time the wet spot spreading across the bottom half of my T-shirt. I fight a smile as I turn around and dispose of the condom in the trash can by the door, careful not to step in the puddle she left on the floor too.

I wasn't kidding when I'd thought she'd exploded, flooded me with her release.

Fuck, that's hot.

I want to see her come like that a thousand times. A million.

As I turn back to face her, she scrambles to lower her skirt and readjust her top. She hastily drags a hand through her hair, pausing as she takes me in again. My pants are somewhere across the room, but luckily, I didn't discard my underwear completely, so I pull it up and fasten it over my hips. Her eyes are zoned in on my wet abdomen.

"I'm so sorry," she murmurs as she stands and lets out a forced laugh. "Normally, I can only do that to myself." Her mouth snaps shut and her eyes go wide, as if she didn't mean to say that.

I'm utterly confused. "Sorry? Why are—"

"Well, that was fun. I'm sorry again about..." She waves her hand at my groin region. "Um, anyway. Have a nice life."

"No, wait—" I start to plead, rapidly searching the room for my jeans. Before I can find them or finish my sentence, she's out the door and gone.

Fuck.

I scramble around Emilio's office like a goddamn cartoon character, searching for my fucking pants. Finally, I find them wadded in the corner behind the couch. I don't even know how they got there. Once I began kissing her, everything became a flurry of moans and flesh and chasing bliss.

I dart out of the office and down the hall while zipping myself up, tucking my shirt in as I beeline toward the front doors of the bar when I don't see her inside. I burst through the entrance, blinking at the diminishing daylight as I look around the parking lot, but she's long gone.

I run a tattooed hand through my hair. "Dammit."

When I head back inside, my friends are shooting me shit-eating grins as I walk to the bar to pay my tab. "I've never seen a woman run out of this bar so fast." Ryan laughs.

"Fuck off," I grumble.

I gave her exactly what she wanted, but something must've happened to make her leave like that. I know it can't be because she didn't enjoy it. I've got the wet spot on my shirt to prove she did. She wanted to fuck and forget, but that woman was anything but forgettable.

I don't even know her name.

She'd claimed she wanted nothing that could tie us together, but now, I'm wishing more than anything I had something that would.

Three – Wildflower

Stress Baking

I stress bake.

This isn't news to me. I've always known I bake when I'm overthinking, but as I stare down at the massive mixing bowl full of brownie batter and the clock on the microwave that reads 1:34 a.m., I realize it may be an issue.

The recipe I'm working from is supposed to make a dozen, but I quadrupled the measurements, and now, I'm wondering what the fuck I'm supposed to do with forty-eight brownies. I don't even have enough pans to bake that many.

My eyes dart around the kitchen, taking in the mess of flour, sugar, and chocolate-covered utensils that accent my sister's counters. I'm suddenly feeling very tired, and I don't know what to do with all this batter, nor do I have the energy to clean up right now. I know, eventually, Monica is going to wake up, and I don't need her seeing what a mess I am. She'll start asking questions about my date, and I don't have the energy to go there right now.

I don't know how to tell her that I ditched the guy she set me up with and fucked some random man in the office behind the bar before running away.

Sighing, I wrap the bowl of batter and throw it in the fridge before I begin loading the sink with dishes. At the very least, Darby and Leo are out of the country, so they won't know if I leave their dishes sitting in the sink overnight.

I pull out my phone, wondering if now would be a good time to call my sister. I think it's got to be mid-morning in Portugal, so she's probably awake, though I'm not sure if I want her to start asking why I'm up this late.

I notice three more missed calls from my dad, plus another text message. He's getting more aggressive, more desperate, demanding Darby and I return his correspondence. I roll my eyes, deleting the text before even reading it. There is a message from my sister sent a few hours ago, likely when she first woke up but assumed I was still asleep.

Dad called me again.

Me too.

You don't think he'd come here, do you?

She replies immediately.

Leo says he doesn't think so. Dad's too intimidated by him.

I chuckle at that, clamping a hand over my mouth as it rings out through the silent house. It's not even because I disagree; Leo's probably right. He's likely the only person who has ever told my father to fuck off straight up and gotten away with it. Everything in my dad's life is categorized by money and status, and Leo has an abundance of both—more than my father could ever dream of achieving. He stole my sister away from her own wedding and humiliated our family, and when my dad demanded Leo bring Darby back, he essentially told my dad to go fuck himself then anonymously bought my grandmother's house out from under him.

My father has never been served like that, and if I were him, I'd stay as far away from Leo as possible. That knowledge gives me an additional kernel of faith that Pacific Shores is the one place on Earth where my sister and I are safe.

My phone buzzes with another message from Darby:

I can't imagine why he'd bother to come after us anyway.

I know exactly why he'd come after me, exactly what he wants from me. But Darby doesn't, so I confirm her claim and tell her I'm going back to sleep before she can ask why I'm awake at this hour in the first place.

My goal was always to get out from under my parents, to leave and start over somewhere new, but my sister's abrupt move to California earlier this summer kind of catapulted that timeline. I couldn't stand remaining in Kansas without her, so the moment I could get Lou and me out, I followed her to Pacific Shores.

Though, due to the messy timeline and lack of planning on my end, Lou and I ended up rolling into Pacific Shores just days after my sister and her fiancé, Leo, left for a surf competition in Portugal, meaning I moved into my grandmother's—well, technically it's Leo's now—house with my daughter, not knowing a single soul in this town.

A few days after settling in with our things, Leo's adoptive mom, Monica, showed up with dinner and introduced herself. Lou immediately became smitten, and I couldn't blame her for it. Monica's cool as hell. Plus, I think she's a little lonely with Leo and Darby gone. Her daughter, Elena, lives in New York and doesn't visit often. Apparently, when Leo told Monica he'd reconnected with Darby after ten years, and they'd be getting married next spring, she was elated. She immediately took Darby in like a daughter—which was great, given that our own mother has never been particularly nurturing—and it now appears that extends to me and my daughter too.

Monica has taken us around town, helped me get Lou registered at the elementary school nearby, and has even started apartment hunting for me. Leo got me set up with a job that I'll be starting once he returns from Europe and I get Lou settled at school. After one particularly late night and a few too many margaritas after Lou went to bed, I explained my dating history to Monica, who then decided I was far too young, hot, and smart to be so accepting of my single status. Now, her goal is to help me find a boyfriend.

I didn't have the heart to explain my deep-seated trust and daddy issues, so I played along, thinking it was something she'd forget. I wasn't expecting her to inform me that she set me up with the son of a friend of a friend—because apparently, everyone in this town knows everyone—and she would be babysitting.

I was adamant about not going, but when she showed up at the house this evening and demanded I leave, I couldn't say no. At the very least, I looked forward to the opportunity to get out of the house and feel like an adult for a little while.

That date ended up going sideways when I walked away on the arm of a stranger, fucked him in the back office, and scurried out like a sewer rat. I didn't even have a ride home, so I ran around the backside of the building while I called my Uber, afraid the gorgeous man whose name I never learned would come looking for me.

God, he was gorgeous, though.

Thick arms, corded muscles, and *all those tattoos.* He's exactly my type, and fuck, if I didn't cling to his body like a bear on a tree branch.

"You could've woken me up, you know?" A voice pulls me from my daydreams, startling me in the darkness.

"Fuck, Monica." My hands fly to my chest. "You scared me."

Leo's mother stands in the doorway leading from the living room, smiling sleepily. When I got home from my date, Lou was already in bed, and Monica had fallen asleep on the couch. I didn't want to disturb her, so I began stress-baking brownies instead.

"I didn't want to bother you. I figured you'd get up at some point."

She smiles at me. "How'd the date go?"

I wince. "I'm not sure there will be a second."

Monica frowns before letting out an exasperated sigh. "Yeah, Colin's a bit of a dud. I'll admit I knew that going in, but I thought it was a good way for you to at least dip your toes into the Pacific Shores dating pool."

"Well...I think I definitely got what I needed out of it."

She flicks a manicured dark eyebrow at me but thankfully doesn't push for further explanation. Yawning, she putters into the kitchen and begins putting dishes in the sink. "Lucy went to bed around nine thirty."

Lucy. Child of many nicknames, my daughter is. With a birth name like Lucille, it's bound to happen. My parents have always called her by her full name. I began calling her Lou when she was a baby because I thought she kind of looked like an old man. Plus, my mom hated the nickname. Darby will sometimes call her Lulu, which Leo has picked up too. Monica, however, has taken a liking to Lucy.

"Are you throwing a party I wasn't aware of?" she asks, cataloging the disaster of a kitchen.

"No. I just bake when I can't sleep, I guess." I shrug.

Monica chuffs. "I told Lou you were meeting a new friend, by the way. So, expect her to ask about it tomorrow. She was very interested to know who you're becoming friends with since, according to her, you don't have any."

I snort. "She's nothing if not honest."

I don't tell her I'm dating, because I don't want her getting her hopes up that I'm going to introduce a new person into her life to fill the void her dad left, only for it not to work out and have her be abandoned again.

And if there is anything I'm certain of, it's that my flings never work out.

So, they never meet my daughter.

"You don't need to help clean up," I say. "It's late."

"Don't worry about it." Monica waves her hand at me as she flutters around the kitchen. "I'm a night owl, and I've been meaning to reorganize here anyway. I mean, who puts Tupperware in the cabinets? It needs to go in a drawer. It's all a mess."

I smile. Darby's going to hate coming home to find her kitchen completely restructured. But it's her mother-in-law, not mine.

"I don't want you to clean up my messes, Monica."

"Cleaning up for my kids is my favorite thing. Reminds me that I'm a mother." She doesn't look at me as she says it, as if the words flow from her mouth so naturally she doesn't think twice about them. I suppose I shouldn't be surprised by it, knowing the way she'd taken Leo in when he was twelve after his mother died and his father left.

It's in her DNA. She doesn't need to have known me for years to care about me.

But it's something so foreign to me I can't help but take a step back as it processes.

"Thank you."

She looks up and smiles at me, knowing the words go far beyond her offer to clean the kitchen. "Once you actually bake these brownies, you can repay me with a fair share of them."

"Obviously." I chuckle.

"Maybe you could take them down to the offices on Monday and introduce yourself to the staff there. I know you've got a few weeks before you start, but it might be nice to familiarize yourself with the space and get to know everyone. You can meet Everett too."

I haven't met Leo's brother, Everett, yet. He's the co-owner of Heathen's Surf Co. I guess he recently took over their family business from his dad too. Between running them both, he's busy. Another reason Monica is a bit lonely, I'm sure.

"Do you know why Leo moved the offices from town hall

over to Heathen's?"

The Pacific Shores Small Business Initiative is a partnership with the city funded by Leo to bring awareness and support to small business owners in the community. When Leo found out I had a degree in marketing and graphic design, he immediately offered me a job as their marketing director. I'm not sure if they actually need the help, or if it's something he made up for me so I'd have a place to work. Either way, I'll be partnering with small businesses inside the initiative to help promote them online.

The initiative was originally based out of town hall, but Leo recently moved it to the loft above Heathen's when he converted it from his studio apartment into a workspace.

"I think he wanted it to feel more homey and comfortable. Plus, it cuts down on commute time for Everett and himself when they have meetings." Monica shrugs. "It's coming along nicely, though. So is Honeysuckle." The flower shop Leo bought my sister. He's currently got the empty space next to his surf store being gutted and refurbished with her vision in mind. She plans on opening early next year. "You should go check it out this week. Bring some brownies and say hello. Just ask for Everett when you arrive; he'll show you around."

She's smiling mischievously to herself, but I'm far too tired to question it.

Four – Wildflower

Get Your Fucking Hand Off Her

Incessant, annoying, obnoxious buzzing comes from my back pocket as I cross the parking lot.

I balance the three containers of brownies into one arm as I pull my phone out. It's my dad again. I know, eventually, I'll need to answer his calls. He has been leaving voicemails, but I delete them without listening. It's just a confrontation I'm not ready for.

He has no rights to my sister or myself anymore, but we didn't think he'd try this hard to get a hold of us after we left. Darby ditching her own wedding humiliated him, and knowing that I hold the key to his livelihood, I thought he'd finally let us go. We embarrassed him, hurt his reputation, and possibly even his business. We thought he'd want nothing to do with us ever again, and we'd be able to put our childhood behind us.

Instead, he's been more persistent than ever.

I'm not ready to face it yet.

So, I hit ignore for what feels like the millionth time in the last month. As I move to put my phone back in my jeans, a text message from him comes through.

I know where you are. We need to talk.

I delete it immediately and pocket my phone just as I step up to the front doors. Heathen's Surf Co. is sprawled across the entrance with an emblem of a wave next to it. The entire boardwalk is lined with wooden, beach shack–looking suites that all share walls. It's that charming, classic, California look. The pier stretches out far behind them, with the Ferris wheel, wooden roller coaster, and a restaurant at its far end. Palm trees line the sidewalks between the boardwalk and Main Street.

Heathen's sits on one end of the boardwalk. The door is painted orange, lines of multicolored surfboards propped up outside to my left. The rumble of construction hums from next door, where work is being done on what will become my sister's business. As I walk inside, I take notice of the dozens of surfboards hanging from the wooden beams along the ceiling. One in the center of the space has Leo's name written across it.

They don't just sell surfboards, though. They've got everything someone wishing to live the California lifestyle could ever dream of possibly needing. Wetsuits and swimwear, clothing, sunglasses, handmade jewelry. They even sell shoes and skateboards. There are professional photos of surfers framed on the walls, along with some beautiful paintings of beaches and the local coastal towns.

"Hi, can I help you?" a voice calls out from the far end of the store.

I walk up to the cashier and set the brownies on the counter. A cute young man with glasses and a nose ring smiles at me.

"Hi, I'm Dahlia, and I'm going to be working here in a few weeks. I just wanted to stop in and introduce myself to the other staff." I hold out a container to him as my eyes filter around the space behind the desk. "I was told to ask for Everett?" The man nods as he pulls out his phone and begins typing away. "I brought brownies. Everyone tells me I'm a great baker, so I thought what better first impression than to—" My nervous rambling ceases as I freeze, taking in the sight before me.

A huge canvas photo hangs above the counter behind the man's head. Two unnaturally attractive men sit on twin surfboards in open waves, smiling at each other. I know one of them is Leo—blue eyes, dimples, and sandy-blond hair. It's the man next to him who has my skin prickling with awareness.

Tan skin. Dark beard. Chocolate eyes. Thick arms covered in tattoos that run the length of his neck to his fingers. From this distance, the ink all morphs together, but I know that up close, he's got roses and thorns on one hand, violets and vines on the other. I took note of them when I watched those hands grip my thighs and lift me onto his...

I try to shake the thought away, but it comes roaring back anyway.

"Lift your leg, cariño."

"You're taking it so well. Come for me."

The memories send flutters straight to my core. I haven't been able to get those words, those eyes, or those arms out of my head over the past few days. I don't even know the man's name, but he'd obliterated me to pieces. Made me... God, I hate even thinking the word in my own head. He made me lose myself in a way no other man ever has.

I wanted nothing more than a quick release. I didn't want to know his name. I didn't want anything that could potentially tie me to him again. I don't have the time or energy for a man in my life right now, in any capacity.

I stare at the photo of the stranger I fucked in a bar, and my stomach plummets as I wonder how the hell he knows my soon-to-be brother-in-law. Fuck. Fuck. Fuck.

He's probably a model, I tell myself. *Or another surfer friend.*

I'm sure I'll never see him again.

The gnawing, prickling sensation in my gut tells me I'm wrong, though.

I realize for the first time that I had stopped speaking mid-sentence, and the cashier has been staring at me blankly for God knows how long.

"Um, who is that?" I ask, pointing at the photo above the desk.

He looks behind him. "Oh, that's—" The bell on the front door chimes as it opens, distracting the employee.

"Dahlia."

I jump at the voice, boxes of brownies falling to the ground. That familiar voice, like a caress of recurring nightmares. It echoes through the chamber in my chest, my past and present morphing together in the worst possible way.

Breath stalls in my lungs, and I become a true statue as I feel his presence at my back.

Too many things are happening at the same time. My mind is going blank. I squeeze my eyes shut, afraid to turn around. Willing him away. Willing him out of my existence.

He can't be here. He isn't here.

"Dahlia." His harsh tone rings through my consciousness again, clear as haunting bells.

I summon all the courage I have left and turn around to face Dane Andrews.

"Why?" is the only word out my mouth.

Why are you doing this to me?

Why can't I escape you?

I thought I was safe here.

"What do you mean 'why?'" His jaw is set, eyes crazed. He steps toward me, and I step back into the counter. "You know exactly why. You ignore my calls and run away? You don't have the right. I've been searching for you. Had to follow you here." Disgust drips from his tone as he spits the words.

"How did you find us?" My voice is hollow.

My father has never frightened me physically, but mostly because I think he has never had to resort to it. He doesn't lose his temper or lash out in fits of rage. He's far too composed. Everything he does is calculated and planned. He uses words to cut and blow and destroy. He knows he could slash me far deeper with his voice than with his hands.

This was supposed to be a fresh start, a way to escape that forever.

But he's here. And I'm alone.

Because everything he does is calculated. He waited until my sister was gone, until he knew I was by myself in an unfamiliar town with nobody to protect me—not the way Darby has Leo to protect her—before he came for me.

My parents have never loved me or my daughter, but they shrouded us in a veil of money and power. That made him feel entitled to me, and more terrifyingly, to Lou.

The only thing more potent than my fear of him is my love for her.

So, I stand up straight and approach him. I'm tall at five-foot-ten, and he's almost exactly my height. I used to shrink myself beneath him when I was a teenager, but now, I lift my head and stretch my neck.

"How did you find us?" I ask again.

"My daughter runs off from her wedding with some D-list celebrity athlete. It's not hard to figure out where she went. Then, you disappear after that shit you pulled a few weeks ago? It wasn't a stretch to assume you followed." He sneers. "Darby finds herself a millionaire, Lord knows you'll be riding those coattails."

Bile burns my throat as I swallow. His words slash through my soul like a flaming blade.

I've forgotten the brownies on the ground, forgotten the cashier standing behind me and the fact that this is supposed to be my workplace soon. I've forgotten why I'm even here, and I'm suddenly overwhelmed with the need to leave. I need to pick up my child. I remind myself that she's safe with Monica, down at the beach not far from here, but I won't feel okay again until she's in my arms and nowhere near his.

"I told you all I wanted was for you to leave us alone. I'm trying to protect *my* sister and *my* daughter. From *you*." I maneuver around my dad. "I don't know what you were hoping for in coming here, but you can leave. Let us move on." I'm impressed at the surprising steadiness in my voice, but I wonder if it's only because I refuse to meet his eyes.

He grabs my arm, holding tightly as I try to wrestle out from under his grip. "Not so quick, darlin'." He smiles down at me, but it's coated in disgust. "We're not done. You've got something that belongs to me."

"No."

He holds me tighter, and it feels like he's about to start dragging me out the door when a slamming noise echoes through the otherwise-quiet shop.

A booming voice follows it. "Do we have a problem here?"

I recognize that voice too.

But right now, it feels more like a beacon than a curse.

Tattooed arms crossed against his chest, stretching his black T-shirt tight. Quiet rage simmers behind those brown eyes as they soak in the scene around us. I'm thankful the store was at least empty, but I'm humiliated that *he's* witnessing it. The man from the bar, who's looking at the grip around my arm with enough heat to melt through iron.

"Get your fucking hand off her."

Five – Wicked

I'm Her Boyfriend. Who The Fuck Are You?

He immediately lets go of her arm and steps back. I preen at the kernel of fear in his eyes.

I can't believe she's standing in front of me, though I wonder if I should be surprised at this point. She blew into that bar like a hurricane, dismantling all of my composure and leaving destruction in her wake when she breezed out of my life just as quickly as she came.

Here she is again, in my business, dessert spilled across the floor, requiring rescue from yet another douchebag. "Need my saving once again, huh, *cariño*?"

Her nostrils flare at the pet name, but I'm not sure what she expects, considering she wouldn't give me her real one. I'd heard enough of the conversation to understand now exactly who the woman standing in front of me is.

I also don't let myself think too hard about the eventual fallout of our earlier actions.

She looks just as pretty in her white T-shirt and denim cut-offs as she did in the bar that night. She's wearing less makeup, and her hair is thrown up in a loose bun. Now that I catalog her features, I realize she does closely resemble her sister—the lips, nose, and freckles—but it's her eyes that have me feeling adrift. A color that doesn't match Darby's. A shade of blue I'm pretty sure doesn't exist anywhere but right inside her irises.

The space around us fades to nothing as I study those eyes—as they study me. I watch the heat rise on her cheeks, the flush running down her neck and disappearing beneath the vee of her shirt. I wonder if she's remembering all the same things I am.

"It never did take you long, did it, Dahlia?" The man next to her scoffs in disbelief as he rapidly looks back and forth between us. I wonder if the hunger on my face is that obvious, or if he just knows her well enough to see it on her too. "Suppose I shouldn't be surprised." I watch her physically flinch at the blow of his words, and then I see red as rage overtakes me. "You've always been a slut."

Dahlia recoils back from him, and I watch as she shrinks in on herself, as the words land.

It sends me into a tailspin, and before I fully understand my actions, I'm on the other side of the room with the asshole shoved against the wall and my elbow on his throat. The piece of shit would be half my size on a good day, and the way he looks up at me with hatred in his stare tells me he's well aware of it too. His skin flushes red as I cut off his oxygen, and bloodshot eyes move from me to the woman standing behind me.

"Don't look at her. Look at me." He listens, and I make sure he's entirely focused on my face before I speak again. "I'm gonna ask you nicely to leave my store." I press a little harder, and he gasps as he fights for air. "You're never going to speak about her like that again. I don't want to hear Dahlia's name out of your mouth. If you continue to bother her, I'm gonna make sure I know about it, in which case, I'm going to be a lot less fucking polite. Are we understood?"

"Who are you?" he gasps between choking breaths.

I smile. "I'm her boyfriend. Who the fuck are you?"

I hear Dahlia gasp at that, but I don't have time to think those words through or watch her reaction, so I keep my eyes on the man in front of me.

He's older; I don't think he's some sort of former flame. I don't think she's been in town long enough to have one. The longer

I stare into his brown eyes, I realize that they might be Darby's eyes. I take in the color of his hair; though streaked with gray, it's the same dishwater blond that matches Dahlia's natural shade.

I think I might be holding her father against the wall by the throat.

There's defiance in his stare. I don't let up, though. I don't move. I don't give him air to breathe, not until he finally gives me a slight nod. I back up and let him peel off the wall. He straightens out his trousers and brushes his hands down his wrinkled button up. "We have things to discuss, Dahlia," he mutters without making eye contact with either of us.

"No, we don't." Her voice is soft and timid. She's scared.

I take a menacing step toward him, and he backs into the glass doors, reaching behind himself for the handle. We both pause as Dahlia's voice, stronger than before, asks, "Why would you corner me here?"

Her father's eyebrows knit together, and a gross smile flashes across his face. "I knew that bastard owned a business somewhere in this town. Figured I'd take a look around until I found you."

I chuckle. "If by 'that bastard' you're referring to my brother, I'd think twice before opening your fucking mouth again."

His eyes go wide, face deepening to a crimson hue. Nostrils flaring before his gaze focuses on the woman behind me, just briefly. "You know what we need to discuss. If you'd picked up my phone calls, it wouldn't have escalated to this. I don't fly out until tomorrow afternoon. I'm going to call you later, and I suggest you answer." He pushes the door open behind him. "I'd prefer not to return to this fucking town, but I *will* get what you owe me." With one last look toward his daughter, he mutters, "And to think, I tried to play nice with her."

Dahlia doesn't respond, and I block the entrance to the store as I watch him leave. I don't take my eyes off the front door until he makes his way down the boardwalk and turns onto Main Street. I watch until he's completely out of sight before I turn back to face her.

Adam's long gone. He texted me when the altercation started, and I came downstairs immediately. I had guessed the woman in the store was Darby's sister when he mentioned she was a new staff member for the initiative, but I had no idea I'd be running into the same woman from the bar. I told Adam to head outside and lock the doors while I handled things so we wouldn't risk any patrons witnessing it. I also didn't want Dahlia to feel any more embarrassed than I'm sure she already is.

I know Adam's a hopeless gossip, so I also make a mental note to remind him later that if he utters a single word about the incident to anyone, I'll have him jobless before the words leave his tongue.

Dahlia is leaned back against the counter, a trembling mess. Her eyes are cast down to the floor, as if she were afraid to look at me. I slowly approach her, squatting down at her feet and picking up the brownies sprawled on the ground. I place each one back in the container before rising and setting it beside her.

"You're Darby's sister." It's not a question.

She finally lifts her head, and all I see is the color blue.

"You're Leo's brother," she says quietly.

I nod.

"Well, fuck."

I can't help the laugh that escapes me.

There's that string I was looking for, I guess.

Six - Wicked

That Never Happened

"This is where the magic happens," I say as I flip on the office lights.

Most of our staff only work for the initiative part-time, so they're out and about or working from home. The space is used primarily for meetings. Leo and I put up some temporary walls to section the loft off into two offices, one meeting room, and one large room with several open work spaces. The desks can be used by anyone at any time. We're not strict on schedules as long as people are getting their work done and picking up cashiering shifts at Heathen's when we need them. Leo's old kitchen works as a makeshift break room. There's a bathroom up here too.

Today, however, the office is empty, save for me. It's a Friday in late August. Most of the staff are playing hooky and already out for the weekend, but I'm not about to be on their ass for it. If I hadn't had to set September's budget for Ramos Automotive, I would've been out on the waves myself. Now I'm glad I was here, and Dahlia didn't have to face her father all on her own.

Dahlia's silent as she looks around the space. She sets the one unharmed container of brownies on the kitchen counter before following me into my office, hovering at the doorway as I step inside. "When we were kids, the entire town was run by mom-and-pop businesses. We knew all the owners. They were our neighbors, family, friends. About seven years ago, my mom's best friend, Ruby, passed away. She owned an ice cream parlor here on the boardwalk, and it went up for lease. They tried putting in a frozen yogurt chain." I lean against my desk. "After that, it was like investors were coming for every small business in the area. They tried buying my dad out of his property, wanted to tear down his business to build a hotel or a T.G.I Fridays. I don't fucking know.

"Anyway, once Leo started making money, he came home and bought out the boardwalk. He was determined to keep the small businesses in place, to protect the people who dedicated their entire lives to this town, our parents included." She doesn't say anything, but she watches me intently as I speak. "The mayor was in agreement with him, so they allocated funds to the Small Business Initiative, but it wasn't enough. Leo provided the rest. We opened Heathen's, our friend August opened the tattoo shop at the other end of the boardwalk, and we promised that we'd only put family businesses in between. The economy has made it hard for us to find anyone wanting to take the leap on signing a lease, though." I shrug. "But we're trying. The initiative also serves to protect other small business owners within the Pacific Shores city limits. We help them with marketing, event planning, sponsorships and advertising. We also provide free legal advice when they need it. Loans for when they're struggling. Really, we're just doing what we can to keep the sense of community we grew up with alive."

I may have overshared. I mean, she'll be working here, so she should know what we stand for, but given that the initiative and the two businesses I own are the only things I have to show for myself, I have a tendency to go overboard when I talk about them—especially to pretty girls I can't get out of my head.

"That's really amazing," she says softly.

I press down the lifting sensation in my chest at her approval.

"Thank you." I push off the desk and gesture around the room. "This'll be your office once you start, so I thought you'd like to see what it looks like. You know, so you can start visualizing how you'll want to decorate and whatnot."

Her brows rise. "But...isn't this your office?"

I shrug. "Yeah. But we've only got two private spaces in this building, and Leo's office is here too. I have a second office at the auto shop, so I can start using that one full time and just come down here for meetings."

"I hate to kick you out of your space."

"Don't worry about it." I smile at her, and she forces one back. All she really looks like is uncomfortable, and I can't tell if it's because of what happened with her dad downstairs or because of her proximity to me.

"Do you want to see anything else? Otherwise, I can walk you out."

"No." She shakes her head, giving another strenuously fake smile. "Thanks for showing me around."

I nod as I lead her out of the office and to the main door. "I'll tell everyone the brownies are from you so they know who to thank when you begin working."

She doesn't respond as I lock the door behind us and follow her down the stairwell that leads to the backside of the boardwalk. I assume she parked in the garage across the street. As we make it back to the doors of Heathen's, she pauses. Her head swivels up and down the road, and I know she's searching for him, to see if he waited for her to leave.

"I'll walk you to your car, *cariño*."

She opens her mouth as if she's going to protest, but she thinks better of it and simply nods. I lead her across Main Street and into the garage on the other side of it. She stops when we reach a mid-size Honda that looks to be a newer model in fairly decent shape.

"This is a good car," I say, then feel stupid for it.

She snorts. "Thank you."

"*Cariño*." She looks at me as she opens the driver's side door. "Do we need to talk about what happened at the bar?"

"No." She swallows. "We need to pretend that never happened. Today is the first day we met, understand?"

I hate hearing that, but I nod, forcing a smile of my own. "Well, I suppose you'd better introduce yourself to me then."

A hint of a genuine grin flashes on her cheeks. I hold out my hand, waiting for her response. She slowly extends her own, and there is a near imperceptible flare in her eyes our skin meets. "I'm Dahlia," she says breathlessly.

"Everett," I respond, running my thumb across the top of hers.

I swear chills rush up her spine at my caress, but she drops her arm swiftly, stepping into the car. "You told him you were my boyfriend."

I swallow, caught off guard by her statement. Her eyes grow wide, as if the words surprised her too. "I didn't know who he was at first," I explain. "I thought if he was someone you'd dated or something, he may have been more likely to back off if he thought you were unavailable."

Her mouth turns up slightly, the first sign of amusement I've seen in her since that night at the bar. "Well, it probably helped more than it hurt. It appears the only men my father seems to be intimidated by are the ones Darby and I are dating."

"Happy to be of service." I wink at her. She gives me a coy smile again as she buckles herself in and reaches for the door handle. Before she can shut the door all the way, I grab the top of the window, holding it in place. "Dahlia, are you sure you're safe with him around? I can follow you home. Or, we can file a report with the—"

"No," she says too quickly. "I'm going to pick up my daughter and go straight home. I know how to lock a door, and he knows better than to try breaking and entering. We'll be okay."

"It sounds like he has expectations to see you again before he leaves tomorrow."

"I'm well known for not living up to his expectations."

I don't feel confident about this, but she doesn't seem like the type of woman who likes to be pushed once she makes a decision.

"We'll take care of you guys." I don't know what else to say, but I know those words are true enough, even if Dahlia wasn't... whatever she is to me now. It wouldn't matter. My family protects each other, and that's what they are to us now. Darby. Dahlia. Her daughter.

My brother. Myself. Our parents. We'll take care of them.

She raises her head, appreciation shining in the raging sea of her gaze.

And fuck, if that look doesn't do something to my chest.

"Thank you," she whispers.

The woman in front of me now is so different from the confident person I met in that bar, as if two minutes with her father sucked all the life from her. It takes everything in me to shut her car door and watch her drive away, to keep myself from hunting that man down myself.

Later that night, I call my brother and tell him what happened with Dahlia and her dad. I'm a little afraid she'll be upset with me for informing them, but that fear subsides when I find out she already explained the situation to Darby. Darby's convinced their dad only had the courage to come around because she and Leo are out of the country, and that made Dahlia an easier target. They were supposed to extend their vacation in Europe after Leo's competition in Portugal next week, but Darby asked to come home right after instead.

I don't want to cross the boundaries Dahlia set between us, so I don't demand they give me her phone number, even though I want it desperately. Instead, I tell Leo to give her mine, to let her know she can text or call me with any kind of emergency, or just if she feels generally uneasy. Secretly, I hope she'll text me just to talk, that maybe I've been as stuck in her head as she has been in mine.

I make Ryan station one of his officers outside their house overnight, just to be safe.

Then, I stay up far too late, waiting for a text message that never comes.

Seven - Wildflower

What A Cluster

I pull up to the curb and shut off my car in front of Monica's bungalow.

I guess their family lived only a few houses down from my grandmother—where I live now—but she and her husband, Carlos, decided to sell once their kids grew up.

The bungalow they live in now looks like something out of a beach bum's dream. It's small, with only one bedroom and an office, but it's perfect for a retired couple. They live in a private community with direct beach access, and they even have a view of the water from their back porch.

I don't knock as I step inside the light pink home. Monica has been expecting me. She set me up with a number of apartment tours in the area today, and I knew it would bore Lou out of her mind to come with me. Monica offered to babysit, and I insisted she didn't need to spend her entire Saturday with my nine-year-old, but she told me she was painting her office anyway and needed the help. I couldn't imagine how my wild child would be of any help at all in a project like that, but I didn't argue.

I took the day to myself, touring four apartments that were all just okay. I didn't love any of them, but I don't want to overstay my welcome in my sister's home, either, so I submitted an application for two and then read a book on the beach while I stuffed my face with a burger. I can't remember the last time I ate a meal or read a book in solitude, and while I don't want to continuously burden Monica with babysitting duty, it was really fucking nice.

"Lucille!" I call as I shut the front door behind me.

Natural light filters through the quiet living room, so I follow the hallway that leads to the kitchen, where I find Monica standing over the stove, stirring a pot of something that smells incredible.

"I had her take a shower because she was covered head-to-toe in Timid Absinthe, and I didn't want to risk her bringing it home in your car."

I chuckle. "So, I suppose she was more trouble than help, then?"

Her eyes light up as she spins to face me. "She was perfect. We got the office painted. We just decided to have some fun after too."

"I'm glad you had fun. Thank you for watching her." She gives me a pointed look, and I know she's about to start lecturing me on why I need to stop thanking her for everything, so I quickly nod to the food on the stove. "That smells amazing."

That look forms into a smile, and she opens her mouth to say something but pauses as we both hear the front door open and close. "Mama?"

The smile she gives me is midnight in comparison to the way her face brightens at that voice. She lights up in a way that's only possible when a mother hears her child call out for her, an expression I'm sure has never graced my own mother's face at the sound of mine or my sister's voice.

I've done a decent job over the last two weeks trying to forget the fact that the stranger who unraveled me in a bar happens to be my brother-in-law's brother. I've fought harder to forget that he's the son of the only friend I've made in town. The friend who was babysitting my child while her own kid railed me against a door. The friend who set me up on the date with the man I bailed on so I could fuck my brother-in-law...in-law? In a bar.

What a cluster.

All the effort I've given to shoving those thoughts from my mind fails me when Monica calls out, "In the kitchen, baby!"

My whole body goes stiff. I haven't spoken to Everett since that moment in the surf shop. Leo gave me his phone number that night and told me to reach out to him if my dad showed up at the house. My father called several times that same night and again the next morning. He asked me to meet him for coffee and promised a cordial conversation in a public setting. I ignored him, knowing he'd fly home that afternoon. It has been a week since then, and luckily, I haven't heard from him at all. Even if I had, I wouldn't drag Everett into it again.

I know I can't ignore Everett forever, especially if I want to try to settle down here in California. For the first time in my life, it's starting to feel like I could have a real place to call home. Darby and I have always done a decent job of blocking out the toxicity in our lives and relying on each other to feel whole. Our house in Crestwell did feel like that at times: a home.

Truthfully, though, we didn't have a support system outside of each other. We got by, but I'm not sure either of us were ever truly happy. And while I haven't spent much time with her and Leo together, I can tell just by the sound of her voice on the phone that she's the happiest she's ever been. I can tell she's feeling settled, complete with him.

I want that too. I don't need it with a man; I know I can find that with my daughter and my sister, and Pacific Shores is the closest I've ever found to that feeling. Building that life with Darby and Leo—with Monica—means Everett is going to be a part of it too. I just think I need a little more time to erase the fact that I also know what his dick looks like.

You can't see someone as a brother-figure if you think about how hard they made you come every time you're in the same room as them.

I hear his footsteps echo across the wood floors and, unsure what to do with myself, I grab Lou's backpack off the dining room table and sit down. Monica picked up registration papers for the local youth soccer league after Lou expressed interest in playing last week.

I feel his presence wash over the space like a wave. My head is lowered, pretending to look through her bag for something, but I watch Everett from the corner of my eye.

"Hi, Mom," he says as she steps up to him. Monica raises on her toes to press her lips against his cheek. He hands her a bouquet of flowers. "The market had the lilies you like."

The deep baritone in his voice rakes down my body the way it did when he was whispering in my ear that night.

Physical chills run down my spine, and I work to shake them off. That seems to catch his attention. "It's good to see you again, Wildflower." He leans against the door frame leading to the kitchen and crosses his ankles as he smirks at me.

"Wildflower?" I scoff, ignoring the way Monica's narrowed eyes are darting rapidly back and forth between us. She turns to the stove without a word.

"I mean, your name's Dahlia, is it not?"

I still can't meet his eyes, bending over as I haphazardly shove the papers back into Lou's backpack. "I don't think dahlias are categorized as wildflowers. They're a bit more curated. Proper."

He hums. "Doesn't fit you at all then, does it? Wildflower is much better."

"What? Like a weed?" I snort.

I hear the scuffle of footsteps and look up just in time to watch Everett push off the wall and stride toward me. He pulls out the chair across his mother's dining room table and spins it around, straddling it backward. Crossing his arms over the top of the chair, he rests his head on them and smiles at me.

I don't like the way his fluid movements make my stomach somersault. I don't like the way he smirks at me like he knows what I look like naked.

Like he wishes he could see it all again.

"I was thinking of something more like colorful. Bright. Resilient. Sprouting up in the places you least expect them and blowing away on the wind just as quickly." That wicked smile morphs into a full grin. "Beautiful, too, of course."

I swallow, schooling my features to appear unaffected. He can't talk to me like this if I want to forget the way he makes me feel.

"Dios mío, hijo. ¿Eres capaz de mantener una conversación con alguien que no consista en coquetear?" Monica gripes from the stove. I have no clue what she just said, but the tone in her voice is one of pure annoyance.

Everett blushes slightly, eyes narrowing on his mother across the room. *"Tranquila, Mamá. Ahora mismo me estás arruinando el juego."*

Monica turns around and points her spoon at her son. *"Deja en paz a la pobre chica. Ella no es una de tus conquistas."* She drops her arm and looks at me, features softening. "I'm sorry my son has no self-control. That's a trait from his father."

I can't help the laugh that bursts out of me.

I catch a hint of a smile on Everett's lips before his face straightens again, and he looks to his mom. "If you're going to bully me, I'm not staying for dinner."

"Yes, you will. I'm making pesto from scratch. Your father would take out your eyes and make you eat *those* if he found I made your favorite meal and you bailed on it."

He leans back, bracing his arms on the top of the chair. I can tell he's fighting a smile. "Speaking of fathers, tell him to get the hell out of my shop and enjoy his retirement. My workers will never take me seriously if they think they're still supposed to be answering to him."

"He's never going to fully let go of that shop, baby. You know that. He will, however, lose his own eyeballs if he doesn't make it home for dinner soon."

Everett grunts in agreement. "He was working on Mr. Michaelson's old Beetle when I left, but he promised he'd be home before we sat down to eat."

Everett's eyes fall from his mother to me, and I can see the way he's fighting it, the way he fails when that gaze roams over my face—my body. I know he can see as I fail to do the same. I study the tattoos across his forearms, which run the length of his hands and peek out the collar of the shirt he's wearing. The veins in his neck strain beneath his perfectly manicured beard, and I can almost feel the way his stubble brushed against my chest.

Chills rush down my spine again, and I catch the tilt of his lips as he watches me shake them off. It's as if he can read my mind, see the moment replaying in it.

Suddenly, his head turns sideways, looking down the hall leading to the back of the house. His eyes soften, and before I can turn around to see what he's looking at, I hear a soft murmur. "Mom?"

I know my face takes on the same expression Monica's did earlier as I turn around and soak in those freckled cheeks, green eyes, and strawberry-blond locks. "Hi, bug."

I open my arms as Lou walks into me, and I snuggle her against my chest. She smells like whatever body wash Monica keeps in their bathroom and a scent that's uniquely my child. I grasp her shoulders and pull her out from me, then tuck a wet strand of hair behind her ear.

"Did you have fun today?"

She nods timidly, and I know she's quiet because Everett's here. She's always shy around strangers. She tucks her head into my shoulder and plays with the chain around my neck.

"Lucille, can you say hi to Everett?" I run my hand down the back of her head. "Everett is Monica's son."

Her eyes flutter up to study the man in front of me. He's smiling softly as he slowly rises from his chair and walks over to us. "It's nice to meet you, Lucille." Squatting down so he's at her level, he holds his hand out to her. "That's a beautiful name. Does anyone ever call you Lucy?"

She looks at me, checking for confirmation that it's okay to return his handshake. I nod so she knows it's safe. I can't blame her for being uncomfortable around men when she's never had one she could trust before.

She softly places her small hand in Everett's large one.

"Monica calls me Lucy. My Aunt Darby calls me Lulu." She glances at me. "My mom calls me Lou."

He chuckles. "You have a lot of nicknames, don't you?"

She blushes, and I understand the reaction. I feel the same way when he smiles at me. Lou nods. "Do you have any nicknames?"

Everett shakes his head. "Nope, I'm not a big fan of nicknames. There are no good ones for the name Everett."

Lou takes on a contemplative look. "I'll think of one. Everyone should have a nickname."

"Maybe I'll have to make a new one for you too, then."

Lou drops her hand, still smiling to herself as Everett stands tall. I glance up at the man in front of me, unable to ignore the way he towers above us both. Everything about him is massive.

"She looks like you," he says.

"Thank you," I respond. Somehow, I know he meant it as a compliment. "You ready to go, kid?" I ask my daughter.

"You two are more than welcome to stay for dinner if you'd like," Monica chimes from the other side of the kitchen.

"That's so kind, but I promised her a movie night," I say as I zip up Lou's backpack and fasten it around her shoulders.

"What movies?" Everett asks.

"Spiderman," Lou says.

He looks at me. "Please, tell me it's the originals."

I smile as I shake my head. "We're Tom Holland girls through and through."

He groans as he tips his head back. My eyes get stuck on the way the column of his throat moves at the sound. Looking back at Lou, Everett asks, "Who's your favorite superhero of all time?"

She contemplates for a moment. "Ironman."

He nods. "All right, good choice."

Their conversation bounces back and forth as I quietly hug Monica and thank her again for watching Lou. I guide my daughter toward the front of the house, Everett on our heels, still entertaining Lou's spiel on Marvel superheroes. She's going through a phase.

Said phase allows me hours to stare at Chris Evans, though, so I can't complain.

"You kind of look like The Hulk," she says to him as we open the front door.

His mouth drops open as he looks at me, appearing almost offended.

I shrug. "Mark Ruffalo's hot."

His features morph into a sly smile, and he winks at me. "Thanks, Wildflower."

"Oh, I didn't say I agreed with her." I wink back.

He frowns as we reach my car, and I help Lou into the backseat. "Bye, Lucille." He waves at her from behind me. The widest smile is on her face, as she waves back at him when I shut the door.

"You didn't need to walk us out," I say as he follows me around to the driver's side.

"Walking you to your car seems to be a new habit of mine." He grins at me. "Plus, I was having an important conversation."

I can't help but smile at that. It normally takes a while for Lou to warm up to someone new, but she seems to have taken an immediate liking to Everett. While I'm glad for that—glad she's finding people in this new place to feel comfortable around—it reiterates the idea that what happened between Everett and me in that bar can't ever happen again.

I open my door and slip inside the car.

"Have you heard from..." He pauses, eyes darting to the backseat where my child sits.

"No, I haven't." I know what my father wants from me, but I also made it clear that as long as he left us alone, the thing he's so afraid of would never see the light of day. I should've known the man couldn't handle being blackmailed, but I'm hoping once he realizes I'm keeping my word, he'll let us move on.

Everett nods, leaning against the car door and running his eyes over the interior. "You need an oil change."

I glance at the service light on my dash. "Thank you for the observation. I'll get it taken care of eventually."

He shakes his head with a sigh. I watch as he reaches into the back pocket of his jeans and pulls out his wallet. He fishes something out of it before handing it to me. I grab a business card with *Ramos Automotive* sprawled across the top.

"The address is on the card. Bring it in as soon as you have time. Ask for me."

"And if I don't?"

He raises a brow. "If you don't bring your car in, it's eventually going to take a shit. If you don't ask for me, then you'll be putting whoever does help you on their boss' bad side."

I roll my eyes.

He braces over the top of my car, giving me a front row view of his flexing, tattooed arms. He drops his head between his shoulders, flashing that mischievous smile. "Goodnight, Wildflower."

The way he looks at me takes my breath away, and I have to remind myself where I am. *Who* I am. I'm no longer just a girl in a bar. He's no longer just a guy. We'll never get to be those two people again. I swallow, reaching for my door handle and slamming it shut.

Everett quickly steps out of the way before I can crush his fingers. I hear him laughing through the closed door.

He stands on the curb, watching me drive away until I'm completely out of sight.

Eight – Wicked

New Bitch In Town

I'm going to kill the motherfucker calling my phone at seven thirty in the goddamn morning.

There's a reason I don't open either of my businesses until ten o'clock.

I hazily reach across my nightstand for my cell phone, groaning as I force open my eyes and squint at the brightness. An unsaved number with an out-of-state area code is on my screen. My mind immediately filters to Dahlia, whom I know wouldn't be calling me for anything less than a true emergency.

"Hello?" I answer.

"I'm sorry. Were you still asleep?" Her voice sounds calmer than I expected but more frantic than I'd like it to.

"Hi, Wildflower." A smile forms on my mouth at the nickname. It's an involuntary reaction. I have no control over it.

"How'd you know it was me?"

"I know your voice, *cariño*."

"What does that mean? *Cariño*." She's practically purring through the phone, and my morning wood does not need the reminder of the way her tongue can roll.

"Dear. Darling. Sweetheart. Whatever you want it to, really."

A soft laugh echoes on the other side of the line. My cock jumps at that too. "How about you just call me by my name instead?"

"Okay, Wildflower." I smile. "What's going on?"

I can almost see those pretty blue eyes rolling in my mind.

"I...I'm sorry to bother you. It's my car... It won't start. Today's Lou's first day of school, and she's already going to be late, which is so not a sign of good parenting for the new bitch in town. Plus, she's already the new kid, and I don't want to make things worse for her by making her late. I tried calling your mom, but I think she's at her Pilates class and—"

"Whoa, Dahlia." I sit up and swing my legs over the side of the bed. "Slow down. It's all right. We'll figure it out." I press my phone between my ear and my shoulder as I throw on a pair of sweatpants and a hoodie. "What time does school start?"

"Eight thirty."

I glance at the clock. "Okay. We have time. I'm on my way over to your place now. You can take Lou to school in my car, and I'll take a look at yours in the meantime."

"I..." She pauses, as if stunned. "Are you sure? I mean, don't you have to work?"

"I'm the boss, baby. I can delegate."

She's quiet for a moment, but finally, she murmurs, "Thank you."

"Of course. I'll be there soon. Just hang tight."

I slip my shoes on my feet, swipe my keys from the hook next to my front door, and whistle like a happy idiot all the way to my Jeep.

Ten minutes later, I pull up to the curb of Leo and Darby's house. Dahlia's car sits in the driveway with the hood up, and I catch a flash of blond hair on the other side of it as I step out of my Jeep. I make my way up the driveway to find her bent over inside the car, inspecting it.

Hands braced inside the hood, she arches her back, creating a curve that sends my mind spiraling. As I enter her peripheral vision, she stands straight up and looks at me. Her blue eyes are wildly bright, and there's a faint glow of sweat on her forehead that she wipes away with a dirty hand. Her breathing is heavy, chest expanding with each inhale she makes.

It reminds me how hard I made her pant when I was inside her.

"It's not the oil," she says without greeting me. "I was just trying to figure out the issue, but I'm stumped."

Fuck. She's so beautiful I think I forgot how to speak.

I attempt to piece my mind back together, to get my cock to calm the fuck down and stop thinking about the way she felt wrapped around me. A crease forms on her brows the longer I go without providing a response.

"Are you—"

"Yeah, no worries. I'll take a look while you drop Lou off at school. Take my car."

I nod behind me. Her eyes follow the direction of my head before going wide. She looks back at me with a horrified expression. "*That* is what you drive?"

I glance back at my orange Jeep. I've still got the top and doors off for the summer. I suppose it's a bit less practical than her Honda, but I'm honestly confused on what her surprise is about. "Yeah?"

"I can't take my child to *school* in that thing, Everett. That's a fucking death trap. CPS will be knocking on the front door before I even make it back home."

I shuffle around her, taking a look inside her car. "Chill, Wildflower. It's just for one day. The Jeep is entirely legal. Plus, the school is about three blocks away. Honestly, you could just walk if you wanted to."

She seems to contemplate that for a moment before shaking her head. "No. I'll drive her." She lets out a long sigh. "God, I fucking hate this."

"What?" I ask.

She waves around us. "My car breaking down. Being unable to take my daughter to school without calling in help. Being stuck. Just..." She blinks and looks away. "Whatever. I'm going to finish getting her ready." She turns to head back inside, pausing briefly to add, "Thank you."

I wait until she's no longer looking at me, until she's almost reached the front door before I say, "I told you we were going to take care of you, Dahlia."

She doesn't respond as I hear the front door click shut.

A few moments later, I hear the patter of small footsteps making their way down the entry of the house. "Hi, Everett!" a sweet, young voice calls.

I pull my head from the hood of the car and look down at two bright green eyes and a soft smile beaming up at me. They're a different color than her mother's, but Lou's eyes have that iridescent glow to them that Dahlia's have, a brightness that must only exist in their genes.

"Hi, Luz." I smile.

"No!" She clamps her hands over her ears. "You can't give me a nickname yet. I haven't thought of one for you."

"Oh. My apologies." I hold my hands up, holding back a laugh. "Have a good first day of school, Lucille."

Dahlia smiles at me, placing a hand on the top of her daughter's head and nudging her toward the street. "All right, kid. Let's go. You're gonna be late." She turns to me briefly. "I'll be right back!"

I wave them off just as Lou shouts, "Oh, my God! This is what you're driving me to school in?"

"Don't get used to it," Dahlia chimes as Lou climbs into the backseat.

I go back to work on Dahlia's car, but I don't miss the burst of delighted giggles as the engine roars to life. I don't miss the way it makes me smile, either.

Nine – Wicked

Sunrise After A Hurricane

"Hey. I grabbed a coffee from the gas station and refilled your tank on my way back."

Her voice startles me as I lift out of the hood to look at her. The to-go cup is extended toward me, a peace offering from giant blue eyes. Her freckles are showing in the morning sun because she's not wearing makeup.

She's pretty all the time, but I like her especially like this, since I know not everyone gets to see her this way. This is how she looks when she's rushed and stressed, and her appearance is the last thing on her mind.

This is how she looks when she calls me because she needs help. And I know she only called me because she didn't have anyone else, but I relish the feeling of being needed by someone like her, someone I know—even after only a few weeks—is stubbornly independent. I relish the feeling of seeing her freckles because they feel like a secret.

"You didn't need to do that," I respond.

She shrugs. "My payment for your assistance."

I think of all the other ways I'd like her to repay me. I don't say that, though.

"I don't need payment."

"Well, here it is anyway."

Stubborn.

"Thank you." I smile as I take the coffee from her extended hand. "How'd you like

driving the Jeep?"

She tries to hide the smile on her face. "It was actually kind of fun after I dropped Lou off at school. When I was younger, I had this dream of living in an old van for a few months, just driving up and down the West Coast and exploring; having the top down and the doors off felt like a few moments of how I imagined that life would look." She stops talking suddenly, biting her lip and looking down at her feet, as if she didn't mean to say it.

I take a sip of the coffee she bought me and fight back a sputter when the taste hits my tongue.

She winces. "I just got it black. You look like the kind of man who doesn't like sugar in his coffee."

I force myself to swallow. "I love sugar in my coffee, actually. But yeah, no. This is good too." I reluctantly take another sip because I don't want her to think I'm not grateful.

Secretly, I'm jealous of whatever creamy-colored, iced, whip-creamed concoction she's got in her hand.

I try not to let my face blanch as I drink, but I think she catches it anyway because she lets out a quiet laugh. "I'm so sorry." The light in her eyes, the brief moment of calm from her panicked morning, makes drinking this shit well worth it. "I have creamer in the house if you want to take a break and come inside."

I'm never going to turn down that offer. "That'd be great. Thanks."

I follow her up the steps and inside. We take a left, through the dining room, and into the kitchen. I'm used to finding the island in the middle of the space covered in blooming flowers that Darby picked from the garden out back, but today, it's centered with a huge, pink-frosting-covered cake.

"Someone's birthday I need to know about?" I ask.

"Nope." Dahlia opens the fridge and bends over while I try not to stare at her ass. "We just thought it'd be fun to make a pink cake. It's lemon with strawberry frosting."

Damn. That sounds good.

She stands straight with a bottle of vanilla coffee creamer in her hand. Shutting the fridge door with her foot, she slides the bottle across the counter to me. I pop the lid off my coffee cup and pour a generous amount inside.

"So, I think it's the spark plug. It's worn down quite a bit, which is odd for a car as new as yours. But the good news is that it's an easy fix. I can run down to the shop and grab you one and then come back and replace it. I'll go ahead and change your oil too." I wink at her. "Should be finished before you have to pick Lou up from school."

"Thank God," she says as she takes a sip of her coffee. "I appreciate all your help, really, but I cannot show up to that school in your Jeep again."

I laugh. "You don't take me as the type of woman who minds the stare of others."

"When it's bitchy parents, I do." She huffs. "A bunch of the other people dropping off their kids were giving me these horrible looks. They don't even know me, and I could tell they're already assuming I'm a terrible parent."

"They're glaring because you're younger and hotter than they are." I shrug. "And because they're wondering why you're driving my car."

She snorts into her coffee. "What? Are you some kind of local celebrity? Everyone knows the car Everett Ramos drives?"

"I mean, my brother is an actual celebrity, so yeah. People around here know our family. Plus, how many 1987 neon-orange Jeep Wranglers do you see around town?"

"Yeah, I guess." She bites the inside of her cheek. "I thought you were going to tell me it's because you've fucked a bunch of them."

"I wouldn't say a *bunch*."

Her pink lips drop open, and I can't help the grin that spreads across my own mouth.

"Does that make you jealous, Wildflower?"

Her mouth clamps shut as she shakes her head. "Of course not. I mean..." She looks down at her hands. "I shouldn't be surprised, I guess."

"Dahlia," I say with enough conviction that she raises her head, eyes searing into mine. "What I did with you at Emilio's was not something I've ever done with anyone else before."

"Me either," she whispers.

"I know." I set my coffee on the kitchen counter and kick my hip against it, crossing my arms. "Plus, if it makes you feel better, since I know you're definitely jealous." She rolls her eyes at me. "Most people only go after me because they think it'll get them closer to Leo."

I don't say it because I'm hoping she'll pity me. I don't even know why I say it, honestly. I hate admitting that, admitting that I'm less desirable, often a tool used to gain access to my brother. To his fame. Money. Status. My flings hoping they'll catch his eye the same way they caught mine. I hate feeling that way about Leo, hate feeling that way about myself.

Something about Dahlia makes me feel safe, though. Maybe it's because I know she's one person who would never use me for that reason, even if I only know that because her sister is engaged to him.

I couldn't look at her as I said those words, but a moment passed in silence, and I found myself glancing up, desperate to read her face and what she thinks of me. Her brows are furrowed, jaw set tight, pouty lips turned downward. There is a quiet rage brewing in her eyes.

As if she were waiting for me to meet her gaze, she finally says, "That's disgusting, and I'm sorry you feel that way. That it happens to you." She shakes her head, taking another sip of her drink. "I can't believe a woman would even think that's a good idea. Sleeping with one brother thinking that it'd make the other want her? That's insane."

I let out a laugh at that. "Yeah... There isn't always logic in their actions, but honestly, it happens a lot more often with the men I date. They think if they get with me, they can befriend Leo, that Leo will offer them some kind of connection to his world."

A surprise look flashes across her face, but I can tell she quickly tries to settle it.

"You didn't know I was bisexual, did you?"

She gives a slight shake of her head.

"Is that an issue for you?" I ask casually. It's not the first time, and likely won't be the last either. I'm used to it, and I'm comfortable enough with myself now that it doesn't bother me anymore, though I can't pretend it wouldn't sting a little to hear it come from Dahlia.

"Of course not," she says. The sincerity in her voice tells me she's being honest, and some storm inside my chest immediately calms. "I just didn't know."

"I've been out for so long, and everyone in my life is so used to it, I guess I don't always think about the fact that new people won't automatically know."

She smiles to herself. "So, are you telling me I'm going to be running into not only other women you've fucked, but potentially some daddies too?"

"It shouldn't matter, right? Because you're not jealous." I smirk behind my coffee.

"Exactly."

Her eyes sparkle with mischief, and lightning electrifies the air between us as we smile at each other. *Fuck*. I want her to be jealous. I know it's messed up, and I don't know what it is about her that makes me feel this way, but I want to know she's bothered by the thought of me with anyone else. Then, I want to tell her she has nothing to worry about because if she said the word right now, I'd be on my knees for her and her alone.

But she told me we had to pretend nothing ever happened between us, and I want to understand why. I know it has something to do with Lou. I'm not sure what it is, or why she feels she needs to hide herself away, as if she thinks she can't choose her daughter and also herself at the same time. She deserves more than that.

My emotions must be written all over my face, because she clears her throat and stands straighter, those blue eyes flashing with guilt and something else I can't sense. "Um, okay. Well, how much do I owe you for that spark plug you're going to go get?"

I swallow all the words I want to say. "Don't worry about it."

"I'm not going to take free things from you, Everett."

"The spark plug costs far less than whatever you likely paid to fill my tank this morning."

She hums at that. "California gas prices are a crime."

"Exactly. So, if anything, I owe you."

She smiles. "I can't argue with that."

"So what made you into cars?"

"I mean, my dad has owned Ramos Automotive since before my sister and I were born. I grew up running around that place with a wrench in my hand. I think it's in my blood." I lean over the hood, plugging the new spark plug in. "But I wouldn't say it's like my dream, per se. I just couldn't stand the idea of my dad giving it up. Of course, there was no chance Elena was taking it over. Leo, either." I pull back and wipe my hands on the towel thrown over my shoulder. "I was a bit lost in my early twenties, so when the opportunity arose, I thought, why not? My siblings both did greater things. This was the least I could do."

"Serving your community and preserving your family's legacy was the least you could do? Seems like a lot to me," she says thoughtfully. "Something to be proud of."

My chest takes flight at that.

"In comparison to an international bestselling author and a world-renowned professional athlete, though?"

"Yes." Her eyes burn through me with such intensity I can't question whether or not she really means that. "But I know what you mean. I'm the black sheep of my family too."

I tilt my head, leaning against the hood of her car. "Well, now you have to tell me more."

I know a little of her story, the things Darby has mentioned. I know Darby came to Pacific Shores that summer when she was seventeen because her parents were afraid of Darby finding out Dahlia was pregnant. I know Dahlia was a trouble-maker and a wild child in her parent's opinion. I also know that by the haunted look in her eyes, there are a lot of things she has never allowed to the surface, maybe even some things Darby doesn't know.

"When I was little and Darby was just a baby, I remember our mother being around a lot. We used to bake all the time. She taught us how to swim in the summer, took us sledding in the winter. My father was trying to build his business at the time, so he was gone often. It was just our mom and us." She twirls her car keys around her finger. "Then, when I was around the age of ten or so, things changed. It was suddenly all about appearances. I don't think it was my parents that changed. I think that it was me hitting the age where it started to become noticeable. What my value was supposed to be in our family unit. No longer a child, but now a prospect to further his success and status." She shudders at the memory. "We had to go to church every Sunday. We stopped baking, and my mother started controlling our sugar intake, telling us we needed to be pretty enough to catch the attention of nice boys.

"I remember questioning my school teacher one day. She was droning on about the responsibilities of women in society: God-fearing wives and mothers." I give her what I'm sure is a horrified expression, because she chuffs and adds, "I went to a private school. Anyway, I simply asked if the boys were being taught the same thing." She lets out an exasperated laugh. "She screamed at me in front of everyone. They called my parents and sent me home early for *speaking out of turn*. When my mother arrived at school to get me, I was crying. I was scared. I couldn't understand what I had done wrong to warrant such a harsh response." Her face turns to stone. "My father came home that night in a rage, telling me I was an embarrassment. He grabbed and shook me as he screamed in my face, asking what the hell was wrong with me."

My vision goes red at the thought.

"From then on, I just...I rejected the idea of all of it. I wanted to cause as much noise as I could. I wanted to scream until they noticed I was the one hurting. I needed attention—needed support and love, and I needed to mean more to them than their reputations. I needed to mean more than status and success." She looks at me, pain in her blue eyes. "And I never did. It's like...I went to one end of the spectrum and Darby went to the other. She tried to make up for all the noise I caused by being quiet and timid and perfect until both of us were so fucked up, there was no way to fix it."

"I'm glad you both made it out of that environment." That's all I can say. There aren't words for the kind of hatred I have for men like her father, and I fear if I allow myself to say anything more, I'll end up disclosing just how much I want to kill him.

She nods. "Me too. I knew...I knew after I got pregnant—which was not a cry for help, just a genuine misuse of birth control—that they'd never be the parents I needed. That, even if I didn't, my child sure as hell would deserve more than they could ever give."

She shudders with something like pain and fear, so I give her the only thing I can offer to help settle the storms raging in her ocean eyes. "You both deserve better, and you're already giving her that."

Soft freckles dance across her nose as she smiles at me, resembling something like the sunrise after a hurricane.

Ten – Wildflower

I Bought A Monstera

"I want to carry it!" Lou exclaims loudly as we finish crossing the street.

I squat down, maneuvering the monstera plant into her hands. "Careful. Hold it from the bottom." The damn thing is nearly as big as she is, and I know she can't see where she's walking through the leaves covering her face.

She wobbles slightly but steadies herself, determined. I place my hands on her shoulders and steer her toward the boardwalk. We slowly make our way to the back entrance to Heathen's. I finally told Lou I'd be starting my new job this coming Monday after Leo and Darby return home from their travels this weekend. I told her I'd have my own private office—something my father never granted me when I worked for him—and she was elated about it, demanded to see what it looked like.

We went out together after she finished school today and bought a plant for the space, a plant I'll likely need to ask my sister to take care of because I do not have her green thumb.

As we reach the back staircase, I pause at the bottom. "All right, bug. You're gonna have to let me carry that thing up the stairs."

She huffs, setting the monstera down on the bottom step. By the way she's panting, I can tell she quickly began rethinking her insistence on carrying it all this way down the boardwalk, but her stubborn nature didn't allow her to drop it.

I hide a laugh at that.

I carry the plant up the stairs and unlock the door with Leo's spare key. I show Lou the space and my office. She jumps around in excitement, spinning in my chair and pulling out every drawer in the desk—which I notice has been entirely cleared out, just as Everett promised it would. I let her play around a little longer before we head out, and I lock up behind us.

"Can we go inside the store?" she asks as we reach the bottom of the stairs.

I'm hesitant after what happened last time, but I know if I'm going to keep this job, I'll be spending a lot of time in Heathen's, likely in all the small businesses in the area. I'm going to have to get used to it, but I'm also not sure I'm ready to face Everett again, not after the emotional information dump I placed on him Monday after he came to fix my car.

I'm normally much better at locking things up. I only open up around my sister, really. Maybe she has been gone too long, and I'm feeling too many things with nowhere to put them. Regardless, though, Everett isn't that person—that place. So I try not to think too hard about why it was so easy to vent to him about all my fears, about my past.

I sigh, checking my phone. It's a half hour before the store closes on a Friday night, so it's unlikely he's the one there anyway. "Yeah, we can check it out real quick."

She skips ahead of me, darting around the edge of the building and to the front doors. I catch up to her just as she stops at the entrance. She takes in the surfboards propped up outside the doors, slowly running her hand along one of them.

"Leo owns all of these?"

I laugh. "Well, I think they're for sale, but he owns the shop. So, yeah. Kind of. He and Everett."

She looks back at me. "Everett too?"

I hum in response. "They're brothers."

Her nose scrunches, a trait she took on from my sister, I

think. "They don't look like brothers."

I maneuver her toward the front door as I pull it open. "Well, they're not brothers by blood. They don't have the same parents. Monica and Carlos took care of Leo when he was a kid, and they've been best friends their whole lives, so they're brothers in all the ways that count."

"Will I have a best friend like that?" she asks. My stomach plummets at the question. She doesn't say it like she's sad, like she's longing for anything, but I know someday—someday soon—she may be. She has always had a tough time making friends, always isolated herself a bit.

Sometimes, I'm afraid it's because she's an only child from a broken home.

I've always been a sister first and a friend second. Everything I've learned about friendship and bonding and communication came from Darby and our closeness. I've never needed any other friends because I've always had her.

Lou doesn't have that, and it breaks my heart that I can't give it to her.

"I hope so, bug," I whisper against the top of her head, planting a kiss in her hair.

I'm not sure she even heard me, her train of thought already barreling down another track as she enters the shop and takes it in. Her head is snapped back, tracing the surfboards hanging from the ceiling, the paintings along the walls. The entire place exists in shades of blue and green and orange, bright and colorful.

I love seeing the look on her face when she discovers something new for the first time.

Her eyes are wide with wonder as she wanders behind a stack of surfboards, sliding her hands along the smooth surfaces and yelling out to me which colors she likes most.

So hyper focused on my daughter, I almost don't hear the caress of his deep voice as he says, "Hey, Wildflower."

I jump around to face the back of the store. Everett is leaning on the counter, hands resting on his elbows as he smiles at me, studying me like I'm his favorite painting. My hands come to my chest—an attempt at calming my racing heart.

I can't decide if it's racing because he *startled* me or because *he* startled me. "Shit. You scared me."

"Mom!" Lou calls from the other side of the shop. "That's a dollar!"

Shit. That stupid swear jar was such a bad idea. It has been draining my wallet for months.

Everett chuckles as he walks around the counter and closes the distance between us. Towering over me, he flashes that wicked grin again. "What're you two doing here?"

"I bought a monstera," I say.

I bought a monstera? Idiot.

Those chocolate eyes and straining arms—tattooed fingers—make me incapable of normal speech sometimes. "I mean, for my office. I bought a plant for my office. Lou wanted to see it, and then she wanted to see the store."

He nods, a knowing smile on his face. Without taking his gaze from mine, he calls, "What do you think of it, Luce?"

Small footsteps pitter-patter toward us until she's at my side. "It's so cool!" She tugs at my shirt. "You have to come look at this one board. I *need* it, Mom."

We both laugh. "What are you gonna do with a surfboard, bug?"

She gives me an eye roll that is far too exaggerated for a child her age. "Surf?"

"You don't know how to surf."

"Leo can teach me."

For the fact that she's never actually met him in person, only having ever spoken on FaceTime, Lou is incredibly comfortable with Darby's new fiancé. I'm thankful for that, for the ease in which she settled into her new reality, but I don't need my sister or my brother-in-law feeling like they have some kind of responsibility over her, not when they're just starting to build their new life together.

I'm not sure Lou understands those boundaries, though. Darby has been so deeply ingrained in every aspect of her life since she was born I'm not sure Lou knows what normal family dynamics are supposed to look like.

"Leo's busy, bug. I don't know if he's going to have time for that. You know they're only going to be back in town for a few weeks before they have to leave again."

Leo has another competition later this year in Hawaii or Africa or...somewhere. I can't keep track. He'll be working with me, training for that next competition, and running Heathen's in the meantime, not to mention helping Darby get her flower shop ready to open and planning their wedding.

I'm already living in their house. I don't need to add this to their plate too.

"I can do it," Everett says. My head snaps up from Lou's pleading puppy eyes to meet his. He has a soft smile on his face, nothing but sincerity in his eyes. "I mean, I'm no record-setting prodigy, but I've spent pretty much my whole life on a board." He laughs to himself. "I always say that the only reason Leo is as good as he is is because he spent so much time trying to be better than me when we were kids."

I can practically feel my daughter vibrating with excitement next to me. "I couldn't ask you to do that. You're just as busy as he is."

"You're not asking. I'm offering." He shrugs. "I could easily carve out...what?" He looks down at Lou with a smile. "An hour a week? Would that work for you, kid?"

She nods rapidly.

"The auto shop is closed on Sundays, so how about Sundays at....ten o'clock?" he asks me.

I give a strained smile. "Yeah, that works." I press against Lou's shoulder and point back toward the swimsuits. "Why don't you go pick out a new one?"

She starts to run off toward racks of children's swimwear when she pauses and turns back. "Okay, but what about—"

"Girlfriend. I am not buying you a new surfboard when there is a strong possibility you will get out there and after ten minutes decide you hate it. We'll rent one until we know it's something you actually want to pursue, then I'll take a look at getting you a new one for yourself."

She lets out a frustrated huff. "Fine."

"I have boards you can borro—" Everett tells me the same time as I say, "You don't really have to do this."

He blinks at me. "Dahlia. Do you not want me giving your daughter surf lessons?" he asks in a hushed tone. "I want to respect your boundaries. If it makes you uncomfortable, then we don't have to do it, of course."

I shake my head. "It's not that. I just...I don't understand why you'd want to. What's in it for you?"

"Something has to be in it for me?" He crosses his arms. "She looks excited. It's the same excitement Leo and I used to have in our eyes when we were two poor, good-for-nothing kids running amok around town and wishing we had boards we could ride waves with." He nods in Lou's direction, and we both turn our heads to look at her skipping around the back corner of the store. "That kind of reaction is exactly the reason we opened this place, the joy we want to spread to anyone willing to accept it. So... that's what I get out of it. The smile on the face of a kid who just discovered how great it feels to be out there on the water."

I swallow slowly. Somehow, I feel like there's more to it than that, but I'm afraid to know what that may be. All I know is the way his brown eyes electrify with intensity as he looks at me spell nothing but sincerity and conviction.

"Thank you," I say quietly, looking away. "I can pay you."

"Don't you fucking dare."

I let my eyes flutter upward, meeting his. I melt beneath his stare, summoning only a nod in response. "It's late on a Friday, and I know you need to close the store. I don't want to take up any more of your time." His eyes soften at that, almost as if he's going to disagree, but he says nothing. "Lucille, you have thirty seconds to pick a bathing suit, and then we're out of here."

She runs up to me with some frilly, bright pink one piece. I carry it to the counter, and Everett tries to argue with me about paying for it, but I argue back. We finally agreed to give me the employee discount.

The bells on the door chime as Lou pushes it open. "Goodnight, Ev!"

"Oh, that better not be the nickname you decided on, Luce!" he calls back. She looks at him with furrowed brows, and he winks at her before his eyes filter up to meet mine. "Ten o'clock Sunday morning. Meet me here."

I nod.

"Goodnight, Wildflower."

"Goodnight," I murmur back.

"That's a good nickname, Mom," Lou says as we make our way back to the car.

Eleven - Wildflower

Your Mouth Must Be Dry From All The Panting

I've always hated the sound of slamming doors.

They remind me of my father, the way he stormed in and out of the house when I did something less than acceptable by his standards. Always me. Never my sister.

The first time he caught a boy in my bedroom, he slammed the front door so hard the glass shattered. The day he found out I was pregnant, he slammed that door again, but the glass didn't shatter—only I did. When he locked me in from the outside. When he never let me leave.

The last time I heard that front door slam was only a few weeks ago, when I went to see him for the last time, the last time before he rushed back into my life unannounced and demanded to see me. He hasn't spoken to me since he left Pacific Shores two weeks ago with his tail between his legs. I don't think he was expecting to find Everett protecting me. I don't think he expected either of us to stay away at all. I think he was holding out hope that Darby was obedient enough to go crawling back. I think he thought I was too dependent on him to run away too.

But I'd been waiting years to get away, waiting for the perfect moment.

When I put my house on the market and it sold, I brought him a check in-person to pay him back for the down payment he'd put on my house when I bought it seven years ago, plus some interest for good measure. Lastly, I informed him of some information I happened to dig up one night working late. He'd made a poor mistake of keeping confidential documents on the network drive for his company, and he didn't know that I'd taken multiple programming classes in college.

I'd spent years looking for some kind of crack in his armor, something that could knock him down from the pedestal he rests upon, and just weeks before my sister's wedding, I found it.

I planned to sit on those files for a while, until the right time. But once Darby ran away, I knew we'd need the leverage, especially once he tried selling our grandma's house out from under her. He drained her trust account, thinking she'd fail on her own. Luckily, Leo had a plan of his own and ended up anonymously buying the home from my father, saving it for all of us. But I knew it wouldn't have been enough.

My father would've kept trying to find ways to ruin Leo, to force my sister home, to prevent me from leaving. We knew better than to believe he wanted us around for the sake of family or because of love. For Dane Andrews, it was—had always been—about control. He couldn't stand the idea of losing it.

So, I went over to my parents' house that day. The house I grew up in. The house that had never been much more than a prison to me. I gave my father that check and told him I was leaving town with my daughter. Then, I explained the documents I was in possession of, and that if he made any move against my sister or myself to bring us back, to prevent us from escaping him and that town, from moving on with our lives, I'd make sure he'd lose everything.

His empire is the only thing he truly cares about anyway.

The thumb drive in my nightstand is the armor I have against him. It's what I used to protect myself, to protect my sister and my daughter. I didn't expect him to fight to get it back, never thought he'd come to hunt me down for it. I told him if he did, I'd turn it in—turn *him* in.

I guess he called my bluff. He must believe I have enough love for him not to hand it over to authorities, even though he's wrong. It's just the only thing I feel I have to protect myself with.

But it doesn't protect me from the scars he left across my heart.

Wincing as a door slams down the hall again, I'm reminded of that particular fact.

I quietly slip out of my bedroom and into the bathroom next door. Lou stands in front of the mirror, her strawberry blond hair a messy halo around her face as she brushes her teeth.

"Stop slamming doors," I hiss quietly. "Your aunt and Leo are still asleep. They didn't get in until very, very late last night."

"Sorry," she mumbles, mouth full of toothpaste.

As excited as I know we both are to see Darby, I'm trying to let them sleep. I stayed up to greet them briefly last night, but Lou had already passed out. I haven't seen my sister since the morning of her wedding, all haunted eyes and hollowed cheeks.

Last night, even in the darkness, she was glowing in a way I've never seen before.

It only served to confirm the fact that my intuition is always right. When I found that note she'd written to Leo in her desk drawer just weeks before her wedding, I knew she'd never planned on sending it to him.

But I did.

He showed up on the day of her wedding and helped her leave.

He showed up because even though they'd only spent one summer together ten years ago, he'd always known she was the love of his life. Deep down, she'd always known it too. She left him all those years ago for me. Because I was pregnant and I needed her.

Seeing her—both of them—now, happy and healed, settles that pang of guilt that had been eating away at me for a decade, the knowledge that she'd chosen me and my chaos over the boy she loved, and the fear that she'd never find that happiness with anyone else.

So, I'm happy my sister is home. I want to hear about their trip to Portugal and the life they've begun building together, but for now, I'll let them sleep.

I finish getting ready for Lou's surf lesson. I throw on a pair of denim shorts and a black tank top before tossing my hair into a loose topknot. I pack a bag with towels, sunscreen, water, and snacks, and Lou meets me downstairs.

She's wearing the bathing suit I bought her on Friday with a pink dress draped over top of it. I take a minute to brush out her hair and braid it back before we grab our things and head out to my car.

"Can we drive in Everett's Jeep again sometime?"

"Maybe."

Lou insists on cranking Taylor Swift as we make the short drive down to the boardwalk. Another phase she's going through, which I don't mind at all. I make her hold my hand as we cross the street and enter Heathen's.

Everett's standing at the counter, talking with the same man I met the first day I came in. I feel slightly embarrassed at seeing him again, but he doesn't mention the incident with my dad, and neither do I. Everett formally introduces him to me as Adam, Leo's personal assistant. He works for Leo part time and fills the rest of his hours here at Heathen's.

I can't help but notice the way Adam stares at Everett like he has stars in his eyes.

I can't help the way it makes my insides twinge a little, knowing that other people look at him that way, find him as desirable as I do, that he may be giving others the same soft eyes, intense attention, and knowing smiles he gives me.

I shake it off as Lou runs up to him with excitement.

"Hey, kid." He smiles at her. "You ready to go?"

She jumps in response. "What board am I using?"

"I've already got everything set up on the beach for us, so you'll see it when you get down there." He moves away from the back counter and leads Lou toward the door, calling over his shoulder to Adam, "Just shoot me a text if anything comes up. I'll be around!"

Lou leads the way, even though she doesn't know where she's going. Everett directs her down the boardwalk steps and onto the beach, with me trailing behind them. A short distance away, I make out an umbrella and towels laid out in the sand. A dark-haired figure sits back in a chair beneath them, and there are two surfboards propped up in the sand beside her.

"Your mom wanted to join?" I ask, hiding a laugh.

"You know how she is."

Once Lou spots Monica down the beach, she takes off in a sprint. Reaching Everett's mom, she takes off her dress and drops it into the sand, showing off her new bathing suit. I can see Monica make the motion of clapping her hands as Lou twirls around.

"She seems really happy, you know," Everett says next to me as we walk at a slower pace. "I don't know a lot about being a parent, but I feel like there is this constant worry that your child isn't fulfilled, that you're not doing a good enough job."

I look at him, but he's watching my daughter. After a moment, his eyes meet mine. Rays of mid-morning sun float across his face, turning those eyes to a shade of molten amber. "From the outside looking in, I can tell she's your whole life, so I wanted you to know that she looks happy. She's full of light, and I think that kind of iridescence only comes from the deep knowledge of being loved."

I realize now that we've both stopped walking. Waves crash against the shore behind me, sea breeze blowing between us, but momentarily, I'm entirely lost in those eyes. I study his face—his long, ridged nose, luxuriously full lips beneath his rough yet soft beard, the smooth, tanned skin of his cheeks, his short dark hair.

He runs a tattooed hand across the scruff of his jaw, breaking my trance. As I begin to study his hands—the intricate artwork that crawls along his fingers and his wrists, looking like flowers and vines—I realize I'll only get lost again in the memory of how those hands felt along my bare skin.

I remember the way he looked at me that night, like I wasn't someone's mom, someone's daughter or sister. I was just a girl in a bar who caught his eye. He looked at me like I was desirable, alluring. That look in his eyes made me feel free and wild and unworried. It made it easy for me to say yes, to throw caution to the wind and let myself go.

The way he looks at me now is no different, as if none of those other factors matter to him. Still, I can't change the fact that they matter in general. I'm not just a girl in a bar. I don't get to throw caution to the wind. I'm no longer wild and unworried. I'm not even sure I'm free.

I break my gaze and look away, back to where my daughter sits on a surfboard in the sand. "Thank you," I whisper. "She is my entire world. Her happiness is my only priority, so..." I swallow. "That means a lot."

I let myself glance at him, just briefly. He's still looking at me. He's not moving, so I begin walking again, breaking the moment of tension between us. As I approach Lou and Monica, I hear the shuffle of something behind me before a flash of tanned skin jogs past me.

Suddenly, I'm met with the unobstructed view of Everett's bare back. He doesn't have tattoos there, not like the ones that crawl up his arms and around his neck. His back is entirely smooth, muscles rippling as he catches up to where his mother and my daughter sit in the sand. I watch his body move with fluidity as he bends down to kiss Monica on the cheek.

"All right, Luce. Help me carry these boards a little closer to the water. I'm going to go through the basics with you on the sand, and then we'll get into the water and practice standing up."

I catch up to them, dropping our bag onto the ground next to Monica's. Lou's dragging the smaller of the two surfboards about fifteen yards from where our chairs and umbrella are set up. "You need to put sunscreen on before you start!" I call out to her.

"Oh, speaking of. I forgot mine," Everett says as I squat down and dig through my bag. "Can I use some of yours?"

"Yeah, sure." I hear Lou jog up to me. Flipping the cap on the lid, I squeeze a generous amount into my palm. I lift my hand to lather her when my gaze is met with the most gorgeous chest I've ever seen in my life.

All the air leaves my lungs on a swift inhale as I look up at him. A fine dusting of hair starts over his chest, trailing down his stupidly perfect stomach, beneath the band of his shorts. Endless ink dances across his muscles when he moves, the sunlight reflecting off his bronze skin with an obnoxiously golden glow. I feel saliva gather on my tongue like I'm a fucking dog staring at a rare piece of steak.

"Ah, Mom. This is my new bathing suit." Lou's voice breaks my trance.

I look down to find that I placed my sunscreen covered palm right into the center of her chest. "Shit. Fuck." I reach into my bag for a towel before wiping off my hand and then her swimsuit. "Sorry."

I ignore Everett's knowing chuckle as he drags his surfboard across the sand and next to Lou's.

"That's two dollars," she says matter-of-factly.

"Sorry," I mutter again as I wipe her down to the best of my ability and glob another generous amount of sunscreen into my hand, rubbing it up and down her arms, legs, face, and ears.

After I finish lathering her up, I straighten out her swimsuit, make her give me a kiss, and then send her running. Everett high-fives her as they pass each other, telling her to sit on the board and wait for him to come back. I can't stop staring at his stomach—the way it flexes when he walks, how his body is all hard lines and fine points and muscle. So much muscle. So much strength.

I think about the way he folded me against that door and held me up like I weighed nothing at all. How I didn't get to see his full body that day, and what a disservice to the experience of fucking him that was.

Because that body deserves to be worshiped. Studied. It's a work of art.

"I brought water," Monica chimes. My head snaps sideways

to face her, her dark brows raised behind her sunglasses. "Your mouth must be dry from all the panting."

I realize for the first time that my jaw has been hanging completely open as I've been watching Everett. I clamp it shut just as he reaches us.

"Can you do me next, Wildflower?" he asks with a grin.

"¿De repente tus brazos dejaron de funcionar? ¿Ya no eres capaz de ponerte tu propio protector solar?" Monica asks with a knowing tone.

He rolls his eyes. *"Mamá, ¿por qué tienes que seguir interviniendo? Sólo relájate."*

"I, uh—" I have no clue what they're saying. I stare blankly at the two of them with the bottle of sunscreen in my hand.

Monica smiles at me. "I'm sorry. We're being rude. Everett can put on his own sunscreen."

He places his hands on his hips, tilting his head toward the sky as he shakes it. I extend my arm to him, handing him the bottle. He takes it without looking at me, and I settle into the chair beside Monica as Everett hands the bottle back.

Our fingers brush when I take it from him, and when my eyes snap up to meet his, they're already on me. He winks as he pulls away.

"Please be careful," I say breathlessly.

He flashes me an easy smile. "She's safe with me, Wildflower. I promise."

And in my bones, I know that's true.

Lou and Everett have just migrated into the water, and all my mother senses are on alert. I'm watching them intently, the conversation with Monica fading out as my focus remains on them.

"I used to be afraid of my kids in the water too," she says. "It got easier as they grew, though. Then, it got hard again after Zach."

"Zach?" I ask, still unable to pull my gaze from the water.

It's not just that I'm hyper-aware of my daughter being in the ocean. It's also the way she laughs constantly when she's talking to Everett, the way he teaches and guides her with kindness, patience, and ease, how happy and comfortable she looks next to him.

"He was one of Leo and Everett's best friends growing up. Elena's first boyfriend." She clears his throat, and my eyes perk up at her use of the past tense. "Leo, Everett, Elena, Zach, and his brother, August, were inseparable from the age of about ten. Darby, too, that summer she was here." She's quiet for a moment. "He was in a surfing accident about three years ago. He didn't make it."

I gasp, breaking my gaze from the horizon and facing Monica. "Oh, my God. I..." I shake my head, unsure of what to say. "That's awful. I'm so sorry."

She nods thoughtfully. "None of the kids could stomach the ocean for some time after that. Leo... He found his way back first. It's something written in his DNA. Everett followed soon after," she says in a contemplative tone. "But Elena... She hasn't stepped foot on the sand since. Went so far as to run away to New York City just to get away from it, I think."

"You miss her," I say quietly. She only nods in response. "Do you wish she'd move home?"

Monica shrugs. "If I thought she was happy in New York, thought she really moved there for her career and not to escape her grief, I'd be happy to have her there. But she hasn't published a book since she landed there. I doubt she's even tried writing one. I think she's hiding from her sadness, and I don't think she'll ever get better by doing that. I think she needs to come home in order to heal." She sighs. "But she's an adult, and she's stubborn as all hell. You'll never convince that girl to do something she doesn't want to. So, what choice do I have but wait for her to figure it out for herself?"

"I'm sorry," I say quietly.

She gives me a soft smile, and I decide to change the subject. "Does your family always speak Spanish to each other? Or only you and Everett?"

She chuckles quietly. "It's interchangeable. Depends on the mood, I guess? The kids took Italian when they were younger too. Elena is a little more drawn to that, as am I, so we try to speak frequently. A few of the other workers at the garage can speak Spanish, so Carlos and Everett converse more frequently in that environment. I think the Spanish comes a little more naturally for him, and with Elena gone, it happens to be what's spoken most often at home."

"Why Italian?" I ask.

"My grandparents are from Sicily," she says. "My mom could speak a little, so I would learn from her when I was a child, but I was never fluent. When the high school the kids went to offered Italian classes, they both wanted to learn for me." She smiles proudly. "So, I wanted to learn for them. I began taking online classes, and we've been practicing together ever since."

Fuck. The man is fluent in *two* romance languages?

"That's beautiful," I say, shaking away those thoughts as I realize I'm literally conversing with his mother.

We're interrupted by the sound of screeching laughter, both of us looking out to the waves. Lou is calling for our attention as she stands on her board, her arms thrown out wide. Everett's about a foot away, waist deep in the water with his hands held up, as if showing her that he isn't touching the board. As she balances on her own for the first time, she cheers, and both Monica and I clap and whistle.

A small white cap breaks beneath her, and just as she loses her balance, Everett's arm shoots out and grabs her around the middle before she can tumble into the water. He steadies the board, setting her down on top of it and giving her a high-five again.

A few moments later, they make their way back to us, dragging their surfboards through the sand. Lou runs into me, exclaiming her excitement. "You did so great, bug," I croon as I wrap her in a beach towel. "Can you tell Everett thank you?"

She turns to face him as I brush my fingers through her wet

hair. "Thank you, Evvy."

He purses his lips. "Oof. Yeah. That nickname is a no for me." Lou rolls her eyes. "But of course, Luce. I had fun." He looks at me. "Does this time next week work again?"

"Sure." I smile, my eyes getting stuck on his glistening, wet skin, the beads of water that run the length of his torso. I track one as it disappears beneath his shorts. "Thank you," I say, breaking my stare and meeting his gaze again.

His smile is wicked and knowing.

"Can we get ice cream on the way home?" Lou asks.

I let out a dramatic sigh, pretending like I'm contemplating it, even though I knew she'd ask. "I guess so. But we'll have to get it to go." She cocks her head at me. "I think there are a couple of people waiting to see you back at the house." I smile.

Realizing she forgot her aunt got home late last night, she jumps up in a flurry of excitement and rapidly begins packing up our things. Everett, Monica, and I all laugh as we begin helping her.

"I can get a head start with her if you want to help Everett carry the surfboards back to the shop?" Monica asks. "I can meet you at the ice cream stand on the end of the boardwalk."

I'm a little suspicious of her encouragement to leave Everett and me alone, but I say, "Yeah, that's fine." Nodding toward my daughter, I add, "Lucille, can you help Monica with the chairs and towels? I'll meet you at the ice cream stand soon."

I kiss Lou atop her head as she scurries off with her hands full. Bending over in the sand, I grab her orange board. Everett grabs his at the same moment, and we both stand tall as we face each other. My eyes stick on his body once again, traveling slowly along the planes of his chest, his broad shoulders, his tattooed neck, before meeting his face.

"You'll need to stop looking at me like that, Wildflower." He smirks.

"Looking at you like what?" I ask, even though I already know the answer. I'm looking at him like I'm hungry. Because I am.

"Like you've seen me naked. Like you wish you could see it all again."

I bite my lip and glance away, willing myself to remember all the reasons I made him promise that we'd never cross that line again.

"I didn't know you could speak Italian."

What a stupid fucking thing to say. I nearly wince at myself.

His laugh rakes along my skin. *"Bella, ti parlerò in qualunque lingua tu mi dica se questo ti farà continuare a guardarmi in quel modo."*

Twelve - Wicked

Longing Looks And Daydreams

I don't think she even notices the way she licks her lips as she looks at me, but the sight of it damn near brings me to my knees as all the blood in my body rushes straight to my cock.

As the words I know she doesn't understand settle inside her, she finally gathers her composure and shakes her head, taking off toward the boardwalk.

Fuck, if I don't love having that effect on her.

"You look at me like that all the time," she mutters from a step ahead of me.

"Yeah, well..." I draw out as I catch up. "I can't stop thinking about it. About you. That night. You sure as fuck don't make it easy to forget when you look at me like you wish we could do it all over again."

Her breath catches at that.

"I'm on my way home. To your brother's house." She lets out an exasperated sigh. "Where I am living. Because he's marrying my sister." She spins to face me. "Your *mother* is my only friend. My life is a mess. My estranged father is stalking me. I'm basically homeless." She throws her hands up. "Not to mention, my daughter *really* likes you. I don't let men meet her. Ever. Because if there is one thing I know with certainty, it's that my flings never work out. I won't do that to her. Or Darby. Or Leo. Or Monica. It's too much." She breaks her gaze from mine, as if rethinking everything she just said. "Oh, right." She scoffs. "And we work together. Are all those reasons enough for you to realize that this"—she waves a finger between us—"would be an astronomically bad idea?"

"No."

"Everett," she groans, throwing her head back.

I love it when she says my name.

I step into her the same time she steps into me—not so close that I'll scare her away, but close enough that she can see my eyes, so she can feel my intention as I close the space between us. "I understand your fears. I respect your boundaries." Her face softens at that. "But just...if you forgot about all the other bullshit for just a second. You're just you. I'm just me..." I slowly reach out and brush her hair from her shoulder.

Her eyes flutter closed at the contact, mouth parting slightly, as if she savors my touch. "I wish I could," she whispers. "But I don't have that luxury. That night was all I had. I don't have the option to just forget who I am and lean into feeling."

"I know." I nod. I brush my thumb across the pulse in her neck. "Just know that it's killing me. If nothing else, if it can't be acted on, know that I wish it could..." I pause, trying to find the right words. "If you change your mind, I want you to know that I'm not afraid of complicated, and I won't hurt Lou. Ever."

She inhales sharply, and I let my hand linger on her collarbone just a second longer before I pull away. I nearly feel the electricity between us in the tips of my fingers, as if the feel of her skin has branded itself onto my own.

I'm swept into the sea of her eyes as she opens them and soaks me in. We let each other see the desire written in our stares for just a moment, knowing this is all it'll ever be between us. She's decided we'll never be more than this: longing looks and daydreams.

I don't think it's just because she's afraid of her daughter being hurt. I think it's because she's afraid of hurting herself. Of being abandoned. Of not being enough for someone, not worthy of the love she so badly wants to receive but refuses to let herself have.

And fuck, if that doesn't make me want to tear down her walls and show her she's worthy of everything. It makes me want to cut through her armor and pull out the wildflower buried beneath it, waiting to bloom.

She takes a deep breath, and I wonder if my intentions are written all over my face.

"I won't change my mind," she whispers. It's a cool challenge I see on her face now.

I scoff. "Then you better stop looking at me like you've been wandering the desert for forty days and forty nights, and I'm the mirage of an oasis. Like you're dying of thirst and I'm the body of water you want to drown yourself in." I give her a slow smile. "Because I want to drown myself in you, too, Wildflower."

Her nostrils flare, but I don't miss the way her eyes widen as I make myself abundantly clear. I've thought that night through enough to understand exactly why she ran out so quickly, and I need her to know she doesn't have to be embarrassed about the way she loses herself. Not with me.

"That was—" She lets out a huff of air. "We're not going there right now." She rolls her eyes. "You think you're a real heartbreaker, don't you, Ramos?"

Her attempt at changing the subject is cute. As if I'm going to forget any time soon the way she squirted all over my cock. As if I'm going to stop thinking about how badly I want to see her come like that again, open and spread out on my bed. But I entertain it because she's pretty when she looks at me with that heated, playful gaze, and I don't want this moment to end just yet.

"You appear to break your fair share of hearts too."

She snorts. "What makes you say that?"

I duck my head so we're closer to the same level. She lifts hers to meet me halfway. Her chest presses against my crossed arms, and we're near enough to share breath. I feel every place our bodies align, as if my molecules are on high alert to her proximity. "The fact that I'm staring at your lips right now and knowing I'll never feel them again... It's breaking my heart, Wildflower."

"Don't flirt with me."

I tsk, giving her a smirk. "Telling me not to flirt with you is like telling me not to breathe around you. It's biological, written in my DNA. It sustains my life source."

Her eyes flare, and I see the challenge in them, the same look she gave me that night at the bar. Her breasts brush against my arms as she raises on her toes, the sensation sending all of the blood in my body straight to my cock.

Her lips are just a hair's breadth from mine, and I feel the softness of her breathing against my mouth. I don't move a fucking muscle, afraid of ruining what may come next. Just like the night we met, the ball is entirely in her court. I wait for her to decide how she wants to play me, knowing when it's said and done that I'll fucking thank her for it.

Her mouth nearly touches mine as she smiles. In the softest tone, pure seduction dripping from her voice, she murmurs, "Then don't breathe."

I let out a shaky exhale as she steps back with a triumphant smile on her face. I'm damn near ready to unleash myself on her, kiss her breathless right here on this beach. She raises her brows at me, as if challenging me to do so.

Suddenly, a chiming noise erupts from her pocket, breaking our moment.

I can't ignore the annoyance that flashes across her face at the interruption, as if she weren't ready for it to end either. She gives me an apologetic look as she fishes her phone out of her back pocket. "It's probably Darby wondering where we are. Are you going to come by—"

She pauses as she stares down at her screen, and all evidence of that wild and fierce woman from a few moments ago vanishes entirely.

She's no longer that girl I met in the bar weeks ago. She's now the terrified woman I found in my shop with a man's grip around her arm. "Is it your dad?" I ask.

She looks up at me with fearful eyes, giving me a shallow shake of her head. "It's not my father..." She sighs. "It's my daughter's."

I feel my eyes go wide as my mouth drops open.

I obviously knew that Lou *has* a dad. I've just never heard her nor Dahlia speak of him before. I've never even heard Darby mention him. I figured he was entirely out of the picture.

"You seem afraid," I say cautiously. Her eyes snap to mine, creased and careful. "Is he dangerous, Dahlia?" My stomach knots as I ask the question.

"No." She bites her lip, looking back to her screen. "Not in the way you're thinking. I just... I didn't..." She huffs in frustration.

"You should answer it," I say. "Figure out what he wants. Otherwise, it'll be eating at you all day. At least this way, we can figure out a path forward, and then you can enjoy having your sister home."

She slides her thumb across the screen, holding the phone to her ear as she says, "There is no 'we,' Everett. This is my mess. Mine alone."

That stings.

"Hello?" she answers breathlessly. She swallows deeply, quiet for a moment as she takes in whatever is being said on the other side of the line. "How did you—" She rolls her eyes. "Of course. You know you don't—" She's cut off. Dahlia glances at me briefly, and it somehow makes me feel like I'm interrupting, but I refuse to leave her here alone. "I don't owe you that." She grabs Lou's surfboard from the stand and begins stalking off toward the shop. I follow behind her.

I hear brief clips of "no" and "how" and "but," though it appears she's interrupted every time she tries to get a thought out. It fucking enrages me.

We reach the front door of Heathen's, and she drops the surfboard onto the ground, placing a hand on her hip as she looks out at the horizon. I watch her jaw tighten, and her refusal to look at me tells me she's on the verge of tears. "Jason, who would possibl—" She stops again, and my heart stops in my chest as she turns to face me, eyes red-rimmed, chest heaving, pure devastation on her face. Fear and fury warp together in her eyes as she looks at me. "No, he wouldn't."

As whatever response she receives filters through her head, her eyes fall closed, and her bottom lip trembles. She doesn't say anything else as she lets the phone fall from her ear and ends the call. I watch her breathe for a moment—rage and worry rushing through me.

"Dahlia..."

Her eyes fall open, and she attempts to shake away whatever emotions are holding her hostage, but I see her fail. "I have to go home," she says quietly, and something about her tone makes me question if she means Darby and Leo's house, or something else entirely.

"Let me take you."

She shakes her head. "No, no. I need to... I just need to get Lou and go home." She runs a hand through her hair, glancing around as if entirely unsure of where she is.

"Dahlia, what—"

"Everett, please." She lets out a sigh. "Thank you for today. I know Lou appreciates it, but I need to go. I'll see you later."

Before I can protest, get on my knees and beg her to let me in, she's turning the corner and making her way down the boardwalk.

I watch her go until she's out of sight.

Thirteen – Wildflower

Lemon Bars & Emotional Scars

"Do you want a lemon bar?"

Leo's lawyer, Malcolm, eyes my outstretched arms and the plate of dessert carefully as he slowly plucks a piece off it and takes a bite.

I've been stress-baking again. Lemons, this time. Lemon cake. Lemon poppyseed muffins. Cinnamon rolls with lemon frosting. Now, I'm onto classic lemon bars. I hope this is the end of my lemon phase, and that after today's meeting, it'll be the end of my current stress-baking phase too.

I smile at Malcolm as his face lights up with the first taste of the dessert. "Damn. This is good."

"That's what I'm saying." Leo pats his stomach beside me. "I'm supposed to be on a strict diet for competition season, but shit."

Darby rolls her eyes. "I think you're fine."

After coming home on Sunday, I hardly kept it together while Lou caught up with her aunt and got to know her new uncle. I was so sure I'd make it home and instantly break down after that call from Jason, but seeing my daughter's face light up gave me the strength I needed to push through.

Knowing me better than anyone on earth, though, Darby could see the darkness in my eyes, and the moment Lou went to bed, I broke down in her arms. Like I have so many times over the years, like she has with me, too.

I didn't tell Lou's father that I was moving out of state. I didn't have any obligation, either. He gave up his rights to her years ago in exchange for forgiveness on all back child support he owed me. I haven't seen him since that day in court. He never called on her birthday, or any holiday, never attended any of her school functions or sports games.

It's exactly how I was able to go nearly two months living here before he even realized we were gone.

He only realized because my father called him. My father. The person who has abhorrently loathed my daughter's dad since the day he met him, even more so after he found out I was pregnant. My father went to great lengths over the last decade to keep Jason away from me—not that he really needed to. Jason didn't want much to do with me, anyway.

Regardless, to learn my dad was the one now bringing him back into the picture, encouraging him to pressure me to move back to Kansas so he can have a place in our child's life... That gut-deep betrayal sliced through me in ways I hadn't known were possible.

The claim that my dad would agree my child is better off with her criminally negligent father than she would be with me was like stabbing a searing blade right through my soul.

I was supposed to start my new job on Monday, but Leo insisted I take another week. The anxiety of Jason's call was eating me alive, along with my father's secrets I'm harboring, causing him to act this way. I knew there was no way I could focus on all of this and learn the ropes at the Small Business Initiative, too, but I hate being that person—the one with the excuses who can't do the job. The one who needs to rely on nepotism from the men in their life to get by.

Leo insisted that the rest of the staff would be fine, though. I insisted I not take more than one additional week from work before I started.

Leo also called his lawyer over to help me sort out the best path forward for dealing with Jason. I can see why Darby loves him so much, why I knew—even without meeting him—that he'd come to rescue her, and that he was a man good enough for my sister.

He's selfless, protective, and kind. He cares deeply about those in his life, and a part of me knows he's going to such lengths for me—letting me live in his house, giving me a job, helping me handle my baby-daddy issues—because he wants to see my sister happy, and she wants to see me happy. But I know there is at least a part of him that cares about me too.

"Now, I can only give you my input as a friend. I can't offer real legal counsel here, as I don't specialize in family law. Eventually, you may need to get your own lawyer if things escalate. I'd be happy to get you a list of recommendations, though."

I nod. "Thank you."

"So, if I'm understanding correctly, your daughter's father has demanded you move back to Kansas so he can take an active role in his daughter's life?"

"Yes."

"But he doesn't currently hold parental rights?"

I shake my head. "He never paid his child support, not once. A few years ago, we went to court over it. I agreed that if he signed away his rights, I would forgive what he owed." I swallow. "He's always been like this, showing up at random and pretending to be World's Best Dad and then disappearing for years at a time. The last time it happened was my daughter's seventh birthday. He showed up after almost a year of being M-I-A. He was drunk and couldn't even remember what age she was turning." I shudder as I remember the embarrassment of that day, the hurt on Lou's face. It was the first birthday party she'd ever had with friends from school, and the scene that her father caused had been the talk of the town the following week.

She wouldn't tell me if anything happened at school afterward, what kids had said, but I don't think it's a coincidence that I never saw any of those friends again.

She has been doing well in Pacific Shores thus far. She told me the kids at school have been welcoming. Her teacher is nice, and I think it helps that Monica is a volunteer librarian there. She's friends with Lou's teacher and checks in with Lou throughout the week.

So far, there haven't been any sleepover or birthday party invitations, but it's only the second week of school, so I'm trying not to overthink it.

"Well, logically, it sounds like your daughter is better off with you and you alone." Malcolm shrugs as he takes another bite of his lemon bar. "Plus, her father doesn't have a legal leg to stand on if he voluntarily gave up rights." He pauses to swallow. "But, I suppose it's possible *your* parents could attempt to file for some kind of guardianship if they have strong legal counsel and unlimited funds. Would be a hell of a fight for them, though." Malcolm shrugs. "*If* that's a route he's looking to take, he may think garnering the support of your child's other parent, regardless of if the man has rights, would be beneficial."

I brace my arms on the counter, my hands flexing. Darby inches across the kitchen toward me, covering her hand with mine. "He doesn't have it in him to go to those lengths."

"What if it's Dad trying to take her from me? As a punishment to us." The words scorch my throat as they force their way out of my body.

"That's not going to happen," Leo says with stern authority when he sees my sister's eyes begin to water over.

I take a breath, willing the shaking in my tone to cease as I say, "Jason said she doesn't have a support system here. Her grandparents, both on my side and his, are back in Kansas. That I uprooted her life without thinking. That I'm a bad mother for doing that. That I'm selfish and she's better off with him." One rogue tear falls from my eye. "And I know those weren't his words. They were Dad's."

My sister wraps her arms around my waist, letting her head fall against my back. "You are not a bad mother. Leaving Crestwell was the best decision for both of you, for all of us. She has a support system here. She has us. This is the only place she'd like to be."

Malcolm nods. "She's getting to the age now where she can testify for herself in court as well. She can voice her opinion, and it'll be taken into consideration. So, as long as you're right about that, that she's happier here..." He reaches out for another lemon bar, and I slide the plate across the kitchen island, meeting him halfway. "Sorry, those are really good."

"Help yourself."

"Better yet, we'll send you home with some because I can't handle having this much sugar in my house," Leo adds, blue eyes glistening playfully, as if attempting to lighten the mood.

"But let's not get too far ahead of ourselves," Malcolm adds, pushing his dark-rimmed glasses up his nose. "You're a far way from court testimonies. Like you said, he doesn't have any rights. I'm sure this will all blow over before we get that far."

Malcolm doesn't know my father, but I nod in agreement, attempting to tell myself and everyone else in the room that it'll be okay.

He must catch my expression anyway, because he continues, "It helps if you can ensure that for whatever support system her father claims to have in Kansas, she has a better one here."

"How so?" I ask.

"Get her in some extra-curricular activities, maybe? Have her meet friends. Birthday parties. Clubs and sports." He takes another bite. "Do you have any family here?"

"No—" I say at the same time Leo says, "Yes."

He gives me a pointed look. "My family is here. My parents and my brother. My brother is giving her surf lessons, and my mom is just...absolutely smitten with Lou. So, yes. They have a support system here."

Malcolm looks at me again. "What about you?"

"What about me?"

"Do you have any friends? Connections outside of Leo and his family?"

I bite my lip. "Not really. I'm starting my new job on Monday, though."

"Good." He nods. "That's good. What about finding a place to live?"

"I'm looking," I murmur.

"Is it bad if she's living here?" Darby asks.

"Not necessarily, but planting roots helps, I think. You should show you don't have any

intention of bouncing from place to place, that you can offer stability. A job is good. Owning a house would be better." Malcolm shrugs.

I nod in contemplation. These were all things I wanted to do for Lou anyway.

My mind wanders back to the thumb drive in my bedside table. I know that's why my father is going to such lengths. It's not the only reason—he'd do anything to have Darby back home with him, the child he considers his true daughter. I think he could honestly give a shit about me or mine.

I can't help but wonder why my blackmail couldn't keep him away, though. He knows what files I have, knows what I have could put him away for years. He knows it's enough that he wants it back, but it isn't enough to keep him quiet.

My only conclusion is that he doesn't believe I have it in me to actually turn him in. That realization only makes me want to do it more, to show him how lethal I can fucking be when he gets my kid involved. He doesn't understand the need to protect, love, and nurture a child. He doesn't have those qualities in his bones. It makes me want to go that much further in my effort to protect Lou. Maybe it'll finally make him understand what we've been missing from him all our lives.

But if I turn him in and he gets out of it, there would be no barrier between him and me—between him and Darby—to keep him from attempting to destroy us again or genuinely trying to take Lou away as a form of punishment.

"What about your mother?" Malcolm asks, breaking me

from my thoughts.

My mom isn't evil like my dad; she's just weak. She never stood up for Darby or me one single time, instead letting our father spew his hatred. She was content to sit back and watch, to play trophy wife and let us wither away. I think if I had never become a mother myself, I might have forgiven her for it, but I know that I'd go to the ends of the Earth for my daughter's well-being. No status, money, or stability a man could provide me would keep me from putting her first. So, seeing my own mom put my sister and me behind herself time and time again only proved my fears that she simply doesn't love us the way a mother should.

"She'll go along with whatever our father demands," Darby answers for me.

"All right." Malcolm nods. "Well, my official advice would be to build that support system. Establish yourself at work. Find a home for your daughter. Make connections. Plant roots, essentially." He wipes his hands. "Play nice. If her father asks for updates on her, provide them. Eventually, if you're right about him, he'll tire himself out and go away. If not, then you fight him, or whomever else, in court." Malcolm looks at Leo. "I'll have my assistant email over a list of family law practices for you to look into."

I thank Malcolm profusely for his help, wrapping up a plate of lemon bars for him to take home to his husband and their kids. As he leaves the kitchen, Leo in tow to walk him out, I feel the weight of the situation bear down on me as I fall against the counter and bury my face in my hands. My sister silently rubs my back as we wait for Leo to return.

The front door shuts, and heavy footsteps pad back into the kitchen when Darby says, "I just don't understand why Dad is going to such lengths. What is his endgame? Does he think threatening us, scaring us, is going to bring us back? Going to make me marry Jackson?"

"Over my dead fucking body." Leo rounds the island and plants a kiss against Darby's forehead. "I think that man has been in control of every aspect of his life for so long he's not capable of comprehending what it's like to lose it, to lose power over other people. He's probably falling apart because, in his brain, if he can't control his own daughters, how is he going to maintain control of all the other people in his life? He thinks the power he held over you and your family is what made people respect him, and now he's lost it. He's probably losing his mind too." Leo sighs. "There is no logic to his actions. He's just scrambling for any ounce of power he can get back, and honestly, he's probably trying to get revenge too."

Leo isn't wrong. For having never met my father, he somehow understands a great deal about the man, though I shouldn't be surprised. He has had a front-row seat to my dad's antics since he was seventeen, seen firsthand the way he broke my sister and me down, how much work it's taken to help Darby piece herself back together.

One thing Leo is wrong about, one thing I can't seem to find the strength to voice, is that my father has another motive for all of this. The documents sitting in my nightstand that could potentially put him in jail for the rest of his life, tear down his business—the only thing he truly cares about...

I have the power to destroy that, to destroy *him*.

The protective instincts in me won't allow me to get my sister involved. I know she'd be upset about me keeping her in the dark over it, and I feel guilty—I'm lying to her about so many things, but I can't stomach adding this one to her plate. I took it upon myself to blackmail our father, something I know she would've never done because she's the better of us. I won't put this on her shoulders.

"Dahlia?" Darby's soft voice filters through my thoughts.

My head whips sideways, clashing with her soft hazel eyes full of worry and concern. I hate that I'm lying to her. I hate it so much that I blurt, "I had sex with Everett."

Her brows knit together, concern morphing into confusion. Her blond hair falls off her shoulder as she tilts her head and crosses her arms. "Okay?"

Leo's face pops around her a second later, his jaw dropped. "*My* Everett?"

"Your Everett?" I ask.

At that, the tightness in my sister's mouth widens into a grin, and she begins laughing. Her entire body shakes with it, and she covers her mouth, glancing down at the floor like she's not able to stop herself. Leo and I are both staring after her with perplexed looks.

"I'm sorry." She giggles, clearing her throat. "That's kind of funny. What made you say that?"

Shaking my head, I say honestly, "I don't know. I felt guilty keeping it from you, I guess."

She laughs again. "When did this happen?"

Leo leans over the counter, bracing his head on his hands, as if waiting for the explanation too.

"Do you remember when Monica set me up on that blind date a few weeks ago while you guys were still in Portugal?"

They both nod.

"You said it was a bust." My sister raises a brow at me.

"The date Monica set me up on was a bust, definitely. That doesn't mean I didn't run into a different guy at the bar who was hellbent on *rescuing* me from said busted date."

"Sounds like my brother," Leo mutters.

"He didn't know who I was," I snap back defensively. "We agreed not to share names. We weren't ever supposed to see each other again."

Leo frowns. "I can't believe he didn't tell me."

"I told him not to. I told him to pretend it didn't happen."

My sister chews on her lip. "So, why are you telling us now?"

"Guess it's not as easy to pretend as I thought it would be." I shrug. "Didn't feel good about holding it in."

My sister smiles knowingly. "That good, huh?"

Leo and I both glare at her, but I don't confirm or deny.

We're all quiet for a moment before Leo busts up with a rough laugh. "So, you're telling me that Monica inadvertently set you up on a one-night-stand with her own son?"

I wince. "Sounds about right."

He laughs again. "You going to tell her about it?"

"I'd prefer not to."

He snorts as my sister asks, "Is it awkward between you and Everett now? You'll be working together, you know."

"It hasn't been," I say honestly. It has been...fun with him. When I'm around him, I laugh. A lot. He makes things feel lighter, although I don't know what things will look like after the way I treated him at the beach. "He took Lou out for surf lessons, and you know he was there when Dad cornered me at Heathen's. He stepped in and made Dad leave." I snort. "Everett told him he was my boyfriend, actually."

Their eyes go wide as they stare after me, willing me to go on.

"He didn't mean it," I quickly add. *I mean, I'm fairly certain he didn't mean it.* "He was just saying it to get Dad to fuck off. Intimidate him, I think."

Neither my sister or her fiancé look entirely convinced, but they nod all the same. Suddenly, Leo slaps his palms onto the counter as he stands straight. "Well, great. I'll let Everett know you'll join him at the Hayes Foundation Banquet then."

"The what?"

My sister's mouth splits into a grin as she lightly claps her hands together.

"The foundation in Zach's name. They raise awareness for water safety, provide free equipment like lifejackets at parks, host training in schools, free swim lessons for children and parents, and help fund lifeguard stations in underserved coastal communities. They have an auction on the anniversary of Zach's death every year." Leo's face tightens as he pushes off the counter and heads toward the hallway to his and Darby's bedroom downstairs. "Heathen's is a main sponsor, and Everett needs a date."

"Why would I need to be Everett's date?"

Leo pauses in the doorway, crossing his arms. "You said that

Everett told your dad he was your boyfriend, right? To intimidate him? Make him leave you alone?"

I nod. "I assume that's what has kept him away thus far. He would never take Darby or I seriously, but a man with more money, status, and power than he has, or a man like Everett who's taller, larger, and more threatening? That's the kind of shit he'll cower under."

"Exactly." Leo's face twists into something like disgust. "I'm not going to pretend this is some kind of star-studded event, but there will be cameras. Some reporters. Anyone who's looking for us will find out we attended. You might as well continue playing that part if you want your father to stay fucked off."

My sister nods next to me. "Yeah, that's smart."

"Plus," Leo continues. "It's never an easy night for any of us. I hate to tell you that I'd like you to be a distraction, but I think it would help if Everett had something else to focus on than the day of the year and the reason for the event."

My heart drops at that. I didn't know Zach, obviously, but the heartbreak is written clear across my brother-in-law's face, the same way it was written across Monica's when she spoke of him. They all loved Zach, and they still feel his loss deeply.

"Of course," I say. "Whatever you guys need."

He gives me a grateful smile. "Okay, I'll let Everett know when I see him tomorrow."

"Actually," I call out as Leo pushes off the door, "can I talk to him about all of this first?"

Leo nods, a small smirk on his face as he turns the corner toward his bedroom.

Inhaling a shaky breath, I pull out my phone and send the message:

Can we talk?

Fourteen - Wicked

I'm Not Scared Of It At All

Can we talk?

My breath catches as I stare at the message from Dahlia. We haven't spoken in four days, not since she very clearly reminded me that she had zero interest in having me as part of her life. I've been giving her space ever since, while not-so-discreetly begging my brother for details on what the hell happened with her ex that spooked her so much.

Leo doesn't tell me shit, though.

"What are you staring at?" My dad's voice breaks my thoughts as I look up from my screen and realize he has been extending the socket wrench I asked for.

Of course. At Lou's next lesson on Sunday?

I shake my head, typing out my response quickly and slipping my phone back into my pocket. "Nothing." I take the tool from him and get back to work on the 1982 Chevy Corvette we're restoring. "Just had to return a text message."

"Your eyes lit up like a kid who just found out they're going to Disneyland for the first time," Dad mutters under his breath. "Someone we should know about?"

"Not yet," I answer honestly.

My dad's head lifts from where he works beneath the hood, surprise accenting his brown eyes. "Well, that's four more letters than I'm used to hearing."

I snort.

"I think that could be good for you, you know," he adds.

"What makes you say that?"

"You keep telling me to let this place go, and part of the reason I can't is because I've been here so long I don't know what to do with myself when I'm not here." He sighs, going back to his work. "But," he continues, "another part of the reason is because you've got a reputation on you, kid." I catch his gaze as he looks at me again. "And some people don't want to work with you because of it."

I roll my eyes. "I'm not offended by people who're unwilling to patronize a business owned by a queer man, and I'm surprised you'd be concerned about those customers anyway."

"You know me better than that." His tone is rough. "Fuck those assholes. They can go elsewhere. I'm not talking about your sexual identity, Everett. I'm talking about your sexcapades all over town and the bruised hearts you leave in your wake."

I fight the twitch in my lips at that. "A bit dramatic, Daddio."

"I am not," he counters. "Debbie Michaelson has been coming here for thirty years damn near, and last week, I found out she drove her ass out to Carlsbad for a goddamn oil change because you 'ghosted' her grandson after two dates, and she doesn't want to upset him by coming here." He steps back from the car and wipes his hands on a rag. "Whatever the hell 'ghosted' means, I don't know, but it doesn't sound good."

I groan. "I told Clay I wasn't looking for something serious." I drop my wrench on the table next to me and stand up straight, stretching my back. "It's not my fault if people misconstrue my feelings when I make my intentions abundantly clear."

"I'm not saying you're a bad guy, kid. I'm not. All I'm saying is that it's a small community, and unfortunately, personal and professional can get mixed up a lot easier around here than in a big city. So, you've got to keep that in mind when fuckin' around town."

"Christ," I mutter.

I've always been one to chase a good time. I'm not afraid of commitment or relationships. I'm not afraid of falling in love. I had a good example of what a marriage should look like growing up, and I've always felt like it was something in the cards for me. But being exposed to such a prime example of what love is supposed to look like makes you realize all the times that it's simply not there. I've always wanted to wait until I found the person I could look at the way my dad looks at my mom.

He has always said that you've got to find that one who makes you feel like every love song was written just for them.

My dad has a habit of stopping when he hears a song that makes him think of my mom, making her dance with him right then and there. Doesn't matter where they are—crowded restaurant, the grocery store, or the kitchen; if he hears a love song, he takes her in his arms and spins her around until they're laughing and breathless.

I always knew I'd never been interested in settling down until I found someone who made me want to do that too.

But I always make my intentions clear. I'm not afraid of seeing someone more than once, and I'm not opposed to a one night stand, either. I like to spend time with people until I simply feel like our connection has run its course. Sometimes, we remain friends. Other times, we go our separate ways. No hard feelings and no regrets.

I make sure that's clear before I ever take a person to bed, but I can't help if feelings get hurt in the process every once in a while. Clay's a great guy, but he's not the person I want to dance in the middle of the grocery store with.

It's not often I get stuck on someone enough to consider seeing them for more than a few times, and as of late, the only thing stuck in my head are stormy blue eyes.

"I'll be more careful," I say. "I know I need to start making the businesses my top priority, and I'll make sure I put the integrity of them first from now on."

I mean the words as I say them, but mostly because I just don't have any desire to even attempt at a casual hook-up right now.

Dad smiles at me, clapping a hand on my back as we exit the garage and enter the office attached to it. "Don't stop having fun. Don't stop chasing your good time. Just...maybe find someone you have a good time chasing over and over again."

"Stop looking at my wife," Leo says two days later as we stand waist deep in the waves, waiting for Lou to meet us in the water for her lesson.

Darby and Leo decided to join today, and the girls are laying out while we take Lou into the water. Dahlia's wearing a good-for-fucking-nothing blue one-piece that matches the shade of her eyes and accentuates every dip and curve of her soft body.

It's driving me out of my goddamn mind.

"She's not your wife. And I'm not looking at Darby. I'm looking at Dahlia."

"She's basically my wife. And they look exactly alike."

I glance at my brother, whose eyes are completely stuck on his fiancée as she rubs sunscreen into her legs. It's perpetual bliss and adoration I see on his face as he watches her. It's the way he has stared at her since he was seventeen, like he always knew, even back then, that he belonged wholly to her.

"I don't see Darby when I look at her. I only see Dahlia."

That's enough to snap him from his trance, and his sharp blue eyes study my face with bemused consideration. "Christ, man," he murmurs as his gaze narrows on me, reading my expression. "You've got a crush on my sister-in-law, don't you?" He chuckles. "I don't think I've seen you have a crush since your obsession with Mr. Vardin in the eleventh grade."

"Dude. He was my bi-awakening. That's a sensitive topic."

"Whatever." He scoffs. "Just stay away from Dahlia. She's got enough on her plate without you drooling over her."

"You don't think she could use someone to help take some of that shit off her plate? Carry some of the weight for her?"

He seems to consider that for a moment. "I think she could, but I don't think that person is you. What's the most you can offer her? A few casual hook ups before you get bored and move onto your next conquest?"

His words land like a physical blow as I stumble back, ocean water lapping at my legs. I think back to what my father said the other day.

Is this really what they think of me?

"Dahlia needs someone who's in it for the long haul, who wants to be around for her, and for her daughter, for good. She's not going to trust someone until she knows they're going to stay." His eyes meet mine. "They were never made to feel like they were enough, and it takes a lot to prove them otherwise. Trust me, until she finds someone who's going to do that, she's not going to open up to anyone, and she does not need you messing with her head in the meantime. Not with everything she's got going on."

"Can someone please tell me what the fuck she has going on, then?"

My brother shakes his head. "That woman has trust issues as deep as the goddamn Grand Canyon, and it wouldn't be right of me to share her struggles without her knowledge. If she chooses to trust you with them, she'll tell you herself."

I don't respond as I ponder my brother's words, my own intentions. I haven't thought much past my attraction, my adoration of her. She's alluring and enticing, and I can't get her out of my goddamn head, but the truth is, I have no idea what the fuck that means.

What I do know, though, is that I think I understand her fears. I understand what it takes to open her up, gain her trust, and win her over. I think I understand just how precious those parts of her are, and what it would mean to hold them. The scariest thing about it is that I'm not scared of it at all. The challenge. The chase. The commitment.

I open my mouth to tell Leo just that when a flash of purple catches my eye. I turn my head in time to find the bundle of red-blond hair barreling toward us with the orange surfboard in her hands. She laughs maniacally as she reaches the water, laying down the board, jumping atop it, and gliding straight toward us.

I pull her between Leo and myself, and Lou looks up at me with those big bright eyes and the sunniest grin on her face.

"You ready, Luz?" I ask.

She nods excitedly, and I lift my head to find her mother watching the two of us with a cautious yet hopeful smile.

It's then I realize loving the two of them may come far too easily.

Fifteen – Wildflower

Aching Ovaries

"What time did Everett say he needed to be back at the shop?" I ask, glancing at the time on my phone before locking the screen and dropping it back into the beach bag.

"Two o'clock, I think," Darby says from her spot next to me. She's on her back, face tilted toward the sun. She looks at peace.

I'm the utter opposite of peaceful as I nod. "All right, we should probably call them in. I have a feeling they lose track of time out there."

My sister chuckles in agreement as she lifts her head, and we both look out to the horizon.

Everett stands about chest deep in the water, calm waves cresting and crashing against his perfect, golden abdomen. Leo stands closer to shore in knee-deep water. Lou takes turns paddling back and forth, coasting through the waves between the two of them.

She's laughing the entire time, and so are they.

"It makes my ovaries ache."

I laugh at that, throwing Darby's dress at her as we both stand. I whistle toward the boys and motion for them to come back to shore before turning to my sister. "Can we get you through your wedding first?"

She smiles softly to herself, hazel eyes catching mine with a knowing glitter. "We can certainly try."

I shake my head as we both giggle.

We begin folding up towels and packing our bags as Leo reaches us with both his and Lou's surfboards balanced on top of his head. Everett follows behind him with my daughter at his side. She jumps ahead of him as she reaches me, barreling her wet little body into my arms.

"Did you see me?"

"I did, bug. You were doing so well." I squat down to her level, brushing the wet strands of hair that came loose from her braid off her forehead.

"Why do we have to leave?"

"Everett has to get to work."

She pouts.

"I wanted to take you to get ice cream, Lulu. But," Leo draws, "if you don't want any, then I guess I'll just go by myself."

My daughter's face instantly brightens, lips parting to reveal a toothy grin as she looks from her uncle back to me. "Can I?"

I shoot Leo a grateful look; he must know what I have planned next. "Of course."

She smiles as I wrap her in a towel. I notice her gaze catching Everett, who's trying to fold up one of our umbrellas but struggling. A small smile accents her cheeks. "Is Everett coming?"

"Do you want him to?" I ask cautiously, noticing the anticipation of her answer sends a sensation through my stomach.

She nods. "Yeah."

"Okay. I'll ask him if he wants to come." I pull her into me and press my lips against her head. "Why don't you help Darby and Leo take the surfboards back to the shop? I'll help Everett with the umbrellas and ask him if he'd like to join us for ice cream and then meet you up there, yeah?"

She nods, and I send her off to my sister, who wraps her in a hug. Darby throws a bag over her shoulder, Lou holds the towels, and Leo grabs the surfboards as they take off through the sand.

I stand up straight and face Everett, who's been waiting with his arms crossed. A different kind of trepidation washes over me as his eyes meet mine. "You wanted to talk, Wildflower?"

I nod. "Yeah..." I take a breath, preparing myself for the conversation coming next. "I'm sorry for how I acted last week. I got a call from her dad, and I was just..."

"Don't apologize. You've got nothing to apologize for."

"Okay," I breathe. "I just... I'm scared, I guess. He hasn't been around in a while, and I don't like the idea of him trying to be involved again."

I almost hate those words as they fall from my mouth. My child deserves a father. I should want her father to be part of her life, but I don't trust his intentions—I never have. I don't have it in me to watch her get hurt by him again, and I can't pretend it wasn't part of the reason I came to California so easily: to avoid the fear of ever running into him, of having him pretend he doesn't know his own daughter and watching that break her.

But purposely keeping her away now that he reached out doesn't make me feel any better.

It feels like no matter what I do, I'm the bad guy.

Everett gives me a soft smile.

I force myself to return it as I say, "Lou just asked me if you'd come get ice cream with us. I think she likes having you around."

His face brightens at that. "Of course, I'll come."

I sigh. "Do you see my point, though? She's beginning to trust you. I don't want her to have expectations of you—or anyone else—that aren't reasonable." I glance down at the sand, afraid to meet his gaze. "Sometimes, it's just easier to keep the distance."

I'm grateful I looked away when Everett responds in a rough tone, "Why do you assume it's unreasonable of her to trust that I'll protect her? That we—as a family—can give her comfort and stability?" I hear him shuffle toward me, pausing until I lift my head to look at him. "You allow her to lean on Leo that way."

"Leo's marrying her aunt. He'll be her uncle."

His face straightens, his commanding presence towering over me. "Exactly. And he's my fucking brother." His arm flutters in the direction of the boardwalk. "We own a business together.

He's my best friend. I'm not going anywhere, Dahlia. You can ask things of me, and so can your daughter." His eyes bore into me, as if ensuring I absorb every word. "It's not unreasonable."

The intensity in them is too strong, too honest. I want to look away, but I can't. I can't ever seem to take my eyes off him when he looks at me this way.

"I don't want to feel like anyone's obligation," I whisper.

"You aren't!" His jaw tightens, and his eyes flare. I feel myself shrink beneath his presence, and as if he can see it happen, his voice instantly softens. "I'm sorry." He runs a hand through his hair. "You aren't." I only shrug as we stare down on the beach, unsure of where to go from here. After a moment of tense silence, Everett finally sighs. "Did you know I lost my best friend three years ago?"

I can't hide the surprise on my face at that, but I nod. "I know. I'm sorry."

He sucks his lip between his teeth, as if he can't decide whether or not to tell me whatever is running through his head right now. On a breath, he finally says, "When that happened, I didn't just lose Zach. We all lost...everything. Zach's brother, August— He won't hardly talk to me anymore. Talk to *anyone*. And my sister..." he scoffs. "I lost her too. Three of the people I love most in the world"—he snaps his fingers—"just like that."

I open my mouth, but words don't come. Telling him I'm sorry doesn't feel like enough.

"Do you know how lonely my mother has been since Elena moved to New York? How big of a gap she has had in her heart? My sister hardly calls. She's basically a ghost at this point. She's my *twin*. So, trust me when I tell you how deep her absence runs inside my soul too."

I don't understand where all of this is coming from, but it feels as if the words are something he's held in for far too long. I say nothing, but I reach across the arm's length between the two of us, running my hand across his skin, a silent plea for him to continue.

"We've all been broken down. Lost and wandering is what it feels like. Then, a few months ago, Leo got that letter." His eyes are on the place where our skin meets, but they snap up to meet my face. "A letter you sent him. It was the first sign of life in his eyes that I'd seen in years, the first scrap of motivation or determination to do anything, like he suddenly found his purpose again." He nods down the beach, where his brother and my sister walk hand-in-hand through the water, my daughter at their side. "She was that purpose. And my mom? I haven't heard her gush and beam about anyone the way she does you three in years, maybe ever. Your presence, you giving her the ability to form a relationship with Lou, that brought her back to life. She has been brighter since knowing you."

Everett faces me, but I watch his eyes lose focus. I don't know what's going through his mind as he whispers, "And I haven't found that purpose yet. My purpose for healing." Suddenly, all that intensity—all that focus—is concentrated on me. "But you know what, Dahlia? Taking that kid out on a surfboard and watching her laugh, watching *you* laugh because of it"—he smiles to himself—"it certainly feels like the sun is shining after years of cloud cover." He sets his hand over where I hold his arm, and I only now realize how tightly I'm gripping him. "So, you're not a fucking obligation. You, your sister, and your daughter, you are exactly what we've all been needing."

Those words—this moment—stretch between us, like an eternity of emotion. I let them soak into my skin and bones. I let myself begin to believe them, because as I look into those sunlit brown eyes, I see only honesty, only conviction.

"I need you to take me as your date to the Hayes Foundation Banquet," I find myself blurting, still attempting to process everything he just said and form some kind of response, though that *certainly* was not it. I clamp a hand over my mouth. "I mean... I—" I shake my head. "It wasn't supposed to come out that way."

Everett's face lights up with surprised laughter. "You're always intriguing me, Wildflower." He softly brushes my hand and spins me so I face the pier. Placing a hand at the center of my back, he guides us forward. "Tell me how exactly that was supposed to come out."

His laugh skates along my skin, instant relief settling over me at the sound. We begin walking along the waves, but his hand doesn't leave my back. "The call I got last week was from Jason, Lou's dad."

"You mentioned that," Everett says quietly.

"My dad got in contact with him." Everett pauses and waits for me to continue. "Informed him that I moved away without telling him. He somehow convinced Jason—who hasn't seen his child in almost three years—that he needs to be involved now." Suddenly, my throat is feeling tight as I try to speak. "They're like..." I swallow a lump of emotion. "Banding together to try and... I don't even know what the motive is, really. I guess to try and make Darby and I move back to Kansas, using my *child* as their pawn."

I don't know how or why the words spill out so easily, but those softening brown eyes may just be the reason.

"Your father is a horrible person," he says with conviction. I can only nod in agreement. "Is it possible Lou's dad has changed? That maybe you leaving made him realize what he'd been missing?"

I shrug. "That's the thing. It could be, but I don't trust him enough to pack my life up again. I don't even trust them enough to visit. I don't need to uproot my daughter for the second time, only to find out Jason doesn't care at all and..." I trail off.

"Have Lou end up hurt," he finishes for me.

I nod.

"It's not an easy position to be in." I feel his fingers flex at the base of my spine, his way of providing some sort of comfort to me. "I think all you can do is your best, though, and take comfort in knowing that your best is good enough. She knows how much you love her, and someday, she'll understand how much you've sacrificed for her. Whether he's in her life or not, she'll know how loved she is."

I don't know how to respond to that, so I don't. I *do* find myself shifting a bit closer to him as I absorb his words. How he innately seems to understand what I need to hear, I have no idea. After a few minutes of silently allowing the sea to lap against our feet, Everett asks, "So, how does all of this tie into me being your boyfriend?"

"I said be my *date*." I sigh. "We met with Leo's lawyer, just to get some guidance on what kind of case—if any—Jason and my father could make. He says they don't have much, but with the right legal counsel and unlimited funds—which my father does have—he could potentially try." Our feet drag along the sand as we continue walking side by side. "I don't understand their motives, so it's hard to know their actions, and I want to be prepared." I bite my lip. "In the midst of all that, I may have accidentally disclosed to our siblings that we..."

Everett grins.

"Anyway"—I roll my eyes—"since you took it upon yourself to say that you're my boyfriend, Leo suggested we lean into that narrative." I lift my head, gaze clashing with his. "He said there will be some reporters at the banquet, and he thought it'd be a good idea if you took me as your date, since my father will be keeping tabs."

I don't tell him what Leo said about Everett needing a distraction from the anniversary of Zach's death, and after all Everett just said, I realize Leo was completely right about that.

"Malcolm thinks that's a good idea?"

"We didn't ask." I can feel Everett's eyes on me. "He said I should plant roots. Establish a life here. Find a support system who could provide the stability and support that Lou's father never could. He didn't say it outright, but I suppose if it appeared I was bringing someone into her life to fill the space he left..."

Everett's breath seems to catch at that, and I realize just how large of a proposition I've just made.

Backtracking, I say quickly, "Which, of course, is ridiculous. That's not what I'm asking." I shake my head. "I just mean... There is no getting *rid* of you now anyway because of the whole—" Everett's head whips to the side, and I lift mine to meet his eyes. They're narrowed and concerned. "I didn't mean it that way. I don't want to get rid of you, I—" I take a deep breath. "I don't know what I'm saying."

"Are you trying to tell me that you've never let someone meet your daughter before, which is why you normally choose to never speak to a man after night one? Are you trying to tell me that was your intention with me? Why you didn't want to exchange names?"

I nod.

"I already knew all of that, Wildflower. So, are you also trying to tell me that based on your dad's reaction..." His jaw ticks in anger at the memory. "The things that he said to you that day at Heathen's, you think he may try and hold our one-night stand against you?"

I hadn't thought of that, actually. Thinking back, my father had called me a slut. Everett referring to himself as my boyfriend would squash any notion my father has of using promiscuity against me.

So, I nod. "I think he'd use anything he could to prove I'm an awful mother, go to any length to get my sister and I back in Crestwell. Get his control back."

Before I have time to process much of anything, two strong arms grasp my shoulders as my body is being turned to face him. He drops his head, brown eyes clashing against mine. "Taking a night off does not make you a bad mother. Going on a date does not make you a bad mother. Having casual, consensual sex does not make you a bad mother. You are wonderful to that girl, and anyone with eyes and a functioning brain stem would be able to see that. You're allowed to be a human being, Dahlia. You are not exclusively tied to that title. You can be a woman. Have a career. Hobbies. Be a friend and a sister. You're entitled to all of those things—to having an identity outside of Lou's mother. There is nothing wrong with that." The near-setting sun casts Everett's face in a golden hue, bright conviction and waring emotion in his eyes.

"Do you understand?"

"I want to," I whisper honestly. "But I'm just not sure that's true."

"How can I prove to you that it is?"

I almost say it then, almost open my mouth and tell him that when I met him, he made me feel like a woman. He made me feel desirable, wild, and free. He reminded me of the person I'd always dreamed I'd be before I saw those two little pink lines while sitting on the bathroom floor.

Oh, how badly I want to be that woman again. How I wish I could take surf lessons. Play pool. Drive an impractical car with no doors so I can feel the wind whipping through my hair as I drive.

But I don't. "That's not what I'm asking of you," is what I find myself saying.

"Let me prove it to you anyway."

"Everett." I shake my head. "It's not about any of that. That's not why I wanted to talk to you."

"I know. You want me to pretend to date you when there are cameras around my brother to threaten your father, to help give the appearance you're providing your daughter with a stable environment and a supportive male role model."

"Yes."

"Great. Can do," he says immediately, as if requiring no further explanation on the matter. "But I'm also going to take you on dates. I'm gonna show you that you can be so much more than just her mother. You can be yourself too."

"Why?" I ask breathlessly.

"Because I want to," he says quickly. Pausing to settle himself, Everett takes a breath. "And because I think this might be in my best interest too, honestly."

I cock my head, interest piqued. "What makes you say that?"

He chews on his lip, looking off to the horizon, almost as if he's nervous. "I kind of have a...reputation. I guess."

"You don't say?"

He rolls his eyes. "My dad has been giving me shit about it. Some of my...past flings have been painting the businesses in a bad light." He swallows. "Leo's been giving me shit about it too."

"Why?" I laugh to myself. "What'd you do, fuck his assistant?"

Everett flinches.

My jaw drops. "You didn't."

"I might have. A little." He winces like he's afraid of my response, but I can only laugh at him. He lets out a sigh of relief at my reaction. "I think it would be a good look if I appeared to be cleaning up my act, making moves to settle down. People like a wholesome family business or whatever."

I chuckle again. "This wasn't what I was expecting when Leo asked me to support the small businesses of Pacific Shores."

An effortless smile breaks out on Everett's cheeks, and I can't ignore the way it sends an eruption of sensation throughout my chest. "Thanks for your service, Wildflower." He winks, and that sensation spreads deeper into my being.

"Do we need to work through the logistics of it all? Set boundaries?"

His face straightens slightly, but whatever thought crosses his mind is shaken away just as quickly as it appeared. "For now, let's go deal with this banquet. Why don't I take you to lunch tomorrow, and we can work it out then?"

"Tomorrow is my first day of work."

"I know." He smiles. "I'll stop by the office and grab you around noon."

We continue toward the pier, though this time, instead of his hand at my back, he simply twines his fingers through my own.

Sixteen – Wildflower

I Don't Mind The Mess

"Are you sure that's necessary?" Leo eyes the boxes in my hands as we stare each other down from the foyer of the house.

"I don't want people not to like me."

"Everyone is going to love you," Darby says behind him.

"That's not historically accurate."

She rolls her eyes as she brushes past us and out the door. Construction on Honeysuckle Florals is coming to a close, which means it's time that Darby gets to work on the decorating aspect of the flower shop. She's dropping Leo and me off at work for my first day, and then she's going out with Monica to get some inspiration on paint and wallpaper.

"Because you never allow people to get to know you, Dal. Now, let's go!" she shouts from the driveway.

"This is how I get people to know me!" I call back.

"By dumping your leftovers on them?" My soon-to-be brother-in-law raises a brow as he pushes off the doorway and follows his fiancée out to his car.

"Rude."

I mean, sure, it's a half-eaten cake, a pan of lemon bars, and eleven of the twelve chocolate chip cookies I whipped up last night. In my defense, the reason there isn't a full dozen is because Leo ate one for breakfast this morning.

I carry the boxes out to the car and climb into the back of

Leo's old red Mustang. I cherish the sea breeze whipping through my hair as Darby drives us the two minutes it takes to get down the hill their house rests upon to the boardwalk.

In another life, I'd own a convertible.

My sister drops us off on the backside of the surf shop, and I follow Leo up the staircase into the Pacific Shores Small Business Initiative offices. "I'm nervous," I whisper.

"You're going to be great." He laughs at me as he unlocks the doors and steps inside, flipping on the lights. "Plus, I told everyone to come in a little later this morning so you don't feel bum-rushed on your first day."

"Thank you." I sigh.

Apparently, Leo and Everett only have three staff members under them anyway. Adam, Leo's assistant who's kind of known as a Jack off All Trades. He picks up shifts at Heathen's, manages Leo's schedule, and runs errands around the office. Then, there is Scarlett, their Event Planner. She works with the city on community outreach and services and acts as a liaison between the local government and the small businesses. Finally, they have Jeremiah, their intern. He's a law student who helps the team look over contracts, negotiations, and general operations.

My responsibility will be to help create marketing plans for local businesses, as well as the initiative itself, and assist Scarlett with event promotion and advertising.

It's not entirely different from what I did working for my father; though, instead of a company led by a corrupt criminal, I'm doing something to actually benefit where I'm living. I wouldn't say I'm passionate about marketing, but I'm fairly decent at it. I majored in graphic design in college, so marketing felt like a natural path to that.

In reality, I'm not entirely sure what I'm passionate about. I love baking, but it has never been anything more than a hobby and a stress reliever.

As I enter my office, I remember for the first time in two weeks my monstera. Fully expecting a dead plant in the corner of the room, I instead find it thriving, long, Swiss cheese–looking leaves pointed toward the morning sun filtering through the window.

"Everett watered it for you while you took that extra week off," Leo says from behind me, as if he heard my smile.

"Oh" is my response as my eyes flicker throughout the room, my mind reeling from the man's thoughtfulness that I'm still not used to. I take in the desk to the right of the door and the filing cabinet next to it. Across from it on the other side of the office is a small meeting table that fits four chairs. Directly in front of me is a window that spans the length of the room, my plant in the corner beneath it.

And on my desk, there's a vase of bright red flowers. Dahlias. My breath catches as I step up to it, running my fingers through the soft petals. A sweet, light, floral scent filters up to me as I pluck the card, which is pinned to one of the stems, assuming it's from my sister.

Leo laughs to himself as a surprised gasp escapes me when I unfold the slip of paper and read the note attached.

Good luck on your first day. I know you'll do great, Wildflower.

P.S. don't forget our lunch date. I'll see you at noon.

\- *boyfriend*

"Now that Honeysuckle is well underway, we need to focus on what comes next. We still have two vacant suites here on the strip. Do you have any proposals that have caught your eye?" Scarlett asks.

Leo, leaning back in his chair and bouncing a small basketball off the door, glances over at her. "Only person who applied in the last six months was Bill Turner. He proposed moving the barber shop to the boardwalk, but I didn't feel it was the best location for it. The boardwalk should be more focused on tourism. Locals love Bill, but not everyone decides they need a haircut while they're on vacation."

"Yeah," Scarlett breathes. "True."

"Haven't had anyone else apply."

Scarlett raises her brown eyes to me, long braids falling into her face. She brushes them behind her shoulder as she smiles, and I wonder if how overwhelmed I am is written all over me.

"Let's set up a meeting next week to talk through a campaign for advertising the two open business suites here and see if we can get at least a handful of proposals submitted by the end of the year."

"Yeah. Of course." I jot it down on the legal pad sitting in front of me. I have a lot of notes written across it, but I have a feeling when I go back to look later, I'll have no idea what any of them mean.

I have three meetings set for next week with small business owners to help them create marketing plans and set up their social media accounts.

"You're doing great," Scarlett says reassuringly.

"Thank you." I attempt to smile back at her.

It's weird working for an initiative that's so small. Nobody has held my position before, so there isn't really anyone around to show me the ropes. I'm being given the freedom to make it my own, and I know that Leo trusts me completely to do the right thing. It's the kind of freedom I've always wanted, but I'm not sure what to make of it now that I have it.

"After lunch, you and I can meet with Jeremiah and go over some of the contracts. Every business is handled individually based on their needs, so we'll make sure you're familiar with everyone before you begin meeting them," Scarlett says.

I nod, adding that to my notes. "What time?" I ask. "I have a..." I shake my head as Leo eyes me knowingly. "I have somewhere

I have to go at noon, but—"

Scarlett scrolls through the tablet in her hand. "How about two? Jeremiah has an opening then. I'll put it on your calendar."

"Sweet." Leo sits up and claps his hands together. "Are we good then? I've got a hot blonde I need to see about a thing."

He's definitely talking about fucking my sister right now.

I roll my eyes and scoff. Scarlett chuckles to herself as she leaves.

Leo winks at me as he strolls out of my office and shuts the door behind him.

About fifteen minutes later, I hear a bellowing laugh from the main workspace. "No, I'm at the shop all day today. I'm just taking a break to have lunch with a pretty girl."

I don't know who he's talking to, but a moment later, there's a light knock on my office door. "You knock as if I can't hear you squawking out there," I call as I stand from my desk.

The door swings open, and I'm met with that playful, wicked smirk. Brown eyes glitter at me beneath thick brows, and full lips invite me in with that smile behind his trimmed and manicured beard. Tattooed arms cross at his chest as he casually leans against the doorway.

He roams the length of my body, eyes snagging on the form-fitting black skirt that runs from just above my knee to my waist, the white blouse I have tucked into it, and the black heels adorning my feet. "You look ravishing, Wildflower."

I try to fight the smile that wants to bloom at his words, but I can't help it. My cheeks flush, and I duck my head to hide it. I swipe my purse off my desk as I brush past him and out the door. He follows close behind, that warm, reassuring hand on the small of my back like he held me at the beach yesterday.

"Thank you for the flowers," I murmur abashedly. "They're beautiful, but you didn't have to do that."

"You're right. I didn't," he says as we make our way down the staircase. "I wanted to. You can allow people to do things for you just because they want to, Dahlia."

I don't know how to respond to that, so I only nod.

"Have you eaten at Surfside Fish Co. yet?" he asks.

I shake my head. "I don't like fish."

He laughs. "They've got more than fish. Soups, salads, sandwiches, burgers. The best goddamn french fries I've ever had in my life."

"Okay." I chuckle. "That's fine. I can pay." It's the least I can do for him agreeing to be my fake boyfriend for the foreseeable future.

"You are not paying, Dahlia."

I scoff as we make our way down the boardwalk. "You can allow people to do things for you just because they want to, *Everett*."

"Are you offering to pay because you *want* to, or because you feel like you *should*?"

"I—" I pause. I mean, I'm not enthusiastic about spending money in any circumstance, really. I do feel like I *should* pay, but it's not like I don't want to, either. "I don't know. Both?"

He laughs as he guides me to the front entrance of the restaurant. "Look, I know the owner here, and it wouldn't be very boyfriend-like of me to make you pay for our first official date."

I roll my eyes. "Small-town values."

"My small-town values and your small-town values are very different, I think. I'm not doing this because of a complex or because I think I'm superior to you. I was, however, raised to be a gentleman, and if my mother knew I was making her favorite girl pay for my meal?" He lets out a low whistle. "That would be the end of me, Wildflower. Then, you'd really be fucked."

I'm embarrassed by the cackle that escapes my throat, but the way his eyes light up in surprised amusement, flaring with something like pride, diminishes it immediately.

We enter the restaurant, and the hostess, of course, knows Everett by name. She blushes when he smiles at her, and I wonder if that's how everyone he meets reacts to his charm. I bite down the rush of nausea that floods my stomach as I think of all the pretty girls and boys Everett has smiled at the way he smiled at me that night.

I have no right to be jealous. At least, not in real life.

We're seated at a booth near the back, next to paneled windows that look out at the beach beyond us. "So, what do we need to discuss, Wildflower?" Everett asks as we look over our menus.

"Jumping straight to the point, Ramos?"

He smiles to himself behind his menu. "I just want to get the heavy stuff over with quickly so I can actually enjoy a meal with you."

His eyes lift to mine just in time to see my face fall as those words settle over me.

"Okay." I swallow. "Well, I guess I just want to set the right expectations and boundaries. Rules. I feel like this has potential to get...messy."

"I don't mind the mess," he says.

"I'm sure you don't, but regardless..." I sigh. "How long do you reasonably expect this to go on? This shit with my dad could last..." I close my eyes. "A while. I don't want to hold you back from your own life indefinitely."

"I'm not going anywhere, Dal. My life is here. My businesses, my family. Whether I'm 'dating'"—he holds up his fingers to gesture quotation marks—"you or not, I'm here anyway."

"Right. But what if you meet someone? I mean, you understand you've got to keep your hook-ups on the down low from here on out, right? I'll be honest, I don't pay a ton of attention to water sports, so I don't know what kind of status Leo really has, but I imagine that he's got some kind of media coverage interested in what he's up to, especially as we get closer to his wedding. That means it won't be hard for my dad to keep track of what we're all doing, and I can't have him finding photos or something of my *boyfriend* with another person."

I take a deep inhale after that long-winded explanation. It almost feels as if I was fighting extra hard to justify why I'm not okay with Everett seeing other people, but I push that thought away.

He drops his menu to the table and lifts his head, brown eyes blazing through me so deeply I think I feel them searing my skin. "I wouldn't worry about that if I were you."

The intensity in his face makes me not want to question him, so I decide to take his word for it for now. "Okay," I drawl. "Can you keep giving Lou surf lessons?"

"Of course," he says immediately.

"She wants to play soccer too. Would you come to games every once in a while?"

"I'll come to all of them." He looks over the menu again.

"All right. And what do you need me to do?"

He pauses for a moment, chewing on his lip. "You only need this arrangement around cameras, but I kind of need it... everywhere. I need the people around town, the ones who've been here years and know my parents—the businesses—to see I've settled down. I need them to believe that when they take their car into my shop, or they come to Heathen's to buy a new board, that they're supporting a family business. We've always been known as that, and I think I've ruined it." His jaw tightens, and his eyes drop. Guilt coats his words. "It turns out people don't want to support a twenty-something bachelor who treats the world like his own personal playground and doesn't give a shit about anyone but himself as much as they want to support a man who's working to provide for his family."

"I can't imagine anyone thinking that of you, Everett."

"According to my father"—he scoffs—"*and* my brother, that's exactly what people around here think of me."

"Leo said that to you?"

"Not in those words, exactly," he murmurs. "But yeah, especially now that he's settling down himself. It's like the same expectations are extended to me. When he was single and fucking around with socialites, it made him a god around here, so I don't think people cared so much about what I was doing. Now, suddenly, he's engaged, and the world has flipped on its axis."

"That's not fair of him to put those kinds of expectations on you just because his life has changed."

Everett shrugs. "I don't know if they're expectations. I just think there always has to be a gossip mill working overtime around here. He carried that weight for years. Except, even when he was at the center of it, everything was kind of okay. He could fuck around and act like a bachelor because he was also setting records, getting rich, and appearing on magazine covers. All the single women in town secretly hoped they could change him, and all the older people in town secretly hoped he'd fall for their daughters. Everyone has always wanted their piece of Leo Graham. There were limits they'd go to on what they'd say and how they'd treat him." He bites his lip. "It's not fair for him to take on that kind of pressure. I'm glad it died down now that he's engaged, but it just means that attention has turned on me, and I don't get the same allowances he did."

"I'm sorry you have that pressure now." I find myself reaching across the table and covering his hand with mine. "I'll do what I can to help alleviate that. I'll even let you buy me lunch, I guess."

A small smile ticks up at his mouth. "Thanks, Wildflower."

I smile back as the server arrives at our table and takes our orders. We talk about everything and nothing as we wait for our food. He tells me about his sister living in New York and the way she self-published her first few books while she was in college before having one take off online. That led to her landing an agent and a publishing deal at the age of twenty-one.

"So, yeah. Record-setting, future legend surfer for a brother, international bestselling author for a sister. Two one-in-a-million kids in one family...and then me." He chuckles at the sentiment, but it's not real. He smiles, but it doesn't reach his eyes.

"What you do is important, Everett. You have not one, but two successful businesses, and you're not even thirty. You provide for your community and support your family. You should be proud." He only shrugs in response. "Your parents seem really proud of you, if that makes a difference."

"I know." He nods. "They're great, and I'm lucky. They don't compare us. I know enough about Darby's life to know that you two didn't have that. I'm sorry."

"You're right. I think..." I sigh. "I think that's why I'd rather it be my sister and I against the world than continue relying on people who manipulate us, who are only concerned about how our existence benefits them." I've never said this to anyone before. I don't know why I let my thoughts spill from my head when Everett's around. "I just want my daughter to have better than I did. That's the only thing that matters to me."

"She already has better. She has you, but it doesn't have to be you against the world anymore, Dal." He pushes his empty plate aside and places his hand over mine on the table like I did earlier. "You've got people here who want to support you. No ulterior motives. No manipulation. I know it's a foreign thing for you, so I get that it's hard to accept, but we truly just care."

"I don't trust anyone," I find myself whispering. My voice nearly cracks as I add, "I don't understand why anyone would ever want to be around me, support me—love me—if they didn't have to. I don't understand why anyone would choose it."

I watch his brown eyes ripple with devastation as he soaks that sentence in, and it's that exact moment that our server returns with the check. I pull my hand back from Everett's and quietly blink back tears as he pays. Once he finishes, he stands from the booth and extends a hand toward me. I take it silently as he leads me outside the restaurant, though instead of turning toward the surf shop, he takes me down onto the pier.

Sea breeze coats my face as birds chirp in the sky above us. The sun is high, piercing the white caps in glittering gold. "I know the best compliment I can give you is that you're a great mother," he says, finally breaking our silence. Everett isn't looking at me; he's looking out at the horizon as we pause at the railing. "I see how much you love her, how much you sacrifice for her. I see the way your face lights up when she says your name, when she smiles at you. I think you're patient, supportive, and loving. You're nurturing, but you also teach her right from wrong, how to set boundaries and when she's crossing them too." He turns to me. "You're a good fucking mom, Dahlia. But you don't need to be all alone in order to be a good mom. I just hope you figure that out eventually."

I look down at the water, watching waves break and crash against the wooden beams of the pier. "I hope I figure it out too." I lift my head to meet his gaze. "I hope you realize that you have a lot to offer, and that you have value regardless of what your siblings—or anyone else—do with their lives. I hope you figure out your worth."

He smiles softly. "Yeah, me too."

Seventeen - Wicked

Let's Never Do That Again

What are we wearing to this shindig?

Haven't decided yet.

I like blue.

For me or for you?

I look good in everything, Wildflower.

But you in a cerulean dress that matches the color of your eyes?

That's enough to bring a man to his knees.

Preferably me.

Stop flirting, Everett.

You know it's in my DNA., baby.

She's wearing a blue dress.

It's more navy than cerulean, but fuck, if it doesn't make her eyes shine like sapphires. The silk fabric clings to her waist and stretches at her bust and hips, accentuating every one of her beautiful curves. Simple, thin straps are tight over her shoulders and appear to cross in the back. The dress hugs her legs all the way down to the ankle, where her feet are strapped into a pair of silver heels.

Her hair is in soft waves at her shoulders, makeup neutral—heavier than her average day but less than she wore to the bar the night I met her—and her lips are painted a glossy, pale pink shade that glistens when she smiles, which is exactly what she does now as she descends the stairs and catches me staring at her. I realize I'm looking at her with a dropped-jaw, wide-eyes, and my heart beating out of my chest so hard it's likely leaving an imprint like one of those old cartoons.

Darby follows her sister down the staircase, wearing a soft yellow chiffon gown that cinches at her waist before flowing to the floor. Short, loose sleeves fall off each of her shoulders, accented with bows, allowing her chest to highlight the gold necklace that hangs at the center of it. A simple golden chain, one that belonged to my brother, now houses a small flower pendant. I notice Dahlia is still wearing the same compass necklace she always has on too.

My brother stands next to me, fiddling with his cufflinks and oblivious to anything going on around him until his fiancée reaches the foyer and steps into him. Taking his hand, she begins to adjust his sleeves for him. I know Darby caught him by surprise when his head snaps up and he rears back, doing a double take before freezing to take her in. Darby smiles as his eyes rake across her body, and she finishes fixing his cufflink.

He steps back quickly before surging forward and grasping each side of her face with his hands. He presses his mouth to hers, backing her into the dining room and just out of sight. "Swear to God, Honeysuckle, I'm gonna get you pregnant later," he murmurs between what sounds like mauled, rough kisses.

I'm thankful that our mother picked Lou up *before* we left, because I think he's so oblivious to everyone else in the room right now, he would've said that right in front of her.

Darby giggles. "Dare ya, heathen."

Dahlia and I glance at each other awkwardly from opposite sides of the small entry space. She remains on the bottom step of the staircase, eyes darting around the room uncomfortably before finally landing on my face. "Please, don't say something like that to me."

I can't help the small laugh that escapes my lips. "I'd never be so forward." She gives me an eye roll, but I don't miss the tilt of her mouth or the flare in her gaze as she looks me up and down.

Leo and I are wearing essentially the same thing: a black tux, though he's wearing a bow tie, and I went with no tie at all, leaving the top two buttons on my dress shirt undone, a simple gold chain hanging off my neck. I watch Dahlia lightly lick her lips as she catches that. I smirk, reaching out my hand in the space between us. She takes it, allowing me to help her down the last step on the staircase just as our siblings round the corner of the dining room hand-in-hand.

Darby's slicked-back bun is slightly ruffled, and my brother's hair is tousled like a pair of hands were just running rampant through it. I hear a small chuff leave Dahlia's lips, indicating she noticed it too. "Ready?" Dahlia asks.

"Absolutely." Leo smiles. "You look beautiful, Dal."

"Nice of you to notice." There's a glimmer in her eyes that tells us the jab was meant in jest.

My brother only laughs as he opens the front door. He leads Darby out first, and I place my hand on the small of Dahlia's back as we follow behind them.

"You look stunning, Dahlia," I whisper quietly in her ear.

"Thank you," she responds breathlessly.

As we reach the car, I open Dahlia's door for her, getting a view of the back of her dress for the first time. Just like I thought, the thin straps cross at her back, leaving most of her smooth, pale skin on display. The tightness of the fabric around her legs extends to her plump, round ass, and I'm fighting back a goddamn groan. It's like this dress was made for her.

"Can I be forward enough to say that you do look utterly fuckable in that?" I murmur against her shoulder as she climbs into the back seat.

I assumed I was being quiet, but the way my brother's head whips sideways, a glare on his face, tells me I failed. Dahlia snorts, not bothering to respond as she slides into the seat and looks up at me with playful eyes, pulling the handle and slamming the door in my face.

My brother grunts in some sort of agreement at her action as he gets into the driver's seat. I round the car to the other side and fall into the back with Dahlia. I don't fucking fit in this thing, but I was told we couldn't take my Jeep because I forgot to put the damn top back on and it would ruin their hair, chief complainer among them being Leo. It's so cramped in the back that I have no choice but to let my thigh press up against Dahlia's, and I've never thought the simple brush of legs could be erotic before, but I swear, my body is on fire in all the places our bodies meet, even through our clothes.

Her breathing is a little labored, making me question if she feels it too. "You're wearing blue."

"New dress," she says breathlessly.

She bought the dress for me. *Fuck.*

Her legs tremble lightly, like she's nervous. I can't tell if that's because of the event we're attending—which I'm nervous about, too, if I'm being honest—or if it's because she's so close to me. My arm itches to grab her thigh and quell her shaking, but I think better of it, balling my hand into a fist instead to fight the instinct.

The annual banquet is always held on the anniversary of Zach's passing, I think more than anything to give his parents a distraction from remembering the horror of that day, and fuck, am I thankful for that too. The first year was brutal. Elena had already run away to New York, August was even more shut down back then than he is now. Leo showed up at my apartment in the middle of the night crying, and we spent the entire twenty-four-hour period on my couch, watching Zach's favorite movies.

Grief kind of feels like a bullet wound that never fully heals. Sometimes, it's just a scar, and then other days, you wake up and feel like it tore right through you again, this gaping hole in the center of your chest sucking the life right out of you. You're never entirely sure which days you're going to find yourself bleeding out and which days you'll feel patched up, but I'm always certain that on the anniversary of the loss, that hole is bigger than ever.

For some inexplicable reason, feeling Dahlia's presence beside me makes it feel like the wound I woke up with this morning is shrinking, little by little.

The foundation, and the banquet, help too. They help distract us, help us feel like we're doing something to make his death less...senseless, but the hurt is still there. Still bone deep. Zach and August's parents hold themselves together—they always have. At his funeral, in the aftermath, and ever since. I only ever saw them fall apart in the hospital when we first received news that he hadn't made it. I watched Sadie, their mother, fall to the floor and scream in a way I never knew was possible—at least until I heard the sounds that came from my sister only minutes after. I watched their father, Alex, tell August it was his fault and storm out of the emergency room.

I don't think Alex and August have spoken since.

Darby's soft voice pulls me from my thoughts. "I tried to get him to come."

I watch Leo's arm reach across the center console and grip her leg, calming any anxiety she may be feeling, exactly the way I wish I could comfort Dahlia.

"I know you did, love. It's not you. He didn't come last year, either. He doesn't come to anything."

Dahlia's eyebrows furrow at the center of her forehead. She glances at me for an explanation, but the energy in the car right now doesn't feel like the right place to discuss it.

Later, I mouth at her.

She nods, turning her head to glance out the window as Leo merges onto the interstate, heading south toward San Diego, where the event is being held. The ocean is no longer visible, but the sun sets to the west, sinking low on the horizon and casting Dahlia's face in gold. She's so beautiful, features so graceful as she takes in the imagery around her. Looking at her makes it hard to breathe, makes me feel like I need to clutch my chest and ensure I'm not dying.

I've met a lot of pretty people in my life, but never someone who makes me feel like that, like they could actually kill me just by existing. Like gazing upon her is such a goddamn privilege, I might as well end it now.

Dahlia's leg continues bouncing nervously, and while I'm not exactly sure if my touch is crossing one of the boundaries she set, I can't stand her being uncomfortable. I know I need to touch her in public, know we have to pretend. In this car, I should be keeping my space because we're only supposed to be for show.

But I can't stop myself from reaching across the seat and taking the hand resting in her lap, lacing her fingers through mine and squeezing gently. Her eyes fall from the window to the place I'm touching her before she lifts her head to look at me. I run my thumb across the back of her hand, not knowing what to do other than smile at her.

She returns it, so bright and beautiful that she eclipses the sun behind her. Silently, she squeezes my hand back.

Only a moment later, her nervous shaking ceases, but she doesn't let go of me.

When Leo pulls up to the valet of the hotel, Dahlia lets go of my hand, leaving me feeling empty. We all pile out of the Mustang, and Darby loops her arm through her sister's, whispering something in her ear that causes Dahlia to smile.

Leo and I trail behind them as we make our way through the lobby of the hotel and toward the ballrooms. "Did you really not know who Dahlia was when you two hooked up in that bar?" he asks, voice sounding accusatory.

"No. I didn't." My own tone comes out pinched in response to his. "Why?"

He huffs, running a hand through his perfectly tousled blond hair. "I'm just trying to figure out how you keep getting yourself into these situations."

He may be projecting a little. He's definitely still upset that I hooked up with his assistant, Adam, last year. Adam is a great guy, undoubtedly the best assistant Leo's ever had. It was definitely selfish of me, and I shouldn't have been so impulsive. Still, Adam and I set clear boundaries before it happened—he knew it was going to be a casual thing. He also promised me that no matter what, he wouldn't quit his job because of anything happening between the two of us, and he has stayed true to that promise over the last year.

It wasn't a big deal, but it could've been, and I understand why Leo was pissed about it.

But it has nothing to do with Dahlia or the way I feel about her.

"She's supposed to feel comfortable here. Safe—" my brother continues.

"Are you insinuating that I would ever make her—or anyone else—feel otherwise?" The words come out as a near-growl. He speaks to me like I'm a fucking child with a hand caught in the cookie jar.

Leo shakes his head. "No. But the way you speak to her sometimes—the flirting—it's like you're playing games. She cannot be played with that way, Everett."

I stop in the middle of the lobby. The girls continue walking ahead of us, oblivious to what's going on, but Leo pauses, too, turning to look at me with concern on his face.

"You know Dahlia as Darby's sister. You see her for what

she's gone through and what she's struggling with. You want to protect her, and I love you for that." My brother crosses his arms as I step into him. "But I met Dahlia and only knew her for exactly who she is. Have you ever considered that she might want a break from being someone's sister? Someone's mom? The daughter of a fucking psychopath? Have you ever thought that maybe she just needs a safe place to breathe? To play? That maybe I'm trying to be that for her? I'm not trying to fuck and forget her, Leo."

My brother flexes his jaw, eyes boring through mine, but he doesn't know what to say.

"Don't you try to be that for Darby too? Make her laugh and give her a safe place to escape the rest of the world?"

Leo's eyes flash with something unrecognizable before he dips his chin in a shallow nod. "But Darby is going to be my *wife*. She's not a meaningless one-night stand."

And that's it for me. An unexpected wave of jealousy slams right into my gut, almost causing me to stumble backward. I pull myself together and walk past my brother without another word. It's not that I'm jealous of him and Darby; I'm just jealous of what they have.

I'm also angry at his insinuation that Dahlia means nothing to me, or that I mean nothing to her. Nothing about what happened between us was meaningless—even if we intended it to be. For me, it happened before I ever learned her name. She'd taken root in my mind the second she sat down next to me at that bar. After that night, all I could think about was how badly I wished there was some way I could find her again. If I could locate the tiniest thread between us, I'd hold on with everything I had until she was pulled into my life again.

Then, suddenly, there she was.

I don't know if I believe in fate. I've never wanted something bad enough to care if it was destined or not. But I remember watching Dahlia run out of that bar and wanting nothing more than to have something—anything—to tie me to her again, only to find her standing in the center of my business, needing my help. I find out she lives with my brother, that she works for me, as if the universe took every tiny string and created a massive knot, placing me right at the center of it. I'm entirely caught up in her, entwined, and I don't want to be untangled.

"Everett." My brother's on my heels, calling my name as he catches up to me. "I'm sorry. I shouldn't have said that. I... Just be careful, yeah?"

I look at him, and I hate the caution I see on his face. I suppose I don't have the best track record to back me up, but I've never intended to hurt a single person in my life. I try my hardest to be easy-going and fun. It's all I've fucking got to offer. I don't have my sister's intelligence or creativity. I don't have Leo's God-given talent or business-savvy mindset. I don't have a whole lot to offer anyone, nothing but myself. For the first time, I consider the fact that maybe I've gotten used to leaving someone before they realize that nothing but myself isn't enough.

For the first time, I realize that I don't want to leave Dahlia before she notices that. I just want to figure out a way to be enough for her.

So, I don't say anything more to my brother as I nod and head toward her like she's a beacon. She's calling to me. She needs me. I've never been needed before. I finally have something to offer her, and I'm going to make damn sure I give her every bit of it she deserves.

There is a small red carpet set up outside the ballroom, a handful of photographers and reporters snapping photos as people enter. A few high-profile athletes are in attendance, and some celebrities, including Leo's friend, Milan, a socialite and influencer whom I make note to introduce Dahlia to later. As my brother and I catch up to the girls, a worker for the event explains how we'll each walk down the carpet to allow for photos before entering the room, and that the four of us are sitting together at a table toward the front.

Dahlia looks at me with wide, scared eyes. I place a hand at the small of her back and give her hip a reassuring squeeze. "We'll let Leo and Darby go first." I chuckle. "That way, we can just copy what they do."

"Who's even going to want to take photos of us, anyway? We're not famous."

I laugh because I get it. I hate doing this kind of stuff too. Leo isn't addicted to the spotlight, but he doesn't mind it. The attention comes naturally to him, always has. I feel like Darby might feel the same way, because she's calm and cool, if not a little excited. Dahlia's like me, though.

"Isn't that the point of this *date*, Dahlia?" I wink. "We're supposed to be seen together. Plus, it's not just for the celebrities. Sadie and Alex use these photos for the Foundation website and to promote other events they put on. It helps."

She takes a deep breath, nodding. They call my brother and Darby up, and the cameras start flashing wildly. Reporters are shouting questions over each other. Even though Leo is the household name, he ushers Darby in front of him with a hand on her back like she's the star to be gushed over.

If she's nervous, it doesn't show. She walks with confidence and a soft smile to the center of the carpet, pausing as photos are taken. My brother sidles up next to her, wrapping an arm around her waist. Darby smiles at the cameras, but Leo's eyes are on her, like she's brighter than all of it. A reporter asks for a look at Darby's ring, and she simply turns sideways, placing her left hand at the center of Leo's chest. The reporters go wild at that, and my brother chuckles, pressing his lips to Darby's forehead. He snakes his arm farther around her body, tugging her in tighter. His hand grips just at the curve of her ass, a borderline inappropriate gesture, but his way of telling the rest of the world that she's all his.

The event staff wave them off the red carpet, and suddenly, it's our turn. Dahlia looks up at me with unsure eyes, and I'm brought back to that timid woman who stared after me with those same bright baby blues the night I met her, the woman who wanted me to take control and guide her.

Dahlia's got confidence, or at least, she appears to at work and with her daughter. She's independent, used to being on her own and doing everything herself. These tiny moments of vulnerability that she tries to hide from the rest of the world—I see them. She's unsure about this, not confident, and she has never had someone to pick that up for her before.

So, I do what I think she needs at this moment, and I take over. Grasping her hand, I lead us onto the red carpet, her eyes on me as cameras begin flashing around us. I pause at the center, and it's not as wild as it was when Leo was up here. Still, the attention is on us for this brief moment. I know Dahlia's hating it as much as I am.

I pull her in front of me, wrapping an arm around her waist. Her hand rests at the small of my back, the top of her head just below my mouth. Her entire body is rigid, so I brush my thumb against the fabric on her hip. Leaning forward until my lips meet the shell of her ear, I whisper, "You don't have to look at them, Wildflower. You can look at me."

I keep my eyes up, smiling at the cameras, but I know Dahlia's head snaps sideways. I can feel her gaze boring through me, and her body softens slightly. I tighten my grip on her, knowing the gesture appears possessive. Allowing my mouth to brush against her neck, I whisper again, "You know, they say you're supposed to imagine everyone naked during shit like this, but I think if I tried doing that, I'd only end up imagining you naked—maybe in nothing but those heels—and I'd really embarrass myself here."

I have no idea if that's the right thing to say, if she's going to get offended, and I'm going to make her anxiety worse, or if that kind of joke is exactly what she needs to relax right now. I think back to what my brother said and wonder if he's right—if I think I'm offering her some kind of reprieve, or if I'm only seeing it that way because I'm desperate to be around her, to make her want me as badly as I want her.

My stomach twists with anticipation as she pauses, but it quickly morphs into the rapid flap of butterfly wings when Dahlia's mouth bursts with bright laughter. The flash of the cameras intensifies at the sound, and I find myself looking down at her, watching her face fall from pinched and nervous to carefree and open.

She catches her breath, meeting my gaze with grateful eyes. Something like pride blooms in my chest, sending warmth throughout my body.

We're ushered off the carpet, and it's Dahlia who grabs my hand now, interlacing our fingers and squeezing gently. "That was awful. Let's never do that again."

"You did great, Wildflower. The hard part's over with." I keep her hand in mine, leading her into the grand ballroom as we maneuver our way toward our table.

I lied, though, because for me, the hard part is just beginning. Walking into this room puts me on alert, makes me start to sweat. I know they start the event with a speech about Zach—his life, the things and people he loved. Then, they play a slideshow filled almost entirely with photos of us as kids. That's the hardest part for me, watching how happy and carefree we used to be. We had no fucking clue what was coming for us. Photos of August and Elena choke me out the hardest because they're still so broken, and I don't know if there is any part of the two of them that'll ever heal.

Last year, they asked me to give a speech, and I nearly broke down in the middle of it. I feel like shit about it, but I told the Hayeses that I couldn't do it again this year. It takes everything in me just to show up. So, I don't know who's giving it, but I know someone will give a speech. Then, the silent auction will begin. It gets a little easier after that. There is dinner and dancing, and the auction items are set up at the perimeter of the room for people to bid on.

Leo is auctioning a private surf lesson, though if this year is anything like last, those bids will come from a bunch of women with little interest in surfing and a lot of interest in an hour of private time with Leo Graham. Heathen's auctioned off a custom-designed board. My parents, on behalf of Ramos Automotive, are auctioning a year of vehicle maintenance. Lastly, I'm offering a classic 1960 powder-blue T-Bird. It was left at the shop, abandoned by someone's granddaughter after they passed away. It needs a ton of work, but my dad and I are completely rebuilding the engine. It won't be ready for a few months yet, but when it is, it'll be damn near priceless.

The lights around the ballroom dim as Dahlia and I make our way to our table, letting us know they're about to begin. I pull out her chair next to Darby and then slide into the other side. Sure enough, the event begins with Zach and August's dad taking the stage. He thanks people for coming and starts in on who his son was.

Keyword: *was*

It's hard for me to listen, to hear all the qualities that Zach bore and all the potential he'll never get to live up to. I find myself zoning out through the speech, and before I know it, the lights are off, music is playing, and pictures are flashing across a projector in front of me. They use the same ones every year, so I don't need to look to know what they are.

Zach as a baby. Zach holding August after he was born. The two of them on the beach as children. All the sports Zach played growing up. Then, pictures of Leo, Elena, and me start popping up after we met them around the age of eleven. My eyes meet my brother's across the table, and I can see the unshed tears in his gaze. He swallows hard before he looks in the other direction. Darby's holding his hand so tightly her knuckles are nearly white, like she's keeping him anchored.

Somehow, I make it through the slideshow without actually crying, but I'm pretty sure I'm completely disassociating with my surroundings in order to make that happen. I didn't hear a lyric of the music that played, didn't look at Dahlia once. I'm only brought back to the moment by the brightening of the lights and the sound of Sadie's voice on the mic. She talks of Zach and how he died, the reason the foundation was established, and how their hope is to never see another parent be told their child had drowned again. She speaks of that day with such calm composure, a stark contrast to how it felt to be there.

The wail is deafening. It pierces through the entire hospital—through my mind and soul. I didn't know a sound like that existed. I also didn't know the people we love could die. Not like this. Not so suddenly and without warning.

Sadie Hayes hits her knees, hunched over on the floor as her body racks with violent sobs. She has just been told that her son has died. He's gone.

Zach is gone.

"What is—" I hear my sister's voice briefly before it goes silent, the sound of the automatic entry doors shutting behind her.

It's almost as if I can feel Elena take in the scene in front of her. I'm hearing through her ears as the doctor says again, "He didn't make it. I'm so sorry."

I refuse to look at her, keeping my eyes on Sadie, because despite how devastating she looks right now, I can't bear what I'll find on my sister's face. I know Elena is taking count of who's in this room.

Who's missing from it.

Leo and I sit next to each other. Across from us, Sadie's on the floor, August—eyes red and withdrawn—kneeling next to her. Alex, their dad, shoots from his chair, looking down at his youngest son as he spits, "You did this" before storming out.

I watch him as he rushes past us, my eyes following him through the doors my sister just entered. When they land on her face, she looks to me for only the briefest moment, as if searching for confirmation that everything she feared has come to life.

All I'm capable of through my streaming tears is a shallow nod. She stumbles back like someone punched her. Shaking her head, she retreats backward through the doors, and the sound barely leaves her lips before she's in a full-out sprint.

But before she's gone, I hear it: the wrangled cry—the broken sob, so hollow and gut-wrenching it shakes me to my core. It rattles my bones and scorches my soul. The sound of death and heartbreak, of someone being torn apart right in front of you. I feel it filter through me because, on some innate level, I feel what she feels. She's my other half, and I already know she won't come back from this.

"Everett?" Dahlia's voice is soft and warm, coaxing me from my nightmares.

I'm warped back to the current moment, realizing that the speech is over, dinner is being served, and the dancing and auction have begun. My brother gives me an apologetic smile over the table, like he understands exactly where I was just then. His eyes dash to Dahlia for the briefest moment before he's pulling back in his chair and standing up. "C'mon, honeysuckle. Let's go take a stroll."

I turn to Dahlia, her face etched in concern, her hand covering mine on the table. "Where'd you go just then?"

I blink, shaking my head as I take a deep breath. "Nowhere. I'm fine."

She tilts her head, blue eyes blazing. "You don't have to pretend, you know."

I huff a laugh. "Isn't that what we're doing here? Pretending."

"Not with that." She shakes her head. "Not with whatever darkness just passed across your eyes. You don't pretend that doesn't exist. You don't hold that in. Not with me."

I feel my throat swelling again, and all I want to do is break down in her arms. All this time, that's exactly what I've been doing: holding it in. I can see Leo beginning to heal. I can see my parents—Zach's parents, even—doing the same, but I'm not there yet, and sometimes, I don't know how to get there or if I ever will. I feel like I'm not just grieving my best friend; I'm grieving two of them, and I'm grieving my sister too. I don't know how to explain these feelings, and sometimes, it feels like I shouldn't be having them at all.

So, I press them down and hold them back, pretend they don't exist.

Dahlia's the only person to see through that, to give me permission to stop, to share them with her. I'm not even sure I know how to do that, but I want to try. "Some days are just harder than others. Today is always a hard day."

She smiles softly, squeezing my hand. "I know. What can I do?"

I blink at her question, because I'm not sure how to answer. Somehow, touching her makes everything a little easier. Looking at her makes me feel better. Speaking with her makes the weight lighter. All she has to do is exist, and I feel like I'm going to be all right.

"Dance with me?" I find myself asking.

She chuffs. "Of course. I can do that."

We stand from our chairs, and she allows me to lead her to the dance floor where soft, classical renditions of modern songs play. Darby and Leo dance slowly on the other side of the room, entirely caught up in their own world, and I imagine Darby's providing him the same comfort I'm so desperate for.

I turn around, pulling Dahlia into me, wrapping both arms tightly around her waist. She lets hers loop around my neck as we begin to sway. "I miss my sister." I sigh, surprised by how easy the words fall from my mouth. "Sometimes, it feels like I'm not just grieving for Zach, but for her too. It's like...I don't even know who she is anymore, like she might as well have just..." I trail off, unwilling to finish the sentence. "That feels heavier today, I guess."

She's quiet for a moment as she contemplates what I've said. Her fingers brush against the hair at my nape, sending chills up my spine. "I get it. I think I would feel the same way. There is this weird connection with siblings when you're so close, and it's hard to be far apart. I imagine it's even stronger when you're twins."

I nod, feeling understood for the first time in a while.

"I'm sorry this brings all that to the surface for you, but I hope next time it happens, you stop dissociating or holding it in. It's okay if you feel like nobody understands. We'll still be there for you." She's looking at my lips as she says those words, but her eyes slowly drag up to my own, searing right through me. "I'll still be there for you."

"Even if all I want you to do is dance with me?"

She smiles. "Even if all you want to do is dance."

I grip her harder, dropping my chin so my forehead brushes softly against hers. "You've made this easier."

"You make things easier too," she whispers.

I let my eyes fall closed, soaking in this moment with her. I know it's not real. It was only meant to be a few camera flashes to fuck with her dad. A few lunch dates to impress mine. That's all this is supposed to be.

But the way Dahlia sighs against me, the way her body meshes into mine—a flawless fit beneath my hands—it feels as if all the fear and grief and stress in our lives melts away. We spin on the dance floor in momentary peace, and I can't ignore the fact that this doesn't feel fake at all.

Eighteen - Wildflower

Just Making Sure He Knows You're Mine

Parents are fucking mean.

I've never been one to fit in with a crowd, really. I had some surface-level high school friends. I thought I'd met my ride-or-dies in college when I fell in with Jason's group, but they all abandoned me once I got pregnant.

People I've never fit in with, though, are the school moms. I've always been a solid decade younger than the majority of them, and especially back home in Kansas, being Dane Andrews's black sheep daughter was like having a warning label on my forehead. I won't pretend I wasn't hopeful things would change once I got to Pacific Shores, but a lot of these people are just as catty, small-minded, and rude as those I dealt with back home.

It started with a parent-teacher night when I was repeatedly asked if I was Lou's sister or her aunt, followed by wide-eyed sneers when I confirmed that I was, in fact, her mother. Then, I showed up on the first day of school in Everett's Jeep, which is apparently well-known. Ever since, it has been cold shoulders and fake smiles, being left out of conversations or glared at across parking lots. I don't have any interest in befriending most of them anyway, but I can only hope their mean streak doesn't extend to their children, because Lou is loving it here.

She has made several friends, though she hasn't asked to see any of them outside of school yet. She doesn't seem concerned about it, so I pretend I'm not either. Today is her first soccer game, and she seems close with most of her teammates. My heart soars as I watch her excitedly run out onto the field and meet up with her friends.

Of course, it's just my luck that the girls she has grown closest with happen to have the moms who seem to make a hobby out of burning holes through the side of my face with their eyes. It's fine, though. Today, I brought reinforcements.

A group of parents huddle in a circle on the other end of the bleachers, stealing glances every few seconds, no doubt hyper-focused on the six-foot-something tattooed mechanic hulking over me. I shift under Everett's arm draped around my shoulder, but I don't remove it. Being this close to him gives me comfort—something I'm afraid to admit to both him and myself.

It's been three weeks since we finalized our faux relationship agreement, two since the Hayes Foundation Banquet. I knew Everett had a friend who died, but I didn't realize how deep those cuts ran. I'm not even sure Leo knows just how affected Everett still is. After we danced, the night went on more smoothly. He seemed present, at least. I could tell Leo was struggling, too, but when we got home that night, he went to bed with my sister. He wasn't alone. Leaving Everett by himself almost killed me, but with my daughter sleeping upstairs and his mother waiting up for us, I couldn't easily invite him to bed with me. Not to mention that having Everett Ramos anywhere near my bed is a detrimental idea.

I'd probably never let him leave it again.

Plus, Lou's getting increasingly comfortable having Everett around. We explained to her that we're friends, and we enjoy spending time together. Neither are lies, but to the adults of the world, we're putting off the air that much more is going on behind closed doors. While Lou may not understand all of that, she's still getting attached to him. Eventually, this fake relationship with Everett will end, and so will my situation with my dad and Jason. Either they'll finally go away and let us move on, which means

Everett will move on too, or they'll win, and I'll have to take her back to Kansas.

Everett may always be around in some capacity. As her uncle's brother. As a friend. But eventually, space is going to exist between us, and I don't want Lou being hurt by that.

A snide cackle of laughter erupts from the circle down the field, pulling me from my thoughts. I glance over to find a group of parents snickering as their eyes flicker back and forth between each other and myself.

"I don't know what I've done to be so offensive," I mutter under my breath.

"You're prettier than they are," Everett says immediately.

"It's okay. I'm Public Enemy Number One," Darby adds from my other side with a chuckle.

I rear back, turning beneath Everett's arm as I look at my sister. "You? The All-American golden girl? How could anyone ever possibly hate you?"

My sister scowls at me, and I wince. I've never been resentful of her, never blamed her for being the good girl, the perfect child, growing up. Rebelling was my way of protecting myself, and conforming was hers. I know she resents that, though, and I know she's still trying to find her way out of it, to figure out who she is.

"Sorry," I murmur.

"It's fine." She rolls her eyes at me. "But I'm not joking. The teller at the bank is rude to me. The barista at the coffee shop downtown always spells my name wrong, and I'm pretty sure she purposely messes up my orders. The owner of the antique store I love glares at me every time I walk through the door."

"Why?" I ask. "Didn't everyone here love Grandma? Didn't they love you when you spent that summer here years ago? What could you have done now?"

"She took Leo Graham off the market," Everett says next to me.

Leo lets out some kind of annoyed growl from next to him. "That's bullshit."

Everett laughs. "No, it's not." He turns sideways at the same time Leo does, the four of us forming our own little circle as we wait for Lou's game to start. "Leo was just starting to gain attention around the time Darby spent that summer here, but by the time he turned eighteen..." Everett lets out a low whistle. "Everyone in Southern California knew Leo Graham and that he'd be a legend."

Leo's cheeks heat as he dips his head bashfully. My sister glances up at him, beaming with pride.

"He was a hot commodity, but he was also like this sad little puppy. Everyone knew about the girl from that summer who broke his heart. Every girl in this town wanted to be the one to mend it." Leo lifts his head, glaring at his brother. Everett only shrugs. "It went on like that for years. Leo got more famous, made more money, and more women threw themselves at him. He dodged them all. Then, all of a sudden, he runs off to steal a bride on her wedding day?"

"It didn't happen like that," Leo mutters.

Everett laughs again. "You come back to town with that same girl from all those years ago, and you retire early just so you can spend all your time with her. You buy her a house, buy her a business, and ask her to marry you after a month together."

"Technically, my grandma bought the business," Darby chimes.

"Logistics." Everett waves his arm in the air. "Of course people are going to take time warming up to you. You got what so many others wanted for themselves, what parents wanted for their daughters. It's all small-town jealousy. It'll pass eventually."

My sister shrugs. "I'm not worried about it. I won anyway."

A slow grin creeps up on my cheeks. "That's my girl." The old Darby would hyper-focus on what others thought of her, would hate herself for the actions and opinions of others, even the things she couldn't control. I'm proud of the growth she achieved and the happiness she found. "But why are the parents at Lou's school being bitches to me, then? I didn't steal anyone's surfer boy wet dream."

Leo snickers. "No, just their tattooed, motorcycle Hercules one."

My jaw drops as I turn to look at Everett. His thick brows furrow, full lips pout, and brown eyes—almost amber in the sunlight—narrow as he scowls at his brother. "Trust me, I'm nobody's wet dream."

He's my wet dream.

I don't say that, though.

"Most of those people"—I nod toward the group of parents—"are so much older than us, though. I thought that was why they didn't like me. Because I'm a trashy teen mom."

"You are not," Darby gasps. "Don't fucking say that shit about yourself."

The three of us gape at her. My sister rarely curses.

"Sorry," I murmur.

"I told you, Wildflower; it's because you're younger and hotter than them. They're jealous." Everett rolls his eyes when he adds, "Plus, the PTO is run by Tana Miller, and you know how she likes to hold a grudge."

Leo scoffs while my sister eyes him curiously. "Who is Tana Miller?" she asks.

"Oh, my dear Darby, I think you'd be more familiar with her younger sister." Everett smiles mischievously. "Amaya."

Darby's hazel eyes bulge.

"Who's Amaya?" I ask now, noticing the way my sister blushes.

"Amaya was Leo's first girlfriend," Everett continues, ignoring the glare from his brother. "She broke up with him because he wouldn't let her...deflower him. But even after they broke up, she still hung around, hoping he'd change his mind." He chuckles. "Until this one"—nodding to my sister—"went ahead and announced to Amaya—in front of a house full of people—that while Leo was hellbent on protecting his virtue from her, Darby had gone ahead and laid claim to it after...what? Five minutes of knowing each other?"

Both of our siblings scowl at him.

I'm just shocked. "You shouted that you let Leo take your virginity in front of a house-party full of people?"

"No," Darby growls.

"She was drunk," Leo continues. "And she didn't tell everyone we had sex. She just implied that I prefer morning sex to evening sex." He smirks. "Which isn't a lie. She's very perceptive."

Darby avoids eye contact with me, blushing as she focuses on the field in front of us, suddenly real interested in a bunch of nine-year-olds kicking a soccer ball. Leo, sitting a row above her on the bleachers, pulls her back against him and plants a kiss in her hair.

I laugh, shaking my head at them. "Why would your ex-girlfriend's sister from five hundred years ago care about me, though?"

"If someone hated your sister, even for an irrational reason, wouldn't you hate them too?" Everett asks.

"Of course," I say. "But I didn't deflower Leo Graham or whatever the fuck that girl is upset about."

"Amaya was queen bee, and Darby's the only person who ever stung her. She was embarrassed and hurt, I'm sure." Darby looks up at him with regret in her features as he brushes a thumb against her cheek. "You didn't do anything wrong, baby. She wasn't kind to you, and that was likely the first time in your entire life you ever stood up for yourself. Regardless, it probably stuck with her. She held a grudge." He shrugs. "Her sister is projecting those feelings onto Dahlia now. Just ignore them; they'll get bored eventually."

We're quiet for a moment as I think through what he'd said.

"Let's also not forget that you're probably getting death glares because the cougars love Everett, and I think some of the single ones secretly hoped they'd be the person to finally tie him down." Leo smiles.

Everett scoffs at that.

"Why cougars specifically?" I snort.

Leo shrugs. "He's kind of known to go after older women. And men, actually."

"Dude."

I laugh. "Well, shoot, maybe this"—I wave my finger between us—"isn't as believable as we hoped it'd be."

I duck out from under his arm, but his strong hand grips around my waist and tugs me back to him. My skin lights on fire where his fingers splay across my midsection, searing me even through my T-shirt. Chills race down my spine at the feel of his hard body against my back, his breath against my ear.

Our arrangement doesn't require a ton of PDA. We go out to lunch a few times a week. Everett always holds my hand or places it at the small of my back. He hovers against me closely or tucks my hair behind my ear if someone he knows is watching. Sometimes, he'll brush his lips against my temple, but I know those moments aren't for show. Those are just for him.

Just like now, as he pulls me back beneath his arms and wraps both around my shoulders. He leans down and lets his lips tickle my cheek as he whispers, "You're older than me, so I think it works out great."

I crane my neck to the side as his breath trickles down my body. He takes the opportunity to tightly press his mouth against my throat, and I know he can feel my hammering pulse there. When his hands, his lips, and his body are against me, it's like the rest of the world fades out. I can tell myself he's doing this because of the parents standing nearby, but in reality, I savor this moment because I love the way he feels. He touches me like he's cherishing me, and God knows I'm fucking starved for it.

So, I let his lips drag along my skin, just briefly. I bite back the moan I want to let out.

"By what? A year and a half?" I chide, though it comes out breathless.

"I don't discriminate, baby," he murmurs against my jaw before pulling away. "Plus," he says louder, clearing his throat, as if just realizing we're in public. A children's soccer game, no less. "I don't have a type. Well"—he pauses, and it's almost like I can feel the smile I can't see as I stand in front of him—"at least not until I met you."

My sister's eyes widen. She watches me curiously, and I can't meet her gaze as I drop my head to hide my blush. A strange weight settles over all of us, like Everett may have just said something a little too real. Thankfully, before anyone can address it, a whistle blows from out on the field, and my daughter's soccer game begins.

We all watch from the bleachers as a bunch of little kids run around in circles on the field, chasing the ball. I don't know shit about soccer, but my eyes are only glued to my daughter anyway. She looks confused, and she trips over her own feet no less than three times, but she's laughing, and that's all that matters.

"Oh, by the way, Lou asked me if I would recruit the three of you to accompany us on Halloween." I sigh. "I think she's afraid of the other kids at school not inviting her, and she doesn't want to feel left out. Of course, I, as her mother, am not enough. She needs a whole crew to join her."

My sister giggles. "What does she want to go as?"

"I need y'all to say yes first."

The boys look at me with perplexed expressions. Hesitantly, all three of them mumble their confirmation.

"She wants to go as Ironman, and she wants us to be the rest of the Avengers."

"Oh, God," Leo groans, and the same time, Everett mutters, "Fuck me."

Darby is cackling as she asks, "Do we at least get to choose who we dress up as?"

I give each of them my most apologetic smile. "Nope. She already decided."

We pause as the crowd cheers, but looking out onto the field, it appears the other team scored. Lou stands in the center of the field with her hands on her hips, looking concerned. Everett slips his thumb and forefinger into his mouth—I try to ignore how hot it looks as his tongue darts out between his lips—and lets out a deafening whistle.

Her little head snaps up, braids swaying side to side. He gives her a thumbs up, and even a field away, I can see her smile brightly at him. Something in my chest erupts at that.

"All right," Leo says as we turn back to each other. "Lay it on us."

"She wants you to be Captain America."

He pops a brow as he nods. "Okay, that's not too bad."

"She wants Darby to be Hawkeye." I turn to Everett, attempting to hide my grin because I know he's going to hate his costume most of all. "She wants you to dress as—"

"Don't even say it, Wildflower." He sighs. "I already know."

I chew on my lip. I know it's a lot to ask of each of them, which is a major part of the reason I've been trying to teach her boundaries. She has to realize that not everyone is going to be as invested as I am, though unfortunately, I think she's already well aware of that, after growing up with my parents and her dad. She just refuses to lose hope that she's going to find people in her life who'll drop everything to see her smile. I hate the idea that someday, she might be as hopeless as I am. I don't ever want to see that happen, but I can't expect everyone in her life to treat her like their own daughter. She has never had healthy relationships with anyone outside of me and Darby to witness as an example. She doesn't understand the role of aunt or uncle, doesn't understand the role of grandparent. I'm afraid that anyone who shows her the slightest glimpse of love and care, she's going to expect the world from.

And that's going to cause her a lot of heartache.

I told her I couldn't guarantee that the three of them would be able to join us, and I tried to convince her we'd still have fun on our own. Secretly, though, I hoped we could give her this experience. Every Halloween she's ever had was either just Lou, Darby, and myself, or some kind of church event my parents would drag us to. Someday, someday very soon, she won't want to trick-or-treat at all. I secretly hoped to give her one year where she felt totally in control, a year where she could make the night everything she wants it to be.

"So, it's a no, then?"

Everett's face softens, and those eyes burn right through me, as if he can read every thought in my head and every expression on my face. "Of course not. You know I'll paint myself green for that kid if she asks me to."

Butterfly wings explode in my stomach, fluttering up through my chest. My throat goes tight, and my eyes burn. I've never had anyone say that to me about Lou before, nobody besides my sister. I turn away, rapidly blinking back my tears before they can surface. This shouldn't be such a big deal to me, and I don't want anyone seeing the emotion on my face, seeing the effect those words—that care for her—has on me.

As if sensing that, too, Everett places his hand on my thigh, drawing soothing circles over my jeans with his thumb. "I've just got one favor to ask."

"Yeah?" I say, attempting to keep my voice from cracking.

"Who're you dressing up as?"

"Black Widow."

I turn back to face him just in time to catch his smile. "That's what I thought." He bites his lip as his eyes dart down to my legs, slowly running the length of my torso before meeting my face again. "I'll be there, Wildflower, as long as I get to see you in some leather fucking pants."

My jaw drops as he flashes me that wicked grin that threatens to put me on my knees every time I see it. The way this man can bring me from the edge of tears to bursting with laughter in a matter of seconds is a whiplash I've never experienced before.

I can't help the giggle that bubbles through me, and Everett returns it with his own as he squeezes my thigh gently before turning back to the game.

We watch the rest of the half in comfortable silence, focusing mostly on Lou while my sister and I make idle small talk when she's not playing. Deep into the second quarter, my attention is snagged when the bleachers we're sitting on suddenly dips with the weight of someone stepping up it. We all turn to see Jeremiah—Everett and Leo's intern—climbing toward us.

"Thought that was you guys," he says, running a hand through the blond curls at the top of his head. "What are you doing here?"

I'm leaning against Everett's chest when I feel him tense. "Watching Dahlia's daughter play."

Jeremiah's brown eyes land on me, softening when he smiles. "I didn't know you had a daughter. Which one is she?" he asks, looking out to the field.

"Number eight. The blond pigtails," I respond.

"She's cute," he says, turning back to us. "I'm watching my niece. She's number twelve on the other team." He points out the small brunette girl across the field. "My sister is sitting on the other side, but I thought I saw Everett's big-ass body over here."

Everett's shoulders shake with his scoff, but he doesn't respond.

Jeremiah quietly greets my sister and Leo, who are wrapped in their own conversation, before taking the seat next to me.

Everett loops one large hand around my thigh and tugs me into him. His grip is a possessive warning, and I watch Jeremiah study where his palm spreads across my leg, the ink along his hands and the way his fingers flex beneath Jeremiah's stare, as if Everett's daring him to say something.

"Are you two—"

"Yes," Everett responds immediately.

God, why is jealousy so hot on him?

I swear I could've caught a glimpse of disappointment flash across Jeremiah's face, but it's gone just as fast. Everett is a brick wall next to me, and Jeremiah looks equally as uncomfortable, though I have no fucking clue what's going on.

Jeremiah clears his throat. "So, how are you liking work so far?"

"It's good. I'm enjoying it." Tilting my head toward the men next to me, I add, "They keep things interesting."

He snorts. "That's for sure."

Jeremiah and I make small talk for a little while, but I can feel the tension radiating off Everett next to me. As the conversation dies down, I lean against him and whisper, "What's your deal?"

"No deal."

"Don't lie."

Everett glances down at me, the corner of his mouth ticking up. "He came over here to make a move," he whispers. "Jeremiah knew you had a daughter, and I can guarantee you that dude has never shown up to a game of his niece's before. He was seeking you out. Didn't expect to find me." He slides his hand deeper down my thigh, nearly between my legs. My entire body shivers at the touch, and I know it catches Jeremiah's attention next to us. "I'm just making sure he knows you're mine."

"I'm pretending to be yours," I murmur. "And I doubt he's interested. He's just being nice because his bosses are around."

"Mm-hmm." Everett's breath is hot against my ear, his nose running the length of my neck until his mouth meets my collarbone. "Pretending." I feel his lips part, dragging slowly against my skin before his teeth nip at my flesh, tongue snaking out to soothe the sting.

"We're *friends*," I bite out, holding back a moan. My body ignites beneath his touch and teeth and mouth.

"Friends," he muses, and I feel his smile against my neck. "Do all your friends make you squirt?"

My veins flood with heat, and he laughs again at the sound of my breath hitching. I can't help the flush of my cheeks and the tension in my core, the fixation on every place his body aligns with mine.

A throat clears next to me, bringing us back to reality. Eyes flying open, I look over at Jeremiah, who's still sitting next to us, jaw tight. My cheeks flush with embarrassment as Everett leans around me. "Sorry, man. Forgot you were there."

His eyes narrow. "Right. Well, I should get back to my family." He hikes a thumb behind him. "I'll see you guys Monday."

"See ya!" Everett tosses out, not bothering to make eye contact.

"Bye," I call before turning to Everett and slapping his chest. "You're such an ass."

"I'm an ass?" he deadpans. "That fucker was looking at my girlfriend like she's his next meal."

Leo snorts next to us.

I open up to yell at him some more—masking my lust with anger because I'm trying to ignore the fact that I'm incredibly turned on—when the final whistle blows, signaling the end of the game.

We all gather our things and climb down the bleachers when Lou runs up to us after her team's post-game huddle. Her pigtail braids bounce at her shoulders as she closes the distance. Despite her team losing in a landslide, she's beaming when she stops in front of me and catches her breath. "You did so well today, bug." I chuckle into her hair, bending down to hug her.

She glances up at Everett as he holds out his hand and offers a high-five. She returns it, laughing as she says, "I heard you whistle at me from *so* far away."

"You did great, kid."

"Thanks, Evo." She smiles mischievously.

He frowns. "Hard pass."

Lou rolls her eyes, ignoring him. "Can you teach me to whistle like that?"

"As long as you never call me Evo again."

She lets out an exasperated sigh. "Fine."

My sister steps up behind Lou and ruffles her hair. "Good job, Lulu. You were awesome out there."

My daughter talks animatedly about the game as we walk back toward the parking lot. There are multiple groups of parents and kids congregating by their cars as we reach Everett's, so when Lou isn't paying attention, chatting with a few of her teammates, he makes a very public display of mauling my neck before heading to his car.

With flushed cheeks and tingling toes, I corral my kid from her friends, not missing the sneers and silence of a handful of their parents. Lou ends up demanding to go home with Leo and Darby anyway, because I have to stop by the grocery store, and she doesn't want to go.

Luckily, the two of them are fine with taking her, because I prefer to grocery shop alone. It's kind of therapeutic when you don't have a child hanging off the back of the cart, asking for every box of sugary cereal and bag of chips in sight.

I reach my car, unlocking it and throwing my purse into the passenger seat. As I open my door, I catch sight of what appears to be a folded piece of paper underneath my windshield wiper.

Knowing that people are watching, I quickly grab it and shove it into my back pocket as I slip inside my car.

I wait until I'm home before I pull out the sheet and open it.

In sloppy handwriting scrolled across the page is a note:

TAKE THE TRASH BACK TO KANSAS

Nineteen – Wicked

Paper Rings

Taylor Swift's voice is deafening as I step inside the house.

I shut the front door behind me and drop my green bodysuit on the dining room table—because lord knows I won't be changing into that until the last second—as I walk through to the kitchen. Leo and Darby are out doing something for their wedding; I don't remember what, but Dahlia is supposed to be home.

As I enter, I realize that it smells like hot chocolate. Not like the packaged one, but like someone heated melted chocolate and milk right over the stove—a warm, delicious, inviting smell.

But it's not hot chocolate I find in the kitchen. It's a fucking mess.

Dirty mixing bowls are scattered along the counter, sprinkles spilled across the floor. There are little brown balls coated in multicolored sprinkles laid out on wax paper-covered baking sheets. I think they might be the chocolate I was smelling.

Despite the chaos, the sight taking my breath away is the sway of Dahlia's hips as she attempts to moonwalk across the kitchen floor, dancing to "Paper Rings." Lou twirls around next to her, belting the lyrics into the chocolate-covered wooden spoon that she holds to her mouth like a microphone.

They're both so entranced by the music and their singing that they haven't noticed me enter the room, and I can't do anything other than stare at them, entirely allured. Dahlia's face is lit up with a carefree brightness that I've never seen on her before, like all her worries have been forgotten. She throws her head back, laughing as Lou wiggles to the floor and back up again.

She's so unbelievably beautiful, it feels like a stab right through my chest.

The warmth in her face, the wild movement in her body, has me physically stumbling back and leaning against the wall, like my legs can't bear to hold me up as I'm buried beneath the weight of her enchantment.

Because that's what she is—fucking enchanting.

I don't know how she could ever question her worth as a woman, her value as a mother, when that kid laughs and sings like she's the happiest girl on Earth. I don't know how Dahlia doesn't see that the only thing Lou needs in this world is her. I don't know how Dahlia doesn't see that she's enough.

The urge to capture this moment and save it forever is overwhelming, so I pull out my phone and take two pictures of them spinning around the room—they still haven't noticed me—before sliding to record video. I capture the song playing, the light on their faces, and their god-awful singing.

Finally, Dahlia spins at a slow enough speed that her eyes catch on mine, going wide as she freezes. Then, she screams, an ear-piercing, blood-curdling scream, which triggers a yelp from Lou. The spoon in her hand clatters to the floor as they both look at me with shocked, scared eyes.

As soon as recognition passes through her, Dahlia's hands fly to her chest, and that fear morphs into vexation. "Fucking Christ, Everett! You wanna warn someone when you walk into the goddamn room?"

"Mom!" Lou shouts. "That's two dollars."

"Godammit," Dal mutters.

"Three!"

"Okay! I get it." She leans over the counter to catch her breath, tapping on her tablet to lower the volume. I have tears streaming down my face as I stop recording, and she lifts her head just in time to watch me slip my phone back into my pocket. "Were you recording that?"

"Absolutely," I choke out through fits of laughter.

She rolls her eyes. Lou runs around the end of the kitchen island and grabs me by the hand. "Everett, we made truffles! You have to try one."

I let her lead me, her hand so small inside my own. She plucks a small chocolate ball covered in green and purple sprinkles from the cookie sheet and places it in my palm. Dahlia watches me curiously, but Lou's big green eyes are basically pleading with hopeful anticipation as I bite into the soft, fudge-like ball.

It tastes like milk chocolate with a hint of something even sweeter, and the truffle absolutely melts on my tongue. It's soft and rich, and explosions of flavor burst in my mouth.

"Holy fuck."

"That's a dollar," Lou says, but the smile on her face is filled with pride. I glance at Dahlia, who's smirking too. I pop the rest of the truffle in my mouth before pulling my wallet from my back pocket, fishing out four dollar bills and handing them to Lou. She scurries over to a jar on the counter and stuffs the money inside.

"Dal, these are amazing."

I swear, I see Dahlia blush. "Thank you. I make them every year."

It's clear she feels comfortable in the kitchen. I wonder if it's therapeutic for her somehow. She made those brownies before her first day of work, that lemon cake that was sitting on the counter the day I came to fix her car. I remember her giving my mom a box of lemon cookies too.

Maybe she just has a sweet tooth, if the insane coffee concoctions she brings into work every day are any indication.

"Do you bake a lot?"

She nods. "I always have. It's a stress reliever, I guess." She tucks a piece of hair behind her ear, turning toward the counter and gathering a handful of dishes before she drops them into the sink.

I grab the broom from the pantry and begin sweeping up the sprinkles as Lou asks, "Everett, are you a Swiftie?"

I smile to myself. "I'd say so, yeah."

Dahlia chuckles from where she washes dishes at the sink. "Lucille is the biggest Swiftie of them all."

"What's your favorite era?" she asks, leaning over the counter and placing her cheeks in her palms. Her deep-green, saucer-like eyes bore into me, like it's the most important question she has ever asked.

"Probably Midnights." I mimic her position before grabbing another truffle and popping it into my mouth. "What's yours?"

"Oh, my gosh," she squeals. "You are *totally* Midnights!" Those eyes light up as a grin overtakes her face. "I'm Lover."

"Oh, my gosh!" I mimic the excitement in her tone. "You are *totally* Lover."

She's practically vibrating with energy, and I can feel Dahlia looking at us out of the corner of my eye, but I'm afraid to meet her gaze for some reason.

"Lucille, why don't you go upstairs and take a shower so we can get you ready for your costume?"

"Okay!" she chimes, mouth full of truffle. The patter of small footsteps ambles toward the staircase at the front of the house.

I wordlessly make my way around the kitchen, grabbing utensils and meeting Dahlia at the sink. She looks down at my full hands, watching as I toss them in with the rest of the dirty dishes before I take the whisk she just finished scrubbing and place it into the dishwasher.

"How did you get into baking?" I ask before she can protest my helping her.

She clears her throat, and I notice that pretty flush back in her cheeks. "When I was pregnant, I...um...I spent a lot of time at home. I got bored easily, especially the first few months, since I was taking a break from school. The only thing that got my mind off ...everything was cooking." She laughs under her breath. "Except I hate cooking. But I love dessert. It started with cookies, and over time, I learned how to perfect recipes and explored more." She hands me a bowl, and our fingers brush as I take it from her. Her skin is soft and warm beneath mine, and I hold it there for just a little longer than necessary. "By the time Lou was born, it had become a source of comfort for me, and then it became something we did together."

I nod. "Why'd you spend so much time at home during your pregnancy?" I pause, glancing down at her, but she refuses to meet my eyes. "Were you sick a lot or something?"

She shakes her head, and her body goes stiff. It's like I can see some sort of memory flood through her, haunting her daydreams.

I place my hand on her lower back, and she flinches at the contact. "I'm sorry." I quickly pull it away. "I didn't mean to bring up something that might..."

"My dad." She shudders as whatever she's remembering racks through her.

"Your dad?"

She finally looks at me, storms raging in her blue eyes. "He locked me in the house. Took away my car. My phone. Cut off all my access to the outside world. He told me I could leave once I agreed to an abortion." Her lips tighten as she swallows and blinks, turning her head in the other direction, fighting back tears. "They sent Darby away and wouldn't let me talk to her, wouldn't let me contact Jason and tell him. It was so fucking lonely. I was trapped."

That word rings through me. *Trapped.*

They locked her in the house like she was their prisoner. Their embarrassment. Their mistake. They tried to hide her away from the world, shame her for what happened. I can't imagine how it'd feel to be in that situation period, let alone because of one's own parents.

I think my heart has broken for Dahlia before. I've seen hurt and fear and devastation in her eyes, and my heart ached because of it, but nothing quite compares to the raging storm and hurricane of despair that roars through my chest now.

"That's why you freaked out about your car that morning," I

say quietly, still trying to process the horror of what she just told me. "It makes you feel trapped. You need to know you have an escape route. The ability to get away."

Her eyes find mine, and though she doesn't let them fall, I see the tears shimmering there, as if it's the first time she has had words to name those emotions.

"Something like that."

"Dahlia." I step toward her. I'm almost afraid to touch her because of the way she flinched before, but I've also learned over the last few months that my touch brings her comfort. I slowly lift my hand toward her face, ensuring she can see it coming. She doesn't shy away from it as I cup her cheek and run my thumb across her jaw. "I don't want you to ever feel that way again. You'll always have a way out, an escape route. You'll always have me to call."

She lets her eyes flutter closed at those words, taking a deep breath and settling herself. "I've never told anyone that before."

"It's safe with me."

As those blue pools fall open, all their depth lands on me, and I'm suddenly sucked inside them, drowning in them. I know then that I'd do anything she asked of me. I'd go to the ends of the earth for her—for her daughter. I'm lost to her storm, and I belong to her sea.

I wonder if that's written all over my face as the softest of smiles highlight her freckled cheeks. "I know."

❧

When we arrive home after trick-or-treating, Lou immediately plops down in the center of the living room floor, dumping her candy out across the rug so she can sort through it.

My parents came by just before we left, to see Lou in her costume—and to make fun of the rest of us in ours. They stayed at the house to hand out Dahlia's truffles, since they don't get many kids coming through their retirement estate.

Our costumes were horrendously embarrassing, but I know that kid was having the time of her life. It was weird that only a year ago, Leo had dragged me to some flashy Halloween party in LA., and despite the frills and status, neither of us really wanted to be there. Even though this year, we were skipping around our neighborhood in homemade costumes, being laughed at by our neighbors, and following three blondes who completely turned our lives upside down, I don't think either of us would've wanted to be doing anything else tonight.

Darby and Leo join Lou on the couch as Dahlia runs upstairs to get out of her shoes. My brother is still wearing his ugly-ass blue pants and Captain America T-shirt, with the little hat and shield to match. I'm pretty certain the only shield Dahlia could find was for a children's costume, so it's way too small for him. Either that, or Dahlia grabbed that shield on purpose so he'd look stupid, which only makes me more obsessed with her.

Darby got away with a pair of black jeans, purple hoodie, and a toy bow and arrow slung over her back. My assumption was that Dahlia would take the same route, but when she appeared at the bottom of the staircase earlier, I was met with a costume that was anything but casual.

Tight, faux leather pants looked practically painted on her, with her lush hips and the dip of her waist hugged by a black athletic jacket. The zipper stopped right at the center of her chest, giving off the smallest glimpse of her flawless, full breasts. Thigh-high, heeled boots with silver stripes ran up her legs, and a matching belt sat fastened at her waist. Her blond hair was sleek and straight at her shoulders, and she even painted her lips cherry red.

The sight of her sent all the blood rushing straight to my dick. As she walked down the stairs in front of my entire family, I watched, slack-jawed and drooling.

"What?" she asked, feigning innocence. "I thought this was what you wanted?"

"Everything I've ever wanted," I found myself saying without much thought.

Thinking back, I don't think I meant to say the words out loud, but the way she had smiled was well worth it. I'll put my heart out on my sleeve—in the palm of my hand—for her if it means she's going to blush and smile at me like that.

If I let myself think too hard about the fact that she's above me right now, peeling those pants off her smooth legs, I'm going to lose my mind. So, I retire to the kitchen, putting away the leftover truffles. I secretly stash a handful to bring home for myself.

I think the evening went well. Lou skipped with excitement to the front door of every house in the neighborhood, sometimes dragging one of us with her. People gushed over her costume—a sparkly red long-sleeved unitard that ran down to her ankles, a silver circle fitted in the center of the chest, a gold belt wrapped around her middle. She also had a golden tutu, an Iron Man helmet propped at the top of her head, and a yellow pillowcase for collecting candy.

I made sure we stopped by Debbie Michaelson's house—the patron of my father's who told him she wouldn't bring her car to the garage anymore after my brief stint with her grandson. I made sure to showcase what a *reformed playboy* I am, taking my girlfriend's daughter trick-or-treating this Halloween rather than getting shit-faced at a party. I made sure to say the girlfriend part out loud, too, mostly just because I like the way it rolls off my tongue, and I enjoy the sound of Dahlia's breath hitching every time I say it.

My favorite moment of Halloween, though, was when Darby dared Leo to take Lou's pillowcase and go up to one door completely by himself. She knows as well as I do how hard it is for him to turn down a dare. The best part was when the owner of the house recognized him and asked him to sign a T-shirt. Caught up in the midst of that, Leo forgot to ask for candy, and Lou sent him back up to the house a second time.

I hear Dahlia call down to Lou that it's time for bed, then the sound of their footsteps ascending the stairs from the front of the house. I know I don't have any reason to stay, but I don't want to leave without saying goodnight to Dal, without having just one quiet moment alone with her.

I decide to make small talk with my brother for a while and hope that Dahlia comes back downstairs before she goes to bed herself. I stop short as I enter the living room, finding Leo and Darby both asleep on the couch. Lou's pillowcase is lying on the floor, candy spilled across the rug.

Both of them are breathing deeply, my brother sitting almost upright with his fiancée sprawled across his chest. One arm splays around her waist while the other sits at his thigh, her hand nestled in his palm.

I watch that hand flex, his fingers tightening around hers, as if, even in his sleep, he needs to remind himself that she's still there. She hasn't left him again.

"Do you think we should wake them up?" Dahlia's whispered words startle me as she appears at my side.

"No." I shake my head. "They look peaceful. Plus, he'll wake up in a few hours when his back goes out anyway."

She laughs quietly as she brushes past me and begins to pick up Lou's candy. Wordlessly, I squat down to help her. Once we finish, she takes everything into the kitchen and, like a moth to her flame, I follow. She's wearing a pair of joggers and a black tank top. I can tell by the way her breasts bounce as she reaches into the top cupboard for a glass that she's not wearing a bra.

My hands are balled into fists at my sides, aching for her touch. I want to step into her, want to feel her body against mine again. I want to grab those lush hips, touch that soft skin. I want to taste her again. I need to be reminded of what those pillowy lips feel like.

"Everett?" Her voice breaks me from my trance.

"What?"

"I said thank you...for tonight." She laughs to herself, and the sound makes my cock jump. She laughs so prettily. "You really went above and beyond in your fake boyfriend duties."

She puts an emphasis on that term, and I decide I hate that

word. *Fake.* Nothing about tonight—the way I acted, the way I felt—was fake or forced.

"It has nothing to do with our arrangement, Wildflower." I find myself rounding the kitchen island, closing the space between us. "I care about Lou," I say, towering over her now. "I care about you. I want you to understand..." I sigh, slowly lifting my hand and tucking a piece of wild hair behind her ear. "Regardless of this arrangement, no matter how long it lasts, I'm gonna be here. For her. For both of you."

Her ocean eyes swirl with hope and hesitation—and the war within them is enough to bring me to my knees. She's searching my face rapidly, looking for the lie that she's so used to being told. I let her search; all she'll find here is honesty.

I drop my forehead to hers, keeping my hold on her face. Both of our eyes close, and I feel her sigh against my lips. I want so badly to kiss her. Feel her. Taste her.

But I don't. I don't close the gap, because as always, the ball is in her court. I wait for her to decide what she wants from me, knowing I'll give her all of it.

It's this moment—with her lips nearly touching mine, her skin beneath my fingers—I realize I don't want drunken nights at the bar or random hook-ups with people I barely know anymore. I don't want surface level. I don't want temporary.

I want to clean candy up off the ground with her. I want to help her do the dishes, to watch her dance around the kitchen with her daughter. I want to hear them laugh together and be the reason for their smiles.

But I know I can't tell Dahlia that, because every promise she's ever relied on has been broken. I have to show her that this isn't an arrangement for me. This isn't fake. She may be mine for show, but I'm hers for real.

All I've got to do is prove it.

Twenty - Wildflower

Say Thank You

The rasp of knuckles sounds from the other side of my office door. They're not hesitant like Adam's, not delicate like Scarlett's, not clipped like Jeremiah's. Leo never knocks.

It's a comforting feeling that I've grown to know my colleagues well enough to understand who's knocking on my door just by the sound.

There is only one person who knocks with the back of their hand, knuckles clattering against the wood in a rough tone.

"Come in, Mr. Ramos," I call from my desk chair.

The door swings open, and he takes up the entirety of the entryway. He leans against the frame in a long-sleeve Hurley stretched tight across his broad chest, a pair of black jeans, and boot-clad feet crossed at the ankles. Eyes glittering with mischief, he flashes me that wicked smile. "Mr. Ramos? I like that." Stepping into my office, he places what appears to be an iced coffee on my desk.

"What's that?" I ask, nodding toward the plastic cup.

"I'm closing up Heathen's today, so I swung through Dutchies on my way over from the shop. I figured you might need an afternoon pick-me-up." He briefly glances down at the cup in his own hand, appearing almost bashful. "I asked them to whip up the most ridiculous concoction they could think of."

I laugh, reaching across the desk and grabbing the drink.

As I take a sip, I'm blasted with the taste of pumpkin, cinnamon, cream, and something else I can't quite place. "Pumpkin spice with cream..." I take another sip. "I can't figure out what else is in here. Something sweet." I drink again. It's fucking good, though.

Everett smiles. "It's supposed to be a pumpkin glazed maple donut...or maple glazed pumpkin donut? I don't remember. I added three shots of espresso too."

"Three shots? Shit. I'm going to be up all night." I can't stop myself from drinking more, though. "Thank you. It's good. Maybe I'll try making some real maple glazed pumpkin donuts... or whatever." I grin at him, nodding toward his drink. "What'd you get?"

"That thing you kept getting last week. The s'mores drink."

I hum. "Toasted marshmallow mocha with a splash of almond." I beckon for him to hand me his drink. "Let me see if you ordered it right."

He rolls his eyes. "I ordered it exactly the way you told me to." He hands the cup out to me anyway, and our fingers brush as I take it from his grasp.

I don't let him see the way I savor the warmth of his skin in these small touches, the way he sometimes holds my hand when he walks me to my car, or when he places his hand on my back as we walk along the pier at lunch. We haven't gone beyond those stolen touches and longing glances in the two weeks since Halloween, haven't talked about that night, how close we came to kissing. It wasn't because anyone was watching or because either of us had something to prove. That moment was private and intimate, just for us.

Everett didn't kiss me. He simply pressed his lips to my forehead and told me goodnight before he let himself out. I told myself I was thankful we didn't cross that line, but I went to bed that night feeling nothing but his absence.

I bring the straw of his drink to my mouth, and I don't miss the way his eyes flare as I wrap my lips around it and take a sip. The warm, rich taste of marshmallow and chocolate hit my tongue, mixed with the hint of coffee and almond, and I find myself letting out a moan.

"Yeah," I say as I pull away, handing his coffee to him. "You ordered it right."

He laughs, and our hands brush again as he takes the coffee from me. He leans back against the conference table, and I fall into my chair, propping my feet up on my desk. I find my eyes stuck on his hands, on the rough calluses on his knuckles, forged by long hours working on engines and covered by intricate artwork framing his fingers and running along his veins. Vines of roses crawl up the backs of his hands and wrap around his fingers. Small stars, trees, and other flowers dot the spaces in between.

I can't help but wonder if there is any rhyme or reason to the designs, if they mean something deeper. I think about all the tattoos that flow through his arms and onto his neck.

"What, Wildflower?" he asks, voice rough and heavy.

My eyes snap to his face, and I realize he was watching me study him. "Oh." I clear my throat, feeling flustered. "I was just... Your tattoos. Do any of them mean anything?"

"Some of them do." He glances down at his hand, flexing it as he studies the ink. "But August owns the tattoo parlor a few doors down. Years ago, when he was still learning, I basically let him use my skin as a practice canvas, so some of the designs are just that—designs he wanted to try out or drawings he made. Some of them mean something to me."

"The flowers?"

He smiles to himself. "Roses on one hand for my sister. Her middle name is Rose. Zach..." He swallows. "Zach used to call her Rosebud. She hated it. Zach and I both got rose tattoos when we were drunk one night. We were just fucking around, provoking her." His eyes close as he shudders, as if remembering something hurtful. "I'm glad I have them now, though. It's something that keeps us connected."

He sets his coffee down on the table behind him and looks at his other hand. "I got the violets on this hand to make up for the other one. They're her favorite flowers, and purple is her favorite color. Plus, Violet is her pen name. So, I got this done the first time she became a bestseller. She has a matching design that runs down one of her arms but ends at the wrist. Mine starts there, so that connects us too."

"You miss her," I say.

He looks up at me, and I see raging emotion in those eyes. "So much."

"I'm sorry," I say quietly. "Has she visited since she moved?"

He shakes his head. "No. Never, though she claims she's coming home for Christmas this year. So, we'll see."

I only nod, unsure what else to say. My sister is my best friend, and I don't know how I would handle not seeing her regularly.

Everett clears his throat, attempting to shake off the heaviness in his voice. "Do you have any tattoos?"

I huff a laugh, rising from my chair and rounding my desk until I'm standing in front of him. I turn around and sweep the hair from the back of my neck, showing him the one piece of ink I have on my nape.

I shiver as the feel of his fingers runs down the length of it. "Why a compass?" he asks, letting his hand linger against my skin.

"I got it on my nineteenth birthday," I say. "I've always liked compasses. What they represent, at least. Lord knows I can't read one." We both chuckle. "I think they're beautiful in a practical way. They have purpose, but they're also symbolic. I don't know." I'm rambling now. His touch makes me unable to think straight. "I got it to remind myself that I'm the navigator of my own life." Everett's hand leaves my neck, and I let my hair drop as I spin to face him. "Which is hilarious, considering that, just a couple of months after getting that tattoo, I found out I was pregnant. Ever since, my life has been heading in every direction but the one I intended."

Everett's eyes are fierce as they study me. "Maybe that just means life was sending you in the direction you were destined for instead." He slowly reaches out and grasps the necklace at my throat, the small golden compass pendant. "Is that the reason for the necklace, too?"

I glance down, watching the way he twists the chain back and forth between his fingers. My pulse kicks up at his proximity—the way it feels when his thumb briefly rubs against my neck. "Like I said, I like compasses," I say breathlessly. He smiles, as if realizing the effect his touch has on me. "Darby bought me this necklace years ago."

"Lou plays with it when she's nervous."

I nod. "Yeah, she's done that since she was a baby. I bought her a matching one for her last birthday, but she lost it. I haven't been able to find a replica."

He hums in acknowledgment but doesn't respond as his eyes stay glued to my chest. Mine are watching his mouth as his tongue snakes out from between his teeth and swipes along his lips. There's hunger in his gaze, hunger and longing and something more.

I watch those deep-brown eyes run the length of my throat, studying the curve of my jaw and the breath filtering through my lips before they reach my own. I wonder if I've got the same need in my face that he's giving me right now.

I hear a shuffle of papers nearby, realizing that my office door is open. Scarlett and Jeremiah are standing at their desks, pretending not to pay attention, even though they totally are. They must've just gotten back from lunch...or wherever they were. I can't remember. Truthfully, I can't remember much past the way Everett's hand feels at my neck.

He drops it, and I step back to create space between us.

We both clear our throats, glancing around the room and looking at anything besides the other's eyes. "Thank you for the coffee." The words come out high and cracked from my flustered voice.

"Always, Wildflower," he says, sounding the same.

Are you awake?

I send the text to Everett, feeling stupid the second it shows delivered. I sound like a fucking teenager.

Am now.

Can't sleep, Wildflower?

No. And it's your fault.

It's just past midnight, and my entire household is dead asleep, but I have enough energy to run a marathon. Not that I actually ever would, of course. I figure, if I'm going to lay in bed all night, thinking about the man who can't seem to ever leave my head, I might as well make him keep me company.

I don't know what you were thinking. Three shots of espresso? You're insane.

Maybe this was my plan all along. 😉

What? Keeping me up all night? Why would you wanna do that?

Maybe I wanted you to text me.

And why, Mr. Ramos, would you want me texting you so late at night?

I dunno...

So, anyway... What're you wearing?

I laugh out loud as his latest text comes through, clamping a hand over my mouth to stay quiet. I bite my lip. God, he's actually making me feel like a giddy fucking teenager.

It has been so long since anyone has been able to make me feel like this.

Shameless flirt.

Only with you, Wildflower. Really, though. I am sorry. For overloading you with espresso.

But also...what are you wearing?

Another giggle escapes me, and I can feel myself blushing behind my phone. I take a moment to consider what to say next and, knowing that it's probably a horribly bad idea, I reach over and turn on the lamp beside my bed before throwing the comforter off my body.

Everett makes me feel young and dumb, which somehow makes me feel carefree and brave and wild. So, I let those feelings guide me as I walk over to my dresser and open the top drawer. I'm wearing a Wichita State T-shirt and a pair of gray high-waisted briefs that are at least three sizes too big, but Everett doesn't need to know that.

I tear through my drawer until I find a pair of black all lace boy-shorts. Changing my underwear and crawling back into bed, I lie on my side, hiking one leg over the other. I lift my T-shirt so just a glimpse of skin shows between the gap of my top and my panties, skin on full display beneath the lace. I bring one hand up to the center of my chest, and angle my camera so that it catches my entire body between my bent knee and my chin.

Before I allow myself to think any further, I snap the photo and send it to Everett.

He immediately reads the message. Three bubbles pop up, letting me know he's typing, before they disappear again, and my stomach plummets. "Shit."

I press and hold down the photo, trying to figure out if there is a way to unsend it, though I know it's too late, and he already saw it. "You're so fucking stupid, Dahlia," I groan into my pillow. Still trying to figure out how to unsend the message, I jump when my phone begins vibrating in my hand.

Everett's contact pops up on my screen—he's FaceTiming me.

I reach across my bedside table and grab my AirPods, connecting them and placing one in each ear before hesitantly answering the call. I check my reflection on the screen, brushing my ratted hair from my face and pinching some color into my cheeks and lips.

"Hi," I say awkwardly, my voice shaking as I hold the phone up to my face.

Everett's sitting up against his headboard, ridiculously gorgeous bare chest staring back at me, brown eyes on fire. "Is that really what you're wearing right now?"

"Yes?"

I watch his throat work as he swallows. "Show me."

There's a challenge glimmering in his face, and I decide to throw caution to the wind, meeting it head-on. I shrug back down the bed so I'm on my back, slowly angling my phone screen down so that my chest, stomach, and legs become visible. My shirt is long enough that it covers the apex of my thighs, but I lift the hem slightly, showing off the black band of the lace underwear against my hips.

"Fuck," he rasps. "That's what you wear in bed at night when you're thinking of me?"

I put the camera back on my face, raising a brow. "Who said I was thinking of you?"

"You texted me."

"Because it's your fault I can't sleep."

He lifts one arm and places it behind his head, biceps flexing with the movement. Flashing me that wicked fucking grin, he says, "You know what they say can help with falling asleep?"

I gasp, feigning offense. "Mr. Ramos, are you proposing FaceTime sex with me right now?"

He bites his lip, hiding a smile. "I'm just saying... As your *boyfriend*, I'm here to assist with all your needs, Wildflower. Whatever it is they may be."

"Fake boyfriend," I correct him and then ignore the way he bristles. "And I'm not sure what you think I need help with, but I can manage on my own."

"I know something you need help with."

I turn on my side, propping my phone up against my pillow. "What's that?"

He smirks. "You're embarrassed about the way you come. That you squirt."

My face flames. I drop my phone onto the bed so he can no longer see it. "I can't believe you just said that."

"C'mon, Dal." His voice is muffled through the speaker covered by my pillow. "You shouldn't be embarrassed about it. Do you have any idea how fucking sexy it is?"

I grab the phone again. "It is *not* sexy."

His jaw ticks beneath his perfectly manicured beard. "Who the fuck told you that?"

I roll my eyes as I turn over onto my back. "I don't want to talk about it."

He's quiet for a moment, contemplating. "Fine. We don't have to talk about it, but whoever he is, he's a fucking asshole, and he's dead wrong."

I don't know how to respond or how to look at him, so I stare at myself in the mirror hung against my bedroom door on the other side of the room. I wasn't lying when I told him it was something I could normally only do to myself. Only once, before Everett, had I...come like that with another man. He definitely did not find it sexy, and he had no interest in seeing me again afterwards.

"Have you ever watched yourself?" he asks.

"What?"

"Have you ever watched yourself...come?"

"God, no." I laugh. "That's horrifying."

His eyes soften as he studies me through the screen. "You really have no idea how beautiful you are, do you?"

I open my mouth, but words don't come out. I don't think there are any to respond to what he said, to describe the way he makes me feel.

"You're so beautiful, Dal. All the time. When you're done up and when you're dressed down. In the middle of the night and in the light of day. God"—he laughs breathlessly—"you're fucking stunning, including when you're coming. I've been blessed to see it, so trust me when I say that."

"I..." I swallow. "I don't know that I'd be able to agree with you, especially if I was watching myself...like that."

His lips tilt up again. "Maybe you just need to be coached through it."

I feel the flush on my cheeks deepen at that. "Everett..." I sigh, but I can't bite back the smile on my lips.

"Like I said...just say the word, baby. I'm here to help." He winks at me, and I feel a shot of warmth flood my core.

He's patient, soft brown eyes burning through me like he knows I'm contemplating something, like he's waiting for me to make my decision. That slow smile overtakes his full lips, and he runs a rough hand across his beard.

I remember what those lips felt like against my skin, the words that mouth whispered in my ear, the caress of those hands along my curves, and the flare in those eyes when he came. I remember how he lost himself inside me, how he reveled in the way I made him feel. I remember the power that gave me, the way it made me feel wild and alive.

I realize that, whether he's watching me or not, my hand is going to be slipping between my legs tonight before I'm able to find sleep, and he's going to be on my mind as I chase that ecstasy.

"Everett," I whisper, voice breaking on his name. "If I were to...touch myself. What..." God, the look in his eyes makes me feel like a timid schoolgirl talking to her crush for the first time. I shake it away and will confidence into my tone. "What would you do?"

"Whatever you want, Wildflower." His voice is like silk, running along my skin in a soft caress. "You want me to talk you through it? Tell you how pretty you are when you squirt?"

I let my eyes flutter closed. "I want you to..." I trail off, unsure how to make the request. I know I won't be able to get myself there, not with him watching, not unless he's giving me the same level of vulnerability. I want his presence—his words and his voice—but I can't be the only one of us crossing this line.

"You want me to fuck myself, Dahlia? Tell you how I dream of you when I close my eyes? Pretend it's your mouth instead of my hand? Or how I imagine I'm fucking your tight, wet pussy again?"

"Fuck." The word flies from my mouth on a moan as my fingers slip between the band of my underwear, feeling the wetness already pooled between my legs. "Yes."

"You have a mirror in your room, baby?"

I nod as I brush my clit, a quiet whimper escaping me.

"Get out of bed and go sit in front of your mirror. I want you to see your entire body."

I throw the blankets off my legs and all but leap out of bed, taking my phone with me. The full-length mirror bolted to the back of my door runs the entire length of it, nearly touching the floor. I sit down, leaning back against the foot of my bed and facing the mirror.

"Prop me up somewhere so I can see you."

Coming up to my knees, I place my phone on the shoe rack next to the door and angle it so the entirety of my body can be seen within the frame. I can still see Everett's face as I fall back against my bed, his eyes glimmering with hunger.

"You listen so well, Wildflower. Doing so good for me, baby." I can see the movement of his arm pumping his length, and I run my eyes along it until it disappears from the screen. His tone turns rough and strained with each movement. "Now, take off that shirt."

I shake my head. "I'm not taking off my shirt."

He pauses, brows coming together at his forehead in concern. "You're not comfortable with that." It's not a question, but I nod. "Why, Dal?"

My name from his mouth settles something deep inside my body. "I had a baby."

He tilts his head. "And?"

I sigh. "And... I breastfed. My... They're not..." My breasts don't look like they belong to a twenty-nine-year-old. One of them is permanently bigger than the other, and they're definitely not as perky as I think most would expect to see from a woman my age. Plus, I have stretch marks and veins and ripples.

"Don't finish that sentence." He sits up straighter, as if he wishes he could reach through the phone and grab my face, force my focus to his eyes. "It is infuriating to me how blind you are to your own beauty." I drop my gaze to the floor, feeling the flush run up my neck. "Look at me, Dahlia." He doesn't speak again until I listen. "I'm going to make sure you understand how pretty I find you. Every single piece of you. Every part of your body that made you who you are. All of it is beautiful to me."

There is such ferocity in his brown eyes, such intent, and I can't bear to do anything other than nod.

He settles back, getting comfortable again. "When I tell you how beautiful you are, you're not going to argue with me about it. You're going to thank me, and you're going to fucking listen. Am I understood?"

I nod again, but his face is still hard as he says, "Now, I'm going to ask you to take off your shirt and show me those tits I've been dreaming about. You don't have to do anything you're not comfortable with, Dahlia, but I'm begging you to let me see that body, baby. Show me what you're afraid of, and watch me fucking worship it."

I don't know if this man took a class on how to say exactly the right thing at the right moment, or if he's just somehow inherently wired to know what I need, but those words have me sitting up on my knees and pulling my T-shirt over my head. Knowing I'm not wearing a bra, I toss it to the side, keeping my eyes closed as I hear Everett's breath hitch. My entire body is on display for him now—save for the lace underwear that leave essentially nothing to the imagination.

I crack one eye open, terrified to see the expression on his face. I try not to be ashamed of my body. I mean, it made an entire human fucking being. But at the end of the day, you don't see stretch marks, cellulite, or misshapen boobs on models. You don't see it on perfect people like my sister, or I'm sure any number of the women Everett's been with.

But when I do look at him again, it's pure captivation I see on his face. His eyes rapidly roam across my body, like he doesn't know where to look, like he needs to soak all of it in before it disappears. His arm begins moving again, and he lets out a groan that echoes inside my ear, letting me know he's fisting his length.

"Dahlia," he rasps, eyes meeting mine. "I speak three fucking languages—*three*—and when I tell you that there is not one word in any of them to describe the way you look right now. You're beyond beauty. You're beyond comparison to anything in this plane of existence. You're something beyond comprehension. Unreal."

"Everett," I whisper. I've never been told something like that before. I've never heard words uttered with such raw emotion, like they're flying straight through his chest and out his mouth. I've forgotten where our conversation was going, what we were supposed to be doing.

All I know is that I'm sitting on my bedroom floor, nearly naked, staring into the eyes of a man who just sputtered poetry without thought because he saw my breasts for the first time.

As if realizing it, too, Everett shakes his head and clears his throat. "Do you want to see what you do to me, Dahlia? Do you want me to show you?"

"Yes." The words come out as a high-pitched squeal, and I will myself to quiet, at risk of waking up my child—or worse, my sister—and having them walk in on the current scene.

Everett smiles knowingly. "Lay against the bed and take off those panties, baby." I listen immediately, falling back and kicking my legs out in front of me. I lift my hips and slip the lace down my legs before kicking it to the other side of my room. "Can you see yourself in the mirror, Wildflower?"

I nod.

"Good. Now, spread those legs and show us both how pretty that pussy is."

His words rush through me, anticipation coiling in my stomach and snapping tight. The buzzing at the center of my thighs has my skin on fire, desperate with the need to touch myself, the need to feel him touch me too. I slowly widen my knees, displaying my sex for us. We both look at where I'm spread, the wetness at my center apparent in the low light.

"*Me moriría de sed por ahogarme en ti,*" he rasps, and I know he can see the way my body trembles at the words I can't understand but somehow still feel inside me. "Tell me how beautiful it is, Wildflower. Tell me you know how pretty that dripping pussy is."

A whimper erupts from my throat, and I can't stop myself as I run a finger through my slit, my arousal coating my hand. "You told me I only had to say thank you."

His laugh is rich and taunting. "Fine. I'm going to tell you how pretty you are, then. Your perfect little cunt is the most beautiful fucking thing I've ever seen. Is it all wet for me, baby?"

"Yes," I moan. "Thank you."

He laughs again. "Show me what makes you lose yourself. Show me what makes you explode the way you did all over my cock."

I bite my lip, feeling the flush rise to my cheeks and spread throughout the entirety of my body. I feel that coil tightening around me, my body begging for release, for sensation. I hold myself still, though, keeping two fingers just above my clit. "You said you'd show me first."

"Fuck." His voice is so deep, it's a near growl. I watch as he flips from his front to his back camera, and I'm suddenly met with his intimidating length. Strong, muscular thighs are partially covered by a dark blue blanket, his room accented in the same low light as mine. His cock—so massive I'm unable to believe it fit inside me—is standing erect, his beautiful, tattooed hand fisting his length hard and fast. "Do you see this, Dahlia? This is all you, baby. Only you on my mind every time I fuck myself since the night I met you."

I bite my lip, hard enough to taste the tang of my blood as I hold back a moan. I slowly lower my hand between my legs and dip two fingers inside myself, curving them to hit just the right spot on my innermost wall, pressing my palm against my clit.

"That's right, baby. Show me what feels good so I know what to do next time."

"You already know what to do," I whisper breathlessly as I move my fingers in and out of myself, picking up speed with each pump. My eyes dart back and forth between watching myself in the mirror and watching his cock on my phone's screen.

His laugh is rough, skating down my skin like a teasing touch. "You mean when I bent you in half and fucked you against that door?"

I let out a hum, watching both our hands as they pick up speed, as we climb toward that peak—toward the freefall into ecstasy.

"But next time, I'm going to do so much more than just fuck you, Wildflower. I'm going to make you forget your own name, forget how to walk straight, forget anything except what it feels like to be filled by me. I'm going to make you gush all over my hand. Flood my face." I cover my mouth to muffle the cries that his words wring from me. I press my hand harder against my clit, increasing the pressure at the center of my thighs as I pump into my core, curling my fingers and hitting the spot I know will make me explode. "Then," Everett continues, voice strained as he grips his cock harder, "I'm going spread that pretty cunt and fuck you until you're screaming my name, until you squirt all over my cock again."

"Everett," I cry, though the sound comes out muffled behind my palm. I feel the building pressure break, feel the climax pool in my hand as I pull out of myself. My toes curl, my vision goes nearly black, but I keep my eyes on the mirror as I bring my fingers to my clit and flick rapidly, guiding myself through my orgasm. I watch my release spill out between my thighs and soak the floor beneath me, watch my flushed, glowing cheeks, and hooded, hazed eyes. I drop my hand to reveal parted lips, legs spread open, body limp. My entire head is foggy as I watch myself ride out my orgasm, slowly bucking against my hand.

It's erotic and raw, and in some far-off awareness, I know I should feel embarrassed by the sight, by Everett watching me unravel for him, but in this moment, I don't feel that. I only feel the pleasure, the sound of his breathing, and the words he whispers in my ear, though I'm past comprehending them.

"Fuck, Dal. Fuck. *Fuck*."

My eyes dart sideways, catching the screen of my phone just in time to watch him pump his cock once more, his own climax ripping through him. I watch his stomach muscles tighten as his release shoots from his tip and drips down his base, gathering on his abs and in his hand. The sight of it nearly sends me into another spiral, wishing that it was covering my tongue. Across my chest. Dripping out of me.

He drops his phone, and I finally pull my hand from between my legs. We're both quiet for a moment as I stand and slip my T-shirt back over my head, stepping into my bathroom to clean myself up. I don't bother with my underwear when I return; I just grab my phone and climb between my sheets. A moment later, Everett's face appears back on my screen. I lie sideways, setting my phone on my pillow, and he does the same, almost as if we're lying in bed next to each other.

I wait for things to turn awkward and uncomfortable, but he only gives me that soft, easy smile that seems to make my bones melt. "Do you believe me now when I tell you how beautiful you are?"

I can't hide the tilt of my lips. "Maybe a little."

I'm not sure I'll ever be able to find my own orgasms beautiful. I don't think I'd ever describe myself that way, but that embarrassment I'm still waiting to envelop me never does. The shame I used to feel after sex when I'd come the way I did with Everett... It doesn't arise. I just feel...satisfied.

"You're so beautiful, Dahlia. So fucking pretty, sometimes I can't believe it."

"Everett," I whisper, caught off guard by a sudden yawn as my post-climax exhaustion settles over me. I realize it's nearly one in the morning, and he wasn't lying when he said orgasms help one fall asleep.

"Say thank you, Wildflower. Then you can go to sleep."

"Thank you." My eyes begin to droop, but through my blurred vision, I can see him smile.

"Go to sleep, Dal."

The sound of my name on his lips feels like a lullaby. I'm not ready to accept his absence yet. I want to keep feeling his presence. I don't want to be alone. "Can you stay?"

"Yeah, baby. I can stay."

His quiet breathing sends me into sleep.

When Lou wakes me in the morning, my phone is dead. I plug it in as I ready myself for work and Lou for school. When

I leave, I notice text messages from Everett, sent just after four o'clock.

I think your phone died. I just couldn't take my eyes off you. See you soon, Wildflower.

Twenty-One - Wicked

I'm Great With Filling!

My brother has beef with other sports.

Fucking weirdo that he is, he finds surfing superior to pretty much anything else. So, I'm not surprised when I enter his house on Thanksgiving morning to find him in a fuss over football being on the television.

Darby rolls her eyes but doesn't respond to him, hiding a smile as she entertains his dramatics. Lou shifts around him so she can get a better look at what's happening in the game, laughing into her cereal as Dahlia glances back and forth between them with a bemused expression. She slaps her knees as she stands and makes her way toward the kitchen.

I take one last look at where my brother and Darby are arguing, though the glitter in both of their eyes makes me question if it's some kind of weird-ass foreplay they've got going on. Regardless, I'm not nearly as interested in that as I am in the woman standing in the kitchen, so I follow her.

She has her back turned, handling something on the counter that I can't see as I lean against the island. "So, football fans, huh?"

She chuckles quietly. "Always have been. My dad had a couple of big-wig clients who'd take us out to Chiefs games a few times a year growing up. They were always business opportunities for him, but he'd drag us along to give the impression he was a family man." I watch her shoulders as she shrugs. "You know, it made him look more personable. Approachable. Less of a corrupt piece of shit. Darby and I always had fun, though." She turns around, and I notice she's holding a large plate in her hands, her blue eyes glittering with something like excitement. "I've got something for you."

"Me?" I ask.

She grins, nodding. As she holds out the tray, I notice what appears to be a handful of donuts with some kind of bright orange frosting and chocolate sprinkles on top. "Maple Glazed Pumpkin Whatevers, I call them."

The laugh that bursts out of me takes us both by surprise, and my eyes shoot up to meet hers. They widen as our gazes clash before she returns my laughter with her own bright melody. We're both breathless when she sets the donuts on the counter and slides them toward me. I take one, and it tastes just like everything else Dahlia creates—sweet, warm, and insanely flavorful. It's like I'm drinking the iced latte she knows I love from our favorite coffee stand. I swear, there are even hints of the espresso flavor within the pastry.

"So good," I say, though it comes out as more of a moan. "Why can I taste the coffee too?"

"The sprinkles," she responds proudly. "They're espresso flavored."

"You are utterly divine."

Her eyes spark at the compliment, and I notice her dip her head to hide the blush my words bring to her cheeks. I seem to always be making her blush, yet she continues to hide it. I never get tired of seeing it, her flustered by me, knowing I'm capable of bringing that kind of reaction out of such a strong, independent woman.

We haven't had another...moment like the one on FaceTime a couple of weeks ago, but we've spoken every single night before we fall asleep.

I reach out to grab another donut, only now realizing I've demolished the entirety of my first one in just a few bites. A small, pink-manicured hand slaps me on the wrist. "Don't ruin your dinner. You can take them home and have them later."

"C'mon, Wildflower."

She's failing to hide her smile as she shakes her head. "Your mother would be upset with me if you didn't eat her turkey because you're filled up on my donuts." She grabs the tray and turns around, giving me a view of her phenomenal ass as she covers the plate. "Plus, I'm making pie I'll want you to try later."

I open my mouth to continue arguing when I'm cut off by the door opening and a loud whistle. "Whose pretty little blue thing is sitting out in that driveway?" my dad calls from the foyer.

"That'd be mine!" Darby chimes from the living room.

My brother bought her a beautiful new car for her birthday last week. Apparently, the car she had back in Kansas was actually owned by her father and, knowing there was no way he'd be willing to give it to her—or any way she'd be willing to go back out to Crestwell and get it herself—Darby has been going without a vehicle for the last few months. That is, until Leo surprised her with a baby-blue, brand-new Mustang, the perfect complement to his classic red one.

They do look fucking great parked next to each other in the driveway.

Laughs ring out from the other room as Dahlia turns to face me again. "Someday, I'm going to make that happen," she murmurs under breath.

"Make what happen?" I ask.

She starts, as if she hadn't realized she said it out loud. Shaking off the surprise, she sighs. "I'm going to buy myself an impractical car I can drive just for fun. Something with no top. No child safety features. Something that doesn't need to accommodate anyone but myself."

"If you ever want to drive mine, Dal, you're more than welcome."

Her gaze softens, lips twitching up in the corner, pretty pink lips that I'd die to taste again. "I'm not sure I'm a Jeep gal."

I raise my brow. "You a motorcycle gal?"

I can tell by the way her eyes flare and her tongue flicks out to run along those pretty pink lips that I'm right on track. "I'm not sure I care enough to get a license and learn all that."

I smile. "I'll take you for a ride any time you want, baby."

We both know I mean that in more ways than one.

Dahlia's cheeks flush, and she looks away. "You can drive a motorcycle?"

"I've got a 1983 Triumph Bonneville sitting pretty in my garage right now." Her eyes flutter, glancing up at me through long lashes. "I don't get her out nearly enough, though."

She hums contemplatively just as my parents enter the kitchen with bags full of food. "Happy Thanksgiving!" my mother sings as she drops everything onto the counter and beelines straight for Dahlia.

She chuckles against the top of my mom's head as my mother wraps her arms around Dal's waist. She's tiny at just above five feet tall, whereas Dahlia has to be at least five eight or five nine. My mother finally pulls away and turns to me. "Hi, baby." She smiles, closing in on me too.

I pull her into my chest. "*¿Y yo? ¿Estoy pintado o qué?*"

"I think we're both second-best when it comes to the three of them," Leo chides as he strolls into the kitchen and begins rummaging through the fridge.

"You know Spanish?" Dahlia asks.

"I can understand it. Can't really speak it, though," he says with his head in the freezer.

"What do you think you're doing?" My mother flicks his ear as she bumps him out of the way with a hip and begins filling the space with everything she brought over.

"Ah," my brother hisses, holding his ear dramatically. "I trained for two hours this morning. I need a snack."

Mom rolls her eyes. "You can wait until dinner like everyone else."

"*Everyone else* isn't a professional athlete."

My mother shoos him from the kitchen, waving her hands in his face as he skips around the island away from her. The stern look on her face slips as she chases Leo around the kitchen, fighting a smile. He skips backward, eyes zoning in on Dahlia's donuts on the counter. "Oh, shit, what are those?"

"Fuck no. Those are min—" I reach out to grab the plate, but not before he swipes a donut and spins, barreling out of the kitchen doorway and back into the living room. He places the pastry between his teeth and gives me a salute then flips his middle finger at me before turning the corner. "He's insufferable," I mutter.

"You're the one who brought him home," Mom agrees.

"I heard that!"

We both laugh at that. I catch Dahlia's face light up, too, but she looks between us like the concept is foreign to her, standing around a kitchen on a holiday, making jokes and messing with each other. I again wonder what it must've looked like to grow up in that house.

"All right." Mom claps her hands. "Everyone not cooking can clear out. We've got work to do." She points at my dad. "Potato peeling." She looks at Dal. "Are you still making the pies?"

She smiles. "Yes, ma'am."

"Okay, you can stay." She lifts her head to me and makes that same shooing motion with her hand. "Out. We need the space. And send in my little helper!" She shouts loud enough that Lou will hear her anyway.

"What if I want to help too?"

Mom pauses, muttering something like "*Dios mío*" before letting out an exasperated sigh. "Never in your life have you offered to help with Thanksgiving dinner." Her eyes filter to the other end of the kitchen, where Dahlia reaches on her toes and digs through a cupboard, pretending like she's not listening and hiding the smile that tells me she is.

My mom looks back at me and raises a brow. I wink at her as I round the counter and close in on Dahlia. She's trying to grab a mixing bowl from the top shelf but can't quite reach it. I press in behind her, lifting an arm to grab what she's looking for. She sighs, falling back on her heels, which puts her body flush against mine.

I bite back a sound at the feel of her ass pressing against my dick, and in an attempt to hold my breath, I lose my own balance. Stumbling forward, I accidentally push us both into the counter, and all of me lines up with all of her. Soft curves brush against my all-too-sensitive cock. I know her body too well to be this close to it and not garner a reaction. Not only have I touched it, felt it, been inside of it, but seeing her touch herself on FaceTime those weeks ago?

Fuck.

I lost my fucking mind watching her come undone at my command, at the soft, quiet whimpers of my name from her lips and the way she looked spread, bared, and naked in front of that mirror. You could've convinced me I'd died and gone to heaven, and I'd be none the wiser. There is no way I can feel the press of her tight ass against me now, knowing it's the same body I'm so fucking desperate for, and not get hard.

With my fucking parents in the kitchen, no less.

A small gasp escapes her lips as I brace my hand on the counter next to her and set the bowl she needed down.

"Sorry," I murmur.

"No worries," she whispers.

Fully aware I should pull off her, I can't seem to do so. I lean away but keep her caged

between my arms. She spins so her back is to the counter. Her eyes lift to meet mine, and I realize I still haven't been able to match the color of those eyes to any shade I've seen in real life.

Incomparable. Just like her.

"So, what are we making?" I ask.

I watch her delicate throat bob as she swallows, and I can tell she's as flustered by our proximity as I am. I think that's what makes it impossible to pull away. She's so hard to read. I can never figure out what's running through her mind, except in these moments. When my skin touches her, she seems to melt beneath it. It opens up some kind of door that's typically shut tight, allows me a sliver of the woman inside—the woman who wants me as much as I want her.

"Pie," she says quietly.

"What kind of pie?"

She pulls her lip between her teeth, eyes fluttering around the room, looking anywhere but at me. "Boston cream. And pumpkin."

I let out a low laugh. "Do you need help with that cream pie, Wildflower?"

Big blue eyes snap to me, growing brighter to complement the blush raging up her neck and across her cheeks.

I hear the clattering of some kind of utensil, followed by an annoyed groan. "No. No, no." Dahlia stands up straight, and I reluctantly pull away from her. My mother drops the celery she was cutting, and I notice my dad standing over the kitchen sink, face beet red as he holds back laughter. "Whatever you two do behind closed doors is none of my business, but I'm not going to spend my *family* holiday listening to you make *cream pie* references and take seductive glances at each other." She points to the living room. "Out, Everett."

"Oh, my God, Mother." I run a hand down my face. "It was a joke."

"Right. Just like I'm sure it was a joke that Colin's grandmother called me after that date I set Dahlia up on and told me that she left him high and dry at the bar, running off with some"—she holds her hands out to make air quotes—"'big tattooed, motorcycle club member.'" She puffs. "I asked her what bar he took you to, and oddly enough, it happened to be Emilio's. The bar owned by one of my son's friends." She flicks her wrist, referencing me. "My big tattooed, motorcycle-riding child."

I roll my eyes. "Why do I feel like that's not a compliment?"

"I swear, I didn't know who he was when it happened," Dahlia says, eyes wide. "And to be fair, Colin was a fucking dud, Monica. You know it too."

Mom's brown eyes soften. "I'm not upset that you're hooking

up with Everett, *carina*. Lord knows that boy could do worse." I scrunch my nose at her, even though she's not wrong. No one's better than Dahlia, and we both know it. "I just have two rules: I don't want to see it, and I don't want to hear it. Same goes for them." She points her knife in the direction of the living room, where I know my brother and Dahlia's sister sit.

"Please don't say 'hooking up' ever again," I mutter.

"Please don't say 'cream pie' ever again," my mom snaps back.

Dahlia's face falls into her hands.

"Deal."

"Deal," she replies. "Now, get out of my kitchen. Go get Lou."

Dahlia laughs beneath her hands, and I snap my arm out to pull her fingers from her face, wanting to see her smile. "What are you laughing at?"

"It's enjoyable to see you get put in your place."

"Okay, I'm being bullied. I'm leaving." Both women are chuckling at me now, and some force outside my control has me tugging on Dahlia's hand, bringing her into me and planting a kiss against her neck.

Her laughter stops, and the room goes quiet. I hadn't realized I'd done it. It was something that felt all too natural to me. Making her smile. Hypnotized by her laugh. Putting my lips on her skin and showing her affection. It's too easy, like something I'm just supposed to do.

I clear my throat. "I'll grab Lou for you," I say gruffly, darting out of the kitchen before the awkward silence can settle in.

"And keep an eye out for August!" my mother chimes. "Should be here any time."

I pause at the threshold of the kitchen doorway, eyes locking on my brother from across the room. Surprise is plastered on both our faces. "How the fuck did she pull that off?" I ask.

"I don't think she did." Leo nods at Darby, whose head rests against his shoulder with a knowing smile on her face. "Something tells me it was all Honeysuckle's doing."

I plop down on the couch next to her, taking Lou's spot as

she hops up and heads into the kitchen. A moment later, my phone buzzes in my pocket.

That was so embarrassing.

I smile at Dahlia's message, typing out a reply.

I notice you didn't correct her when she said we were 'hooking up.'

Well, we are 'dating.'

I never realized how much I fucking hate quotation marks until this moment.

Might as well live up to the assumptions, no?

I hear her giggle from the kitchen.

You're insatiable.

Let me know if you need help with that cream pie. I'm great with filling. 🤠

Another laugh echoes through the house, and I know I'm smiling at my own phone like a goddamn idiot.

"What are you two doing?" Darby asks me.

Now I'm the one blushing.

The sound of knuckles clamor at the door, and all seven

people in this house shout, "Come in!" at the exact same time. My parents, Dahlia, and Lou are too busy in the kitchen to answer it, Leo, Darby, and myself too comfortable on the couch to move.

I hear the door open and close before August's frame rounds the staircase into view. He stands awkwardly at the edge of the living room and waves at us. "Hey. Happy Thanksgiving."

He's tall and lean, with dark, unruly curls tousled messily on his head, and green eyes that dart around the room beneath his black-rimmed glasses. He's got an eyebrow piercing he didn't have the last time I saw him, and two more piercings on each of his ears. Though unnoticeable, beneath his long-sleeved tee and dark-wash jeans his body is covered in more tattoos than even mine.

I open my mouth to greet him when the pressure next to me on the couch suddenly lifts, a flash of blond hair darting past me. I catch the surprise filter across August's face too when Darby suddenly leaps into his chest and throws her arms around his neck. "I'm so happy you came," she murmurs.

He stills momentarily before slowly wrapping both arms around her waist. His eyes close as he lets out a sigh, the kind that tells me it might've been a long, long while since he has been hugged by someone.

August's been an irreparably broken shell since the moment they pulled his brother's body from the beach a little over three years ago. He shut out everyone, including me and Leo. We tried for the solid first year after Zach's death to be there for August, but he refused to answer our calls. He'd ignore us when we showed up at his house, his business. He wanted no part of the foundation set up in his brother's name—not that his father would've allowed it, anyway.

He wouldn't even talk to my mother, and that bothered me most of all.

Leo and I look at each other, and I know the same thought is running through his head. *Maybe we didn't do enough*. Because the way he hugs Darby tells me he's starved for connection.

Leo clears his throat, standing from the couch and walking

over to them. It's a little awkward, the way he and August wrap their arms around each other. "Hey, Augustus. It's good to see you."

"Yeah." August sighs. "You too."

I stand, too, but as I cross the living room, I notice Lou peeking her head around the kitchen door, taking in the sight of the new visitor she hasn't met yet. I smile, reaching out my hand. "Hey, Luz."

Her green eyes go wide as she turns to me. "Hi."

"Do you want to come meet my friend?"

"Your friend?" she murmurs.

"Yep. Since I was as old as you are." I beckon her with my outstretched hand. "C'mon."

I remember her hesitation the day she met me. I remember Leo telling me she was the same way when she met him, too, and our dad. She's not comfortable around men, for understandable reasons. I don't know what kind of feeling it is that erupts inside me when she rushes around the corner and takes my hand, but something inside my bones feels settled.

She feels safe with me.

Keeping Lou's tiny hand in mine, I give August a one-armed side hug before stepping back to give the girl at my side space. "Lou, this is our friend, August. August, this is Lucille, Dahlia's daughter."

August gives her a genuine smile, holding out his hand. "It's nice to meet you, Lucille."

She keeps her fingers tight in my palm but extends her other arm and returns his shake. "You too," she whispers. "You can call me Lou."

He grins, his own emerald eyes showing the most emotion I've seen in years. "Okay, Lou. Happy Thanksgiving."

Lou returns his with a shy smile, hiding her face against my side. It's less nervous, almost more...bashful.

"Lucille?" Dahlia calls out. I hear her voice grow louder, and even though I'm not facing the doorway to the kitchen, I suddenly feel her presence there.

I feel her pause as she takes in the scene. Leo has his arm slung around Darby where they stand next to August, and I watch Darby's eyes lock on to something behind me. A knowing smile rises on her face.

Lou, still glued to my side, turns her head back toward her mother. "Hi, Mom."

"Hi, bug." Dal steps up to her other side, eyeing me with some expression I can't decipher before turning to August. "Hi."

"Auggie, this is Darby's sister, Dahlia."

He chuckles, a sound I haven't heard in fucking years. "I can tell." He extends his hand toward Dal. "You two look so alike."

"Thank you," the girls say together.

"And you look just like your mom too." August looks down at Lou again.

She lifts her head, swiveling back and forth between Dahlia and me, as if she's not sure how to respond.

I smile at her. "Your mother is the most beautiful person in the world, Luz. That was a compliment, so you can tell him thank you."

Darby's eyes widen, and my brother's mouth drops open. I hear Dahlia's breath hitch, but she doesn't respond. Lou's little cheeks pinken, and she can't meet August's face as she murmurs, "Thank you."

I think she might have a fucking crush on the guy.

"You're welcome," August responds, seeming confused by the entire ordeal.

August hasn't been close enough to any of us to understand the situation surrounding the girls' dad and our "arrangement," but I wouldn't be surprised to hear his clients have been talking about Leo and me during their appointments with him. It's a small town, after all.

So he may very well be under the impression Dahlia and I are together, meaning that the shocked expressions everyone is giving me now are probably extremely confusing.

"Augustus?" my mom calls from the kitchen. "Is that you?"

"Yeah, Mama!" he shouts back.

"You better go see her before she blows a gasket." Leo grins.

August nods. "Yep. You're right." He darts around me, waving at Lou and Dahlia. "Nice to meet you. I'll, uh, I'll be right back."

As soon as he rounds the corner and disappears, Dahlia's mouth drops open, and she turns to her sister. "He is so fucking hot."

Darby grins, nodding rapidly.

"Please," I mutter at the same time my brother throws his head back and groans.

A half-hour later, the eight of us are sitting around the formal dining table. It was Dahlia and Darby's grandmother's, one of the few pieces of her furniture Darby and Leo kept in the house when they bought it.

My dad sits at one end of the table, flanked by my mom and August on either side. I sit beside my mother, with Lou between me and Dahlia. Darby is next to August, Leo on her other side. Darby whispers in August's ear every so often, like she's checking in on him.

"August, your parents are in Palm Springs for the holiday?" my mom asks.

He swallows hard before taking a sip of water. "Sounds like it."

"That must be fun for them," she murmurs quietly, and I can hear the hint of disgust in her voice that she's trying to mask. None of us know the true details of where his relationship with them stand, but we know the blame that was placed on him, by his father in particular, after we lost Zach. My mother has a hard time hiding the way she feels about that.

Changing the subject, she looks back and forth between Leo and me. "Have either of you talked to your sister yet today?"

I shake my head at the same time Leo says, "I called her on my way back from the gym. She didn't answer." *No surprise there.*

"Maybe we can all video call her after dinner," my dad

suggests. "I'm sure she'd love to talk to you, Augustus."

It's at that moment August is tilting his glass of water against his lips, and when the words filter through his ears, the glass falls from his hand, clattering against the table as he begins coughing.

"God, are you okay?" my mom gasps.

Darby pats his back, concern on her face. My brother and I give each other looks across the table. There's another piece of the puzzle we've never been able to fit together: something happened between our sister and August, something bad. Neither of them has ever opened up to us about it, won't tell us a goddamn thing.

Leo thinks they're both just too tied up in their own grief, but I think there's something more. Before, they were inseparable, attached at the hip an understatement. It was like they spoke a language only the two of them could understand. None of us could come in between their friendship, not even Zach.

But after he died, the mere mention of each other's names became nuclear.

"We'll call Elena later," I answer finally. August shoots me a grateful look.

The table goes back to awkward small talk, and when everyone's finished eating, Darby and Leo begin clearing plates. Clean-up is their designated job, since neither of them can cook for shit and were of no help preparing dinner. I technically didn't do anything either, but I'm hoping nobody will notice.

As their seats vacate, August offers to help them, and Lou scampers off into the kitchen to get pie for Dahlia and myself, although I'm fairly certain she just wanted a reason to follow August. I slide into her seat next to Dahlia, desperate to be closer to her. My parents are at the head of the table, chatting amongst themselves as they continue eating.

"So, what's the deal with August?" she asks quietly.

I had a feeling the question was coming. "I don't know the full extent of it. I know that the day Zach..." I sigh. "Elena said some things to him that made no sense. Still doesn't make sense to me. Neither of them will talk about it. Talk to each other." I shrug.

"I'm in as much of the dark as you are, but before Zach...they were *best* friends. I'd never seen two people closer."

"That's awful," she murmurs. "And everything with his dad too? I can't even imagine." She's quiet for a moment, brow furrowing. "How could anyone treat their own child like that?" She laughs cynically to herself. "Not sure I'm the one to be asking that question, actually."

"You think your father would treat you that way too? If something so horrible had happened?"

Dahlia bites her lip, eyes going a bit hazy as she stares down at the table. "I mean...it's not the same. It really isn't. But..." She huffs. "After Darby left her wedding, my father blamed me. I told him I had sent Leo the letter. I was the reason he showed up in town. He told me I ruined his chances of ever getting to walk his daughter down the aisle, that I had taken that from him."

"He has two daughters," I mutter through clenched teeth.

"That's what I said." She laughs again, but it's not genuine. "He told me he didn't. He only had one in his eyes, that he'd felt that way for a while. That no good man would be willing to bother with me. That I was ruined, damaged goods. That any man who'd ever want to take that step with me wouldn't be worthy of my father's blessing anyway. Therefore, there was no reality in which I'd be walked down the aisle by him."

I'm going to fucking kill this man.

I hate him. Disgust coats my throat at the thought of Dahlia having to endure those words, that pain, from someone who's supposed to love her. I glance briefly at August as he re-enters the dining room and decide I hate his dad too. I hate any person who could make their own child feel that way.

Dahlia continues staring at the table, at her hands folded together in front of her. She's completely unfazed by the things she's saying, and I know it's only because she's numb after a lifetime of hearing it all. I place my hand over hers, brushing my thumb across her knuckles.

The touch seems to break her out of her haze as her head

snaps up to look at me. I let myself drown in the oceans of her eyes, hoping she sees the sincerity in my own. "You're worthy, Dahlia. You're worthy of everything."

And my words seem to open some kind of gate inside her, because that numbness disappears, and I watch those beautiful, bright blue eyes fill with tears. She blinks hard, willing them away, but one escapes. Cascading down her soft cheek in slow motion. I reach out and catch it with my thumb. Nuzzling her face into my hand, Dahlia closes her eyes and lets out a shaky sigh.

We stay like that a while longer, letting her take whatever comfort she finds in my touch. Only the pitter-patter of small footsteps hurling through the dining room is enough to pull her away from me. She smiles at her daughter as Lou sets two slices of pie on the table in front of us, her own face smothered in chocolate.

"Thanks, Luz." I smile at her.

She huffs. "I've come up with all these cool nicknames for you, and you hate them. The only one you can come up with is Luce? I wanted a better one, Everett."

She climbs into one of the chairs across the table from me and leans over it, dipping her finger through the whip cream on her mom's slice of pumpkin.

"It's not *Luce*, like short for Lucille. It's *Luz*. L-U-Z. It means *light* in Spanish."

Both of the girls turn their heads to me, surprise on their faces.

I only smile wider. "Because you're like a burst of light, all bright and warm. You're *la luz*."

Lou's cheeks redden, and she hides her face behind her hair. "Oh, okay. That's a good one, then, I guess."

"You guess?" I laugh.

She shrugs, but I can see her coy smile through the curtain of her hair. I turn to her mother, but Dahlia's speechless, staring at me with emotion on her face, fighting back the tears once more. I place my hand back over hers, whispering against her ear, "She's the light, and you're all the colors, Wildflower."

Dahlia and I didn't talk much more after that. After Leo and Darby finished the dishes, and all the dessert was devoured, we sat around the table and played an extremely heated game of Monopoly, which resulted in my brother nearly flipping the table with his over-competitive, dramatic ass.

A phone call from my sister had August on edge the rest of the night, and he decidedly had to use the bathroom at that exact moment. Now, August is quiet, my dad is drunk and bellowing George Strait in the kitchen, and Lou is quite literally passed out face down at the kitchen table.

Dahlia rubs her back where she sits between us, and some kind of strange contentment rushes through me at the sight. It's like sitting here, with the two of them, is where I've always been meant to be.

"Dahlia, do you have any formal culinary experience? You're an incredible baker," August says.

"Oh, thank you." Dahlia blushes, and it kind of enrages me. I know he didn't mean anything by it other than a genuine compliment, but I don't like the thought of anyone else making her blush like that. "I don't. I just got into it when I was pregnant, and it has been a hobby ever since."

He nods thoughtfully. "You could've fooled me." He takes another bite of the Boston cream pie and points his fork at me. "You know what would be good for one of the empty suites on the boardwalk? A cafe. A coffee shop with an ocean view? It would bring so much traffic to the area and make a fortune."

"You know, that's not a bad idea. I think a lot of people were wary about replacing Sweet Rue's after Ruby passed, but there is definitely a demand for that," I say.

"I think a chain would be a terrible idea, but another small business? It could work." August shrugs. "Maybe we could even contact her kids and see if they have any of her old recipes on hand that could be incorporated, maybe as a way to honor her?"

Leo rounds the corner at that moment, snapping his fingers at us. "You're fucking brilliant, Augustus." He nods toward me. "We need to get with Scarlett and talk about this idea."

"Why don't you do that in the office when you return to work? You're shouting, and we've got a sleeping child at the table." Dahlia laughs quietly.

I look down at the strawberry blond sprawled out next to me. "That can't be comfortable for her. Do you want me to carry her up to bed for you?"

She smiles at me with enough gratitude to bring me to my goddamn knees. "Yeah, maybe. We can wait until everyone leaves, though."

"Speaking of, I should probably head out," August says.

"Oh, no. I wasn't suggesting—" Dahlia starts.

"No, I know." He smiles. "It is late, though, and I've got to open the shop in the morning."

To my surprise, August hugs both Dahlia and me before he stalks into the kitchen. I hear him say his goodbyes to my parents, along with Leo and Darby, who're still boxing up all the leftovers. When he returns, hands full of Tupperware, Darby's with him. She walks him to the door and hugs him again as he leaves.

As softly as possible, Dahlia helps me lift Lou into my arms, and she hardly stirs. I'm pretty sure she ate way more dessert than she let on and has fallen into some kind of sugar coma. She's completely limp as I carry her bridal style up the stairs. Dahlia navigates me to her bedroom. I slowly lay her down in her bed, and I know I should probably leave, but I can't.

Instead, I watch from the doorway as Dahlia settles her in and covers her with blankets. She kisses the top of her head, sitting at the edge of Lou's mattress for a prolonged moment, stroking her hair.

I can hear my parents downstairs saying their farewells. I can hear the television shut off, the glow of the lights on the staircase dimming. The night has ended, and that means it's my turn to leave, too, to go back to my quiet townhouse on Pacific Street. Except the quiet I used to find peaceful only feels lonely now. An empty house feels isolated, and all I want to do is stay here. I tell myself it's because today is a holiday, and I want to prolong the time with my family, but as I watch Dahlia whisper into her daughter's ear, I know it's simply because I don't want any of these moments with her—with them—to end.

Twenty-Two - Wildflower

Guess You're All Losers, Then.

Staring at the galaxy projector on my desk, I quickly realize that my shit excuse for parents really know nothing about their granddaughter at all.

In the newest round of whatever game my father's playing, he mailed Lou a Christmas gift. It arrived yesterday afternoon, and I quickly stashed it in my car before she got her hands on it and saw who it was from.

A card in the box stated it was a gift to "help her sleep at night," whatever the fuck that means. The most cynical parts of me think it's some kind of message, but what that message may be, I have no idea. What I do know is that Lou has never needed a nightlight. She can't sleep in anything but pitch black and total silence. She's also afraid of outer space and has a deep fear of aliens. This thing would scare the shit out of her, and you'd think that being a part of her daily life up until six months ago, my parents would've caught on to that.

I don't know if they're clueless or cruel, but either way, this thing has got to go. I brought it with me this morning to drop in the toy donation bin outside Heathen's when I leave.

My father texted me this morning asking if I'd received the gift, and I told myself I would call him to get to the bottom of whatever fucking game he's playing. Thus far, I've not had the courage, but I've got to leave in an hour to pick up Lou early from school, and I'd rather this not be hanging over my head all afternoon.

Taking a deep breath and summoning all my strength, I pull up my father's contact and press call. He answers on the first ring, not bothering to greet me, cutting straight to the chase. "Dahlia, I assume you received the Christmas gift for my granddaughter?"

"Yep," I drawl. "Guess this is the year we're pushing her to get over her fear of the solar system, then?"

"What are you talking about?"

I roll my eyes, leaning back in my chair. "She has been scared of outer space her entire life. And she doesn't use a nightlight. If anything, this gift would traumatize her, not help her sleep better."

He's quiet for a moment, as if this information genuinely caught him off guard. "Your mother bought it." *Of course, he'd blame my mom.* "She researched good gifts for a nine-year-old girl." He clears his throat. "Maybe if we knew her better, had the opportunity to actually speak with her once in a—"

"I'm going to stop you there," I say. "You had nine and a half years to get to know her, and you never tried. You wanted nothing to do with her unless you needed to play the role of grandparent to further either your social or economic standing in Crestwell. You could've used any of those times to ask her questions about herself, gauge her interests."

"Dahlia." My father's tone is clipped and stern. "Do not victimize yourself here. You had no problem passing her off to us when you wanted your free time."

My stomach drops at that. *He's so full of shit.* I never passed her off to anyone. He'd demand time with her and had my mother coax me into it by telling me I deserved a day off.

"Not to mention all the financial support we provided you over the years."

Angry tears sting behind my eyes. Never have I encountered a person with quite the knack for manipulating the truth. The fucking king of gaslighting.

"Why are you doing this to me?" I ask.

"You know why, Dahlia."

I bite my lip, furiously wiping at my eyes and willing the emotion from my voice. Anything to appear unaffected by him. "Are you telling me that if I gave you back those files right now, if I burned that thumb drive, destroyed it, you'd leave us alone?"

"Despite what you may think of me, the gift for Lucille was genuine. I'll never not want a relationship with my grandchild." *Liar.* "But once we put this blackmail nonsense behind us, if you prefer I cease contact with you and your daughter, I'll respect that." He pauses before adding, "I could get Jason off your back too. You know, he's quite upset with your decision to move his child out of state without informing him."

"So, you admit you told him in order to fuck with me?"

He clicks his tongue. "Don't cuss, Dahlia. It's unbecoming."

My hand tightens around the phone against my ear, yearning to crack it in half. He's impossible to talk to, impossible to battle with. It makes me want to scream. Despair and fear and dread war inside my bones, fighting for their place on top as I realize I'll never win with him. I'll never escape him. He'll never stop having this control over me, this ability to put me in my place and make me want to cower.

My phone vibrates, and I pull it away momentarily to check the notification. A message from Everett pops up across the screen, letting me know he's on his way over to Heathen's from the garage. I breathe a bit easier, knowing he'll be here soon, and this conversation with my father will be over; it brings me some ounce of comfort.

"You know who loves my unbecoming mouth, Dad?" I smile, feeling a wave of bravery wash through me. "Everett. You remember him, don't you? The man who had you pushed up against the wall, his elbow against your throat as you gasped for air?"

My father scoffs. "Whatever game you're playing doesn't faze me, Dahlia. I'm not interested in your flavor of the week."

"I've been enjoying him for many weeks now, actually."

"Save yourself the slightest amount of dignity, will you?"

His tone drips with pure disgust. "I mean, I gave up hope for you some time ago, but you speak of being the village whore like it's something to be *proud* of." He sighs. "I don't know where we went wrong."

His voice is a razor blade along my skin, all of the bravery and courage and comfort dripping from my body, like blood seeping out of the wounds he leaves behind. I've lost another battle.

"I'm hanging up," I choke out, shaking with the tears I can no longer keep at bay.

As I pull my phone from my ear, I hear him say, "Don't act like that, and I won't have to respond so harshly. Have a civilized conversation for once and see how far we might get."

"Okay, fine." I will the trembling out of my voice as I say, "What do I have to do to never speak to you again? To get Jason off my back? To get you to leave us alone?"

"Give me back the thumb drive," he says immediately. "Ensure there are no duplicates of the information you obtained and prove that to me. I'll happily fly back out there to collect it myself."

"Really? That's it?"

"I want a conversation with your sister. I want to see her—without him around."

Of course, he does. Of course, he wants to see his golden child. His true daughter. He's all too happy to throw me away for good, but he'll fight for Darby.

"That's not up to me. That's up to her."

He lets out an incredulous laugh. "Is it? Because she seems to make every decision based on your guidance. If you told her to sit down and give me a chance, you know she would."

"You are terrified," I scoff. "You're getting desperate. You know the moment she's married, you'll have well and truly lost her. Once her last name is Graham, you'll lose any chance you think you still have of getting your perfect child back. That's what this is all about, isn't it? We both know I'm only really blackmailing you to keep you away from her." I can't stop the hot tears from running down my cheeks now. I want him to hear the emotion in my voice, hear how much he has broken me. "And from Leo. Because I know you better than you think I do. I know there are no lengths you won't reach to get that control back. I mean, fuck." A wretched laugh escapes me. "You're using your own grandchild as a weapon. Bringing Jason back into the picture? Threatening my custody? That's all a ploy, right? Hoping to get her and me back in Kansas with the assumption Darby will follow? You know how awful Jason is, and you'd actually put Lou at risk if it meant the slightest possibility of Darby coming home."

My voice cracks, nearly three decades of heartbreak flooding out of me.

The black sheep.

The lost cause.

The ruined goods.

Worthless.

"All because the only thing you've ever really cared about is her." I swallow, my throat constricting.

My father doesn't bother responding.

"Well, unfortunately for you, all I've ever really cared about is Darby too. So, no deal. Leave me alone. Leave my child alone. Leave my sister and my brother-in-law the fuck alone. Or I'll take your precious little files, with all your fucking fraud, right to the authorities. I hope you've cleared those offshore accounts, Daddy."

My father doesn't deny anything I've said, doesn't try to hide it or cover it up.

At least now I know exactly where things stand.

He simply responds, "You won't do that, Dahlia. I know you won't." There's a pause, and I know it's because he's readying himself to drop whatever bomb will obliterate me next. "Because you're still holding out for the one thing you've never gotten from me..." I can feel his cruel smile, can see it in my mind. "My approval."

A sob rips out of me, and I clamp a hand over my mouth to stop it.

How did I get here?

How did I let him win again?

"All you've got to do, Dahlia, darling, is come back home. All three of you."

I can't listen to another word of it. I can't keep playing his games. I pull the phone from my ear, ending the call before tossing it across my office in a fit of frustration. Another wail escapes me as I sink to the ground behind my desk.

Suddenly, my door is thrown open, and Everett appears. His eyes work rapidly to take in the scene before stopping at my face. Cataloging my tears, my trembling limbs, and heaving breaths, he's immediately slamming the door closed, taking purposeful steps to remove the space between us. When he reaches me, he sinks to his knees.

"What happened, Wildflower?" My mouth opens, but it's another sob that escapes. His eyes are frantic, darting around the room in search of the source of my pain. He sports a desperate expression when he looks back at me, pleading and begging for an explanation. "Tell me who did this."

I shake my head; words are beyond me.

Leaning back against the wall, Everett wraps his arms around my waist and pulls me against his chest. I fall into his lap, my tears soaking his warm skin as I bury my face in his neck.

One of his hands comes around the back of my head, soothing me as he brushes his fingers through my hair. "It's okay, baby. I've got you."

"Can you come in with me?" I ask. "I can't deal with Tana alone right now."

Everett gives me a soft nod from the passenger seat of my car as I pull into the school lot. In addition to all of the other shit I've been hiding, I haven't told anyone about the note left on my car after Lou's soccer game weeks ago. It never happened again, so I figured it wasn't something worth getting everyone up in arms about.

I'm convinced it's the other parents from Lou's school, their weird, sick way of hazing the new girls in town. I can't be sure that the note was aimed at me and me alone; they could've been referring to Darby too. But apparently, happiness and regularly scheduled orgasms have provided her with a no-fucks-given attitude, because she has taken well to ignoring the rumors and sideways stares.

The people whispering around town that she's pregnant—that Leo only proposed so early to do the right thing by her because she trapped him—particularly upset me. As if these fucking assholes have any idea what she has gone through.

Despite Everett and Leo's insistence that Tana's disdain for me is due to some teenage grudge, I refuse to believe anyone is actually that petty. Plus, the real answer is clear as day to me; I'm used to it. I had a kid at nineteen. Even though I'm twenty-nine, and she can't be a day over thirty-five, she's only ever going to see me as a trashy teen mom.

Tana also happens to be the receptionist at the elementary school, meaning in order to sign Lou out, I've got to interact with her. I don't want to believe that Tana and her group of petty parents would be the ones leaving threatening notes on the hood of my car, but I can't imagine it being anyone else.

Well, that's not true. My father would do that, but he's not here.

So, that leaves them. With everything else that's gone on today and the need to plaster a happy smile on my face when I see my kid, I can't face Tana alone.

After breaking down in Everett's arms in my office, I told him everything about the conversation with my dad—leaving out the blackmail, of course. Because nobody knows about that, not even my sister. I know if I told Darby and Leo, they'd insist I return the thumb drive to get my father off my back. Darby wouldn't support me turning him in. Despite all he's done to us, she wouldn't be able to do that to him. As pathetic as it is, he might've been right in assuming I can't do it either.

I know she and Leo would insist they fight this battle themselves. Leo has no fear, but he doesn't know my dad. That man used me once before to tear them apart, and they lost ten years because of it. I can't risk him finding a way to do it again. I owe that to the two of them.

I told Everett everything else, though, every gross detail of my father's words and motives. For the first time in my life, I allowed someone else to see how worthless I am in my parents' eyes. The throwaway kid—the lost cause.

He held me through it, whispering reassurances in my ear. I could see rage and devastation on his face, but he didn't voice any opinions of his own. He only listened.

I've never had someone do that for me either.

"Anything, baby." He reaches out to take my hand, running his thumb over the back of it. "Do you want me to just go in and grab her? You can wait in the car."

I tighten my fingers around his. "You can't." I sigh. "There is an approved pick-up list, and anyone not on it can't leave the building with the student. The only people on my list are Darby and your mom."

He nods, opening the passenger side door and rounding the car to open mine. He holds his hand out to me, pulling me from the car and lacing his fingers through my own. He doesn't let go as we walk through the parking lot and into the school.

Tana's head snaps up from her desk as we step through the front entrance. The cheerful greeting on her face dies as she realizes it's me before she recovers with a false smile. "Dahlia, hi." Long dark hair is pulled back into a clean bun, her brown eyes crinkling in the corners when she forces a grin. "What can I help you with?"

"I'm here to pick up Lou. I'm sneaking her out a bit early." I don't mean for my tone to come out flat and hard, but it does anyway. I can't fake it today.

Everett's hand tightens around mine, as if he can sense it too.

Tana begins typing something into the computer in front of her. "Is there an official reason you're picking her up before the school day has concluded?"

"Because I'm her mother, and I can take her out of class if I'd like to," I snap back.

I can feel the judgment seeping off her. I understood the undertones in her question, her questioning of my parenting skills because I'm letting my kid play hooky.

Truthfully, I don't have a good reason for taking her out other than it's the Friday before Christmas break, and I've done this ever since Lou started school. I take a half day from work, I pick her up early, and we make gingerbread houses while watching our favorite holiday movies. I realized pretty early on that childhood flies by far too fast, and missing three hours of school is a small price to pay in exchange for family tradition.

Especially when I brought her into a shit excuse for a family, with no tradition to speak of. This is our tradition with my sister, and for the first time in her life, she asked others to be included. She wanted Leo, Everett, and their parents to join us, and there was no way I'd take that away from her, even if it meant she was missing class.

Tana's hands pause on her keyboard, and her eyes flutter up to me. "When I sign her out for the day, it asks me to enter a reason for the absence. I was only asking."

"Sorry." I sigh. "She's, uh, she's not feeling well."

Tana humphs but doesn't say more.

"While I'm here, can I go ahead and add a couple of people to her pick-up list as well? You should have Darby Andrews and Monica Ramos already listed."

"We do," Tana responds without looking up from the computer. "Who would you like to add?"

"Everett Ramos and Leo Graham."

Her head snaps up at the same time Everett's whips sideways. "Really?" Tana asks.

I turn to face Everett. "If you'd like to. I just figured..."

I trust you is what I really want to say.

And again, like the man can read my mind, he smiles. "Thank you."

Tana snorts, shaking her head. "And to think we were all taking bets on how long you two would last." She smiles at me, but I see the sneer beneath it. "Looks like you're proving us wrong."

"I'm sorry, what?" Everett asks, tone dripping with disgust. "You were placing bets on the relationships of parents your children go to school with?"

"N–Not just me," she backtracks quickly. "Just some of the other parents from the soccer team. It was all in good fun. No harm meant."

"It's fucking weird," he mutters.

Tana has the good sense to look embarrassed. I remain quiet, though, because I'm in no way surprised.

After a moment of awkward silence, she clears her throat and says, "I've added Everett and Leo to the approved pick-up list. Her teacher has been notified that she's leaving early. She should be up here in a few minutes."

"Thanks," I respond, tone clipped. "We'll wait in the lobby."

As I turn back toward the doors, Everett calls out, "Oh, and Tana—whoever bet on forever is going to win the pot."

"Nobody bet on forever," she chimes back.

He laughs under his breath. "Guess you're all losers, then."

If I'm not mistaken, I think I hear her gasp at his comment, but we're both laughing as we push through the office doors and out into the school's lobby. Everett takes a seat beside me as we wait for my daughter.

"You know, maybe when this whole fake dating thing is over, I can hire you on as my bodyguard instead," I muse. "You really handed her ass to her."

"Don't be silly, Wildflower." He smiles at me as he tosses his arm over my shoulder and pulls me against his chest. "We're gonna have to date forever now so we can prove those assholes wrong."

Twenty-Three - Wicked

A Safe Place For Her To Land

I've thought of about a hundred and twelve different ways I'd like to kill Dane Andrews.

Gruesome, deranged, messy ways I'd rip him limb from limb and watch him bleed, the kind of things only a man my sister writes about in her books would be capable of.

I guess that depraved kind of creative darkness is a family trait.

I've hated that man since Darby first spoke of him when we were kids. I hated him when Leo told me all the things he'd done to keep her away. I hated him when I saw him in my business with his hand around Dahlia's arm. I've hated him every time she has spoken of him.

But until I walked into her office yesterday and saw those tears streaming down her face, watched her body shake with sobs and tremble with fear, I'd never dreamed about killing someone. I'd kill him, though. I'd kill him for how broken he has made her.

I'd kill him without a second thought.

Then spend the rest of my life trying to put her back together.

If all I get out of life is a chance to do the latter, I'll take it happily, but fuck. I'd like to kill him.

Those are the thoughts that plague me as I pull up to the curb outside the boardwalk businesses and park my car. They follow me to the front of the empty suite beside Heathen's, still in the thick of refurbishment.

I push open the door, finding the space is littered with boxes, paint, and tarps. They've been making great headway on the opening of Honeysuckle Florals, Darby's flower shop, and are on track to open early in the new year. I add two more boxes to the pile in the middle of the main room, full of photo prints from up and down the California coast.

Leo bought them off a friend of ours, a landscape photographer who owns a gallery in Venice Beach. We've got several of his canvases hung up around Heathen's, and Darby wanted some for herself too.

"Honeysuckle!" I call, knowing Darby's supposed to be here.

"In here!" she responds from somewhere toward the back of the building.

I maneuver around the boxes and equipment until I reach the small office in the corner. It's a complete one-eighty from the rest of the building: walls painted a soft yellow, with a bright, multicolored rug and matching throw pillows on the cream-colored couch to one side. There's a desk on the other end of the room, bookshelves and filing cabinets set up behind it. Potted plants line the windowsill that looks out to the pier beyond the boardwalk.

"Damn." I let out a low whistle, turning slowly as I take in the space. "It looks great in here, Darbs."

"Thank you," she says from behind her desk, where she appears to be organizing some paperwork. "It's too early to get started on the shop itself, since we're not finished painting, but I figured I could put my office together. I was itching for something to do."

"You're doing great." Hitching my thumb behind me, I add, "I left those canvases you bought from Carter in a box in the main room. Do you want them somewhere else?"

"No, we can leave them there for now." She lifts her head, smiling at me. "Thanks for going all the way up there, by the way.

I know it's a far drive."

"It was no problem." The garage is always slow just before the holidays, so I had a free day earlier this week. I was happy to take the trip out to Santa Monica. "I owed them a visit anyway."

She nods, sinking down into her desk chair. I fall back onto the couch behind me and sprawl out.

"So, I wanted to ask you something."

"Yeah?" Darby asks, not looking at me as she continues sorting through her files.

"About your parents."

She pauses, hands stilling on her desk as she slowly raises her eyes to me.

"Dahlia had a call with your dad yesterday, and it sounds like he wrecked her pretty bad. I..." I run a hand through my hair, suddenly nervous. I don't know that Dahlia would want me talking about this behind her back, but I'm at a fucking loss. "I just want to help her, and I don't know what to do."

Darby sighs. "I don't either. Sometimes, it's hard for even me to talk to her about it, like she thinks it's something she has to battle on her own."

"Why does she feel that way?" I ponder.

"I don't know." Darby breathes defeatedly. "When you spoke to her, did she mention anything about my mom? Or has she only talked to my dad?"

"She only mentioned your dad. I don't think she's had contact with your mother at all."

"That's what I thought." Darby chews her lip. "My mom has been reaching out to me, and I want to talk to Dahlia about it, but I'm afraid to bring it up."

"Why?" I ask.

She looks at me, sadness in her eyes. "Because she thinks our parents love me more."

She thinks your parents don't love her at all.

"I'm afraid it would hurt her feelings if she knew my mom was trying to make an effort with me and not with her."

"Don't take this the wrong way, Darby," I say. "But *is* your mother trying to make an effort with you? Or is it your dad using her as a means to an end?"

"No, you're right." Her tone is sad, and it breaks my heart that either of them has to go through something like this. I couldn't imagine being unable to trust my parents. "I don't know either. I've always had a soft spot for my mom, though. She has one for me, too, so I guess there might be part of me holding out hope that she's really trying."

"Why would she try for you and not Dahlia?" I ask. I don't mean for my tone to come out cold and rough, but it does.

"My mother is terrified of Dahlia."

That takes me by surprise.

"I think she always has been, but even more so after Lou was born," Darby continues. "Dahlia has always been so...so fearless. She always stood up for herself, refusing to cower beneath the influence of our father." She sighs. "But when Lou was born? She became unbelievably brave and strong, something our mother never was. Our mom used our dad as an excuse to check out and leave us to protect ourselves, and when Dahlia became a mother too... Well, our mom's weaknesses became glaringly apparent. She watched Dahlia protect and nurture and love—all the things she had never done—and Mom knew she'd never be forgiven for it."

Darby shrugs, looking at me with sad eyes. "I was weak like her. I craved his acceptance, did whatever I could to please him, bit my tongue and hid my tears. I won't call my mom a victim, and I don't know if I'll ever forgive her either, but I *understand* her. We never had the strength my sister possesses."

"You're strong, Darby," I say.

She gives me a shallow nod. "But not like Dahlia."

No, not like Dahlia.

But perhaps if she hadn't lost the things she had, if she'd ended up in the same position at seventeen, she would've found that strength for her child too.

There is a longing on Darby's face that makes me wonder if

she's thinking the same thing, so I don't voice that thought out loud. Instead, I ask her, "What can I do to help Dahlia?"

Darby gives me a soft smile. "Listen. Don't push. Be a safe place for her to land, because I don't think she's ever had one of those before. I think she trusts you, which is a foreign concept to her. So just...keep being that."

"I can do that," I say, even though I'd already planned on it.

"And don't tell her about my mom," she adds. "I'll tell her myself."

I nod. "Speaking of siblings, Leo is supposed to be around here somewhere, isn't he?"

"He's picking up dinner. We're eating down at the pier tonight after I'm finished here."

Well, fuck. I planned on breaking some not-so-great news to my brother while I was here. I figured why not have two shitty conversations back-to-back so I could get them over with. I hate the thought of ruining their date night, but I'd rather not hang onto the information.

"All right, I'm going to try and catch him in—"

"Catch me where, brother?" he asks, appearing in the doorway with a paper bag in hand.

"Catch you before the two of you go have dinner." I bite my lip, rubbing the back of my neck. "I've got some news. But I, uh..." I glance between him and Darby. "I don't want to put a damper on your night."

"Wouldn't worry about it," he chimes, walking around Darby's desk and smacking a kiss against her cheek. "I'm about to eat pad thai on the beach, and then I'm going to go home and get laid. Hard to put a damper on that."

Darby snorts, but I see the blush she's hiding.

I blow out a resigned breath. "You talk to Elena lately?"

Leo cocks his head. "Not since last week. Why?"

"She called me earlier today." I sigh. *Guess now is as good a time as any.* "She's not coming home for Christmas."

All the playfulness present a moment ago immediately drops

from his demeanor. "You're fucking kidding me."

I break eye contact, hating the look on his face. "No. I'm not." I rub the sudden tension from my jaw. "She claimed she was asked to do some holiday signing event in Brooklyn."

He scoffs. "You know that's bullshit."

"I know."

I hate the anger in his tone, though I understand it. I'm angry too. I'm more devastated than anything, but I'm not surprised, and that might be the worst part.

Leo rumbles frustratedly, "I'm getting tired of this, Everett. I know she was put through the ringer, but at what point do we stop making excuses? At what point do we start dishing out the tough love?"

"I'm pissed too," I agree. "But imagine if you were in her shoes. Imagine if Darby—"

"No." Leo snarls. "Look..." He sighs quietly. "All I'm saying is that I'm done with the bullshit and the lies, pretending she's okay when she's clearly not." He glances at Darby, who's quiet by his side, appearing to be in deep thought of her own. "I'm done with the grudges too. She can skip Christmas, but if Elena doesn't show up for my wedding?" Leo swallows roughly, eyes darting away from me as his next words leave his lips. "Then I'm done with her too. She can consider herself down a brother."

"Leo." I swallow the sudden heaviness in my throat, unable to say more.

He ignores me, leaning in to press a kiss against the top of his fiancee's head. "I need some air. I'll meet you at our spot" is all he says to her before he stalks out of her office.

Darby watches him leave before turning back to me, sorrow in her eyes. "He didn't mean that. He's just upset. He was really excited to see her."

"I'm upset too."

She nods, giving me a sorry look. "I'm going to go check on him."

"I'll walk you out." I sigh.

Twenty-Four - Wildflower

A Whole Damn Village

My stomach twists as my phone lights up with a call where it rests on the counter while I finish frosting Lou's birthday cake.

When I asked her what flavor she wanted, she couldn't decide. So, I ended up with a three-tiered cake: a bottom chocolate layer, a middle lemon and vanilla layer, and a top layer of red velvet. "For the adults," she'd said.

She was adamant that she did not want a theme for her party this year, as she was *too old for that.* She wanted pink, white, and gold decorations, and she wanted the party outside. She also wanted face painting but vehemently refused a clown. Being born in late January, Lou has never had an outdoor birthday party before. Kansas winter wouldn't allow for it. I wanted to make this one as special as possible, her first birthday in California and away from her old friends—not that she had many of them.

She has been fitting in well at school, has a handful of classmates attending her party today. My heart soared when she asked me to pick up invites for her to pass out to her friends, and I nearly cried when I saw that every single person she invited had RSVP'd. I think she's secretly nervous, which is why she has been so unable to make decisions regarding the party.

Darby and I have done as much as we can to make it the best birthday she's ever had.

Though the biggest hindrance to today's success is calling

now. I sigh, setting my knife on the counter and sliding my thumb across the screen to accept the call before wedging my phone between my shoulder and my ear. I don't want anyone to hear that Jason's calling me, because I haven't decided if I want to let him talk to his daughter yet.

She and Darby are out buying snacks now, anyway, but should be home soon. Everett and Leo are setting up the bounce houses we plan on surprising Lou with in the backyard.

"Hi," I huff into the phone as I answer.

"Hi, Dally." His tone is warm as the familiar nickname rolls off his tongue. "I know I said I'd call later today after her party, but I was hoping I could speak with you first."

Jason hasn't spoken to his daughter in years, but he has been checking in via text message regularly since we moved. His sudden reappearance and concern with her well-being coinciding with a new alliance with my father isn't lost on me.

Which is why I've been hesitant to tell Lou her father is suddenly calling, and why I haven't let her speak to him. He began getting worked up over it around the holidays, so I bought myself time by agreeing to let him video call her on her birthday—after her party, so there is no chance of it being ruined.

"What's going on?" I ask.

He's quiet for a moment, as if contemplating what to say. "I just wanted a moment to tell you I'm sorry for how I reacted when I found out you left, for how I've been acting ever since."

"You mean like how you demanded I move back to Kansas so you can have a presence in your daughter's life when and if you feel like it?" I snort, smoothing out the edges of her cake. "Or, do you mean when you supposedly went to my parents behind my back and asked them to support how terrible of a mother I am so you can try and take her away from me?"

"For all of it. It was wrong of me, and I'm sorry."

That has me pausing, and I find myself at a loss of how to respond.

"Before you moved away, I was trying. It has taken me a lot

longer to grow up than it should have, but I knew I needed to be better for her. For both of you." His voice nearly breaks with some kind of emotion, but I can't decipher what. "Then, when I found out you left without even telling me..." He sighs. "I snapped. I freaked out. I spoke with your dad, and he validated all my feelings. He was hurt by your leaving too and—"

"Do not talk to me about my father. Ever." The knife falls from my hand and clatters against the counter. "You have no fucking clue what that man has put me through because you were not there. You do not get to seek out his opinion of me, my life, or my decisions. Do not speak about him to me."

Rageful tears sting the corner of my eyes, and I blink them away, unwilling to let Jason know the depth of the scars they left on me.

"You're right." I hear shaking in my ear, like he's nodding. "I'm sorry. Your parents were awful to you, to both of you." I know he means my sister when he says that. "And I never should've listened to him. He fueled my fire and encouraged me to act out. Once I realized I'd been manipulated... I needed to think things through."

"And?" I ask, taking a deep breath, bracing myself for whatever point he's trying to make.

"And," he drawls, "I want to be a part of her life, in whatever capacity she's comfortable with, and I'm hoping you'll let me do that. I'm not going to tell you to come back—at least, not right now—but I'd like to speak with her regularly. I'd like to have a visit too."

"I have never been the one keeping you from her, Jason," I snap. "I've always kept the door open. You are the one who has abandoned her over and over again. Do not put this on me like I'm some kind of monster. Every trust issue I have was placed there by you. I won't let you twist the narrative around."

"That's not what I'm saying, Dahlia," he groans. "I take responsibility for everything I've done over the years. I wasn't ready to be a father, and I needed time to grow up. I'm ready now, and I just want to do whatever I can. For both of you."

I scoff, lacing my fingers together on the countertop. "That's wonderful, Jason. I'm so glad you took the extra decade to prepare yourself for fatherhood. I, unfortunately, did not have that luxury. I had to step up from the jump. You remember that day, don't you? Ten years ago? I was in the hospital, nineteen and terrified, birthing our child, with only my eighteen-year-old sister there to hold my hand. You were...getting drunk in someone's basement? Am I recalling that correctly?"

"I know, Dally. I know. I was such a fuck-up, and I did so wrong by you." His voice trembles, as if the memory pains him. "That's why I'm playing by your rules here. Whatever I can do to try and make it right."

I swallow hard, working to compose myself, to bite back the memories of fear and isolation that my daughter's birthday dredges up. I try to remain present, remember that she's here, that her happiness is worth more than any heartache I've encountered. But my birth experience was not a pleasant one. I was with my sister when I went into labor, and she was the only person who was there with me throughout the birth. She called Jason at some point, but he had no interest in any of it. Darby took me home to my parents' house afterward, and while they acknowledged their grandchild, they refused to acknowledge me.

I was nothing but a nuisance. An embarrassment. Damaged potential.

I was deemed worthless to my child's father and a disappointment to my own.

I've spent much of the last decade trying to convince myself that I can be anything else.

Willing away those memories and that emotion, I clear my throat. "So, are you telling me you're no longer threatening to file for joint custody and take her away?"

"I stand by the fact that she's better off in Kansas. I believe it's a better place for a child to grow up." I hear him gulp. "But for now, I just want to get to know her. Maybe you could bring her out for a weeken—"

"I am not taking her back to Kansas. Never."

"I'm not telling you to fucking stay, Dahlia," he snaps. "If you'd let me finish a goddamn sentence, I was going to suggest bringing her out for a weekend so I can spend some time with her. It's the least you could do."

"The *least I could do*?" I seethe.

"Yeah?" he continues. "God, you should've seen how devastated your parents were at Christmas when you didn't bring her home, when none of you came home. Your mother was heartbroken."

"Don't fucking talk to me about my mother."

He scoffs in my ear. "Oh, I'm aware. Your parents are off limits, because you refuse to believe you're anything but a fucking victim. I get it."

"Fuck you, Jason."

"My parents were upset too. They deserve to know their granddaughter just like I do." He laughs roughly. "I honestly don't even get it. There is nothing for you in California. You're isolating her. She deserves to grow up with her family."

A family she doesn't fucking know!

His parents, while around slightly more often than he was himself—which was exactly zero percent of the time—were far less involved than even my parents were.

I might be mostly alone here in California, but I was completely alone in Kansas.

For the first time in my child's life, she isn't isolated, even if the people loving her aren't family.

"What do you honestly have going for you there that you didn't have here? You had a good job, a house. You have nothing in California."

"My sister is here," I say, setting my phone on the counter and pressing the speaker button so I can decorate the cake with both hands.

"Your sister isn't Lou's parent. You need to think about what's best for her, not what's best for you."

That one sentence is all it takes for the tears to bubble over and stream down my cheeks. It's the insinuation that I don't think about what's best for my daughter every second of the day, that I haven't put her before myself every minute since she was born.

"That's where you're wrong, Jason." My voice shakes with each word. "Darby is the only person I've ever had, the only constant in my life. She's the only one who has ever loved me. She has been my co-parent and my life partner. She gave up everything for me and our child, far more than you ever have." I angrily wipe my cheeks, upset at myself for letting him hear the effect his words have on me. "So, I go where she goes. She's my person. She's Lou's person too."

"Darby has her own life partner now," he says quietly. "Her own life."

A breathless sob escapes me at that.

"Darby doesn't have a life partner. She has a whole damn village." I jump at the voice coming from behind me. It's hard and brash, but it sounds like salvation as it runs along my skin. "It's Dahlia's village too."

The clip of footsteps echoes on the hardwood floors as he enters the kitchen. The warmth of his body wraps me in safety when I feel him stand behind me. Turning, I look up at Everett's soft brown eyes, etched with concern.

"Hi," I whisper.

He tucks a piece of hair behind my ear. "Are you all right?"

Leaning into his touch, I nod.

"Who is that?" Jason asks, voice sharp and cold.

"Her boyfriend," Everett responds just as brashly.

Jason lets out a sharp, unconvincing laugh. "This doesn't concern you."

With his eyes still on me, Everett responds, "Everything with Dahlia concerns me."

"For now," Jason scoffs. "Unlike you, I'm going to be tied to her for the rest of my life. If I want to have a conversation with the mother of my child alone, I'm entitled to that."

"Not if she feels unsafe."

I'm falling so hard for this man.

Way too hard.

The phone goes silent, as if he's taken aback by Everett's response. "I'm not going to hurt you?" Jason says like it's the most ridiculous thing he's ever heard.

Because he has no idea that his aggressive behavior could have instilled a sense of fear in me, just because he never physically laid a hand on me. It's the same thought process my dad has: it's not abuse if you're not touched. Men like them have no idea how many different ways you can abuse a person—not just their body, but their mind. Their spirit.

"I know," I say anyway. Turning to Everett, I add, "We're almost done talking, and then I'll come find you."

His eyes rapidly dance back and forth between mine and the phone on the counter, assessing the situation. I can tell it pains him. He wants to push, demand to stay, and it has nothing to do with authority or power or possession over me. It's simply protection. He doesn't trust the man I'm speaking to. But rather than fighting me on it, he accepts my decision, taking a step back.

"I'm okay, Everett." I lean up to press a kiss to his warm cheek, keeping my hand on his hard chest. "I promise."

He cups the back of my head, holding me against him a moment longer. "I'll be outside if you need me."

It's silent until Jason hears the sliding door slam in the background. "Never going back to Kansas because of your sister, right?"

"I'm never going back to Kansas for a lot of reasons."

"And he's one of them?" Jason asks.

There's nothing fake about the way I say, "He might be."

He's silent for a moment before he finally says, "I know you think you're hiding away out there, Dahlia, but trust me, you're not that hard to find. Next time someone tells you to come back home, you should consider listening."

The line goes dead before I can respond.

Twenty-Five - Wildflower

All Three Of Us

"He loves her, you know," my sister says, leaning over the porch rail as we look out into the backyard.

Despite it being late January, the sky is bright blue, broken up only by the occasional floating cloud. It's not warm, per se, but holding the party outside was doable. The view from my sister's backyard is stunning. The property backs up to a cliff's edge, lined with lavender bushes that are already beginning to bloom. The deep blue horizon line stretches out far beyond us, clashing with the sky.

It's normally a peaceful place. Darby and I will sit out on my grandmother's old porch swing on Sunday mornings, drinking coffee and listening to the crashing of the waves.

Today, however, the view is obstructed by two massive bounce houses, hollering children, the smell of carne asada—from the tortas Everett's friend Emilio cooked for the party—and the pounding of music. Mostly Taylor Swift, per my daughter's request.

My conversation with Jason had me shaking, on the verge of tears. I don't know if what he said was a threat or a warning. I don't know if it has something to do with my father. I don't know anything at all. My life is utter chaos, and I feel like nobody sees that but me.

I'm out here in the middle of the ocean, drowning, flailing my arms and screaming for help, but no one can hear me, and my haunted past is pulling me under.

Registering my sister's words, I drag my eyes to the bounce house shaped like a castle, following her gaze where it rests upon the two people inside it. Lou sits cross-legged in the middle of the space while Everett jumps around her on all sides, attempting to lift her as high as possible.

He's the one person who seems to be holding onto my life vest—who seems to breathe oxygen back into my water-filled lungs.

The sound of Lou's laughter filters above all else, floating through the air and bringing a smile to my cheeks.

"She's hard not to love," I respond.

"So are you." I glance at Darby, her hazel eyes fixed on my face. "I think he might love you too."

I scoff. "You're insane."

"Look at all he does for you. For her. You can't convince me there isn't something there."

There is definitely something here. A mutual attraction, absolutely. But love? Ridiculous.

"It's an arrangement, Darby. He does these things—dates me—for appearances. He's getting something out of it too. It's an agreement, that's all."

My sister lets out an unconvinced hum. "You really believe that?"

"He said his reputation was beginning to negatively affect his business." I turn to face her, crossing my arms. "Are you saying he's lying?"

"No." She shakes her head. "He does have a reputation, just like I do. Like Leo does. But after six months here, I've found that people stare at me a whole hell of a lot less than they used to. They've moved onto whatever other small-town gossip caught their attention." The breeze kicks up, blowing her long blond hair into her face before she tucks it behind her ear. "I think the average resident cares a lot less about their local mechanic's sex life than he lets on. I think he was smitten with you from the moment he met you, and you gave him the perfect scenario to court you without scaring you away."

I give her an incredulous look. "Court me? It's not *Bridgerton*, Darby."

"Is that not what he's doing? I know you're not too stupid to see it, Dal." Her eyes filter across the lawn. "He's infatuated with you. I mean, is he not flirting with you constantly? He's practically begging to fuck you."

A small laugh escapes me at that. "He is. I've never had trouble with men wanting me that way. The trouble lies with them accepting all the baggage that comes with it."

Sorrow flashes across my sister's eyes. "Well, the way it looks to me right now, he's handling all your baggage and none of your... delicates." Her lips twitch up in the corners. "And he's still here. That tells me all he really wants is...you."

"I'm a packaged deal."

"Look at him right now." I pull my gaze back to Everett, watching him laugh with my daughter. "If anything," my sister continues, "he's more smitten with her than he is with you. I think he knows exactly what comes from being with you, and he wants all of it."

I don't often allow myself to dream up scenarios I long ago deemed impossible, but something deep inside me pulls at my chest as I watch the man I've become so allured by, the man who makes me feel so safe, laughing with my daughter. I think that tug might be hope.

My heart feels like frozen soil, like flowers gone dead in winter's frost.

A lifetime of being iced out by those who are supposed to love you tends to do that to a person, I think. A lifetime of poison leaves little space for one to bloom.

Meeting Everett feels like planting seeds, like the hope of spring.

But there are some places so cold seeds are useless, places so dark that the sun never shines. I think I may be one of them.

"I'm not sure I'm capable of giving anyone all of me, Darby."

My sister looks at me like she wants to understand, and while she faced her own kind of demons in the haunted house of our childhood, mine are just...different.

She was saved by the love of her life.

I had to be saved by her.

So, my sister doesn't argue. She only grabs my forearm where it's crossed at my chest and squeezes lightly. "I think if there is anyone out there worth trying for, it's him."

I nod but don't respond. We watch the party unfold for a moment longer before Leo comes jogging up to us, dimples gleaming with the grin on his face. "Okay, I finished setting up everything in the garage. Are you guys ready?"

I smile at him. "Yep. Let's do it."

I call out to Lou. Everett knows the plan, helping her out of the bounce house as Leo, Darby, and myself walk around the far side of the yard. Monica and Carlos are already in the detached garage, smiling as we enter. August is here too, to my surprise. I had invited him to the party but hadn't expected him to come.

I assume it was my sister's doing.

He's spent most of the day with her, and I noticed him speaking with Monica after Darby joined me on the porch. He's been quiet, reserved, though he smiles at Lou as she walks through the door.

"You ready, Luz?" Everett asks, standing behind her with his hands over her eyes.

"I thought we were opening presents outside?"

"This one is too big to bring into the backyard, so we thought we'd give it to you here first." Leo beams as he stands next to the table in the center of the garage with the bright pink, sparkly surfboard laid across it.

There are boards hung against the walls and across the roof, dozens of them. Most of them seem to be custom-made, and I wonder if they're something Leo won during his competitions throughout the years. I can't think of any other reason why one person would need so many. There are all different sizes, colors, and even shapes.

Another table is shoved against the corner beneath a rack of boards with rags, wax, and resin? I think. Leo talks about fixing up his boards a lot, but I only half pay attention.

Lou's been begging me to get back in the water for the last few months since we halted her lessons with Everett back in October. The weather is too unpredictable right now for surfing, according to Everett and Leo. Lou doesn't seem to understand this, though, since Leo is still in the water almost every day. Even though he technically retired last summer, he had pre-scheduled competitions through this spring, so he's still training. Plus, he's spent almost every day on the water since he was younger than Lou, and I'm sure he can handle the waves and the weather.

My anxiety, however, cannot.

I told Lou she had to wait until May before she could take any more lessons, and I'm hoping her birthday present from Leo will help her get excited for it.

Everett removes his hands from Lou's eyes, and I watch as they go comically wide, her mouth dropping open in astonishment. "Is this for me?" she all but squeals.

"All yours, bug," I reply. "From Leo."

She runs full force into him, wrapping her arms around her waist and screaming, "Thank you! Thank you!" into his stomach.

Everyone is laughing, and I feel tears stinging in the corners of my eyes as Leo pats her back and steers her toward the table. Lou slowly runs her hand over the board, taking in the way her name is sprawled along the side, multicolored flowers dotted across it.

"So here's the deal, kid," he says as he steps up next to her. "You'll get to break in the brand-new board later this spring with Everett, but only if you help me out in the meantime."

"Help you out?" she asks him.

"Yep." He smiles. "Every day after school, you're going to meet me here in the garage, and I'm going to show you how to properly take care of a surfboard. I'll teach you how to wax, check for damage, and fix your dings."

"Dings?" she snorts.

"Dings," Leo confirms. "Does that sound like a deal?"

She nods enthusiastically. "This is the best present ever."

"Rude," Everett says, though there's a smile on his face. "You haven't seen any of your other gifts yet."

"Well, I already know they won't be as good as this one." She scrunches her nose at him.

"Guess we better go check them out, then." My sister smiles.

Lou wraps her arms around Leo's waist again, whispering, "I'm going to pretend I like all my presents the same amount, but I think this one will be my favorite still."

He pats the top of her head, bending down to whisper in her ear, though it's loud enough that we all hear it. "Your secret is safe with me."

The eight of us filter out of the garage and back to the party. I hear August quietly wish Lou a happy birthday as we exit the back door. My heart breaks a little as he adds, "Don't ever go out in the ocean by yourself, okay? No matter how cool your surfboard is."

She cocks her head at him, as if considering his advice before she nods. "Okay, I won't."

My heart breaks a little more when Everett pats him on the back and says, "We wouldn't let that happen, Auggie. She'll be safe."

August dips his chin, tossing both hands into the pockets of his dark jeans. His voice is gruff as he murmurs, "I'm going to step inside and grab something to drink."

Everett nods, grabbing my hand and interlacing our fingers as we make our way across the yard. August parts from the crowd, heading inside the house on his own, and I wonder if he feels safest that way, keeping a distance from any connection that might hurt him if it's lost.

Everett pauses in front of a group of parents standing around the food table, Tana leading the charge of them. "Hey, she's going to do presents now."

Six sets of eyes fall to the place where Everett's and my hands are clasped before Tana raises her head. "Okay, cool. We'll be right over."

We don't miss the elevated whispers and the quiet snickers as we walk away, but Everett only squeezes my hand tighter.

I push the thoughts from my mind, gathering around the table stacked high with gifts. Lou is already tearing through wrapping paper. Patience is not her forte. She does a great job at enthusiastically thanking everyone, though.

Darby got her a bracelet-making kit and a coupon for a jewelry date, just the two of them. What Lou doesn't know is that my sister's gift is in tandem with mine—to make friendship bracelets for the Taylor Swift concert I bought Lou tickets for later this year—but I'll be giving her that gift later. It definitely beats Leo's surfboard, and I don't want to bruise his ego.

August gets her a coloring book, but it's filled entirely with black and white drawings he made himself. Different animals, landscapes, and some abstract designs. He included a box of colored pencils. She blushed when she thanked him. I think my daughter might have her first crush, and I'm not sure how I feel about it.

I can't say I blame her. August has that shy, damaged boy vibe and the soft smile that makes you think you might be able to fix him. Plus, there are those dreamy green eyes and that look that says he'd destroy you in bed but take real good care of you afterward.

Though, it's nothing in comparison to the way I feel when Everett wraps his arms around my waist, nuzzling his chin into my shoulder and sighing contently as he watches my daughter open her gifts, like there is no place else he'd rather be.

When Lou finally gets to the small box in the middle of the pile, Everett shouts against my ear, "That one's from me, Luz!"

"What is it?" I ask quietly as we watch her tear it open.

"You'll see."

The box is a black cube. A jewelry box, I realize. Lou cocks her head as she studies it, unsure of what to make of it. I feel the same. Finally, she pops it open, but I can't see what's inside. All I hear is her shocked gasp, and I watch as her green eyes—wide as saucers—lift to Everett. I'm a little afraid of what her reaction will be, because ten-year-old kids typically aren't big fans of jewelry. At least, not real jewelry, and that box definitely doesn't look like it was bought at Claire's.

"Where did you find it?" she asks.

I look at Everett. "Find it?"

But his eyes aren't on me, they're on her, smiling in a way that reminds me of unfiltered sunlight. "I had it made."

She rounds the table, bypassing all of her friends and the other parents, making her way to me. Nestled on a white cushion is a necklace. It's a simple chain, with a small gold medallion in the middle. A star sits in the center of it, with prongs sticking out in four directions.

A compass.

Identical to the necklace around my throat right now. The matching one of which Lou lost a year ago, and I'd been unable to replace. Something I mentioned to Everett only once.

"How?" I ask, shocked.

He gently plucks the necklace from the box in Lou's hands and motions for her to turn around. "I remember you telling me she was upset when she lost hers. So, I had Darby take a picture of yours, and I took it to a jeweler in San Diego." Lou lifts her hair from the back of her neck as Everett fastens the chain at her nape and links it together. "I asked them to remake it."

I think I'm in love with him.

That thought comes out of nowhere, sucker-punching me directly in the gut, so hard it takes my breath away. Or maybe that's just him, the way he's smiling at me. "Everett," I gasp. "That's so..." I don't have words. "That's so thoughtful."

He lifts his hand, brushing his thumb softly across my cheek before looking back down at my daughter again. "Do you like it?"

She wraps her arms around his waist, hugging him. "So

much. Thank you."

He seems a bit surprised by the physical contact. Lou, like me, has never been much of a hugger. It's well known she's not comfortable around men, but that must be changing around Leo and Everett, because she has been incredibly affectionate today. "You're welcome, Luz."

"Which one should I open next, Mount Everest?"

Leo snorts. "Good one, Lulu. Let's keep that one."

"Absolutely not," Everett dead-pans. He reaches across the table, grabbing another small box and handing it to my daughter. "Who's this one from?"

"That's from us." Monica claps her hands together happily.

She quickly tears the paper off the medium-sized box and throws it aside, revealing the packaging for a polaroid camera. I bite back a laugh as she turns it in her hands, inspecting it curiously as she tries to figure out what it is.

Lou glances up at Monica. "Can I try it?"

"Absolutely, kiddo." Carlos smiles, squatting down to show her how it works. "Go ahead and take a photo."

Wedging herself between me and Everett, Lou says, "Let's take a picture!" She hands Everett the camera as I lift her into my arms, and he holds it up to his face to take a photo of the two of us when Lou says, "No. A selfie."

"Of me?" he asks, popping a brow.

"No." She rolls her eyes. "Of all three of us."

"Oh." I swear, I see a bit of blush rise to his cheeks, and I can't bite back the grin that comes to my face. Everett wraps one arm around my waist, pulling me into him with Lou between us. She places one hand on my cheek and the other on Everett's, smooshing our faces together as Everett holds out the camera and snaps the photo.

I hear a couple of awes from parents standing around as the flash goes off. Setting Lou down, I glance up to see Monica staring after me with what looks like tears in her eyes. My sister is smirking, as if to say: *I told you so.*

"That's so cool!" Lou exclaims as the photo prints, and she watches the image appear in real time. She barrels into Monica's and Carlos's arms. "Thanks."

I pluck the photo from her sticky little hands. "I'll keep this safe while you open the rest of your presents, okay?"

Forty-five minutes later, the backyard is littered in torn-up wrapping paper, and the table is covered in cake. Sugar-crashed kids start turning lethargic, and people begin clearing out.

Once I'm sure everyone has had their fill, I take the remaining cake inside the kitchen so I can put it away. I promised our coworkers at the office I'd bring all the leftovers to work on Monday.

I'm separating each flavor of cake into separate Tupperware containers when I hear footsteps enter the kitchen behind me. "*Fuck*," Everett hisses. "That carne asada was so good. I told myself I wouldn't like it, because that fucker will never let me hear the end of it now." He saddles up next to me at the counter, smirking at me in his wicked way.

"You a big fan of Emilio's meat, Ramos?" I smile.

He shoots me an incredulous look. "He's not my type."

"Hmm," I hum, knocking him with my shoulder. "What is your type?"

His voice is rough against my ear as he leans down, pressing the heat of his body into my back and whispering, "Lately, pretty blondes with smart-ass mouths."

"Oh," I say casually, pretending like the feel of him doesn't set every molecule in my body on fire. "So, Leo."

He presses closer, harder. Bracing his hands on either side of the counter, boxing me in front of him so I'm unable to escape, his next move is bolder than we allow ourselves to be with each other. He's brazen as his teeth nip lightly at the base of my ear. "You're just filthy, aren't you, Wildflower?"

Fuck.

I drop the knife I was using to cut the cake, and Everett laughs as it clatters against the counter, giving me away. Trembles rock through the entirety of my being at that sound, following it as it cascades down my skin and pools in my core.

My composure around him is hanging by a fucking thread.

“What is your type?” I find myself asking, the words coming out just above a whisper. “When it comes to...men.” I’m not even sure why I ask, the feel of his body and the sound of his voice rendering me incapable of logical thought. I realize it’s something I’ve been curious about.

“I pride myself on not having one. I like who I like,” he whispers sensually, as if he’s playing some sort of game. “Though, I do tend to be drawn to pretty boys. Why? What’s your type?”

“Tall. Rugged. Handsome.” I don’t bother lying. I notice his grip on the counter tighten. “I like tattoos. Beards. Wicked smiles and dirty mouths.”

He lets out a soft groan, the feel of it vibrating against my neck and setting my skin on fire. “I like lots of beards too.”

“Shoot.” I let out a breathless laugh. “I guess I don’t do it for you, then.”

He chuckles against my jaw, and I feel one of his hands at my waist. “Baby, you have no fucking clue what you do to me.”

Moving way too fucking slowly beneath the hem of my shirt, calloused knuckles drag along my bare skin. My legs feel weak, and my breath hitches as his hand continues to climb. I’m ready to beg him to move faster, to give me more.

More touch, more sound, more sensation.

Just. More. Always more from him.

It’s not possible for me to hold back the moan that rips from my throat as Everett’s hand slides beneath my bra, my nipple hardening against his palm. I arch into him, writhing against his front, feeling the hardness of his arousal pressing into my ass. He groans at the friction, lips latching onto my jaw as he begins to kiss his way down my neck, mouth gliding along my shoulder and teeth nipping at my scorching skin.

“God, Dal, you taste so fucking good. So sweet. I need to taste you everywhere.”

I whimper at his words, grinding against him harder. He pins my hips with his free hand, pinching my nipple with the other. Rolling against me in the same delicious rhythm he fucked me with all those months ago, I feel his cock press into me.

I can't believe we're doing this here, right now. I don't know how we got to this point, but I do know I don't want to stop. I'm trying to consider how I can get him upstairs and out of his clothes before anyone notices us. "Everett," I cry out as he rolls his hips again.

"Tell me what you need, baby." His teeth sink into my flesh.

"Shit," I hiss. "I need..." I just need him. "I need—"

Tufts of laughter filter in from outside the kitchen.

I gasp, pressing away from Everett, but he holds me steady. So smoothly, he spins us around so we're facing away from the counter and in the direction the voices came from. Positioning me directly in front of him, he holds one arm at my waist and tucks a wild strand of hair behind my ear just as Tana walks in with Jeremy and Marshall—the dads of a friend from Lou's class—in tow.

Tana's eyes widen as the three of them stumble in. I'm sure my skin is flushed, and I can feel the neckline of my T-shirt askew. I realize Everett is holding me in front of him to block his hard-on, though I don't think the notion is hiding anything at all.

"Sorry," she drawls, eyes narrowing. "We wanted to let you know we were about to take off..."

"Oh, great," I say breathlessly. "Thank you so much for coming. She loved the gifts."

Jeremy and Marshall smirk knowingly. "Thanks for having us."

"Will we see you at the science fair next week?" Tana asks in a sickly sweet tone.

"Yep!" I say at the same time Everett adds, "We'll both be there."

She pops a brow, giving an insincere smile as they make their way past us and toward the front of the house.

"Goddammit," I mutter. Stepping away from Everett, I lean against the counter, dropping my head into my hands. "That is the exact opposite of what this arrangement is supposed to be conveying."

Everett sighs, but one hand remains at the center of my back, continuing to rub gently. "What do you mean, Dal? This is exactly the purpose of this arrangement." The word comes out as a near growl, as if he hates hearing it. "To convince people we're together."

I nod tightly. "*And* to convince people I'm not a horrible mother whoring herself around. Getting felt up at our child's birthday party hardly sends a wholesome message. What if something like this gets back to my dad?"

"Baby," Everett breathes. "First of all, nothing is getting back to your dad. Secondly, you're allowed to have a break. Take a moment for yourself. You're allowed to feel good in this life and not apologize for it." He stops rubbing my back, instead spinning me around so I'm facing him before pulling me into his chest and wrapping both arms around my shoulders.

I feel safe when his familiar scent envelops me—the way his chin fits perfectly at the top of my head and he lightly sways us back and forth, as if he's rocking the anxiety from my body. I nuzzle into his warmth, taking that moment he claims I'm entitled to.

"We weren't fucking in the kitchen, Dahlia, and we hardly even touch around Lou. There is no world in which any person—including those bitchy parents—would be able to convince anyone you're a bad mother. And even if someone tries, I'm going to be right there next to you the entire time. I'll fight with you, fight for you. I'm not going to let anyone hurt you, Wildflower."

I grasp the fabric of his shirt at his back, tugging him into me tighter, breathing him in, savoring his touch until I feel like I'm whole again.

Hours later, when the inflatables are taken down, the trash is cleaned up, and the birthday girl is passed out cold in her bed, I walk Everett to the front door. He stayed and helped the entire time, washing the dishes with me even after my sister and Leo called it a night.

He asked if he could help me put Lou to bed again, the same way he did on Thanksgiving, on Christmas Eve after a party we threw for the local small business owners, and again on New Year's Eve when Lou and I both passed out on the couch before midnight.

We helped her hang the polaroid of the three of us on the bulletin board she keeps above her bed. Then, she insisted on reading two chapters on the *Nancy Drew* series she was gifted by Elena. Even though she has never met Lou, she had the box of books delivered this week. In the card, she noted it was the series that made her fall in love with reading as a child.

Lou then asked if she could read one of Elena's books, and though I've never gotten my hands on any of them, the way Leo, Darby, and Everett's faces blanched at the question told me Lou certainly should not have her hands anywhere near Elena's writing.

Everett sat at the edge of Lou's bed while I read to her until her faint snoring interrupted me on page five.

Now, we stand in the foyer, the brisk night air filtering through the open door as he stares after me. "Thanks for everything today," I say quietly. "The necklace you bought her is beautiful. I know she loves it."

"I hoped she would." He smiles. "I'm always here, Wildflower, for whatever you need. But I hope you know"—he lifts his hand, taking my necklace between his fingers and sliding his thumb across the metal—"that there is no place I'd rather be, and nobody I'd rather be spending my time with than the two of you. It's not a chore to me. It's what I want to be doing."

I nod, my breath catching as his fingers make contact with my skin when he places the necklace back at the center of my chest. We're standing close, close enough that if my breathing becomes any more rapid, our chests would be brushing.

I watch Everett's eyes roam from my neck and focus on my mouth. He takes a deep breath, as if settling himself. His tongue snakes across his lips, and for one second I think he's going to lean in and kiss me. I'm sure of it, so sure that I close my eyes, bracing for the warmth of his touch and the feel of his tongue I remember from that night all those months ago.

Instead, he sighs, seeming to think better of it. My eyes fly open, and the expression on his face looks pained. "I'll see you on Monday," he whispers. "For that meeting with Dawn Patrol." A surf wear brand that wants to partner with the shop. Well, with Leo, in particular.

I nod, hiding my disappointment.

He presses his lips to my forehead just briefly before walking out into the night. I watch him until he rounds the corner of the garage and is out of sight. Shutting the door, I flip off the dining room light and turn to head up the stairs when I'm startled by a quiet, yet somehow aggressive, knock on the door.

Knowing it can't be anyone else but him, I open it.

Everett's breathing heavily, eyes wild, and only one thought filters through my mind: he came back to kiss me.

He's going to kiss me.

He looks positively feral.

But he doesn't ravish me, doesn't close the gap between us.

No, he slowly holds up a crumpled piece of paper.

"Who the fuck did this, Dahlia?" he asks, voice heavy and strained.

Written across the page in black ink is one word: *WHORE*

Twenty-Six - Wicked

You're Invaluable, Everett

"You're angry."

My eyes filter to my brother, staring me down with confusion on his face, before they flutter back to Dahlia's office doorway, where I watch her sort through the reports she'll need for our meeting in ten minutes.

Dawn Patrol, a well-known surf wear brand, is looking to do a collaboration with Heathen's. A line of boards and apparel designed in partnership with us. Well, with Leo. He'll be the face of the campaign, obviously. I'm not entirely sure why I need to be here, but apparently, as the co-owner of the business, my presence is required, even if it's not necessarily important. Plus, Dahlia is here.

Technically, Dahlia doesn't have to be here either. She works for the small business initiative, not Heathen's itself. With her background in marketing, though, Leo thought it would be a good idea to have her involved, to help determine the benefits and impact this partnership could have on our store and the boardwalk as a whole.

She looks nervous, chewing on her lip as she reviews a piece of paper laid out on her desk in front of her. She's dressed professionally, in a black pencil skirt that hugs her thighs flawlessly. A deep-red V-neck blouse with long sleeves is tucked into that skirt, clinging to every one of her curves. She finished off her look with a pair of black pumps that have me damn near salivating. I want that skirt hiked up to her waist. I want those legs wrapped around my head and those heels digging into my back.

Fuck.

I swallow, attempting to readjust myself inconspicuously.

Yeah, I am angry—angry with her, and the way she looks makes me keep forgetting. "I can't believe she didn't tell me, that this has been going on since *October*."

"It's not because she didn't trust you," Leo says. "She didn't tell anyone, not even Darby.

I think she genuinely thought it was no big deal, especially since, prior to Saturday, it'd been a one-time thing."

"Then I'm angry at her for being so fucking obtuse to her own safety."

"I'm sure she would've told you about the notes once she found the second one. I mean, if you hadn't found it yourself."

Across the office, I know she can't hear us, but her head snaps sideways all the same, meeting my face. She gives me an apologetic smile, and I only nod back. Saturday night, she hardly even seemed upset at the note we'd found, like she was numb to it. Those kinds of names. That kind of harassment. She said she's convinced it's the other parents at Lou's school just trying to remind her how unwelcome she is.

When I asked her why they'd go so far, her only response was that it's nothing new.

That made me see red.

I'm angry at her for not telling me, but more than that, I'm angry she thinks this is normal, that she believes she deserves this somehow. I'm also scared. I'm so afraid of her being hurt, afraid of things going so far that she runs away, that she begins to feel unsafe in the place I've always felt safest in. That Pacific Shores stops feeling like home to her. I want her to feel at home here. I want her to feel at home with me.

"I'm sorry I doubted your feelings for her." My brother's voice breaks my focus, and I realize I've been staring after Dahlia again.

"I'm sorry I told you to stay away from her."

"Forgiven," I murmur quietly. I can't blame my brother for that, not with the way I typically behave, with how important I can now see Dahlia has become to him. Not with all the scars I now know she bears.

"I love you," he adds.

I look at him, blue eyes soft and sincere. The small smile that comes to my lips isn't forced when I respond, "I love you too."

Leo's unafraid of affection, and I suppose I'm the same. My mom drilled it into us from a young age. It took a while for Leo to say those words to her after his mother died and his father abandoned him.

My mom, however, told him she loved him the day his father called and informed her he'd fled the state and left Leo with us, that he wasn't coming back. She sat all three of us down—Leo, Elena, and me—and told us Leo wasn't going anywhere. Then, she told him that she loved him. I don't think he'd heard the words since before his mother's passing a year prior.

My parents fought for guardianship so Leo wouldn't have to go into foster care. My mom told him she loved him every morning when we left for school and every afternoon when we returned. I don't remember when he began saying it back to her, but I do remember the first time he said it to me.

The day Zach died.

It was as if Leo was afraid I'd be next, and he needed me to know. He has been that way since, so I always say it back. I make sure he knows too.

Thoughts filter to my sister. The affection my mom placed on Leo and me didn't seem to leave its mark on Elena. I think her love language was silent giving. Necklaces she made us, palm readings, or in-depth analysis of our birth chart. Poems she'd slip beneath our doors in the middle of the night, ones she'd write about being bonded, protected, and accepted. Her love was in her written words.

Until it wasn't.

Until love became so foreign to her that the words died with it. The act of love, the gift of it, ceases to exist. There are no more poems, no more books. She hardly remembers to call and check in, and as much as I want to be angry at her for it, I know it's happening because she's broken.

Because for Elena, the word love was always a question.

And all the answers died with Zach.

"Good morning," Dahlia chimes, breaking me from my thoughts. She's followed into the office by two reps from Dawn Patrol, and Leo's agent, Lynn. "Are we ready to get started?"

Leo and I stand, greeting everyone and shaking hands before we all take our respective places around the table. Dahlia sits across from me, flashing a closed-lip smile before diving into her presentation. As I watch her speak, I realize that as much as I want to be angry at her, I can't. She has been broken too.

A half-hour later, Dawn Patrol is deep into their proposal, and I'm attempting not to fall asleep. They've been going back and forth with Lynn negotiating Leo's commission. They argue that Leo's pending retirement devalues him, while Lynn attempts to argue that his value has increased since his announcement, that his decision to settle down and start a family has made him more relatable and personable.

When they finally settle on a number, the Dawn Patrol rep dives directly into design aspects and which products will be featured throughout the campaign. My eyes grow heavier.

"I'm sorry," Dahlia interrupts, her sweet voice snapping me awake. "Are we not going to discuss Everett's commission for this campaign as well?"

Everyone looks at her like she has grown three heads, including me.

Lynn clears her throat, leaning in and saying quietly to our half of the table, "Leo is being commissioned for his personal brand, his name and likeness. He'll be inputting additional time into the campaign. Photoshoots, interviews, and so on."

Dahlia cocks her head, and instead of addressing Lynn, she

turns her attention to the Dawn Patrol representatives, whose names I can't remember. "Why isn't Everett, as the co-owner of Heathen's, being asked to participate in the campaign as well?"

One of them, a round bald man who appears to be in his fifties, straightens his tie. "Well..." He coughs. "Excuse my... my bluntness..." I hold up my palms to let him know I won't be offended by whatever he has to say next. I've heard it all before. "Leo Graham is a household name, a living legend in the name of surfing. Everett is..."

"The other half of this company?" Dahlia snaps. "The person keeping it afloat every time Leo jets around the world? Everett is the person who has stood by Leo since before he was *Leo Graham*. Who housed him when he was orphaned and let him borrow surfboards when he had nothing. Who sat out on the waves with him every day so he could become the living legend you speak of." Dahlia's jaw sets, eyes wild with emotion. "There would be no *Leo Graham*, and no Heathen's, if it not for Everett Ramos."

"Dal," I whisper. "It's fine—"

"No, it's not." She looks at me, and I see so much conviction in her gaze I dissolve beneath it. *She's standing up for me.* Turning to my brother, she murmurs, "Sorry."

"Don't be sorry. You're completely right, Dal. In fact"—a slow grin spreads across his mouth as he turns to Lynn—"Everett's cut matches mine, or I'm walking."

"Leo," Lynn hisses. Looking back at the bald man, she smiles tightly. "Can we have a moment?"

"No, I don't need a moment," my brother continues. "Everett will be included in all marketing for the campaign, and you'll pay him whatever you pay me."

"We simply don't have the budget allocated to—" the other Dawn Patrol rep, a younger woman with dark hair and frown lines, begins.

"Then pay me less. Just make sure whatever you are paying me, my brother gets the same."

Lynn's face falls into her hands, but Dahlia is smiling proudly at Leo.

"Yes, well. Of course. We can figure out how to make that work." The bald man begins rapidly sorting through papers before he glances up at us. "My main concern is the campaign. We planned on launching with a photoshoot of Leo in the line, and as I said before, he's a household..."

"You're telling me that if you took that man's shirt off and plastered him on a poster, it wouldn't catch attention?" Dahlia flutters a delicate hand in my direction. "They don't need to know his name; they only need to look at him. I'll bet he can sell anything Leo can."

My brother laughs. "Your confidence in me is astounding, Dahlia."

She smirks, giving him a side-long glance. "Not everyone likes a pretty boy." Glancing back to Dawn Patrol, she shrugs. "You'd reach a wider audience that way."

The two reps look at each other, raising their brows in silent conversation before the bald man nods once. He stands, extending his hand to me. "I think we've come to an agreement, then."

I rise, returning the gesture. "Looking forward to it."

I'm not, really. I've got no desire to model alongside my brother. He made me do it once before the shop opened. We had a photographer come take photos of us to hang up in the store, and I hated every minute of it. I don't enjoy that kind of attention, and I don't need money badly enough to beg for a cut of Leo's deals. But watching Dahlia stand up for me like that, watching her believe I had the same value my brother has, awakened something inside me. I've always come second to him—until her. So, if she wants me to take this campaign on, then I'll do that. For her.

We finish out the meeting, approving the designs Dawn Patrol mocked up. Leo and I sign a contract under Lynn's reluctant eye. Once the conference room clears and only my brother, Dahlia, Lynn, and me remain, I say to Dahlia, "Do you think we could talk in your office for a moment?"

My brother is shooting me a devilish smile as Dahlia nods

silently and follows me across the room toward her office. I hold the door open for her as we walk inside, slamming it shut the moment she enters.

Grabbing her arm, I spin her so she's pinned between the door and my chest. Bracing my arm on the wall above her head, I lean in close. Her eyes flutter upward, two blazing sapphires that see right through me.

"Nobody has ever done that for me before."

"What?" she whispers.

"Stood up for me." My voice turns rough as I add, "Seen my value."

She slowly lifts a hand, wrapping it around the nape of my neck. My body shudders beneath her touch as she brushes her thumb against my skin. "You're invaluable, Everett."

All of my resolve melts as those words burn into me. My head drops, nose grazing against her cheek and lips pressing into her jaw. I inhale her paradise scent, feel her skin on my mouth as I whisper, "I need to kiss you now."

She lets out a soft laugh. "Finally." I pull back to look at her, a blush running up her chest and into her cheeks. A teasing smile accents her lips, her ocean eyes on fire. She's the most beautiful thing I've ever seen, and she believes *me* invaluable. "Are you going to—"

I steal her words, capturing her mouth with my own, and when she lets out a surprised moan, I steal that too. I inhale her breath, devouring her lips in a kiss that is fervent and desperate and far too long awaited. I want to absorb her touch, imprint her on my skin.

I attempt to do just that as her lips move against mine—soft, warm, and addicting. Dragging my hand down the door, I tangle it in her hair behind her head, tilting her face up slightly so I can kiss her deeper. She opens for me on a moan, and I let my tongue slip inside her mouth. My other hand runs the length of her body, slipping behind her back and grasping her perfect ass outside her tight skirt. I pull her into me, pinning her between my hand and my hips. She hisses when she feels my hard length press against her stomach, and I take the opportunity to slip her bottom lip between my teeth and bite down.

"Everett," she whimpers, the sweet music in her voice singing along my skin and opening all my senses. I'm hyperaware of her—the strands of hair between my fingers, the feel of her flesh beneath my palm, the wet warmth of her tongue inside my mouth, and the drag of her breasts against my chest.

I'm consumed by her.

I know this will destroy me later, but in this moment, I revel in my wrecking.

Dragging my lips from hers, I kiss my way along her jaw and down her neck. She bucks her hips against me when I hit a soft spot behind her ear. She does it again when I nip at the hollow of her throat. I catalog these places—these moments. I mesmerize all the little things that bring her pleasure, praying she'll let me do them again.

"Do you"—I pepper kisses down the center of her chest—"have any idea"—dragging my lips along her sternum until I reach the V of her shirt—"how long I've craved doing this to you?" I glance up, finding those flaming eyes hooded and hazed. "What torture it is to be in your presence and not ravage you the way I do in my dreams?"

She throws her head back against the door, running her fingers through my hair and sending shivers down my spine. "Me too," she breathes. "I think about it all the time, about watching you come all the time."

"Fuck." I rapidly drag my mouth back up her body, finding her mouth again. Her hands land at my back, digging into me as if she wants to pull me closer. I wonder if she feels as consumed as I do, if she's also searching for a way to bind our beings.

I slide my hands up her bare thighs, taking her skirt with me as I wrap around her legs and hoist her up. She's pinned between the door and my body again, reminiscent of the night we met. Though then, I didn't know her name, had no idea how ingrained she'd become in my life.

I know we've kissed before, but *this*? Holding her against me when I know her name, feeling her lips when I've seen her tears, knowing she's losing control with me when she's afraid to do so in any other aspect of her life... *Fuck*. It's different. Kissing Dahlia is a privilege, one I didn't know I had before, and something I'm damn sure I'll never take for granted again.

"I wanted you to kiss me Saturday night," she murmurs against my lips. "I was so sure you would when you came back to the door, but you didn't."

I capture her lip between my teeth again, dragging slowly as I let it go. "Because I knew once I kissed you, I wouldn't be able to stop," I moan into her mouth, and she takes the opportunity to flick her tongue across my teeth, eliciting another sound from me. "I knew I'd want to taste you, and I wasn't going to do that with our siblings downstairs or with your daughter two doors over." I kiss along her jaw again. "Not when I need to hear you scream my name."

She hums, letting her head fall back so she can bare her neck. I nip along it, taking her soft skin beneath my teeth, feeling her buck against my erection. "What about now?" she asks breathlessly. "What do you plan on doing now?"

"Now, Wildflower," I growl against her flesh, "I plan on devouring every inch of you. I won't stop until you're crying out for me, and I don't give a fuck who hears it."

"Anyone ever tell you you've got a filthy mouth?" she whimpers.

I smile against her lips. "Let me show you all the wicked things I can do with it."

I pull us back from the door, marching across the office with her in my arms before sitting her down on the desk. I hear items go falling to the floor beneath us, but we're both past caring. Dahlia leans back, bracing her hands on the wood and widening her legs for me to step between them. I move slowly, tracing my tongue along her jaw and down her neck, moving between her breasts again, my mouth meeting the fabric of her top.

When I reach for her blouse so I can untuck it from her skirt and pull it off her, Dahlia's desk phone suddenly rings. We pause, and she looks up at me with lust-hazed eyes, flushed cheeks, and swollen lips. I think I could come from the sight of her alone.

"Don't answer it," I snap.

She nods rapidly, and the chiming stops just as I dip my head to continue my descent down the rest of her body—until the goddamn phone starts ringing again.

I sigh against her chest, feeling her body tense beneath my mouth.

"Answer the fucking phone, Everett!" It's my brother's voice that booms from the other side of the door. "Adam is downstairs, and he'd like to go home. He's wondering where you are, since you're *supposed* to be relieving him."

"Goddammit," I mutter.

Moving back up, I take Dahlia's face between my hands, planting a soft kiss against her mouth. "I'm so sorry," I say, pressing my lips to each cheek. "I'm sorry." Then her jaw. "I've got to go cover the desk." Then her nose. "I'm sorry."

"Don't be," she says breathlessly. "We were probably getting a little carried away for the workplace anyway."

I pull back to smirk at her before planting one more kiss on her mouth. "Don't leave for the day until I come back, okay?"

She nods. "I've got to pick up Lou from your mom's at five o'clock, though."

I forgot Dahlia had asked my mother to pick Lou up from school today, since she wasn't sure how long our meeting with Dawn Patrol would last, and Darby's working on the finishing touches for the flower shop before it opens.

"I'll be back before then."

"Okay," she says, giving me a coy smile as I stand and readjust my hard-on.

Just as I reach her office door, I find myself doubling back. She's surprised as I take her face between my palms again and kiss her one more time. "I can't get enough."

She's laughing by the time I finally make it out the door.

Twenty-Seven – Wicked

Not Finished With You Yet

Please. Please. Please.
Can you pick up Lou from Mom's?
At five o'clock. PLEASE.

You're desperate.

Unashamedly so. Please, Leo.

Fine, but you owe me.

The minutes tick by painfully slowly as I wait until it's time to close the shop. Leo comes down the stairs just before five o'clock and lets me know he informed Dahlia he'd go pick up Lou. Then, just after five, I see Scarlett and Jeremiah leave together.

Jeremiah doesn't speak to me anymore. I don't give a shit.

Because I know Dahlia's up in that office by herself, waiting for me, not for him.

It's five thirty-three when I lock the doors and close up Heathen's. We're supposed to be open until six, but I haven't had a customer in over an hour, and I know if Darby was sitting in that office upstairs, wearing a tight-ass skirt and waiting for my brother, he'd do the same fucking thing.

I quickly close the till and balance the books before shutting off the lights and bounding up the staircase two steps at a time. The office is dark when I slip inside, only the dim glow of Dahlia's office light glowing behind her closed door.

I enter without knocking, and she looks up at me from behind her desk. The blue light of her laptop reflects on her face as she cocks her head. "Leo asked me to stay late, that he'd pick up Lou, but I don't kno—"

"I'm not finished with you yet." My steps are purposeful and quick as I round her desk and spin her chair to face me. She watches with me with wide, shocked eyes as I slowly lower to my knees in front of her. "I told you I was going to devour every inch of your body, show you all the things I can do with my mouth." I press my lips against her outer knee, keeping my eyes on her. "Are you going to let me finish what I started, Wildflower?"

"Everett." She tosses her head back, her delicate throat moving as a moan crawls its way out. "This..." Her body tenses as I brush my lips up her leg. "Is supposed to be...." Her fingers knot in my hair. "Fake."

This woman must be doing something to me, the way she causes me to have a visceral fucking reaction to a single word. I swear to God, I'm going to obliterate *fake* from her vocabulary.

I pull away, letting my mouth hover just above her skin, far enough away that it denies her the satisfaction of my touch, but close enough that she can feel my breath as I whisper, "That's not what I asked. Tell me: do you want this?"

Her back arches, legs clenching around me. "Yes," she whimpers. "But—"

I stand swiftly, cutting off the rest of her sentence. She looks up at me, blue eyes bright like stars in the dim lighting. Her pretty pink lips part slightly as I grasp her arm and tug her up. She follows my lead, standing before, allowing me to grab her shoulder and spin her around, pressing her between my body and the desk.

She gasps as I bend her over, one hand pressing between

her shoulder blades while the other runs the length of her back, fingers dipping into her waistband. "I'm going to make you come on my fingers." I grab her skirt with my other hand. "After that, you're going to come all over my face." I pull the fabric down her thighs, letting it tangle at her ankles while I stare after her perfect, round ass, now covered only by the thin, good-for-nothing strip of her black lace thong. Catching my breath, I finally add, "Then, I'm going to ask you again if you think this is fake."

Sliding back up her body at a torturously slow pace, I snag the hem of her blouse. Dahlia doesn't hesitate when she lifts her arms and lets me pull it over her head, tossing it to the floor behind me. I reach around and take her full breasts in each of my hands, rolling her pert nipples between my fingers over the fabric of her bra. "Does that sound good to you, baby?" I nip at her ear, peppering kisses down her neck to her back.

As if words are beyond her, she only responds with a terse hum and the nod of her head. I continue moving down her back, kissing, nipping, and suckling her sweet skin, eliciting tremors and moans from her mouth as I go. As I reach the band of her underwear, I take it between my teeth and squat to the floor, dragging it with me until it's bunched at her ankles along with her skirt. My cock is painfully hard as I take in the sight of her above me. She's still in her heels, her legs slightly spread but restrained, hands braced on her desk as she leans over and puts herself on display for me. Her pussy is already wet—dripping just for me.

"Fucking masterpiece." The words leave my mouth before I even realize I'm speaking them aloud, and when Dahlia turns her head slightly, looking down at me with those bright eyes and that playful twitch of her lips, all my resolve shatters.

I run my hands up her legs until I reach her ass. Standing behind her, I take her flesh in my palms, running my hands over her soft skin. "You have such a pretty ass, Dahlia." I grab her roughly, spreading her open. "Has it ever been played with?"

"Yes," she moans.

"Do you like that?" I ask, gathering saliva at the tip of my tongue.

"Yes."

I groan at her answer. *I think she's fucking made for me.* I part my lips just slightly, letting my spit slowly drip out of my mouth and land between her cheeks. She gasps at the sensation, crying out as I circle my thumb around her tight bud, pressing in lightly.

"Do you like it when *I* play with your ass, Wildflower?"

"Please," she breathes, bucking backward, as if to force me deeper.

"Fuck." My cock jumps at her begging, and I'm so fucking desperate for her, I may lose myself without even being touched. "You're so good for me. You're gonna listen to me, right, baby? Gonna do what I say like a good girl?"

"Yes." She bucks back against me again.

"Promise?" I ask, pressing my thumb inside her.

"I promise!" she cries as I slip past the tight ring of muscle. Her breathing picks up, chest heaving as I pump my thumb in and out of her.

"Is your pussy wet for me, too?"

She only nods, and I stretch my hand down between her legs, teasing her entrance with my middle finger. *Fucking soaked.*

"Potrei annegare in questa figa. Muori qui. È mio. Tutto mio."

Shit. Am I speaking Italian? She drives me insane. My mother would weep to know I'm utilizing all those years of lessons to talk like this right now.

I slowly push my middle finger inside her, pumping twice before adding another. I set a rhythm between my two fingers in her pussy and my thumb in her ass, picking up my pace as I feel her begin to tighten and tremble around me.

"Everett," she moans. Body trembling, I steady her with a hand on her hip. I feather my lips along her back, feeling her shudder and tense beneath my mouth as she clenches on my fingers, reaching her peak. "Yes. Please. Faster." She chants as I fuck her with my hand and brush my lips along her skin.

"Look at you." My voice comes out gruff and strained. "Both

holes filled, and you're begging for more. You're perfect, aren't you?" I nip at her neck, fighting the urge to buck against her with my hips, desperate for my own release. "So needy for me."

I continue my pace with one hand, using my free one to tangle in the back of her hair and lift her so she's flush against my chest. She lays her head against my shoulder, looking up at me with lust-laced eyes. "I'll bet you like it rough, don't you, baby?"

Her lips are parted slightly, small whimpers escaping them with each thrust of my fingers into her body. She nods, and I move my hand around her throat, gripping just tight enough to make her catch her breath. "You take my fingers so well, Dahlia. I can't wait to watch you take my cock again."

Her eyes flutter closed, and I feel her throat work against my palm as she moans at my words. I begin moving faster, curling my fingers and pressing hard against the spot I know will make her come undone. Her entire body begins to tense as a garbled, "Everett!" escapes her mouth.

I lean into her, my lips hovering right over hers. "Come for me, Dahlia," I command. "Squirt all over my hand the way you did my dick. I want to feel you, baby."

Her mouth falls open, eyes shut as her pussy tightens around my fingers, and I feel her begin to lose herself. I press my mouth to hers, swallowing her moan before taking her lip between my teeth and biting down, dragging as I pull away. A tremble rushes up her body, and I feel her getting close. I wrap my arm around her middle, feeling her legs weaken. "That's it. Let go, Wildflower. I've got you."

I curl my fingers again, pumping hard and fast a few more times until I feel her become impossibly tight, gripping my fingers hard enough that they can no longer move. I feel the pressure building inside her, the way her body racks with quivers, and a cry tears from her throat as that pressure bursts.

She goes slack, falling forward, supported only by my knee between her legs and my arm around her waist. I feel her release rush past my fingers, flooding my hand. I hold her tightly as she rides it out, muttering unintelligible words like fuck and God and my name.

It's the most beautiful thing I've ever heard.

Once she's entirely spent, I slowly pull my fingers from her body. As I step back from her, she turns around and leans against the desk. Eyes at half-mast, a faint glow of sweat accenting her face, she looks up at me with a heaving chest, watching with rapt attention as I stick my middle finger in my mouth and suck her off my skin.

The taste of her is heady and addicting. She's intoxicating.

She tastes like she fucking belongs to me.

Her eyes are fixated on my mouth, breathing increasing as she watches me. The straps of her bra hang limply off her shoulders, her breasts spilling out of the cups with each rapid movement of her chest. A flush runs up her neck, blooming on her cheeks and making her eyes appear even brighter in the dim light of her office. Lips swollen, she takes one between her teeth, biting down as we study each other.

"You're so beautiful," I find myself saying.

"So are you," she responds breathlessly.

I'm smiling when I surge forward, grabbing her hips and setting her on the desk as my mouth falls on hers. She laces her arms around my neck, pressing us together as I kiss and kiss and kiss her. I move my lips along her jaw and down her neck, reaching around her back to unclasp her bra. She slides it off her arms and lets it fall to the floor as I take one of her hardened nipples into my mouth, sucking and nipping and gently biting.

"Everett," she breathes as I move across her chest to service the other one.

"You are so beautiful," I say again with her breast between my teeth. "I've been dreaming about doing this to you"—I suck her into my mouth roughly, pulling away with force—"worshiping your body like this. You deserve to be worshiped, Dahlia."

I brush my lips along her skin, falling to the floor in front of her. I look up at her, knowing there's pleading desperation on my face, and she meets my gaze with a mirrored expression. "Your body is my new religion, baby." I wrap both arms around her legs, gripping her inner knees. "Now, spread those thighs and baptize me."

Her breath hitches, but she opens for me immediately, baring her perfect, wet pussy. She's glistening with arousal and the aftermath of her first orgasm. My cock rages at the sight of her—the need to be inside her. I press my hand to my groin in an attempt at relieving the pressure.

"Yes," she whispers. "Do that."

I look up, meeting her hooded eyes as she watches me. "What, baby?"

"Touch yourself." She's so quiet, I almost can't hear her. She's so timid in moments like this, and it drives me wild.

I palm my cock again, and she bites down on her lip, a flush coming to her cheeks. I understand why she made the request. She seems under the impression that she can only take pleasure if it's also being returned. I noticed it the night she touched herself on video for me. She wanted me to go there with her. She needs the level of vulnerability to be matched, and I think it's because she needs to know I want to give this to her as much as she wants to take it. She's so afraid of being a burden, of not being desired.

That drives me mad. It's infuriating, and I want to obliterate every person who has ever made her feel that way about herself.

"Dahlia," I rasp. "Do you need to see what you do to me? What the *taste* of you does to me? Do you need proof of how desperate I am to hear you cry my name again?"

With hooded eyes, flushed cheeks, and parted lips, she nods.

I reach down, unbuckling my belt, slipping it through the loops and tossing it aside before unzipping my pants. I watch her breath stop as I pull out my cock. It's painfully fucking hard—aching for her, just like the rest of me. I swipe the moisture gathered at my tip and swirl my thumb around the head. Gripping my base, I pump myself once, twice.

"I need all those doubts to leave your pretty head. I've been thirsting for this pussy, and now, I'm going to fuck myself while I devour it. Can you let me do that?"

Her head falls back on a moan. "God, please."

Pushing her legs open with one hand, I move between her thighs. I start at her center, dipping my tongue inside and feeling her sweet arousal coat my senses. My cock jumps at the taste of her. The smell of her. The sight. I squeeze my tip, willing myself not to come already.

I drag my tongue up the length of her, settling over her clit as I flick once. "And that's the last time I hear you say the word 'God' tonight, understood? You need to call out for someone, Wildflower? You say my fucking name."

Her legs tighten around my head, and a soft whimper leaves her mouth.

"Say it for me, Dahlia," I growl, mouth hovering over her clit, denying her the sensation I know she desperately needs.

"Everett," she breathes. "Please."

It's all I need to descend on her. I circle her clit with my tongue in the same tempo I fist my cock. She continues chanting my name as I pick up my pace, working her faster. "That's it. Keep going."

Her moans grow louder, body tensing and tightening as I wrap my lips around her bundle and suck hard. I gently nip her with my teeth, causing her body to bow off the desk, hand flying to the back of my head and holding me there.

"Fuck, yes, Dal. Use me, baby. Fuck my face. Take what you need." My words vibrate against her center as she bucks against my face, using it to fuel the friction that makes her come undone. I stick my tongue out, letting her grind over it to find her pleasure.

"Everett." She pants. "Everett...I'm going...I'm going..."

Knowing she's close, I begin pumping my cock faster, hoping I can hold out and go with her. I drag my free hand up her thigh, holding her open with my shoulder. Splaying my palm against her upper abdomen, I press down lightly, adding just enough pressure to make her explode.

I take her clit between my teeth again as she continues to move against my mouth. As I bite down gently, her entire body tenses. She cries out louder than she has all night, legs wrapping around my neck and tightening almost painfully. Pleasure zips down my back and gathers in my spine, red hot and blazing. I fuck myself faster, feeling Dahlia tremble above me.

The moment she falls back against the desk, her body quivering as she cries out, I move my mouth to her core, slipping my tongue inside her. Her fingers knot in my hair, heels digging into my back, her entire body clinging to my face as if it's her center of gravity.

That red hot heat explodes into white hot pleasure, my mind going fuzzy and blank as my climax barrels through me. I feel my release coating my hand just as Dahlia's floods my mouth. I keep my tongue inside her, letting her ride out her orgasm on my face. She's still calling out my name, tightening around my tongue, drowning me in her pleasure, and I think it's the closest I've ever been to heaven. I'm still spilling into my hand, pumping myself, lost inside her.

"Quiero vivir, ahogarme y morir entre tus piernas, cariño."

I don't even know what the fuck I'm saying, what language I'm speaking. All I know is I can't get enough of her, of the feel and taste and sound of her. I'm addicted, and I don't know how I'll ever recover from this. I didn't even get inside her, and I know with certainty that I'd die for this, to do this to her—with her—every day for the rest of my goddamn life.

"Everett...Everett..." she continues moaning as she falls down from the clouds. Body still shaking, she finally begins to loosen her grip around my head.

I kiss along her thighs as I pull back from between her legs. I pull a box of tissues from Dahlia's desk and clean myself up before tucking my cock back into my pants and standing. Dahlia slowly pushes herself up to sit. Her eyes are bright and sated, full lips offering me a soft smile.

I grip her chin and drop my mouth to hers. Her wetness is

dripping off my lips as I grasp her jaw, and her mouth drops open. I gather up a mixture of my saliva and her release, and she sticks out her tongue, as if she already knows what's coming.

I spit into her mouth.

I swipe my thumb along her bottom lip, smearing the remnants of my cum. "Tell me, Dahlia—does this taste fucking fake to you?"

Her eyes flutter shut, her delicate throat working as she swallows. "No," she murmurs.

I close the distance between us, taking her lips gently. She whimpers, clinging to my chest as my mouth moves against hers, so soft in contrast to everything we've just done.

"Everett," she whispers, pulling away. Her gaze meets mine briefly before dropping to the floor. "I don't know if I can offer more than this. I don't know if I'm capable of it..." She sighs, eyes fluttering upward. "I'm just... I'm really fucked up."

Everything inside my being shatters at those words, but I force a smile anyway. Taking her face between my hands, I kiss her nose, her cheeks. I run my lips along her jaw.

She told me she'd ruin me. I told myself she'd destroy me. I should've fucking listened, because that one sentence wrecked me.

I move my mouth to her forehead, pressing my lips there too. "I'll take whatever you're willing to give, as long as whatever you are giving me is real."

She nods against me, and I feel her hand tangle in the fabric of my shirt, right over my goddamn heart. I've known what I was getting into with Dahlia since the day I learned her name. Even if she can't give me all of her, I can give her all of me. I don't think anyone ever has.

But I will.

I'll be patient, until she knows she's safe. Her body, her heart, and soul, all of her is safe with me. I can't break down her walls with a wrecking ball, I need to pull them apart brick by brick. Each one she gives me is a gift I know she has never given anyone else. So, I can be patient, no matter how bad it hurts me, because the only thing that would hurt more is losing her.

Dahlia doesn't give her love or her trust freely, because it has always been taken for granted. All I have to do is show her I won't. I'll earn it, and once I have it, I'll cherish it, starting with her trust, because she needs to know she has someone on her side.

"And if you get another note on your car—or anywhere else—you tell me immediately, okay?" I whisper against her forehead. "You don't deal with it alone."

She nods. "I know. I'm sorry. I'll tell you if it happens again."

That's my girl.

But I don't say it. Because she's not mine yet. Not truly.

I am, however, irrevocably hers.

Twenty-Eight - Wildflower

Save A Wave, Ride A Surfer

"Good morning, my little flower child." I smile as my sister flops down into the beach chair next to mine.

"Whoever convinced me it was a good idea to open a business and plan a wedding at the same time needs a swift kick in the ass." She rubs at her eyes, squinting in the morning sunlight.

"I think that'd be him." I nod toward the horizon, where her fiancé stands shirtless, leaning against a propped-up surfboard. Leo smiles when he catches sight of my sister, shooting her a wink.

He and Everett are in the middle of their Dawn Patrol photoshoot, and while Leo is a natural behind the camera, Everett looks increasingly uncomfortable. He looks hot as hell—bare skin oiled and tattoos on display—but his demeanor tells me he'd rather be anywhere else. His eyes continue to catch mine, and in those moments, he looks more like he'd rather be all over me again instead. In the two weeks since our initial meeting with Dawn Patrol, since he dropped to his knees in front of my desk and made me see stars, Everett and I have had approximately twelve office make-out sessions, but I have had zero additional orgasms.

We agreed to sex, but I vetoed any more workplace...*incidents.* We have coffee in my office between meetings, or some days, I'll take my lunch down to the auto shop, and we eat in his office there. We talk and laugh. We kiss—a lot. But the first time we have sex—well, the second time—I'd like to be in private, with an unlimited timeframe. And a bed.

I don't want Everett over when my daughter is home. I don't want him in my bed when she's across the hall. I think she has caught on to the idea that there is something more than friendship going on between us but exposing her to that level of intimacy feels permanent. I don't want her thinking Everett is more to her—or to me—than what he is now. I don't want her thinking he's going to be in our lives forever when it's quite possible he'll stumble upon the love of his life on any given day and his priorities will change.

I won't break my daughter's heart by allowing her to believe a man is filling the void her father left until I'm confident I've found a man committed to being that for her, who'd stay for her even if he left me. I'm not always so sure I deserve love, but I know with certainty that my daughter does.

So, despite finally agreeing to hook up again, Everett and I have yet to do the deed. Darby and Leo have been too busy opening the flower shop, and even though I'm fairly certain Monica and Carlos would babysit for me any time I ask, the idea of saying, "Hey, can you watch my kid while I fuck yours?" seems to be a bit much for me.

Everett has been patient. I'm hopeful now that Honeysuckle Florals is open and Leo finally hired a wedding planner to help them out, I'll be able to convince them to take Lou for a night so I can stay with Everett. Though, another obstacle I can't let myself think about is how I'd even go about explaining that to my daughter.

I shake those thoughts away and glance at my sister, who's rubbing sunscreen into her tanned legs. "The grand opening was great, and it appears business is already booming."

Honeysuckle has been flooded with customers since its opening last weekend. Her store is all shades of pastel, with buckets of flowers lining the entrance and paintings in the windows. Walking inside feels like a warm spring day, like instant peace. She's exactly what the boardwalk needed. Darby has been dead set on handling things herself, refusing any marketing assistance from me or help from the small business initiative to get things up and running. She was determined to do it all on her own.

I think the flower shop became her way of proving she didn't just leave our hometown—our parents or her ex-fiancé—because Leo showed up one day and rescued her. She was on a journey to finding herself for a while, and all he gave her was the push she needed to take the leap. Darby's entire life, she has been taken care of, programmed by our father to believe she wasn't capable of doing so for herself. By taking care of her, he controlled her, and then he passed that control onto his associate Jackson when he essentially arranged their marriage.

The one time in Darby's life she found the courage and bravery to go against my parents was the summer she spent here in Pacific Shores. With Leo. Then, when she found out I was pregnant and locked in the house by our father, being forced into an abortion I didn't want to have, she stole our grandmother's car and attempted to make the drive from California back to Kansas—to rescue me. But not before she experienced her own kind of irreversible trauma, which ended a shattered spirit when my father was the one to ultimately cart her back to Crestwell.

All that courage and bravery—all her wild nature—died that day. I wasn't there, but I saw it in her eyes when she came home. She'd been broken, and seeing her here—thriving, laughing, living, and dreaming—it's like she has been put back together.

As much as Leo saved her, I know she wishes she could've saved herself first, and I think taking on this business is her way of doing so. Taking on this venture is brave and courageous, and while she might be my younger sister, I often find myself wishing I could be more like her when I grow up.

"I'm proud of you, Darby," I find myself saying.

She whips her head to the side, surprise in her hazel eyes. Her features soften as she smiles at me, reaching out to take my hand. "I'm proud of you too."

I squeeze her fingers before pulling away. "Where is my child, by the way?"

My sister laughs, throwing on her sunglasses and leaning back in her chair. She promised Leo she'd try to step away from the shop for a few hours this morning to watch the photoshoot, and Everett demanded I be here too. He said since I was the one who threw a fit about him not being included, it only makes sense that I also suffer through it. Although, I'm lying on the beach, watching Everett pose shirtless, so I'm not entirely sure what he meant by suffering.

"She's still assembling the little five-dollar bouquets for me." Darby smiles. "Monica is in there helping her, though. Once they run out of flowers, they'll probably come down here."

I nod, settling back in my own chair. It turns out that ten-year-olds aren't particularly interested in early morning photoshoots, and since they're doing it in front of the pier, I told Lou she could hang out in the flower shop instead, as long as she stayed with Monica or Darby.

The prospect of my daughter growing up in a town like this makes me smile. Having an aunt and uncle with shops on the boardwalk. I picture her growing up running around, working there in the summers when she's a teenager. It warms something in my chest. I want her to feel at home here. I want this town to be her home.

My eyes drift to Everett again. The director has both him and Leo knee-deep in the waves, the pier stretching out into the ocean behind them, and the morning sun bright on their faces. The water appears a translucent blue, lapping against Everett's hips and complementing the tone of his skin. He stretches his arms over his head, muscles in his stomach and chest flexing with the movement. My tongue sticks to the roof of my mouth as I watch him move and pose. Despite clearly being unfamiliar and uncomfortable with modeling, he looks flawless.

I study his arms and think about the way they feel holding me up when he wraps me around his hips and kisses me breathless. I watch his hands and think about the way they felt inside me, how they look when they're grabbing me, running along my skin.

I watch his chest move with his breath, reminding me of the way it feels pinned against mine when he presses me into a wall, the way it feels like he's breathing life into my body when he kisses me. My eyes finally find his face, and I realize he's watching me too. Smiling wide, he winks.

"You're drooling again, *cara*."

The sound of Monica's voice has me jumping in my chair, a gasp flying from my throat as my hand flies to my chest. "Fuck, Monica. You scared me."

"Mom," Lou drawls from where she stands next to Everett's mother. "A dollar."

Monica smirks at me. "I figure you'd have heard us coming, but you were...distracted." Darby chuckles from next to me. "You're no better," she chides my sister.

"I'm allowed to drool." Darby winks at me, raising her hand to flash her engagement ring.

I roll my eyes and take the beach bag from Monica's arms, unpacking Lou's towel, sunscreen, and her book. Darby and Monica talk softly about operations at the flower shop. It's the first time Darby is leaving it with only her staff—two college students she hired on—and I can see the nerves rippling off her, but Monica quietly assures her while I set up a spot for Lou between our chairs and beneath the umbrella.

Once Lou's settled in the sand and reading her book, my sister glances at me. "I..." She sighs. "I wanted to let you know that I've spoken to Mom."

I look at Lou to make sure she's not paying attention. I rarely mention my parents, and she rarely asks about them. They say kids are intuitive, and I think it's always been clear that my parents saw my child as nothing more than my biggest mistake. I think she always knew their love and affection was conditional, the same way I'd been able to see it since I was a child myself. She doesn't miss them, I don't think, but I try to recognize their existence as little as possible. Luckily, Lou is so engrossed in *Nancy Drew*, she's not paying an ounce of attention.

"Why?" I ask my sister. An uneasy sensation takes over my body.

"She called to congratulate me on the wedding," Darby says. "She found out from a tabloid. I felt kind of bad about that."

"You have nothing to feel bad for."

She nods. "I know. I just... I think she's a victim too. I know she's not perfect. She wasn't even a good mother. I just can't help but wonder what she'd have been like if he wasn't around, the same way I wonder if I would've become her if it wasn't for him"—she nods toward her fiancé in the waves—"or for you."

"You would've always found your way out," I say with conviction. "You're stronger than her." I shrug. "I can't find it in myself to care that she was weak. I can't find it in myself to accept that as an excuse." I know it's harsh, but it's true. "As a mother myself, there isn't anyone on this planet that could put me in a position where I would treat my child the way..." I trail off. My mother may not have been the one who locked me in the house or told me I was worthless. She may not have been the one to throw things or break doors, but she never stopped him, never defended us. "There is no amount of fear that would drive me to be like her, no amount of approval I could seek to do the things she's done or act the way she has." I look into my sister's eyes, glimmering gold in the sunlight. "I'm not sure there is anything that can be done at this point for me to forgive her either."

Darby lets out a long breath. "I think I might want to try. Not for her or for him, but just for me. I feel like it's what I need to let go of that part of my life and embrace everything I have now."

"I get it," I say, because I do. I understand why she feels the way she does, I just don't have it in me to feel the same. "But if she starts guilt-tripping you into coming home, if she brings up him, or Lou—"

"I've set clear boundaries. She knows I'll cut her off without a second thought." She chews on her lip. "Plus, she said Dad doesn't even know she's contacting me."

I nod.

"Will you be upset with me for speaking with her? Forgiving her?"

I grab her hand again, holding tightly. "Never. As long as you won't be mad at me for being unable to let it go."

"Never," she responds.

&

I'm half asleep before something dark covers the brightness behind my closed lids. I open one eye and find Leo standing over us, water dripping down his shirtless chest as he places his hands on his hips and smiles.

"Hi." My sister laughs. "Are you done?"

He shakes his head. "Just taking a break while they torture Everett." Swaying on his feet, he looks almost giddy about something, filled with anticipation. "Did you ask her yet?"

"Oh." Darby sits up. "No, I forgot. Lulu?" My sister shakes my daughter's shoulder.

"What?" Lou glances up at her, face scrunched and appearing aggravated for her reading time being interrupted.

"Wow." Leo lets out a slow whistle. "That's the same look Honeysuckle gives me when she's reading about cowboys and I try talking to her." My sister rolls her eyes, letting out a snort. "It's a little insulting, honestly," he continues. "Like, what could a cowboy offer you that I can't?"

"You know what they say," I chime. "Save a horse."

"That's weird. I thought the term was 'save a wave, ride a surfer.'"

Darby cups her hands around her mouth, letting out a low, "Boo."

Leo crawls over my sister, straddling her chair as he begins shaking his hair over top of her, water droplets flying all around him.

"Stop!" Darby shrieks with laughter. "You're getting me wet."

"Hell yeah, I am, baby." He nuzzles his face against her neck, kissing along her jaw. "I bet your cowboys can't do it like I can."

"¡Ya basta! Hay niños y suegras presentes," Monica shouts from Darby's other side. I'm not sure exactly what she's saying, but I assume it's something like "shut the fuck up" because that's what I'm about to start yelling too.

"Lo siento, mama," Leo mutters, climbing off my sister. Darby's cheeks are flushed, but her eyes glow with adoration.

He wraps his arms around my sister, lifting her and taking her seat before setting her down on his lap. My daughter looks back at them both with a scowl. "You guys are being loud."

"Sorry, Lulu." Leo laughs. "We have a question for you, though."

She lets out an exasperated sigh. "Okay, what is it?"

She has been really into those *Nancy Drew* books, and she gets irritable when interrupted.

"Will you be our flower girl?" My sister beams.

Obviously, we all expect Lou to say yes, but in a few weeks, Darby has a dress fitting at a bridal boutique in downtown Los Angeles. Apparently, she found her dress when she and Leo were in Portugal last summer, and it's being shipped to LA I thought it would be fun to bring Lou with us and let her pick out her dress while we are there. I told Darby and Leo she'd get extra excited if they made a big deal out of asking her, and Leo tends to make a big deal out of everything.

My daughter only lifts her brows at Leo and her aunt. "That depends," she says. "Is the wedding actually going to happen this time?"

Darby rears back, face deepening with shock. "The snark on you, kid."

"Lucille," I snap. "That was rude."

My daughter glances up at my sister before murmuring, "Sorry."

Leo only laughs. "It's okay to change your mind about something if it's not the right thing for you, Lulu." He strokes a hand down my sister's hair. "Sometimes, it takes a person a little while to figure out what's right for them, but it's okay to change your course if you find something better."

She seems to contemplate that for a second, regret flashing across her face. "And Jackson wasn't the right person for Aunt Darby?"

"Exactly."

"But you are?"

"Obviously."

"Why?"

"Because I'm cool?" He says it like an obvious answer, but there is a glimmer of amusement on his face at my daughter's questioning.

Lou gives him a bemused look, glancing at my sister for more of an explanation, like she's not entirely convinced. Darby laughs. "He's my person, Lulu."

"And that's who you marry? Your person?"

Darby smiles. "Yep."

Finally, she nods. "Okay, I'll be your flower girl."

My sister stands from Leo's lap, then squats down to the ground where Lou sits, wrapping my daughter in her arms and pressing a kiss to the top of her forehead. As she pulls away, Lou turns to me. "Is Everett your person, Mom?"

I feel my eyes all but burst out of my head, mouth dropping open. I glance at my sister, to Leo and Monica. All of them hold the same expression, eyes darting back and forth between Lou and me. Everett and I have been doing very little to hide our chemistry, not that it'd even be possible to ignore at this point, but I had no idea how openly I'd been wearing my emotions. Nerves explode through my chest at her question, but the answer on the tip of my tongue is: I hope so.

Knowing I can't admit that to her—to any of them—I simply stare, mouth gaping like a fish. "Oh... I—um." Frantically looking at Darby, I plead for help with my eyes. She only shrugs, like she has no idea how to respond either.

"Because I think he'd be a good one," Lou continues.

My mouth clamps shut, mind reeling. "Really?"

"Yeah." Lou nods nonchalantly, settling back on her towel and reopening her book. "If you married Everett, I think that would be cool."

Leo, Monica, and my sister blink rapidly, jaws dropped. None of us say anything, attempting to act casual at the suggestion my daughter just made. Nobody says a goddamn word, the silence thick and palpable between us. Eventually, though, Leo and Darby look at me with shit-eating grins, and I notice Monica's eyes growing a little watery.

I have no fucking clue how to react to any of it.

I turn my head, looking out at the horizon just in time to find Everett jogging over to us, none the wiser. I wait for him to slow to a stroll, to stop in front of me, but he doesn't. He continues running, barreling right up to my chair and grabbing me beneath the arms.

"What are you doing?" I gasp as he lifts me into his arms and tosses my body over his shoulder. Our family watches us curiously as he begins heading back toward the waves.

"I told you I was going to make you suffer with me." He laughs.

"See? They act like you two," I hear Lou say as Everett runs away with me in his arms. "I think he's her person because they're loud and annoying."

My chest flutters at those words, heart beating harder as Darby adds through laughter, "I think you might be right, kid." She gives me a knowing smile, but before I can react to any of it, Everett lowers me, holding me tight against his chest as he barrels into the ocean.

The water is stinging cold, nipping at my toes and legs, clinging to my clothes, biting my cheeks and nose. As swiftly as he pulled me under, Everett rises out of the water again. I throw my arms around his neck, legs wrapping around his waist. "What the *fuck*, Everett?"

The water is damn near freezing, it feels like. It's late

February, and despite being in Southern California, it's nowhere near swimming weather.

Everett only laughs against my ear. "You were looking a little sleepy over there. Relaxing too hard, I think." He adjusts his hold on me, scooping his hands beneath my ass. "I thought a little polar plunge could wake you up."

"You are crazy," I mutter.

He pulls back from my neck, smiling at me in a way that feels like spring, eyes a warm shade of amber in the bright light of the midday sun. All of him is warm, and despite being chest-deep in the frigid ocean, I don't feel the cold at all.

"Crazy about you."

I'm fully aware of our family watching us right now, including my daughter. I've tried to set boundaries, to keep her from realizing how deeply I feel for this man out of fear for her doing the same and both of us ending up broken later. It appears I've failed at that, though, because she has fallen for him as hard as I have.

"I see the way you look at me, Wildflower, and I want you to know that I'm seeing you the exact same way."

That's not possible, I think to myself. Because he's like the spring—warm and bright. I'm like the winter, like the water we're standing in now, frigid and cold.

"How am I looking at you?" I ask him anyway.

He drops his forehead to mine, and I can feel his lips move against my skin when he says, "Like you can't fight it anymore."

I can't. I should. For the sake of both of us—for all of us—I should.

Maybe I'm weaker than I thought, because instead of pulling away like a stronger, smarter woman would, I get closer. I feather my lips between his, cupping the back of his neck and pressing his mouth against mine. He groans, opening for me. The kiss is quick but deep, full of unspoken words neither of us know how to say.

I hear the distant whistles and cheers of our family from the shore.

All of us seem to be rooting for inevitable disaster.

Twenty-Nine - Wildflower

Are You My Good Boy?

"I saw his entire ass, Everett."

Laughter roars from the other side of my phone. "Wait—" He breathes through a fit of chuckles. "Can you explain the logistics to me again? I'm having a hard time picturing it."

"Why do you want to be picturing it?"

He only laughs harder. "Dammit, Dal. Just explain to me what happened again."

I sigh. "I walked inside the house after dropping Lou off at her friend's and..." I wince at the memory. "I turned the corner into the dining room to find... Well, I'd rather not repeat it. The point is, I saw Leo's bare ass and heard sounds coming from my sister's mouth that I never want to think about again."

"No, but—" Everett wheezes. "What was the position?"

"Why are you asking this?" I damn near shout, tears beginning to sting my eyes as I fight to hold back my own laughter. "I am traumatized, and you're supposed to be comforting me!"

"You said they were in the dining room." Everett's choking on the other end of the line. "Why would they be fucking in the dining room? Like...were they on the floor? The table? A chair? I need to know the logistics of this, Dahlia. It helps me understand the level of severity."

I'm laughing in earnest now. "My sister was laying on the table and Leo was standing and..." I shake my head. "Please don't make me explain anything else. It was horrifying." I'll never get the images out of my head.

"And now you're sitting outside on the front porch?"

"I didn't know what to do!" I exclaim. "I had to get the fuck out of there."

"You could've gone upstairs." He's laughing at me again.

"I panicked. I don't even have my car keys. I think I threw them."

I stretch my legs out on the front steps of the house, leaning back on one arm as the other holds my phone against my ear. My first thought when I ran out of the house was to get in my car and go find Everett. I was hoping to see him tonight anyway, but once I was outside, I realized my keys were no longer in my hand. So, I sat down on the porch and called him instead.

There is no reason I should have to suffer through this alone.

Once Everett finally catches his breath, he asks, "Where did you throw your keys?"

"At Leo, I think."

He begins laughing again.

"I'm hanging up."

"No, no! Don't hang up, baby. I'm sorry."

I snort at him just as my phone dings. I see I have a text message from my sister, letting me know I'm clear to come back inside the house. "Darby told me to come inside, but I'm scared."

He chuckles. "You'll be fine. At the very least, you've got to go get your keys so you can pick up Lou later."

"I don't, actually. She's staying over at her friend's house all night." A girl from school named Sofi. I've never been a huge fan of sleepovers, but the kids have been begging me for months. Sofi's parents are kinder to me than most others at Lou's school, and after letting her spend a handful of afternoons over at their house, I finally gave in.

"All night?" Everett asks.

"Yep," I hum, gathering up the courage to say what comes next—the whole reason I wanted to call him in the first place, really. "So, I was thinking—"

"Hey, Wildflower, I actually just pulled up to the bar. I'm meeting up with Ryan and Emilio to get a drink tonight. Can I call you later?"

Disappointment slams into my gut. My heart falls, and my stomach plummets to my feet. I swallow, attempting to sound unaffected. "Oh. Yeah. Sure. Have fun."

"I'll call you in a bit," he says again.

"Cool." I hang up.

Sea breeze, normally comforting and warm, blows across my arms, feeling prickly and cold. A sick feeling settles inside my stomach as I stand and head back inside. I softly open the front door, hoping my sister and Leo have retreated back to their bedroom, and I can quietly sneak up to mine. Instead, I find them both standing in front of the staircase, giving me awkward smiles.

Leo extends his hand toward me, my keychain hanging from his finger. "I believe these are yours. You hit me in the back of the head with them."

"Sorry," I murmur. "When you see a grown-ass man on top of your baby sister, the protective instincts kind of kick in."

The corner of his mouth tilts up. "The choking was consensual, Dahlia."

"I didn't see that." I shudder at the image it provides. "But thanks for letting me know."

My sister snickers, though her cheeks are bright with a blush. "I'm sorry. We assumed you'd be going to meet up with Everett after you dropped Lou off, and I guess we thought we'd have the house to ourselves for longer."

"Well"—I step around them, maintaining a wide berth—"I'm not meeting up with Everett. Sorry about ruining whatever else you two had planned." *I really need to get back to apartment hunting.* "I'm going to bed."

I don't miss the frown they both give me, but I don't give them the chance to push as I begin bounding up the stairs. Once I'm inside my room with the door shut behind me, I sigh against it. I hadn't told Everett about Lou's sleepover plans earlier because I wasn't sure I was going to follow through with allowing her to do it, and I didn't want to disappoint him.

I suppose I don't have any real reason to be upset with him; he had no idea I'd end up child-free for the evening. But it has been three weeks now since we've had any sort of hook-up, over six months since either of us have had sex—not since the night we met in that bar. I guess I expected him to drop everything for me, and there is no reason for me to hold him to that expectation. It just stings when I know I would've done it for him.

Not just because of the sex, but because I've been dreaming about what it'd feel like to fall asleep in his arms since the day I met him, especially since we began our nightly video calls back in November. I fall asleep to his face nearly every night, and I've wanted nothing more than to know what it'd feel like to drift off on his chest, heartbeat steady against my ear.

Disappointment and rejection coat my throat, and when I swallow, it feels as if all that emotion is stuck inside. I push past the choking sensation, breathing away the thickness and the heavy sting of tears behind my eyes. I refuse to cry over something like this.

Inhaling deeply, I step off the door and set my phone down on my nightstand before entering the bathroom. I decide I'm going to do a face mask, order Chinese food, and binge watch some awful horror movies or something. Yep. That's what I'm going to do.

I'm halfway through washing my face when I hear an incessant pounding that sounds like it's coming from downstairs. I turn off the faucet and dry my cheeks with a towel before tiptoeing back into my bedroom and quietly open my door, just enough to hear the commotion.

Irrationally, when I hear any kind of pounding on my door, I assume it's my father. I know that can't be true. I know it doesn't make sense, but the cowardice in me doesn't want to risk it. So, I wait, hoping Leo will answer instead. I can't see downstairs, but a moment later, I hear the front door creak, and two male voices begin speaking in hushed tones.

The door shuts, and the lock clicks. Laughter rings throughout the house before I hear Leo shout, "C'mon, Honeysuckle! Let's go take a walk down to the pier. I have a feeling this house is about to get real loud tonight."

Now, it's the stomping of footsteps up the staircase that has me backing away from my door. It flies open just as the back of my knees hit my bed, and suddenly, he's standing in front of me. He leans against the frame casually, his broad chest and thick arms taking up the entirety of the space around him. Muscles flex beneath his shirt, threatening to rip it to shreds. My eyes rake up his chest, snagging on his neck, watching his throat bob as he swallows. The tattoos on his skin seem to dance with the movement. As I find his eyes, I realize he's doing the same thing to me.

My skin pricks beneath his gaze, and I'm now aware that all I have on is a T-shirt. His fingers flex, fist clenching at his side, like he's fighting to stay still.

Like he wants to grab me.

"I thought you were meeting your friends," I say.

Everett cocks his head. "You honestly think I'm going to find out that I can get you all alone tonight and choose to spend my evening drinking shitty beer with a bunch of assholes in a dive bar instead?"

I pick at my nails, pretending to be unbothered. "I mean... That's what you said you were doing."

"I was fucking with you, Dahlia." He crosses his arms. "I had already been sitting in the bar parking lot when you called. I pushed you off the phone because I didn't want to talk and drive, and it had become imperative that I get my ass over here as quickly as possible."

I roll my eyes, glancing up to find a playful look in his. My instinct is to block out my feelings and pretend I don't care, pretend it doesn't matter to me if he's here or not. But I'm so goddamn sick of pretending. I spend my whole life pretending. Pretending I don't fear I'm a bad mother. Pretending I don't feel lonely. Pretending I'm not head over heels for the man standing in front of me.

Pretending I'm not afraid he's going to grow tired of me and walk away too.

I don't have the strength to pretend anymore, so I let him see all the vulnerability I'm used to hiding. I wear it plain as day on my face. "It made me feel like you didn't want me."

Everett's shoulders drop, jaw going slack, brows knitting at the center of his forehead. Deep-brown eyes fill with worry and regret. "Dahlia." He takes half a step into my room before stopping himself, and I realize it's because I haven't invited him in yet. "I'm desperate for you. I don't just want you. I fucking crave you." He shakes his head. "I'm so sorry. I was just... I thought..."

He was just playing around. He thought I'd find it funny.

I think if I wasn't so damaged, I probably would have. Everett makes me want to be playful and confident. He makes me want to be wild and have fun. I let my insecurities get in the way of that, because in the six months I've known this man, he's never done anything but show up for me time and time again. Remind me how badly he wants me. Look at me the way he is right now, everything he feels written across those brown eyes.

He makes me want to believe that I'm all the things he thinks I am, that I'm confident, desirable, and worthy, and I hate that I doubted him—doubted myself.

I let out an exasperated sigh. "Well, I guess you're just going to have to prove to me how desperate you are, then," I say, sitting back on the foot of my bed and crossing my arms. "What would you do for a whole night alone with me?"

"I'd do anything." He hesitantly steps into my room, pulling my door shut behind him, but he keeps himself pressed against it. "Anything you want, Wildflower."

I lean back on my forearms, and my shirt hikes up high enough to reveal the orange panties I'm wearing. I rub my legs together, drawing his attention there. "Would you beg?"

"Beg?" He huffs a laugh. "I'd fucking crawl."

I smirk.

Everett's jaw drops before snapping shut as he slowly lifts a brow. "That's what you want, Wildflower? Do you want me on my knees, pleading for another taste of that pussy?"

My breath hitches as I watch him slowly—so fucking slowly—slide down the length of my bedroom door until he hits his knees. "I'm entranced by you, Dahlia." He falls forward, bracing his weight on his arms. "Allured." He begins crawling at a glacial pace across the floor. "Obsessed."

Desperation and pride and subservience reflect on his face as he moves toward me. This man—masculine and strong—is crawling for me, at my mercy. It awakens something inside me, something I think may have been dormant my entire life. I never knew someone could crave another the way Everett appears to crave me, the way I know I crave him. I've never known a desire like this. I've never *been* desired like this.

My heart pounds erratically against my chest. Electric heat sparks in my blood and flows through my body, settling in my core. Part of me wants to meet him on the floor and show him how much I need him too, but something else—something I've never felt before—likes the control I have over him, the power he lends me.

Just as Everett reaches my feet, I pull them up onto my bed and sit up. "You know, because you convinced me you weren't coming over tonight...." I smile to myself as I decide what I want to do next. "I decided to play with my toys instead."

I keep my eyes on Everett, watching as his darken. He stays at the foot of my bed, studying me intently as I lean back and reach into the drawer of my nightstand, pulling out my vibrator. It's thick, long, and bright pink. "But maybe if you're lucky, I'll let you watch."

I crawl across my mattress, matching his earlier stride. His tongue snakes out to trace his bottom lip, breathing growing heavier as he takes me in. When I reach the end of my bed, I come to my knees again. Setting my toy down beside me, I slowly lift my T-shirt over my head and let it fall to the floor in front of him.

Where I used to fear this level of exposure, I now revel in it. All because of him.

I tower over him in nothing but my panties, and his gaze lingers on my body, eyes glued to my bare skin. I can see the outline of his cock through his joggers, massive and hard. The heaving of his chest and the quick, desperate breaths filtering through his parted lips make me feel powerful, playful and wild.

"Everett," I drawl, pulling his attention back to my face while I pick up my toy. "I think I need to get this nice and wet. It'll slide into my *tight, hot* little pussy so much easier that way." I smile as I watch his eyes flutter at my words, near-black with lust.

He's so lost in me right now, so pliant and willing to give me whatever I want. The way he looks at me makes me feel...beautiful, like I can take pleasure without shame, like I can bloom without wilting.

I run the bright pink toy through my palm, inching closer to the edge of the bed. With my free hand, I reach down and grasp his chin. I try to express my intention with my eyes, but the look in his tells me I can do anything I want.

"Open up for me, baby."

"*Fuck*." His jaw drops immediately.

"Are you my good boy?"

He frantically nods, sticking out his tongue as I slide the toy between his lips. I come alive beneath his gaze, sensation flooding through my core as I move my vibrator in and out of his mouth. He suctions his lips around it, bobbing his head in rhythm with my thrusts. The heat in his eyes radiates all across my flesh.

"You're good at that, aren't you?" I ask.

He hums around the cock in his mouth.

I allow him to continue sucking on it for a few more moments before I pull it away. I fall back on my bed, and he immediately moves to follow, but I stop him with a foot on his chest. "No, no." I click my tongue. "You're still in trouble." I settle back against my pillows, lifting my legs as I pull my underwear off and kick them in Everett's direction. "So, I'm going to make myself come, and while I do, you can beg me to let you make me come again when I'm finished."

"Fucking hell." Everett watches me intensely, chest heaving and jaw dropped as I slowly spread my legs and run my vibrator through my soaked center.

"Take your shirt off," I demand as I flick the switch on the toy. I start with a low vibration, circling my clit slowly, though the vibrator is doing much less for me right now than Everett is. Crossing his arms, he grabs the hem of his tee and pulls it off his head. Suddenly, I'm greeted with cut muscle, tanned skin, and all those fucking tattoos. "You're being so good for me."

He bites his lip, nodding rapidly while he watches me play with myself from the foot of my bed, still on his knees. I press the button twice, upping the level of intensity as I slowly slip the toy inside me. It fills me, pressure building in my stomach. The vibrating sends flutters to my clit, but it's Everett's hungry gaze that radiates sensation all throughout my body, lighting me on fire.

"Fuck," he groans, head falling back and eyes falling shut. "I swear to God, I'm going to punish you for this torment later."

I laugh breathlessly. I don't doubt he will. I know the man prefers to be the one in control, and he's relenting that power to me for my own satisfaction, which only makes me want him more. My toes curl as I start to pump inside myself faster. "Eyes on me," I command.

"Fuck me," he growls, head snapping down to meet my gaze again. "Dammit, Dahlia. Please. Let me touch you." He sits up, stretching over my bed to get a closer look, though his knees remain on the floor. "I'm being such a good boy for you, baby. I deserve my reward."

Those words send heat shooting through my spine. Pleasure coils in my core, drawing tight. I feel myself rapidly climbing toward that peak. "Keep telling me what you deserve."

He nods, licking his lips. "I'll make you feel so good if you let me, Wildflower. I'll worship that perfect body." He's panting as I move faster, pleasure sparking through my veins. My eyes are fighting to remain open and fixed on him. I'm so fucking close. "I'll make you see stars. Send you straight to heaven." He swallows thickly, moving closer. Mouth hovering over my ankle, he presses a soft kiss there. "I'll claim that pussy like it's mine, because we both know you belong to me."

With those words, my orgasm slams into me unexpectedly. Everything goes taut, and suddenly, I'm exploding, crying out for him as I'm swept up in the wave of my release. My back bows off the bed, and I ride it out before pulling my vibrator from between my legs and tossing it aside. Just as I open my eyes, before I've even had the chance to catch my breath, Everett's shooting across the bed and coming over top of me, like his own band just snapped.

He falls between my legs, and I know he can feel my wetness through his sweatpants, the way I can feel his hardness pressing against my stomach. His weight settles over me like a blanket, and I look up to find those amber eyes staring blazing through me. "You gonna let me make you feel good, Wildflower?"

I don't even answer. I simply grab the nape of his neck, fingers twisting in his hair, and haul his mouth to mine. He moans. I swallow it. His tongue slides against me, teasing and coaxing the same noise from my lips. I run my hands along his bare chest, feeling the muscles in his back move as he reaches up to grab my headboard. I savor the warmth of his skin, how smooth it is against the tips of my fingers, the way it elicits flames on mine wherever we touch.

He moves along my jaw and down my neck, lips dragging against my flesh and leaving fire in their wake. "Have I proven what a good boy I am, baby?" He bites into my collarbone, and I inhale sharply at the sting. "Are you going to let me fuck you now?"

He presses his hips into mine, hard length flush against my center. "Please," I whimper.

My hands continue their descent down his back, dipping into the waistband of his sweats and pulling hard. He laughs against my neck, pulling away and standing from the bed. His eyes don't leave mine as he slips them off, along with his underwear. Suddenly, Everett Ramos is standing in front of me completely naked, all broad muscle, smooth, tattooed skin, and the proud length of his hard cock. I feel my cheeks heating as I take him in, but I can't look away.

"You're beautiful," I whisper.

"Fuck," he groans. "Let me take control now, Wildflower. Can I do that?"

I nod, and it's all he needs before pouncing back on me.

All of his skin aligns with mine, absolutely nothing between us now. It has never been like this before, and my mind catalogs every place we touch. His hand comes behind my head, lifting it so he can press his mouth to mine. Our noses graze and our lips clash, my hands holding his arms as his chest presses against my breasts, his cock against my low belly. Our thighs and legs and toes align. My entire body is on fire. Nothing has ever felt this way before.

"I need you," I whimper.

He nods against me. "I know, baby. I know. I need you so bad." He pulls back, looking down at me with those soft brown eyes. An infinity of intimacy sparkles in his gaze. He brushes his thumb along my skin and smiles. "I've got condoms in my wallet."

He moves to get off me, but I squeeze his forearm, holding him steady. "I have an IUD," I say quietly. My mind is screaming at me. I've never done something like this before, but some baser instinct knows I won't be satisfied unless there is nothing in between us at all. "And I'm in the clear."

His eyes go wide, and he swallows thickly. "I'm clear too."

"You have to pull out, though," I add, hoping he doesn't press.

"I won't do anything you don't want me to do, Dahlia," he rasps. "Do you understand?"

I nod.

He shakes his head. "Tell me you understand. I need to hear you say it. Do you want me to grab a condom?"

"I understand. If you do something I don't like, I'll say so." I squeeze his arm again. "I don't want to use a condom, but I understand if you do. If you don't, then I want you to come anywhere you'd like...except inside me."

He flicks a brow. "That gives me a lot of options, Dahlia."

"Maybe you can try all of them and decide which you like best."

"God-fucking-dammit." His head falls against my chest. "You're perfect. I swear, you're perfect for me." He pulls back, sitting on his knees and fisting his length in one hand. "I've never fucked without a condom before. Never really wanted to."

I open my mouth to backtrack everything I said before, thinking I've gone too far, but he continues before I have the chance, "Until I met you. Since that first night, Dahlia, I've dreamed about it. What it'd be like to fuck you raw, to feel you come all over my cock."

My jaw snaps shut, a sound of need erupting from my throat. That seems to be all he needs as he swipes his length through my center. His head flicks against my clit, and a moan falls from my mouth.

Leaning forward, he grabs the back of my neck and pulls me up. "I want you to watch me enter you for the first time bare, Wildflower. I want you to see what we look like joined together." Keeping one arm braced on the mattress beside me, he knots his fingers in my hair, pressing our foreheads together. My nails dig into his arms, and we both look down to where his cock notches at my entrance.

He slowly slides inside me, and I watch his length disappear between my legs little by little, stretching me open and filling me up until I'm deliciously aching with him inside. Once he's fully seated, and I feel him hit my most inner walls, a rough moan flies from my mouth, and he catches it with his own, tongue slipping between my lips as he leans forward, both of us falling onto the mattress. His hand stays behind my head, softening my landing. His other arm stays braced on the headboard, keeping his weight off me.

Everett begins moving in and out of me in perfect rhythm. I hook my legs around his back and lift my hips to meet his thrusts. "*Estas tan mojada. Tan estrecha. Eres perfecta, cariño,*" he rasps against my lips. "*Todo lo que siempre he querido. Te necesito para siempre. Dime que eres mía. Por favor. Mía, cariño. Sé mía.*"

His words send sparks across my skin. Fireworks explode behind my closed eyes, a flood of heat spreading to my core. I feel myself tightening around him as he continues pumping deep inside me, that pressure building at my center. "*Mierda. Me estás matando.*"

"What are you saying?" I moan, desperate to understand him.

He shakes his head against my mouth. "I don't know. I can't..." I lift my hips, meeting his thrust again. "Fuck. I can't think straight. It's too good, Dal. It's too." Thrust. "Fucking." Thrust. "Good."

My nails dig into his back as my body tenses and trembles, rapidly climbing toward that peak. Everett sits up, towering above me, though he doesn't stop moving. Gripping my hips hard enough to bruise, he slams into me again. My moans grow louder, more urgent, as his soft palms run down my thighs, hooking beneath my knees and pushing my legs forward, forcing his cock even deeper.

"Everett," I cry. He's so deep, I can hardly breathe, as if his being is buried inside my soul. I don't think I'll ever get him out. I know this is something I'll never feel with someone else. I could die from this, from his movement and his breath and his cock hitting all the places that make me lose my mind.

I feel myself nearing that edge, and when he places my legs on his shoulders, folding me in half, I begin free-falling into bliss. I throw my head back on my pillows, eyes screwed shut, stars dancing behind my lids. Suddenly, it's the pad of his thumb I feel on my clit, rubbing tight circles. That's all it takes to send me spiraling, body tightening, that pressure in my core ready to burst.

"Fuck, Dal," he groans. "Fuck. Fuck. I can feel you, baby. I can feel it."

I can't form coherent words; all I can do is scream. I think something like *Everett* and *coming* and *Jesus-fucking-Christ* is flying from my mouth, but I'm not sure. An orgasm rushes through me, and I get the faint sense of emptiness, but I'm too far gone to tell, my climax already flooding my senses. Suddenly, I feel something wet and soft at my entrance, and I cry out as my body bows off the bed. Heat licks up my spine, and I'm shattering beneath him, all over him.

I open my eyes to find Everett's face between my legs, tongue inside me, lapping up my release, causing another orgasm to crash over me, filling his mouth and soaking my sheets.

"Everett. Fuck. Everett." My hands tangle in his hair, and I'm too far gone to stop myself from grinding on his tongue as I ride out the remnants of my climax.

Once I'm entirely spent and too sensitive to handle the sensation of his mouth on me, I push his head away with my hand, and he sits up on his knees. He swipes a thumb across his lips, revealing a wicked grin where my release still drips off his chin. "If I stayed inside you while you were coming like that, I was going to come too." He gives me a playful shrug. "Plus, I couldn't resist getting another taste."

My eyes roll back, and that fluttering sensation spreads throughout my core again. "Why didn't you want to come?" I find myself asking.

That wicked grin turns devilish. "Because I haven't punished you yet." Before I can even comprehend his words, he's gripping my hips and flipping me over so I'm on my stomach. "Lift that ass in the air, baby." I comply immediately, and one broad hand lands between my shoulder blades, pressing my face into my pillows.

He grabs both of my arms, pinning my wrists behind my back. Placing my hands palm down on each side of my ass, Everett roughly demands, "Spread it for me, Dahlia."

Thirty - Wicked

What Have I Become To You?

"Spread it for me, Dahlia."

She listens, grasping each one of her ass cheeks in a hand and pulling them open. A soft moan floats out of her mouth, muffled by the pillows. I have a perfect view of her wet, satisfied pussy, still leaking for me, and her tight ass, begging to be played with too. The sight alone is enough to make me blow my load, but I hold back, because I'm nowhere near done with her yet.

I gather saliva on my tongue, letting it drip down between her cheeks the same way I did all those weeks ago in her office. She hisses at the sensation, a low, guttural moan erupting from her mouth as I run my finger through her wet pussy and up to her ass, smearing her release around the tight hole. "You said you like your ass played with, yes, Wildflower?"

"Yes," she whimpers into the mattress.

I laugh roughly, slipping my pointer finger inside. "Has your ass ever been fucked?"

"Just with fingers."

I grunt in approval, unable to help the possessive pride that washes over me. "I'm going to be the first man to fuck this tight ass." I'm going to be the last, too, but I don't say that. "Not tonight, though." I laugh again. "Well, at least not with my cock."

I hear her gasp as I continue pumping into her, leaning across the bed to grab her vibrator. I pull out of her, holding the toy while

I knot my freehand in her hair, twisting and hauling her up so she's flush against my chest. The sound of surprise that falls from her mouth is sweet and soft, causing my cock to jump, flexing at her back.

I pull her head until it snaps back, big blue eyes fixed on me. They're the color of the sea after a storm. I smile at her, bringing my mouth to hers and planting a soft kiss there. As I move back, I nudge the toy between her lips. Her eyes, still on me, widen with surprise. "Open for me, baby," I mimic her words from earlier, and she listens effortlessly. "Can you taste your pussy?"

She moans around the vibrator, eyes fluttering closed as she nods her head. I pump the toy in and out a few times before dropping it down her chin, dragging along the column of her neck. "I'm going to fuck your ass with this," I say, circling her pert nipple with the bright pink dildo, "while I fuck your pussy with my cock." She shudders as I move to her other breast.

"God, I love these tits. You're flawless, Wildflower." Slowly, I slide the toy down her stomach and between her legs, swiping it back and forth between her slit. "Look at you, Dal, getting this all soaked." Once the vibrator is good and wet, I pull it out between her thighs, moving quickly as I press her back down on the pillows. She moans into the bed, and I rub the toy along her ass.

My cock is fucking throbbing. I was so close to coming, I had to pull out. Then, as I watched her squirting all over the bed, I couldn't stop myself from getting another taste of it. Now, I'm aching to get back inside of her.

"Are you ready, baby?" I ask.

"Yes," she cries.

Flipping the switch, I set the vibrator to a low, dull level and press it lightly against her tight hole. She groans, and I move as slow as I can, spitting again. The tip of the toy slips inside her, and she cries out at the intrusion. "You okay, Dal?"

"Yes." She nods into the mattress. "Good. So good."

I hum in approval, pressing it in another inch before retreating. I continue this motion, feeding it into her little by little, until she can comfortably take it all the way. Her moans grow louder with each thrust of the toy inside her. Once it's fully seated, I turn it up to the highest level.

She jumps at the sensation, crying into the pillows as her body flies forward on the bed. I grip her hips and pull her back to me, delivering a light smack to her ass. "Stay still, baby."

Her body begins to tense, and I grip her side as I slide back inside her pussy. She's so fucking wet. I begin thrusting, picking up a punishing pace as I fuck her with my cock and her toy in sync.

"Everett," she moans, my name sweet fucking music coming from her mouth. "I'm so full."

"I know, baby. You're taking it so fucking well." Her hands claw at the sheets, body quivering beneath me. I can feel the vibration of the toy against my cock, and I'm pulsing so hard, it hurts. I know I'm not going to last long in this position—her ass in the air, her pussy filled with me, and soft moans flying from her mouth. She's so goddamn tight, so wet and warm. "You feel so good, Dal."

She cries my name, her thighs trembling wildly beneath me. Pleasure zips down my back, settling in my spine, and I know I'm about to lose my goddamn mind. I said I was punishing her by fucking her ass and her pussy at the same time, but I'll be damned if I don't make her come like this.

"Reach between your legs and touch your clit. Give me one more." My tone comes out gruff and commanding. She immediately listens, small hand sliding beneath her stomach. "That's my good girl."

I start fucking her harder, faster, matching the rhythm of her fingers beneath us. Her body tightens, voice growing hoarse with the volume of her moans. I grip her ass with both hands, folding forward and pumping into her with everything in me.

"Come for me, Dahlia," I growl, desperate to feel her lose herself one more time before I do. I bring my mouth to her shoulder, biting down. I'm so deep at this angle, the feel of the vibrator so intense, I'm damn near cross eyed.

Finally, her entire body stills, pussy gripping my cock impossibly tight, almost as if she's swelling, that pressure readying to burst. "Everett!" she screams, and that's when I feel it happen. The gush of her release is so intense, it pushes me out of her as she climaxes. Her body erupts in quivers, going slack as she sinks into the bed.

White hot pleasure explodes at my base, and my cock pulsates. I grip my base, a groan flying from my throat as I pump myself, spurting across her ass and her lower back. I keep fucking my hand, expelling every last drop of my release across her skin, reveling in the way it looks to mark her. "Fuck. Dahlia. Yes, baby."

Her body shakes beneath me, the vibrator still going off inside her. I pull it from her ass, and she lets out a long sigh as I click it off and toss it onto the floor. Both of us are panting, attempting to catch our breath. I drag my lips across her sweat-slicked shoulders, kissing the base of her neck.

"Are you okay?" I whisper against her ear.

She nods. "I think I'm dead."

"No, baby." I laugh. "Just thoroughly fucked." I kiss her shoulder a few more times, still coming down from the high of fucking her, the unreal feeling of being inside her, of watching her come undone around me. I sigh contently against her skin before pulling back and standing from the bed. Darting into her ensuite bathroom, I grab a washcloth from the shelf above the toilet, step back into her bedroom, and wipe off the remainder of my release from her back and ass.

Dahlia rolls onto her side as I toss the towel inside the bin in the corner of her room. She gives me a soft, sated smile, and the look on her face has my cock stirring again. In the low light of her room, with flushed cheeks and swollen lips on display for me, I think she's the most beautiful thing I've ever fucking seen. Still, I notice that she keeps an arm draped across her chest, hand tucked beneath her breast and covering herself.

"Why are you hiding from me?" I ask, nodding at the way her arm is positioned.

She swallows, shrugging shyly. "They're all droopy when I lay on my side without a bra on. I've got to hold them up."

I cock my head. "Are you doing that because it's more comfortable for you, or because you think I won't like the way they look naturally?"

Her eyes drop, answering the question for me.

I don't respond. I simply walk up to the bed and bend down, scooping one arm beneath her knees and the other around her back. She looks at me with a confused expression, but I haul her into my arms anyway. She wraps hers around my neck as I carry her into the bathroom, before flipping on the shower and setting her down inside the tub. She stands in the corner, arms hanging in front of her body, hands clasped together, studying me as I wash my hands then test the water, making sure it's warm enough before stepping inside with her and drawing the curtain behind me.

I softly press my hand against her shoulders, guiding her beneath the running water. "Is it too hot? Too cold?"

"Perfect," she murmurs.

I smile, standing behind her. I pull her hair back behind her head, letting the shower wash over her. Grabbing the shampoo from the shelf next to me, I pop the cap and squirt some into my hand. Rubbing my palms together, I then begin massaging my fingers through her hair, lathering the product until it foams.

As we let the shampoo rinse, I kiss her shoulder before following my previous step with conditioner, keeping to her ends. Next, I grab her body wash, and I realize it's the thing that always has her smelling like coconuts and my personal paradise. I spin her around to face me before dripping the soap into my hand. Starting at her shoulders, I softly run my hands along her collarbone and down her arms, spreading the bubbles across her skin. "You know what I love about your body, Dal?" I ask.

She hums, seemingly transfixed on all the places I touch her, but when I lift my head to meet her eyes, she does the same.

"Everything," I say quietly. "You know blue is my favorite color?" She shakes her head, and I nod. "I love blue because it's so varied. There are a thousand different shades of it in the ocean alone, depending on the depth of the water and the color of the sand, the way it reflects the sun and sky. It's ever changing, always beautiful. I love the color blue because I convinced myself I've seen all its shades. Living on the beach, in a place with as much sunshine as is found here, I've seen every variation of the sea and sky." She blinks at me, and I dissolve beneath the intensity of her gaze. "But the shade of blue staring back at me right now?" I let out a breath. "That shade only exists inside your eyes. It's my favorite one."

Her breath catches, but I continue, sliding my hands down the center of her chest. "I love your lips because when they touch mine, I'm reminded of what it's like to feel something. I love your mouth because it says such sweet things to me." I smile. "Such filthy things." She blushes. "I love your mind because it challenges me and intrigues me and makes me think about the world differently. I love the way your brain works. I love the way you speak and think and feel."

Next, I cup her breasts in each hand. "I love these," I say. "Because they're beautiful and full, and they make me hard as fuck." She dips her head, hiding a bashful laugh. "But I also love them because they fed your daughter. They made her healthy and happy, and that's important to me. I understand why you struggle with the way your body looks now, but I need you to know that I find every piece of you perfect, even the things you see as flaws. When you feel like you have to hide from the rest of the world, I don't want you to feel like you have to hide from me."

When Dahlia looks at me, there is emotion shining in her eyes, but she only nods.

I slowly move down her body, squatting to my knees so I'm face to face with her navel. I run my thumb across the puckered scar at her abdomen. She shudders at the touch. A few faint stretch marks run along the length of her torso. "I love this because it grew one of my favorite people." I flutter my eyes up to her, and she's staring down at me with tears in her gaze. "I admire so much about your body, Dahlia, but most of all, this." I touch the scar again. "The strength and bravery it took to carry her, to birth her, all on your own. You deserved better. You deserved love and support. But even without it, you're an incredible mother. She's an incredible kid. I'm in utter awe of you every day. These scars only add to that."

Her mouth falls open before clamping shut again, as if the words are lost on her.

"I love these legs too. I love the way they feel wrapped around my face." I smirk. "I love that they carried you into that dive bar—right into my life." I press a kiss to her thigh. "When I look back on that night, I realize I think I'd been waiting for you all along. I just didn't know it yet. I was going through the motions. Living, but not thriving. No direction. No purpose. Then, you walked in with that fucking guy, and my world flipped on its axis. You're the only thing I've seen ever since."

"Everett," she whispers, her hands finding their way through my hair.

"I knew your name. Years ago, Darby talked about you all the time. Her wild and free older sister. Her best friend. She talked about how much you'd love Pacific Shores and all of us. How much she missed you." I bring my hands to her hips, holding her tight against me. "I knew your fucking name, Dahlia. You were so goddamn close, and yet so far away from me. If I had asked more questions, asked to see a picture, would it have clicked?" I breathe against her soft, sweet skin. "Would I have seen your face and known instantly what you would become to me? Could I have been the one to save you from that house? Help you escape it?"

I voice the thoughts that haunt me in the deepest darkness of the nights when I can't sleep, when I listen to the sound of her breathing on the phone and revel in the peace my presence brings her.

"What have I become to you?" she whispers, as if she's afraid to ponder those questions too.

I lift my head and find my whole world in that sapphire gaze. "My purpose."

Thirty-One - Wicked

All My Nights, Preferably.

I'm pulled from the best sleep I've had in years—maybe ever—by the sound of rustling and a prolonged groan. I crack one eye open, adjusting to the darkness. In the moon-lit room, I can make out Dahlia's form sitting up in bed, and as I raise my head, I find her beautiful face cast in the blue light of her phone.

She's frowning, sliding a thumb across her screen and holding it to her ear. "Hello?"

I shuffle next to her, rising up on an elbow and catching her attention. Even in the muted colors of the night, Dahlia's blue eyes are bright as stars. Her brows are pinched, and she chews on her lip nervously as she studies my face.

Everything okay? I mouth.

She shrugs, eyes going unfocused when she zones back into the conversation. "Hi, Amy. Is everything okay?"

Her leg is bouncing up and down, and my stomach twists in knots as I try to think of ways to quell her anxiety. She's biting her nails while she listens to who I assume is the mother of Lou's friend. I run my hand up and down her thigh, halting her trembling limbs.

She sighs at my touch, and I take it as a sign to sit up and wrap my arm around her shoulder as she leans against me. I can faintly make out the woman's voice while she explains that Lou supposedly had a bad dream and wanted to come home early from her sleepover.

I have no fucking clue what time it is, but it has to be early. Dahlia and I fell asleep sometime just before midnight. Once I was on my knees in the shower with her, my head found its way back between her legs again, and I didn't come up for air until she was coming on my tongue. After that, she had her way with me, mouth like fucking heaven around my cock as water pounded against my chest. I'll never be able to get the way she looked—soft, pink lips, bright eyes, and skin wet and smooth as she sucked the soul from my body—out of my head.

When we finished, I changed the sheets while she got ready for bed, and then we laid together, watching stupid movies and talking about nothing. It felt...easy, like it was always meant to be this way. It felt like something I could do every night for the rest of my life, and even if it became inconsequential—routine—I'd never grow tired of it. I'll never be bored with Dahlia—listening to her speak, watching her laugh. Something about her feels etched into my bones, like I found something I didn't know I was searching my entire life for.

I've always thought Pacific Shores was home to me, but now, I wonder if it's just where I live. Because falling asleep beside her... That was the first time in my life I've felt that soul-deep belonging I think truly bears the meaning of the word. She feels like home.

"I'm so sorry." Dahlia sighs, breaking me from my train of thought. "I'll head over to get her right now." She looks at me then, and I realize the moisture welling up in her eyes as she nods, says goodbye, and ends her call.

"What's going on, Wildflower?"

She raises a shaking hand to her face, wiping away her tears before they have a chance to fall down her cheeks. "It's not a big deal," she says. "I don't know why I'm overreacting. Lou just decided she wanted to come home."

"What time is it?" I ask.

"Just after four." She throws the blankets off her legs and stands out of bed before rummaging around the room rapidly as she searches for clothes. "She had a bad dream, or so she says. She never has bad dreams." Dahlia hops on one foot as she pulls a pair of underwear up her legs. "I shouldn't have let her stay the night somewhere. I should've known she wasn't ready for that." Her voice cracks, and I know she's fighting back tears again. "Or maybe I shouldn't have coddled her so much."

"Baby, don't cry." I don't know what to do, how to help her. "Do you want me to go get her?"

She pauses, almost like she's contemplating it, before shaking her head and grabbing a sweatshirt from her closet. "No. That would just confuse her."

"Do you... Do you want me to leave?" I ask as she pulls her hoodie on. When her head pops out of it, I see devastation on her face, and then she crumbles entirely. Her face falls into her hands, and her shoulders shake with silent tears. I'm jumping out of bed and rounding her room before I tug her against my chest. "Dahlia. Baby," I hush her. "What's going on?"

"This is so stupid," she cries into my neck.

"What's stupid?"

She shakes her head. "I feel horrible."

I'm so fucking confused. I'm sure she's tired—groggy and confused, worried about Lou. It's not an ideal ending to our first night together, but I don't know what's got her in tears or feeling bad about it.

"It's okay, Dal. We'll have more nights together." *All my nights, preferably.*

She sighs, stepping back from my arms and wiping at her eyes. I watch as her mask falls into place. The vulnerability that she still only gives me glimpses of disappears. "I don't want you to leave," she says firmly. "But I'm not ready for her to see you spending the night here."

"I understand." She moves her head to nod, but I'm quicker. Taking her face between my hands, I add, "But I need you to stop hiding from me. I need you to tell me how you feel right now and let me help you work through it. You're done bottling that shit up."

I prepare myself to watch those walls lock into place, for her to become stubborn and guarded like I'm used to. There is a hardness to her features that makes me believe she's about to do exactly that, but instead, she softens, nuzzling her cheek against my palm. "I..." She takes a breath, and I think she's about to say something, but she must think better of it, because she pulls away. "I've really got to go get her."

"All right." I swallow, allowing her space to step back and slip on her shoes. "I'm going to stay, though. I'll keep out of the way and make sure she doesn't see me when you get home, but I'd like to stay. I want to be here for you when you get back." She looks up from her feet, and I watch her throat work as she contemplates what I've just said. "Please, let me be here for you, Dahlia."

Whatever thread of resolve she was hanging onto seems to snap, because her eyes go soft and misty, her lips tremble, and she gives me a slight nod before slipping out of her bedroom. I listen to her descend the stairs and grab her keys, leaving through the front door.

While Dahlia is gone, I sneak downstairs and make her a cup of chamomile tea. On my way back up, I notice that Lou's bed doesn't have any sheets on it. I assume Dahlia was going to wash them while she was away for the night. I find the bundle in the dryer and warm them up then make her bed for her.

I'm just finishing when I hear the front door unlock, followed by the sound of hushed voices. I slip down the hall into Dahlia's bedroom, shutting myself in her bathroom just in case Lou comes in. The voices seem to bypass Dahlia's room, and it's another ten minutes of silence before I hear her door creak open.

"Everett?" she whispers.

I exit the bathroom to find her sitting on her bed, eyes appearing bloodshot, body drooping with exhaustion. "How's she doing?"

"She's fine, I think." Dahlia shrugs. "Embarrassed."

"She has nothing to be embarrassed about."

"I know." She sighs. "I think it was just a bit much for her.

She's a homebody. I think being outside her safe space is scary for her. It probably would've been better for her to have a sleepover at her own house first." Dahlia's voice cracks as she adds, "But this isn't her house. I don't even have a home for her."

Her face falls into her hands as a soft sob breaks from her throat.

"Dal," I whisper, sitting down beside her. I don't know what more to do than wrap my arms around her back and pull her into me, allowing her to cry against my chest. "This is her home, both of you. Just because Leo's name is on the deed doesn't mean you don't belong here. It was your grandma's house, and he bought it exactly for this reason, so that her family could continue to make it theirs."

She doesn't respond, but the tears continue to fall. I don't know how to make this better. "She could have friends over here any time. You know they wouldn't care."

She sniffles. "Leo's a celebrity. I can't have random people invading his space like that."

"D-List at best." I snort. "Lou could have friends sleep over. Nobody is going to give a shit."

A small laugh bubbles out of her, and I instantly settle at the sound of it.

"I was so frustrated by her," Dahlia continues. "I just wanted one fucking night to myself. One night without having to worry about her." Her voice breaks again. "I feel so guilty for being upset. A mother shouldn't want space from her own child. I don't want to ever make her an imposition. I know what it's like to feel that way, and I don't ever want to do that to her."

Short, rapid breath filters from her lips, and I know it's because she's trying to stay quiet. She's afraid of her daughter hearing her break down.

"You've never made her feel that way." I press my lips to her head. "You're her safe place. She knows that." I stand from the bed, reaching for the hem of her shirt. She looks up at me with red-rimmed eyes but lifts her arms without hesitation. I pull her hoodie off and toss it into the hamper in the corner of her room before pulling back the sheets. "Get into bed."

I hear the shuffling of blankets as she gets comfortable, and I round the room to the other side, grabbing the tea I made from her dresser.

As I crawl in beside her, I pass her the mug. "Chamomile with honey."

"Everett." She sighs. "Thank you." Taking a sip, she asks, "You made her bed too, didn't you?"

I nod. "You're her safe place, but I want to be yours."

Her hands tremble as she places the tea on her nightstand and turns to face me. "Why?"

Because I love you so much it fucking hurts.

I open her arms and pull her into me. "Because you deserve it. Because you make me feel safe too."

Her head falls against my chest, her hand over my stomach. I inhale the scent of her coconut body wash and savor the feel of her warmth against me.

"I feel safe with you," she whispers. We lie in comfortable silence for a while longer as I stroke her hair. Only the unsteady rhythm of her breathing lets me know she's still awake. It was just a few weeks ago that she told me she was afraid she couldn't offer me more than sex, but whatever has happened tonight feels like a whole hell of a lot more.

I'm not sure if she realizes that yet, so I decide not to say anything.

"Why do I feel like a bad mom all the time?" she asks, so quiet I'm not entirely sure she's even addressing me.

"The fact that you even have these kinds of thoughts proves exactly how good of a mother you are," I respond anyway. "You question it because you care, because you've been navigating this alone her whole life, and because you didn't have an example to go off of." I press my lips to her forehead. "You're an incredible mother, Dahlia. Coming from someone who grew up with a great one, I can say that with certainty. Anyone who knows you, who sees you with her, would agree. There's no need to worry your pretty breath with thoughts like that."

She sighs sleepily. "Breath isn't pretty."

I huff a laugh at the random train of thought, hoping it's a sign that what I've just said has gotten through to her.

"Yours is," I continue. "When you moan into my mouth, it tastes pretty. When you breathe against my neck, it feels pretty. When you whimper as I push inside you..." I groan. "Most beautiful fucking sound I've ever heard." She turns her head, nuzzling into my neck, and it's as if I can feel her smile against my skin. "Everything about you is pretty, Wildflower."

"Not everything," she whispers. "Everyone has some ugly in them too."

"Then show me yours." I tuck a piece of hair behind her ear. "I want to see it. I want to see all of you." I know there's nothing about her I'd ever find ugly, even her darkest parts. But as long as she's convinced there are pieces of her that need to be hidden, I'm going to work to convince her to let me see them anyway.

Maybe someday, I'll help her find a way to see beauty in every aspect of who she is.

Dahlia pulls away from my neck and looks up at me. Every conceivable emotion shines in her eyes—fear and sorrow and insecurity, but also gratitude and vulnerability and something that looks a hell of a lot like love.

"Why would you want to see my ugly sides?" she asks.

I smile, running my thumb along the soft skin of her cheek. "Because showing me your ugly and watching me stay is the only way I'm gonna prove to you how real this is."

I watch her search my face the way she always does, looking for the lie. I know it's her defense mechanism, what she trained herself to do because of how much of her life has been spent being lied to and manipulated.

So, I don't just tell her the truth in those words—I let her feel it too. Snaking my fingers around the back of her head, I pull her into me. Her lips land on mine with a soft and delicate caress. She moans, opening for me as my tongue sweeps in to meet hers. I let out a groan at the taste of her, and she matches my sounds as she inches closer to me, hand knotting in my T-shirt.

"Everett," she whimpers, pulling away. It's a smile I see on her face now. "We've got to be quiet, and I can't be quiet when you're doing that to me."

I chuckle, moving down the bed and tugging her against me so we're both lying on our sides, facing each other.

She stares at me for a while, running a finger down my nose and over my lips, studying my face. I wonder if she catalogs me the same way I do her, wanting to engrain every detail of the other until it's tattooed in our minds, almost like we're afraid we'll lose it.

"You're sure you still want real now that you've seen what it looks like?"

"What do you mean?"

"Waking up at four in the morning when my daughter needs something." She laughs sarcastically. "Sex once every three weeks." Swallowing hard, she adds, "Knowing that I'm always going to put her first."

"First of all, Dahlia, I wouldn't want you so much if you didn't put her first. That's one of the things I lo–like most about you. I want what's best for Lou every bit as much as you do, and I hope you know she's my priority too." I watch her eyes gloss over as she nods. "Secondly, I waited six months to have sex with you again. Three weeks is nothing. I'm not in this because I want to fuck you. I'm in this because I want *you*. Period. Plus, after you walked in on Leo and Darby today, they're definitely going to be owing you one, and I plan on using that to my full advantage." She stifles a giggle, rolling her eyes. "Lastly," I continue, "I let you put a dildo in my mouth tonight. It's going to take a lot more than your daughter needing you to scare me away."

Her jaw drops open, face flooding with heat even in the dark. "Did you not like that? I thought..." She drops her gaze. "I thought you would've been into it."

I give her an easy smile. "Because I'm bi?"

"Yeah," she says quietly. "I thought you'd probably..."

"Sucked a dick before?"

"Yeah." She's so fucking bashful, it's cute.

"I have." I grab her chin and tilt her head upward. "And I was into it." I place my thumb on her full bottom lip, pulling it down as she watches me with wide, sparkling eyes. "But I also like to be in control. It takes a lot of vulnerability for me to be submissive like that. I've never allowed myself to be that way with someone before."

"Oh." Her pretty little mouth pops open, and suddenly, my cock is hard. "So...why did you let me?"

"Because it makes me feel good to see you feel good." My tone is turning rough, and I know we can't fuck again with the house this goddamn full of people. "Because I know that you don't take much for yourself," I continue, reveling in the way the soft skin of her thigh slides between my legs. "Peace. Rest. Pleasure. You do a lot of shit for a lot of other people, and I want you to feel comfortable taking what you need from me. I think you need that power and control sometimes, and I want to give you that. I want you to feel safe taking it."

"I've never thought of it that way before," she says on a breath. I watch her pupils dilate, and I wonder if she's replaying the night in her head the way I am. If the brush of my thumb against her lips reminds her how it felt in her ass. If she's remembering the way she wrapped her mouth around my cock in the shower, or the way she took it as I pounded into her from behind.

The memories are delicious and enticing, but I summon the will to remain on topic, knowing there are more conversations to be had about how far we'd gone.

"If you decide you didn't like what we did tonight, we don't ever have to do it again. If you decide you want to do more, then we'll try it." I slip my thumb into her mouth, and she wraps her lips around it, licking the pad of my finger. *Fuck*. "I want to explore with you, Dahlia." My words come out a near growl. "I want you to feel comfortable exploring with me. I want you to show me everything..." I pull my hand away from her mouth and replace it with my lips. "Not just in the bedroom, but in all aspects of your life. I'll be your safe place to land."

"I know," she says quietly, a radiant smile stretching across her face.

I return it, feathering my lips against hers again, kissing her softly. "Go to sleep, Wildflower."

"What about in the morning? Are you going to sneak out before she wakes up?"

I turn on my back, bringing her face to my chest and placing my hand on the top of her head, running my fingers through her hair. "I don't want you to worry about that, okay? I'll take care of everything. Shoulder some of it onto me from now on." Pressing my lips against her temple, I add, "For now, just go to sleep and know I'm right here."

She stills for a moment, as if contemplating whether or not she can trust me. Finally, she silently nods, settling against my body. My entire being comes alive at that knowledge.

I lie in the dark, listening to the sound of her breath long after she falls asleep.

Thirty-Two - Wildflower

Little Thread Of Gold

"Okay, but do you know what the invisible string theory really is? It can't be your favorite song if you don't know what it means." The deep, familiar voice resonates with me as I step off the bottom stair into the dining room.

I woke up in bed alone, on my own. Lou and I have a deal: I wake her up on school days, but she wakes me on weekends, normally before eight o'clock. When I got out of bed ten minutes ago, it was ten thirty-seven. I don't think I've slept in that late since before she was born.

I scrambled into clothes and ran into her bedroom to check if she was still asleep, only to find her bed empty. That's when the smell of cinnamon and sugar hit me. Assuming Everett had snuck out early this morning, I wasn't expecting to find him in bed with me when I woke up, even if I wished he was. The last thing I imagined, though, was that I would hear his voice coming from the kitchen when I descended the stairs.

I stop inside the dining room, knowing they can't see me yet. From the angle where I stand, I can make out half of Everett's tall, broad body standing next to the stove with what appears to be a bowl of pancake batter—based on the flour, sugar, and eggs covering the counter—in front of him. My daughter sits beside him, legs dangling off the edge as she watches Everett cook. Taylor

Swift, of course, floats quietly through the room.

"Wait, it's a real thing?" she asks.

"It's a real hypothesis some people believe in."

"What's a hypothesis?"

"Okay...I actually am not smart enough to explain that to you. Ask your middle school science teacher in like three years." Everett laughs. "Let me think of an example of an invisible string, though."

They're quiet for a few moments, and I can't help but watch them as he pours batter onto the griddle. Lou watches him while she plucks cut strawberries from a bowl and pops them into her mouth. I move to the side so she doesn't see me, not wanting to interrupt their conversation.

"Okay, I've got it," Everett says. "Do you know how your Aunt Darby met Leo?"

"She lived here with my great grandma when she was a teenager."

"Right. While your mom was pregnant with you."

"Oh." Lou pauses. "I didn't know that part."

"Yep," Everett continues. "So, listen to this: if your mom hadn't gotten pregnant with you, Darby never would've spent that summer here in Pacific Shores. In this very house. She never would've met Leo. Then, she never would've moved back here and Leo never would've bought this house. You and your mom never would've moved here. I would've never met your mom, and you and I wouldn't be sitting here right now making pancakes."

He's quiet for a moment, and I wonder what Lou's face must be expressing to all that. I can feel my own stomach flipping upside down and inside out at his words.

"Why would Aunt Darby come here because my mom was pregnant with me?"

My stomach drops. Only silence answers her question.

It goes on so long, I'm about to step into the kitchen, but I'm stopped short when I hear Everett clear his throat. "Well, you know...being pregnant is hard on the body. A woman grows an entire human being in her tummy, and that's a lot of work. Sometimes, she can get sick or tired. She'll need to be taken care of. I think..." I hear him huff. "I think your grandparents wanted to make sure your mom had plenty of space to feel comfortable, and I think they wanted to make sure they could take care of her. I think they also wanted your aunt to have a fun summer while your mom worked on making you."

Those are all horrendous lies, but the truth of that summer and the way my parents treated my pregnancy isn't something I ever want Lou knowing. If she'd asked me that question, I'm not sure I would've been able to answer it, not sure I have the ability to lie about them that way, even in the spirit of protecting her. The fact that Everett knew exactly how to answer in a way that both protected Lou and respected me has my knees ready to buckle.

"The point I'm making," he continues, " is that you're an invisible string, Luz. Without you, none of us ever would've met each other. Do you know how much happiness and love you've brought into our lives just by existing?"

Butterflies explode in my chest, and I find myself clenching my heart with my hand.

"Your life?" Lou asks, her voice quieter than before.

"Absolutely. But not just mine. Leo and Darby. My mom. She loves you so much, it's almost scary." My daughter laughs at that. "You're that little thread of gold." There's some shuffling in the kitchen, and Lou laughs again. "Don't forget that, okay? You're meant to be. You're a fucking cool kid, and I want you to remember that if anyone ever tries telling you otherwise, got it?"

My soul feels like it's been set on fire, body raging with need to touch and love both of them, to see the bright look I know that Everett's words have put on my girl's face.

"Am I allowed to call myself a fucking cool kid?"

Everett cackles. "Not in front of your mother."

I'm fighting back tears, trying to calm my pounding heart when I turn the corner and enter the kitchen. "What can't you do in front of your mother?" I ask, keeping my voice steady.

Lou's eyes go wide, spotting me first. Everett turns, and there's a smile on his face when he takes me in. I can't help but return it, closing in on the two of them. I kiss my daughter on the forehead, and when I step away, I find myself being pulled into a pair of strong arms.

"Morning, mama." He smiles down at me, kissing me lightly on the lips.

"Are you the reason I wasn't woken at the crack of dawn by my child today?" I ask.

Everett winks. "I heard Lou had a rough night, so I thought I'd stop by and make you guys breakfast."

"He slipped a note under my door asking me not to wake you up and to come downstairs and help him," Lou adds. "We were going to surprise you with breakfast in bed, but you ruined it."

"Oh," I gasp dramatically. "I'm so sorry to ruin your surprise." I wrap my arms around her head as Everett goes back to finishing the pancakes. My heart feels like it's about to explode out of my chest, and I allow myself to dream of this moment being the norm. For the first time, I let myself see it: going to sleep with Everett at night, waking up with the two of them every morning, watching my daughter love and trust a man who protects and loves her right back.

I want that reality so badly it hurts, but the pessimist in me tells me it's far too good to be true.

Thirty-Three - Wildflower

Better Start Running, Wildflower

The bell on the red door chimes as I enter the lobby of Ramos Automotive. Sophie, one of Everett's mechanics, greets me from the front counter. "Hi, Dahlia." She smiles, green eyes crinkling in the corners.

"Hey." I wave. "I'm meeting Everett for lunch today. Is he in his office?"

I begin to step toward the backend of the building where his office is located when she stops me. "No, he's actually still outside working on the reno for the 1960 T-Bird." She runs a tan fingertip through the end of her dark ponytail. "He and Carlos both get so carried away with that thing. Can you believe someone just dumped it here?" she asks exasperatedly.

I don't know what a 1960 Birdie or whatever the fuck she just said even is, so it's hard for me to relate to the shock in her tone, but I respond, "No, that's crazy."

She smiles at me like she can tell I'm full of shit, but she holds out her hands. "Here, hand me your boxes, and I'll set them in his office for you." Nodding toward the glass door behind her, she adds, "You can go grab him from the bay."

"You sure?" I ask.

"Yeah." She laughs. "You might be the only person capable of pulling him away from that car."

Everett's staff have gotten to know me over the last few

months, since I come down here for lunch about once a week. He spends a lot of time in the office above Heathen's as well, since we have regular meetings there. I like coming down here when I want to get off the boardwalk, though.

I thank Sophie as I hand her the paper bag filled with sandwiches I picked up from Everett's favorite spot downtown, and then I enter the deck through the glass door behind the counter. A few of his other workers greet me when I pass by. There are three cars in the garage currently, all seeming to be at different stages of repair or maintenance.

Everett doesn't seem to notice my approach, but I see him on the far end of the deck, bent over the hood of an old, classic-looking teal blue car. The Birdie, I assume. As I get closer, I notice his face is pinched in concentration, staring down into the hood. He's got an enticing gleam of sweat on his brow and neck. His arms are bare, straining outside the black cut-off T-shirt he's wearing as he braces against the side of the vehicle. His full-sleeve tattoos ripple beneath his weight, and I find myself clamping down on my lip to bite back a literal swoon.

I'm starting to wonder if Sophie sent me back here so I could get a look at this man in action, and if that's the case, I'm going to need to send her a thank you card.

When I reach the car, I lean against the driver side door. I'm fairly certain he didn't notice me walking up, can't see me from behind the hood. "'Scuse me. Sir?" Hearing a smack and then a groan, I continue, "I'm looking for a mechanic. I'm in need of a full-service tune-up. You know, pipes oiled and rack lubed." Everett's head pops around the lifted hood, eyes wide. "Nuts. Bolts. Whatever." His brows are in his hairline as he stares after me. "There's something there. You get what I mean," I finish, fighting a smile.

The entire deck falls silent before echoing laughter erupts throughout the garage, followed by claps and whistles. Everett's look of shock slowly morphs into something resembling endearment, and finally, a smirk flutters across his lips.

"I'm not sure I do, ma'am." He rounds the front of the car, closing the distance between us. "You might have to show me."

"You askin' for a look under my hood?"

"Always, Wildflower," he rasps, snaking an arm around my waist and tugging me against him. He appears to be done with my little ruse, because his mouth falls on mine, hot, soft, and needful, like he hasn't kissed me in years.

I love playing this way with him. I used to be like this all the time, pushing boundaries and not caring who heard or stared or judged. Everett makes me feel that free again, but part of me wonders if he's attracted to this version of me—the one with a sharp tongue and quick impulse, the one who's experimental in the bedroom and likes to banter when it's just the two of us—and if he could truly fall for all of me.

The anxious, insecure mother. The woman who struggles with her body image and what she wants to do with her life. The girl with trauma, who will never stop questioning if she's good enough at anything she does and whether or not she deserves love.

I'm a lot to take on, and as much as I love flirting, laughing, and having fun with Everett, a part of me feels so sure that the rest of it will catch up with us eventually, and he's going to walk away.

I sigh against Everett's lips. "I brought you lunch."

"You're incredible." He smiles. "I completely lost track of time. Let me finish up here, and then we can head into my office."

I nod, and he steps back, resuming his former place at the hood of the car and picking up whatever tool he was working with before. I walk up next to him, watching his nimble hands move beneath a pair of thick black gloves.

His gaze is fixed on the vehicle, entirely focused, but he's addressing me when he asks, "What's got you all flustered, Wildflower?"

"You?" I say it like a question, waving my hand in his direction. "All sweaty and muscled and working on cars. You're like a walking, talking wet dream."

He smiles to himself, biting down on his lower lip. "You

know that's not what I mean, *cariño.*" Gaze still fixed on the car, he continues, "You got that faraway look in your eye after I kissed you that tells me you're overthinking."

"How do you read me so well?"

That stops him. His head snaps sideways, eyes finding mine. "Because I study you. Because I want to know you better than anyone else does. Because I want to give you exactly what you need, tell you exactly what you need to hear, without you having to ask. Mostly because I know you won't."

His gaze turns intense, eyes of molten chocolate rushing through me.

"I'm afraid that now you've had me, you'll realize I'm not worth keeping." The words tumble from my lips, because I can't hide anything from his sure-fire presence. I know he'd get it out of me, no matter how hard I'd try to fight. I know there's no point in that anymore anyway, because I always melt beneath his heated stare. "I'm terrified because now that the chase is over, I'm not going to end up being what you dreamed of in your head."

I expect Everett to do one of two things: he's either going to go soft, pull me against his hard and steady chest, and speak those insecurities out of existence with reassuring words, or, he's going to get frustrated with me. As he lets out an exasperated sigh and stands straight, I assume we're going with the latter.

"Better start running." He's still looking at me, his face entirely expressionless as he slowly brings one gloved hand to his mouth, taking it between his teeth and pulling it off.

"What?" I ask.

"I said"—he takes off his other glove, tossing both on the work bench next to him—"you better start running, Wildflower." Grabbing the hem of his cutoff, he lifts it to his brow and wipes a bead of sweat from his forehead, providing me with a glimpse of his tanned, toned stomach. "When I catch you, I'm going to fuck all those doubts right out of your pretty mouth."

My jaw drops open. Butterflies flutter through my chest, sparks ignite in my stomach, and heat pools at the center of my thighs. Everett's face is entirely serious—stern, confident conviction in his features. He means every word he says. The slow rise of his brow has my blood racing through my veins, and suddenly, I'm turning on my heel and sprinting through the bay.

We were talking quietly enough that I know his workers didn't hear our conversation, and their confused faces as I run by them, dodging equipment and darting between vehicles, is confirmation. I hear Everett laugh roughly, his footsteps growing louder as he gains on me. I fly through the glass doors that lead back into the lobby, catching the eyes of several patrons and Sophie. "Dahlia?" she gasps. "Are you—"

I move around her, and her question is cut off as Everett barrels through the door behind her. I'm the one laughing now as her eyes bulge from her head. I run through the aisle of tires and toward the back of the building where Everett's office is.

"I'm taking my lunch break, Soph!" he calls, voice getting louder as he catches up to me. "Field any calls and don't let the guys bother me!"

Her laughter follows us as I reach his office door. I fling it open, trying to shut it behind me, but he's on my heels, catching the door and slipping inside. His office is small—desk at the center of the room, two chairs in front of it, a bookshelf where he keeps financial records and employee files against the back wall.

I spin around, backing into his desk until I'm leaning against it. His predatory gaze tracks my every movement from where he stands against the door, reaching behind him and turning the lock. The click of it sliding into place is deafening. I'm prey, and I've been caught.

"On your knees," he growls.

"Keeping your promises, huh?" I ask breathlessly.

"I'm a man of my word, Dahlia," he rasps. "I mean what I say, and I think you need to be reminded of that. So, I won't ask you again. On. Your. Knees."

His tone is primal and electrifying, and I'm instantly lowering to the floor.

He steps up to me in two long strides. His gait strong and purposeful. When he stops in front of me, I lift my head, my gaze clashing against his brown eyes with enough heat between them to light the room on fire if we stared long enough.

"Take off my belt," he commands.

My fingers shake, but I immediately comply, reaching for the hem of his pants. I slowly unfasten the leather and slide it through the loops of his black jeans, feeling the bulge of his raging cock beneath my palm. My mouth waters at the idea of having it in my mouth again.

As soon as I slip the belt off, I move to toss it onto the floor beside me, but he reaches out and snatches my wrist. "We're not done with that." Leaning down, he presses a quick, hard kiss to my lips. "If I do something you don't like, you tell me, understand? Say no. Say stop. If your mouth is full"—he smirks—"you tap me on the thigh twice. Yeah?"

I nod.

"Good." He kisses me again before pulling away and standing straight. "Now, wrap that belt around your neck." My breath hitches, curiosity and anticipation shooting through my core. "Put yourself on a leash and remind me what a good girl you are."

Heat explodes between my legs.

I take the end strap and slide it past the buckle, pulling it all the way through until the belt is tight around my throat. Everett's eyes are on fire as I hold the strap out to him in silent submission. He lets out a low groan, wrapping it around his fist and tugging me toward him.

With anyone else, this would be humiliating, but with him, it's fucking enticing. I want to be at his mercy. There is vulnerability and trust in acts like this, and knowing he's doing this for my pleasure, to help me let go, gives me faith in his control of the situation.

I want to explore like this with Everett, knowing he's going to take care of me, guide me through all of it, pushing the boundaries together until we find new levels of pleasure than we could've ever imagined, that we'd never be able to find with anyone else.

"Take my cock out, Dahlia," he demands roughly.

I pop the button on his jeans, keeping my eyes on him as I slowly unzip and tug them down his thighs. His hardness tents his underwear, thick and long. I dip into the waistband, letting my nails tickle the skin of his hips, and he lets out a hiss at the sensation. I drag his underwear down his legs, too, and his cock springs free, hard, throbbing, and already glistening with moisture. My tongue sticks to the roof of my mouth as my throat goes dry.

Part of me can't believe this is the same man who crawled across my bedroom floor and begged to fuck me. He stands before me now so tall, rugged, and masculine, arms straining, the tattoos on his hands flexing where he wraps the belt around his knuckles. As he pulls it tight, my throat constricts, and my mouth falls open, sucking in air.

His other hand snakes behind my head, fisting my hair and holding me still as he slides his length between my parted lips. He's hard and hot against my tongue, pushing in slowly until he reaches resistance at the back of my throat. I lower my jaw, suction my cheeks around him, and force him just an inch deeper. He's nowhere close to being all the way inside, but it's enough for him to let out a low, strained groan. The sound is like kindling to my skin, lighting my body on fire.

Everett's head falls back, throat working as his eyes flutter shut. I flick my tongue across his base and attempt to pull back, but he tightens his grip on the belt around my neck, causing me to choke and sputter. "Stay." I still myself, and he moves his hips away, until just the tip remains in my mouth, before thrusting back in. "Good girl." A feral smile accents his lips as he brushes a hand over the top of my head, pushing my hair from my face. "You're such a pretty little pet."

I can't help the moan that tears from my throat at those words. The sound vibrates along his length, and he lets out a twin noise at the feel of it. He keeps the reins tight around me and begins a punishing pace, fucking my mouth with abandon. I can do nothing but take it. The control he has over me sends a flood of arousal straight to my core.

Each time he pushes deep, he holds there until my lungs seize and my throat constricts at the lack of oxygen. Then, he moves again, allowing me to breathe. A string of curses fly from his mouth as he moves faster, harder, deeper. My eyes are watering, nails clawing into the flesh of his thighs. Everett drops his head, amber eyes searing through me, hazed with lust and passion and something fierce.

"You think the chase is over, baby?" he growls. "Fuck, no. I'm going to be chasing the high you give me for the rest of my life." He thrusts deep, pausing. "You're such a good girl for me, choking on my cock." I moan again, and his lips tick upward into the wicked smirk that sets my soul on fire. "I'm keeping you, Wildflower. You're mine," he rasps. *"Se mia per sempre."*

He picks up his pace, thrusting deep into my throat—roughly and with purpose. I hollow out my cheeks, sucking hard and wrapping my tongue around his length as it moves in and out of my mouth. "Fucking dammit, Dahlia," he moans. "I'm going to—" His eyes are bright as he stares down at me with that unspoken question.

I squeeze his leg, attempting to nod my permission through the grip around my neck. He pulls on the belt, forcing it even tighter, his fingers knotting in my hair and pulling tight. The sting is electrifying. My vision goes blurry, but I fight to keep my eyes open, desperate to watch him come undone, to watch him lose control.

"C–Coming," he grits out through clenched teeth, and suddenly, his body is spasming around me, cock jerking in my mouth before his release coats my tongue, shooting hot and fast down my throat. His thighs tremble beneath my palms as I swallow everything.

My mind still hazy and clouded, I think I may hear him whispering my name again and again, but by the time the belt loosens around my neck and his fingers leave my hair, the room is quiet. He pulls his cock from my mouth, and I lick the remnants of him from my lips as he watches me with hooded eyes.

Everett tucks himself back into his jeans before reaching his hand out to me. I take it as he hauls me to my feet and slides the belt off my neck, letting it fall to the floor beside us. "You're incredible, and I think I'm obsessed with you," he says, taking my face between his hands. "Was it too much?"

I laugh. "No. I liked it." Gripping his forearms and pulling him closer so that his mouth hovers over mine, I whisper, "But later, I'm going to walk you like a fucking dog."

He smiles against my lips. "Yes, ma'am."

Thirty-Four - Wildflower

Having A Crisis Over My Dying Twenties

Have you given any more thought to my proposal?

I sigh, deleting the text message and locking my phone before slipping it back into my purse. I should really just block his number, but the thought terrifies me somehow. I'm afraid of the damage he would do if he truly lost his access to me.

Plus, if he wasn't tormenting me, he'd be tormenting my sister.

"You haven't heard from Dad recently, have you?" I ask.

Her hands tense on the steering wheel, and I watch her glance in the rearview to check on Lou in the back, ensuring her earbuds are in. The music is so loud I can hear it from the front seat, so I know there is no way she's listening.

"No, not in months. I've been emailing with Mom." Her eyes flicker in my direction. "Only every few weeks. Not often."

I nod. "And she never brings him up?"

Darby shakes her head. "Not at all. We mostly talk about wedding stuff. She seems...she seems happy for me." Chewing on her lip, she adds, "I suppose it's hard to convey tone in an email, but she at least appears enthusiastic."

"That's good." I force a smile.

I'm not getting married, but even if I was, I doubt it'd be enough to warrant a check-in from my mother. I shuffle uncomfortably in my seat, attempting to physically shake off the unease.

"You okay?" Darby asks.

"Yeah," I lie. "It's these damn panties you have me in. They're so uncomfortable."

That's not a lie.

Today is my thirtieth birthday, which is terrifying as fuck all on its own, but I'm being forced to spend the day in some upscale Beverly Hills bridal boutique, trying on dresses. The dress shopping I don't totally mind; it's just not how I'd prefer to spend my birthday. Plus, Darby insisted I wear the same undergarments I plan on wearing for the wedding itself so I can make sure everything fits correctly with my dress.

The panties are uncomfortable as hell, and my sister put me in one of her sundresses, which rides up on my thighs that are already sticking to the hot leather of her car seats.

I'd rather have spent my birthday lying in bed, having a crisis over my dying twenties and watching *Love Island*, Season Six specifically. It should've been my sister's birthday spent at her wedding dress fitting.

"I promise, you'll thank me for it later." She smiles to herself, eyes on the interstate in front of her.

We had to leave early to make our appointment, because apparently, she couldn't get her dress delivered at any other location than the one in Los Angeles, a nearly two-hour drive from Pacific Shores.

An hour and a half later, I'm lounging on the plushest couch I've ever had the pleasure of sitting on, stuffed with eclairs, watching my daughter twirl around the room in a poofy white dress with cap sleeves and gold accents. She picked it out as soon as we arrived and has refused to take it off.

Darby's in the back with her wedding coordinator, Macie, getting into her dress. I offered to go back with her, but she told me she wanted to surprise me. I know that's something typically done with the mother of the bride, but we don't have that option, so I'll have to do.

I tried on my dress when we first arrived—something Darby and I had picked out online. It's simple, sage green and satin, with off-shoulder sleeves, a wrap around the midsection, and tight at the waist and chest.

It made me feel beautiful, and I couldn't stop thinking about how Everett will react when he sees me in it. I still hate the underwear I have on—a silky thong that's supposed to smooth out any lines, but the wedgie it gives me is unreal.

Darby also forced me into a blue floral dress that has my breasts just about spilling over the top. *It's your birthday. You should feel beautiful,* she'd said as she thrust it into my arms before we left this morning.

It is *my* birthday, but somehow, I can't say no to her.

I'm smoothing out the fabric of the dress on my legs as Macie's head pops around the corner, her shoulder-length curls shaking with the movement.

She's a stunner, the kind of beautiful that makes you stop and catalog every single one of her features—bright hazel eyes, full lips, and a megawatt smile. Today's the first time I've met her, and I find myself sweating a little every time she speaks. I mean, she's one of the most approachable and personable people I've ever encountered, but I think I've got some kind of girl crush because she makes me nervous as hell.

I met her boyfriend, Dom, once when he stopped by Heathen's to have lunch with Everett and Leo. He rendered me speechless too. I'm both excited and terrified to see what kind of kids they cook up together someday, because holy shit... Talk about a beautiful couple.

"Are you guys ready to see her?" Macie asks, practically vibrating with excitement.

"Yes!" My daughter claps her hands together.

She smiles, ducking back down the hall before returning a moment later with my sister in tow. Breathtaking doesn't even begin to describe Darby, but as I struggle to catch my own, it's the only word that comes to mind.

Pure white strapless satin fits her chest and waist like a mold made for her before cascading to the floor in smooth, flawless rivulets. She has on matching gloves to just above her elbow. It's effortless, elegant, and so utterly *her*.

What's truly striking, though, is her veil. Her hair is slicked back into a tight bun at the nape of her neck, and tucked into it, falling down her back and over her shoulders is a lace veil, embellished with flowers. Honeysuckles, I realize as I get a closer look. Small yellow, pink, and red honeysuckles are sewn into the fabric. They're sparse at the top, growing more frequent as my eyes drag down the length of it.

Macie helps her stand onto the platform in front of the mirror before bending down and fluffing out the bottom of her dress and smoothing down her veil.

Macie steps back to stand next to Lou and me, and the three of us watch Darby take herself in. I can see tears pricking at her eyes as she slowly runs her gloved hand down her waist, smoothing out the dress. She takes a deep breath before turning to face the three of us.

"Well? What do you think?" My sister's voice shakes as she asks the question, trembling with emotion.

"It's so much better than your last one," my daughter answers, ever honest. "You look like a princess."

A tear begins to bubble over, but Macie's on it with a tissue in hand, extending it toward Darby. She takes it, dotting at her eyes. "Thanks, Lulu."

"You look unbelievable," I say, feeling heavy with my own emotion. "How do you feel?"

She turns around again, meeting my eyes in the mirror. I'm taken back to the day of her wedding to Jackson, the way she looked at me through the mirror back then, to the devastation and hopelessness written across her features.

I'll never stop being thankful for the man who showed up at that church and helped her get away, because the way she looks at me now is full of hope and happiness. Because of him.

"It's everything I've ever wanted," she whispers. "Do you think he'll like it?"

"I think Leo's going to lose his goddamn *mind*," Macie chimes enthusiastically. "He better watch his back, because I might just steal you away for myself."

My sister grins. "Well, you know how pretty he thinks Dom is. They probably wouldn't miss us."

We all laugh as I pull out my phone and begin snapping pictures of her for Monica, who was upset she couldn't come with us today due to a former engagement with her book club. Our appointment was originally set for the beginning of the month, but Darby had to reschedule it last minute, and the only day they had available before the wedding was my birthday.

Macie helps my sister step off the platform, and I wrap her in my arms. "You look so beautiful," I whisper. "I'm proud of you."

"Thank you for being here." Her voice breaks on the words.

Darby and Macie head back to the dressing rooms, and I do the same with my very reluctant daughter. After a partial meltdown, I finally convince her to get out of her dress. The boutique staff pack our things for us while we say goodbye to Macie. We trade hugs, and she vows to set up a lunch date for the three of us, plus her best friend, Penelope.

It has been so long since I had friends, I almost forget how to act. It's another thing I convinced myself I don't deserve and can't find, but for the first time in a while, I feel hopeful at the prospect of it.

My sister is giddy as we grab the dress boxes from the reception counter and head out. Giving me a manic smile, she asks, "Are you ready to go?"

"Yes?" I cock my head at her. "Are you okay?"

"I'm great!" She's giggling as I push open the front door, and I look back at her like she's crazy.

Turning in the direction of where she parked her Mustang, I'm momentarily blinded by the mid-day sun, but as the brightness clears my vision, I'm stopping—stunned.

Parked in front of Darby's car against the curb is a vintage motorcycle, and standing beside it is a six-four monster of a man. Brown leather jacket over his shoulders, in a black tee with beige trousers, Everett is beaming at me as he leans back against the bike with his ankles crossed. In his hands is a massive arrangement of flowers—wildflowers, the names of which I wouldn't know, and the unmistakable dahlias erupting out of the bouquet.

I turn to my sister and daughter, who're both looking after me with shit-eating grins. Without saying anything, Darby slides the box with Lou's and my dresses from my hands, and Everett steps onto the curb, extending the bouquet to me.

"Happy Birthday, Wildflower."

Thirty-Five – Wicked

Kick Rocks, Bitch.

"Thought we could take the long way home," I say with a smile as Dahlia stares after me in stunned silence.

That seems to snap her out of her trance, and she shakes her head as she looks down at the flowers I thrust into her hands.

Darby helped me pick them yesterday. I stopped by Honeysuckle just before closing, and she assisted me in creating an arrangement of the most colorful wildflowers she had, along with bright orange dahlias, until we ended up with a bouquet that reminded us of her sister.

Dahlia was not excited about turning thirty. She didn't want gifts or a cake or a party. She said the only thing she wanted for her thirtieth birthday was to remain twenty-nine. I know Dahlia lost so much of her youth when she became a mother, so we thought the best thing to give her would be the reminder that she's still young, and she can be as wild as she has always wished to be.

Darby and I planned all the things I have in store for her today, starting with convincing her that she had to spend her birthday at a dress fitting, but in reality, Darby rescheduled the appointment on purpose so we could get her out to LA and I could surprise her with the bike.

I'm assuming the dress Darby forced her into was a gift to *me*, because she looks fucking beautiful in blue.

Dahlia eyes the bike behind me, no doubt cataloging the

two helmets I have propped up on the handlebars. Lou pulls the flowers from her mother's hands. "We'll take these home for you."

I was hesitant to let Lou in on the surprise, but Darby insisted. I was afraid she'd end up spilling the beans, but the look on Dahlia's face tells me she didn't.

"Thank you for the flowers." Dahlia steps into me, and I press a light kiss to her lips. "But I cannot get on *that* in front of my kid," she says, nodding at my bike.

I smile; I knew she'd say that. "Luz, what did we talk about?"

Lou peeks her head around the bouquet that's damn near the same size she is. "Motorcycles are dangerous, but you're a professional, so we're safe with you."

"Right." I nod. "And?"

"If a boy ever asks me if I want a ride on his motorcycle, I tell him to 'Kick rocks, bitch.'"

Darby and I laugh. "Exactly." I look at Dahlia. "See? We're good."

Dahlia gives me a deadpan expression, eyeing the bike again. I take off my jacket, pulling her into me as I wrap it around her shoulders. "Put this on. I'm taking you somewhere special for your birthday."

She looks back between myself and her sister, unsure of what to say.

"Go," Darby urges. "We have plans today anyway. Don't we, Lulu?"

"Yep!"

"We won't even miss you." Darby smiles.

I reach behind me, grabbing one of the helmets before placing it on her head and fastening the buckle under her chin. "I'm serious, Lucille," she shouts behind her. "You are not to ride on a motorcycle. Ever. These things are death traps."

"Everett said he'd take me on a ride when you guys get home."

Her nostrils flare, eyes growing wide as she glares at me.

"*Around the block,* Luz." I wink at Dal. "Twenty-five miles per hour. Tops."

"Are you two going faster than twenty-five miles per hour?" Lou snipes back.

"Absolutely not," we lie simultaneously. Dahlia's lips spread into a grin.

After ushering her over to my bike, I help her get on the back before I throw on my helmet and straddle the seat in front of her. "Hold onto me, Wildflower," I say as I start the ignition and raise the kickstand with my foot. "You ready?"

Her arms band around my waist, holding tightly as I feel her nod against my back.

Darby flashes me a knowing grin, waving as I pull out onto the road and take off with Dahlia on my back.

Thirty-Six - Wildflower

Sunshine, Blue Horizons, And Him.

Warm, spring air whips at my face, gusting through my hair. The roar of the road is deafening, drowning out all other noise, firmly placing my mind inside what feels like a bubble of sunshine, blue horizons, and *him*.

My hands lock around his waist, holding tightly as he flies down the coastal highway. Each time we're stopped or slowed, he takes a hand off the handlebars and wraps his fingers through mine or brushes them up my bare thigh, keeping me securely in the moment with him.

I'm not sure where we are, but I know we went west out of LA, and about a half hour later, I could see the ocean. We've been speeding down the 101, right along the beach's edge, for about forty minutes now. Towering green mountains are on one side of me, the endless sea on the other. The sun is at its peak, glittering across the white caps like diamonds. Palms line the highway, swaying in the breeze. The world smells like sea salt and fresh air.

I don't know where Everett's taking me, but I don't much care, not with the way his body feels against mine—safe and warm, with the breeze and the sun and the smell of the ocean. I imagine I'd go just about anywhere with him.

The bike comes to a crawl as we turn off the highway and enter some state park I don't catch the name of. The one-lane, paved road winds up the mountain, and we ride along the cliffside to the top of it. Everett turns, shimmying his bike around a locked gate, clearly intended to cut off access to the gravel road that continues toward the peak.

It's still too loud for me to ask what he's doing, so I just hold onto him tightly, anticipation fluttering in my stomach until we reach the top and he brings his bike to a stop at the edge of a ridge, the Pacific stretching on for an eternity in front of us.

He kills the engine, taking his helmet off as he spins in the seat, grinning down at me. "How was that, Dal?" he asks, unbuckling the strap of the helmet beneath my chin and pulling it off my head.

"It was..." I find myself at a loss for words. I told him I had dreams of driving up and down the West Coast when I was younger, how I longed for a car that was impractical for a mother but could make me feel wild and free again, how much I dreaded turning thirty because it reminded me of the loss of my youth.

All these tiny words I said in passing but never expected him to remember.

In one afternoon, he had me feeling all the things I thought I'd been missing, obliterated my fears, and made my dreams come true.

He gave me everything and then some.

He's... "Beautiful," I say.

He hops off the bike, grabbing my waist and throwing one of my legs over as he helps me down from the seat. Reaching into the fabric case strapped to the back of his motorcycle, Everett pulls out a backpack. Holding firmly onto my hand, he takes off toward the cliffside.

"We're not even there yet, baby." He turns back at me, the sun hitting his face at the perfect angle, allowing me to see his amber eyes through his sunglasses.

"What do you me—" I'm cut off when we reach the edge.

The ocean extends in front of us, wide and blue, but what has me halting, losing my breath, is the rolling hills of bright flowers. Like the sun and sky clashing together, the fields stretch beyond us, meeting the ocean at the horizon. Yellow, red, and pink dot the landscape in front of us, with an overwhelming number of orange flowers taking up the space.

Wildflowers, I realize.

Everett takes my hand, navigating us down a narrow dirt path between the flowers. "Careful not to step on them," he says. "It's a fragile ecosystem, which is why it's not open to tourists anymore." He leads me along until we reach a small patch of plain grass within the blooms. After taking a blanket from the backpack and spreading it out on the ground, he sits down, pulling me beside him.

"How did you find this place?" I ask, settling in against his chest as he drapes his arm around my shoulders.

"My dad used to take us here all the time when we were kids. It has been a while, but I remember the wildflowers peak around this time of year and..." He shrugs. "I don't know. I thought of you, I guess."

He seems almost bashful at the admission. After reaching into the bag he brought with us, he pulls out a small cooler before opening it to reveal a container of chocolate-covered strawberries.

Very messily made chocolate-covered strawberries.

"Those look homemade." I laugh.

"Luz and I made them."

I look up at him, watching as he plucks one out of the box and holds it to my lips. "You? Made these with my daughter?" I ask just before he slides the strawberry between my lips. I bite into it, feeling the sweet juice coat my tongue, mixing with the rich chocolate. "When did you do that?"

"Yesterday," he says simply. "I told you I was at the garage, but I actually spent the day with her and my mom at my parents' house. We wanted to make you something for your birthday, and she said strawberries are your favorite."

"They are." I don't know what else to say. It's spring break for the school district, and Monica offered to watch Lou so I wouldn't have to take the week off work.

I had no idea that Everett had taken Friday off from his own business to spend time with my daughter, to plan a surprise for my birthday.

I've never had anyone do something like this for me.

With him still holding the strawberry to my mouth, I lean forward and take another bite, keeping my eyes locked on him the entire time. His flare with heat as I wrap my lips around it, pulling back slowly.

He runs the fruit across my jaw and down my neck, skating it along my collarbone, leaving behind the melted chocolate before popping the remainder of it into his own mouth. He never takes his gaze from mine, and my breath catches as he leans in and drags his tongue across my skin. Flames erupt across my flesh.

I cup the back of his neck as he licks and nips across my throat, sucking the chocolate away. A primal moan tears from him as my fingers tangle in his hair, pulling his mouth to mine. He catches my lips in a fierce kiss that is such a contrast to the way he delicately lays me back on the blanket and hovers his body over mine.

"Happy Birthday, Dahlia," he murmurs into my mouth as he continues devouring me.

Wrapping my arms around his neck, I cling to him like a lifeline, and he wraps an arm around my waist, holding me just as tightly. His lips move from my mouth, peppering soft kisses along my jaw.

"You guys didn't need to do all this for me," I say breathlessly.

Everett pauses, pulling up to look at me. Eyes bright with conviction bore through me as he says, "We wanted to." I watch his throat move as he swallows before adding, "We love you."

My heart hammers so erratically in my chest I know he must feel it too. The pounding between us is enough to make this mountain crumble, because we both know he just said exactly what I think he did.

I brush my thumb across his jaw, savoring the way his stubbled skin feels beneath my hand—rough and soft, like him.

I study all his perfect features, knowing I'm so far gone I'll never come back.

"Why did you do all this for me, Everett?" I ask again, knowing he understands the question hidden beneath my words.

I watch him slowly lick his lips, buying himself time before taking a deep breath and pulling up, taking me with him so we're both sitting now, facing each other with our limbs entwined.

"I know you said you can't give me anything more than your body. I understand why that is. I don't expect anything more." He looks down at where my hand is pressed against the blanket, and he slowly places his over it. "But that doesn't stop me from wanting to give you everything. All of me." He slowly drags his eyes from our joined hands to my face, meeting my own. "You deserved to know that you're loved, Dahlia. Loved by me."

"I'm not easy to love," I find myself saying.

"Loving you is the easiest thing I've ever done. The hard part is that you won't let me." Reaching up to softly cup my face, he continues, "My love isn't fickle, Dahlia. I'm not afraid to fight for you. For us. Every second of every day, if that's what it takes. I'm not afraid of imperfection or reality. I'm not afraid of your broken pieces." He runs his thumb along my cheek. "I'm broken too, but together, we can be whole." Everett smiles, emotion glistening behind his amber eyes. "You're everything I've been searching for my entire life and never believed I'd find. I know you think you're not worth fighting for, baby, but just give me the chance to show you you're wrong."

My eyes fall closed, soaking in his words as I nuzzle my face into the palm of his hand, allowing myself to absorb everything he just said, every emotion in his gaze, the power of his presence.

I feel all the same things he does—maybe even more—but I don't know how to make myself say the words. "I don't know how to be selfless with my love," I admit quietly. "When I was a child, that word was never used, I was never taught how to express that feeling, or what it even was."

Everett's brows knit together at his forehead, concern and

confusion etched into his beautiful face, but he nods for me to continue.

"When I got older and began to understand what love is—the weight of loving someone and all that meant—I quickly realized I was not loved the way a daughter should be by her parents, and I think that's why they never used it." I pause, biting back the trembling in my jaw, the rising emotion. "When I fell for Jason, I finally realized what it meant to be in love and how heavy that could be. I trusted him. I gave him what I had been told my whole life was the most valuable part of me—my body. I gave him all that pent-up love I never got to express." A tear I failed to hold back spills over, cascading slowly down my cheek. Everett immediately stops it with his thumb, swiping it away. "It was like...once he had it, it lost its value. He didn't want it anymore, and he certainly didn't want to give me his. I chased and chased him, desperate to get back all that love I gave away."

I take a breath, swallowing the sob that wants to claw its way out of my chest. "Then, I had Lou, and I realized what the true value of love is, how what I thought I'd experienced before hardly scratched the surface of the depths I feel for her. All she simply had to do was exist, and she already received everything I had left to give."

I close my eyes, knowing I'll crumble beneath the weight of Everett's stare. My eyes well with tears, and I let them fall this time. I allow myself to weep as he pulls me into his chest, wrapping his arms around my back, attempting to quell the trembling in my limbs.

"What was wrong with me that my parents had never done the same? What was wrong with me, and the half of me in her, that made her father unable to give either of us a drop of love?"

Everett doesn't respond, because answers to questions like that can't be found.

He runs his hand down the back of my head, hushing my cries and rocking me in his arms. I take a moment to compose myself, letting out all the emotion I've held back my entire life—

things I've never shared with another soul because I've always been so afraid they'd see whatever my parents had, that they'd realize I'm not worth loving.

Finally pulling out of his embrace, I'm the one cupping his face in my hands now, ensuring he's looking directly at me as I say, "I've been left to ponder that my whole life. I've been drained of it, and there is hardly enough left for myself most days. I don't know how to give any more. I don't know how to say the words. I'm afraid if I do, I'll lose myself."

He drops his head so our noses brush together, and I feel him smiling against my lips. "You don't have to say them to me, Wildflower, but I'll give you all of mine just the same." Bringing his hand to the back of my neck, he brushes his fingers along my skin. "I'll show you that love is endless. It's infinite. I'll show you that you're worthy of it. I'll love you enough for the both of us until your well is overflowing."

Warm air rushes from his lips, sending shivers across my flesh. I shudder beneath the weight of his emotion—of his love.

"What if that takes a while?" I ask.

"You're my wildflower." He lets out a breathless laugh. "You blew into town one day on a whim and planted yourself right inside my soul. You're rooted in me now, baby. I don't mind waiting to watch you bloom."

I sigh against his lips, feeling him smile as he closes that sliver of a gap between us and takes my breath away with his kiss.

"I've been waiting my whole life to love you, Dahlia. We've got nothing but time."

Thirty-Seven – Wildflower

My Compass, Wildflower.

Hours later, we remain sprawled out on the blanket, watching the sky fade from bright blue to softening pastels as the sun lowers on the horizon.

We talk but not much, instead soaking in each other's skin and breath.

One rogue thought enters my mind, and I find myself voicing it out loud. "What if my dad wins in the end? What if he somehow gets me back to Kansas? Makes me take Lou back there?"

"He won't," Everett answers firmly, turning to face me. "But if he did, I'd go with you."

I lift my head, gazing down at him. *There is no way I heard that correctly.* "You'd move to Kansas? For me?"

"And for Lou."

"But this is your home, Everett."

Brown eyes burn straight through me as he shakes his head. "No, this is where I live. Where I grew up. Where my family is. That's all true." He tucks a piece of hair behind my ear. "But you and your daughter are my home." Dragging his hand down my neck, he grasps the necklace at the center of my throat. "You're my compass, Wildflower. I'll follow you forever, because that's where I find home."

"Everett," I whisper, sitting up and tossing my leg over his waist so I'm straddling him. His hands find my hips, holding me in place while I grasp his face. Despite knowing I'll butcher the words I say next, I find the courage because I don't think anything else will suffice. *"T-Ti ho...a-aspettato per tutta...mia vita."*

He cocks his head at me, a bright smile stretching across his cheeks. "Is that Italian?"

"Your mom has been teaching me." I glance down, feeling embarrassed. "I think it's cool you guys can speak so many different languages. I...I thought maybe I could learn too." Slowly dragging my eyes up to meet his, I add, "For you."

Everett lets out a soft laugh, biting his lip as he shakes his head. "You are—"

"And I know that Spanish probably would've been the more practical option, considering our proximity to Latin America and all but... Well, your mom seemed really excited to have someone to teach Italian to. Plus, Italy is at the top of my bucket list, so maybe if I ever get to go someday, I can order my own pasta or something..." I trail off, realizing I'm nervous-rambling again.

"I've been waiting my whole life for you," Everett rasps. "That's what you said."

"I've been waiting for you all my life." I nod. "Or...I think."

He begins laughing, locking his arms behind my back and pulling me flush against him. Ravishing me with teeth and lips and tongue, Everett kisses me until we're both breathless. "This is real," he whispers into my mouth.

I swallow the words on a moan. "Real. We're real."

He groans, pulling away. "I've got more birthday surprises for you, and I don't want to get carried away right now." He slowly lifts me off him, then gathers our leftover strawberries and throws them back into the bag before we both stand and fold up the blanket.

Taking my hand, he leads me out of the endless field of orange wildflowers and back to the peak of the cliffside. I'm stopped dead when we reach the top, transfixed on the exploding sky. The sun sinks beyond the horizon line, a collage of cotton candy–colored clouds reflected on the ocean below it.

"That's so beautiful," I say.

"Yes, you are." I turn to look at Everett, unable to stop my smile as I find him staring back at me, unaffected by the world around us. "C'mere," he says, ushering me over to the back of his motorcycle.

He grasps my hips, lifting me so I'm sitting on the end with my legs dangling off the edge. He steps between them, reaching down into one of the cases next to me and pulling out a small box.

"I wanted to give this to you privately, because there is a chance you may not accept it, and I want you to know if that's the case, we'll understand. I wanted to make sure you feel comfortable."

"We?" I ask, flicking my brow.

He smiles, the setting sun reflecting on his face with a golden hue. "It's from Leo and me. Well, and Darby, too, technically."

Confused, I look down at the box as he sets it in my hand. Popping off the lid, I find a key chain, with one singular key on it, nestled in the center. Raising my eyes back to him, I only tilt my head.

"It's the key to the boardwalk suite next to Honeysuckle."

"Why?" I ask, having no idea where he's going with this. How this is supposed to be a gift to me?

"Do you remember at Thanksgiving when August suggested a cafe on the boardwalk?"

I nod.

"Well, we had those meetings you suggested... We just didn't include you in them."

I frown. "Who's *we*?"

"Leo, Scarlett, Darby, and me. August came to the first couple as well." He grips my hips a little tighter. "We agreed that the best option for the boardwalk would be a coffee shop, and that led to talks of a bakery, and well..." He smiles. "You're the best baker we know."

"But I'm not a baker." I shake my head, at a loss for words. "And I don't know a damn thing about small businesses."

"Baby," Everett laughs, "you're the marketing director of a small business initiative, and I'm your boss. Don't say that to me."

My mouth clamps shut. "I...I don't know what to say."

"Say yes," he murmurs, feathering his lips against mine. "Let me tell you a secret, Wildflower."

"Hmm?" My eyes flutter shut, head dropping back as his mouth connects with my jaw.

"We don't know anything either. Not me or Leo. Not Darby. We're winging it every day, but we figure it out. Together. Because we're a family." He drags his lips along the column of my throat. "You love baking. It's how you relieve stress. It's your therapy. It's the way you show your love to those in your life. It's your passion, and that shines through in everything you make. You're good, and we want you involved, but we're serious about what we're doing here. It's our family legacy, and we wouldn't offer this to someone if we didn't have faith in them. We're not in the business of failing." He pulls back, looking down at me with bright eyes. "We're giving you this because we believe in you, because we think it'd make you happy, and because you should know it's never too late to find your calling."

Something soft and warm settles over me, like a blanket being wrapped around my shoulders in the cold. Like a sense of belonging, something larger than myself telling me I'm exactly where I'm supposed to be. Whatever compass I've been following—while not the direction I intended—finally helped me reach my destination.

"How... How does it work?" I ask.

Everett presses a quick kiss to my forehead. "As soon as you think of what you'd like to name it, we'll help you get a business license. Our gift to you is that we'll cover renovations, get the building up to code and refurbished with a kitchen. Once it's ready to open, you'll take on a lease from Leo, just like your sister has." He grabs my face with both hands. "The rest of the details, we can work out later. All I need you to do right now is say yes, Wildflower."

"I can't believe you guys want me for this."

"We believe in you, Dahlia." He presses his head against

mine, flaming eyes blazing right through my soul. "But you've got to believe in yourself, too."

I nod against him. "Okay, I'll try."

He smiles wide and bright and beautiful. "That's my girl."

I'm the one pulling him against me now, sealing our lips together. He lets out a deep groan, opening for me as my tongue sweeps in, dancing with his. He still tastes like chocolate and all my dreams coming true. He tastes warm and enticing and like he was always meant to be mine. That bone-deep feeling of destiny washes over me once more, and for the first time in my entire life, I think I feel true contentment.

"Thank you," I whisper into his mouth. "This is better than I ever could've imagined for thirty."

I feel him smile. "I'm not done yet, baby." Hand snaking around my back and grasping my ass beneath my dress, Everett tugs me flush against him, his hard body aligning flawlessly with mine. His lips drag down my neck before he reaches my collarbone, sinking his teeth into my flesh and causing me to arch and moan. He continues down my chest, using his free hand to tug the cups of my dress down, allowing my breasts to spill over the top of it.

Dark lashes flutter upward, brown eyes on fire in the fading daylight as he looks at me. His tongue snakes out between his lips, landing a teasing flick against my exposed nipple. A moan cascades from my lips, my hips bucking against his, feeling hardness in the places I most need it. He sucks my entire breast into his mouth, then pulls away with a delicious tug.

"One last present for you," he rasps. "But for this next gift, I need to know: would you rather receive it sprawled out on my bed, or right here and now?"

I let out a sigh when his face falls back between my breasts. "I think I have a good idea of what it'd look like in your bed," I whimper as he swirls his tongue around my other nipple, "but you've got me curious about how you'd give it to me on the back of this bike."

He pulls away, smiling wickedly as he places one hand at the center of my chest and slowly pushes me backward. "Lay down." I do as he says, falling flat onto the leather and arching my back over the saddle of the seat. "Lift your arms above your head." His other hand slides tortuously slowly down my bare thigh, hooking beneath my knee and lifting my leg to wrap around his hip. "Hold onto the handlebars."

I imagine the view I present to him now: laid out on his motorcycle, my breasts spilling out of my top and my dress hiked up to my waist, the sun setting on the ocean behind my back. My breath flies from my lips in short, intense bursts, anticipation stirring in my core and driving me mad.

Everett towers above me—both pure love and feral lust in his features. He's breathing just as rapidly as I am when his hands reach the buckle on his belt, releasing it before unbuttoning his jeans. He lowers them just enough for his cock to spring free—hard and glistening with arousal.

He reaches between my legs, pulling my panties aside and running a finger through my center. "Mmm," he groans. "Just what I thought. Soaked for me."

Feeling a flush run to my cheeks, I bite my lip and nod.

Everett guides his cock between us, and I lift my hips to grant him entrance. We let out a simultaneous moan as he slides inside me, burying himself to the hilt in one thrust. Falling forward, he fists one hand in the fabric of my dress where it's bunched at my midsection, using it as leverage to fuck me hard, both our bodies slamming together with the delicious sound of flesh meeting flesh.

It's wild and fierce and ferocious, the way he claims my body with a punishing pace.

Using his other hand to reach behind my head, he knots his fingers in my hair and pulls me up so our faces press together. Heat shoots through my core, setting fire to my veins, reaching every inch of my body. Tightening my legs around his hips, I lift mine to meet him thrust for thrust, desperate to be closer, so entwined that there is no untangling the two of us.

"Tell me it's real," he growls into my mouth.

"Real," I breathe.

"Tell me you're mine."

"Yours," I moan. "I'm yours."

"Fuck," he whimpers. "Mine. You're mine."

"Yours."

With each thrust of his body into my own, he whispers against my lips.

"I."

"Love."

"You."

"Dahlia."

An unexpected orgasm slams into me as those words filter their way into my being, etched into the fabric of my soul, tattooing themselves across my heart. My hands fly off the handlebars, grasping behind his back to hold him closer to me as I unravel. The wave crests, pure ecstasy washing over me as stars cloud my vision and my body goes taut.

"Everett," I cry. "Everett. Everett."

I cling to him, feeling his cock pulsate inside me as ripple after ripple of pleasure rises and crashes, sparks dancing along my skin. I can't see or think or comprehend. There is only this moment. Only him. Only those four words and the connection of our bodies. The binding of our souls.

"Dahlia," he whimpers, bringing me back to reality. I realize he's gone still, his hips straining in an attempt at pulling back, but the lock I have around his waist isn't letting him move. "Baby, I'm going to—"

I loosen my legs, and he pulls back, fisting his cock in one hand. "Can I—" His voice is strained, cutting off his words.

The feral look in his eye tells me what he wants—what he needs. I sit up, pulling the straps of my dress down my arms and lowering it entirely to my waist. I press my breasts together, nodding at him in silent submission.

Claim me. Mark me. I'm yours.

I don't say the words out loud, but I know my eyes send the

message he's looking for when his head falls back, a moan loud enough to rock the mountain we sit upon tearing from his throat as he loses himself.

Ropes of cum shoot across my chest, painting me in his release. "*Fuck*," he groans, chest heaving, legs trembling as he falls against the back of his bike to hold himself up.

A moment of silence passes as we both float back to Earth, catching our breath. When he lifts his head, those brown eyes are hooded and satisfied—alight with love and awe.

He reaches out, fingers dancing along the hollow of my throat and smearing the release spread across my skin. "You look so pretty with a pearl necklace."

Shocks shoot through my core at his words, eliciting a moan from me. He takes the opportunity to slide two fingers past my parted lips, forcing me to suck his cum away.

His smile is fierce as he slowly pulls out of my mouth, reaching into the backpack and grabbing a spare T-shirt. He softly wipes the remnants of his climax from my chest before throwing it back inside.

Everett wraps a hand around the back of my neck, bringing my mouth to his as he kisses me hard. "My plan was to fuck you from behind so you could watch the sunset." He laughs, and I just realize that it's now near dark.

"This view was better, anyway." I smile.

Thirty-Eight – Wicked

She's My Peace

We arrive back at my brother's house much later than expected. My plan was to get Dahlia off that mountain before the sunset so she could watch it at my back as we took Pacific Highway home.

It was far too easy to lose track of time, though, even as I watched the sun sink low in the sky when she was wrapped up in my arms, and we were lost inside those wildflowers. I didn't want to rush the gift—offering her a bakery of her own. I'm not sure I fully conveyed what it means to me, and to my brother, to invite her into that. If she goes on this adventure with us, she's truly solidifying herself as part of our family. Opening that cafe means that she has to stay here in Pacific Shores, that she's going to stay close to me.

In my head, it answered the prayer I've been pleading for since I met her: she's mine.

When she agreed, the sun setting like a golden halo around her shoulders, she was so earth-shatteringly beautiful that I lost myself. I didn't intend on taking her right there on the ridge, but when she looked at me with those smoldering blue eyes—brighter than the sea behind her head—it felt like kismet, laying her back and showing her just what she is to me right then and there.

Mine.

Yours.

I love you, Dahlia.

She hadn't said it back, but I didn't expect her to, not after all she'd told me when we talked. I don't expect her to say it for some time, but that doesn't mean I won't keep loving her with everything in me. It doesn't mean I don't feel it when she looks at me, when she touches me, when she clings to me like I'm the only thing anchoring her to the earth.

I know what we have goes beyond words, beyond language.

After pulling into the driveway, I kill the engine and help Dahlia with her helmet before lifting her off the bike. We sneak into the darkened house hand-in-hand, assuming everyone is asleep by this time of night. I let Dahlia in before me, then lock the door behind me.

"Monica?" I hear her gasp.

Spinning, I realize there's one lamp turned on in the corner of the living room, and my mother is curled on the edge of the couch with a book in her hand. She lifts her head at us, smiling, but I see the way her eyes are swollen and red.

"¿Por qué estás llorando?"

She shakes her head. *"Estoy bien."*

"No," I say, stepping toward her.

My mother holds her hand out, snapping the book in her lap closed before getting up from the couch. "How was your birthday?" she asks, wrapping Dahlia in her arms.

Dahlia looks at me over Mom's head as she returns the hug, a twin expression of confusion and concern on her face. "It was perfect," she says quietly.

"What'd you guys do?" Dahlia dips her chin, attempting to hide a coy smile. Shaking her head, Mom walks into the dining room, beckoning us to follow. "You know what? Never mind."

"What're you still doing here?" I ask. "Where are Darby and Leo?"

"Down at the beach."

"I've never met two people with less self-control," Dahlia mutters under her breath, causing a laugh to bubble out of me.

"Not like that," Mom chides, rolling her eyes. "Leo's...upset."

"What happened?" Dal and I ask at the same time.

"Sit down."

"Is Lou asleep?" Dahlia asks suddenly.

My mother nods. "She's in bed."

"Dad?" I ask.

"At home." She crosses her hands on the table in front of her as Dahlia and I sit down on the opposite side. "I wasn't planning on being over here so late. Stopped by to drop something off when Elena called. Leo stormed out, and I offered to stay with the kiddo until you got home."

"I'm sorry." Dahlia sighs.

"You've got nothing to be sorry for. That's what families do for each other," Mom says simply, glancing up at Dahlia with sincerity in her eyes.

She lets out an exhale next to me, as if that kind of care is a foreign language she's just learning, as if she's still struggling to understand it. I grip her thigh beneath the table and squeeze lightly.

"Elena's not coming, is she?" I ask.

My mother's bottom lip trembles, and I watch her swallow thickly. She only shakes her head, unable to say it out loud.

My face falls into my hands, three years of disappointment and devastation cascading over me like a monsoon. The weight of that bone-deep weariness is suffocating.

Memories—sudden and painful—flash across my mind.

"You can't leave," I pleaded.

"I can't stay here."

"This is where you live."

"It's where he died."

"We're all hurting, Elena. We need each other to heal."

"Watch someone you've let inside your body get buried and then tell me what the fuck I need, Everett."

"You don't get to monopolize grief."

"I'm not. I'm monopolizing guilt."

I still don't understand what she meant by that. The morning after that argument, she was on a flight to New York City, one I hadn't even known she booked. I didn't see her again for eight months, not until Leo and I took a trip to New York.

By that time, she seemed content to pretend Zach had never existed in the first place.

She hasn't talked about him since.

"What are we supposed to do?" I ask, my tone coming out rough and broken.

A soft, warm touch lands at the center of my back, moving in soothing circles.

"I think that's something to discuss tomorrow," my mother says quietly. "It's still Dahlia's birthday; let's not ruin it with this." I hear her chair slide out from the table. "I've got to get home and tell your father. We'll get together tomorrow and talk this out."

I nod, palms pressed against my eyes as I fight back tears and the scream I want to release.

"Should I wait up for my sister and Leo?" I hear Dahlia ask.

"I told her to text me when they came back up the hill. I think they'll be fine." I feel my mother's lips brush against the top of my head, her hands running through my hair softly. "Ti amo, tesoro," she whispers.

"Ti amo, mama."

The front door shuts a moment later, and that soft hand at my back moves up to my neck, tugging me against her chest as she cradles my head. Her breath is shallow and steady—comforting.

"Do you want to talk about it?" Dahlia whispers.

I shake my head. Words are lost on me at this point.

I feel utterly hopeless. They say when someone leaves their hometown, they only come home for two reasons: weddings and funerals. If we can't get her back here for the happiest day of our brother's life, we'll never get her back at all.

If New York was healing her, if it's where she was meant to be, I'd try harder to understand, but I know the reason she hides out east is because she's *not* healing. She's letting all of her wounds fester. She's fucking killing herself.

And I'll be damned if the only way I get her back here is by her own funeral.

I take a deep breath, knowing it's unfair to Dahlia for her birthday to end this way, not after I worked so hard to give her a perfect day. Pulling my head from my hands, I look at her, and she's smiling softly at me. "Come on," she says, standing from her chair and grabbing my hand. "Let's go to bed."

I pause, eyes fixated on her outstretched arm and the direction she pulls me, toward the stairs. Her room. "You... You want me to stay?"

A grin splits her face, light shining in her blue eyes. "Yeah, baby. I want you to stay."

A little while later, as Dahlia's breath—heavy with sleep—lands against my chest, I don't feel quite so hopeless. I run my fingers through her hair, and the darkness doesn't feel quite so all-consuming. The exhaustion isn't quite so heavy.

In my arms, she's my peace.

Thirty-Nine - Wicked

Hi, Lele.

I fucking hate New York City.

It's loud. And cold. And I can't see the goddamn sky. I'm suffocated by this smog.

Why do people live here?

After taking a look at the address saved in my phone again, I squint up at the building in front of me, confirming I'm at the right place. There is a buzzer on the door, but the entrance is broken, so it's not even locked.

I easily walk right in before climbing the four flights of stairs until I reach door marked 402. I vaguely remember her apartment from when Leo and I visited last year, but I'd get lost trying to find my own feet in this city, so I'm proud I actually found it.

My knock is followed by a muffled string of expletives and rough shuffling. I glance at the time on my phone. It's just after eleven. Elena's always been a night owl, but damn.

Finally, I hear the turn of a latch and slide of a chain before the door creaks open. Eyes so similar to mine glare at me through an inch-wide crack. Brows furrowed, she looks me up and down, but the moment the recognition hits her, she stumbles backward.

The door slowly swings open, revealing my sister as she covers a hand with her mouth, eyes wide with shock and brimming with silent tears. "Everett?"

"Hi, Lele." I smile.

My heart about stops at the sight of her. She looks exhausted, thin and pale, and sad. But knowing she's here in the flesh, that she's breathing, actually in front of me after nearly a year apart—my bones settle at that. They say a lot of bullshit about twins, but it can't be denied that the connection I have with her can never be duplicated. She always felt a little like my other half, despite the fact we couldn't be more different. Without my sister, it feels like a big chunk of who I am is missing from me, like I'm always walking around the world, wearing only one shoe. Something just isn't *right.*

I take the deepest breath I've been capable of taking in a long, long time, and I open my arms to her. One quick glimpse of vulnerability flashes across her face as she steps into me. At hardly five feet tall, she barrels into my chest, wrapping her arms around my waist. I bring my arms around her head and hold her to me, knowing the moment I let her step away, she'll be wearing that mask again. She'll hide all her emotions like she always has—though it's worse now. She'll probably realize she's pissed at me for turning up unexpectedly.

I squeeze her one more time, hearing her sigh against me before she pulls away. Just as I expected, rage now simmers in her eyes. "What the fuck are you doing here? Why didn't you call me first?"

There are a lot of reasons I didn't call her first. If I had, she would've found an excuse not to see me, to not let me in. She sure as fuck would've found an excuse not to do what I'm about to make her do. I don't say that, though, because she's irrational when she's furious. "Thought it'd be more fun to surprise you."

She rolls her eyes just as a groan echoes through her very small apartment, followed by a sleep-mused, "Baby?"

For the first time, I take note of our surroundings. Elena's entire unit is about the size of my bedroom. It's a studio with a couch under the only window—a kitchen with nothing more than a half-sized fridge, a hot plate, and a sink, plus a bathroom I'm fairly certain I couldn't even fit inside. On the other side of me is a small television, her desk beside it. Books are piled all around the floor, along with various stacks of paper. The kitchen counter is littered with take-out boxes, the floor covered in dirty clothes.

The far end of the apartment holds her full-sized bed, and I now realize the pile of blankets heaped on top of it are not blankets at all. They're a man, likely the source of the noise I just heard.

I turn back to my sister, raising a brow. She doesn't look the least bit embarrassed, striding back over to her bed in nothing but a T-shirt and—I pray to God—a pair of underwear beneath it. Sliding the comforter off the man, she wraps it around her shoulders before patting his ass. "Get up."

Completely naked, this guy rolls over to face my sister, giving me an unfortunate view of his flaccid dick. I lean back against the farthest wall from her bed, crossing my arms. The man slowly opens his eyes, blinking around the room. He smiles sleepily at my sister, but the moment his gaze lands on me, he scrambles back on the bed, reaching for the sheets that are no longer there.

"Oh, shit!" He flies out the bed, stumbling toward his jeans. "Oh, fuck." He jumps into them, urgently searching the floor for the rest of his clothes. "I swear to God, man, I didn't know she had—"

"He's my brother. Calm down." Elena sighs, looking uninterested. "But you do need to go. Sorry. He showed up unexpectedly."

The man pauses, looking back and forth between us. "Your brother?" His eyes track my body, starting at my feet and making their way upward, likely taking note of our size difference. "That's worse!"

I snort. "If I gave a fuck who my sister was sleeping with, I would've lost my mind a long time ago."

Elena glares at me as a look of confusion takes over Nameless Man's face. He finishes dressing in awkward silence before my sister leads him to the door, ushering him out before slamming it behind him.

"Thanks for that. I was afraid I was going to have a hard time getting him to leave."

"How long have you known him?" I ask.

"What time is it?"

"Eleven thirty."

Elena nods. "About twelve hours then."

"Christ, Elena," I mutter.

She laughs. "You're one to talk."

That's true. The last time I hooked up with someone I didn't know, I fell hopelessly in love with her, which might be more embarrassing than the nameless one-night stand itself.

"So..." she drawls as she grabs a pair of sweatpants off the ground and hikes them up her legs. "How are you doing? Why are you here? When do you leave?" She smiles at me sarcastically as she falls back into her bed.

"I'm great." I take a slow spin around her apartment. "Is the furniture yours or did it come with the place?"

"Came with the place."

"So, what? Just the clothes and books are yours?"

Her eyes narrow, studying me intently as she drawls, "Essentially. Why?"

"Great." I smile. "Less we have to ship that way."

She sits up straight, tucking her knees against her chest. "What the fuck are you talking about?"

"You're coming home, Elena. Today."

She laughs, stopping the moment she realizes I'm not joining her. "Are you kidding?"

"No," I say, moving to step into the door.

"I'm not going anywhere."

"Yes. You are."

She swings her legs off the bed, leaning toward me. "You can't make me do a goddamn thing."

"Fine." I expected this to happen. I have a plan in place, so I remain calm. "I can't make you do anything." I slide down the door until I'm sitting against it, raising my legs and letting my hands rest on my knees. "I can wait until you're ready to work through whatever shit is going on in your mind. I'll sit right here with you."

"You are blocking my door," she growls. "You show up to my fucking apartment without warning, demand I pack up my whole life, and then *block my door* when I say no? Who the fuck do you think you are?"

"Something tells me you didn't have many plans today anyway, Lele. In fact, I'd be hard-pressed to believe you have any plans any day," I say simply. Her nostrils flare, but she turns her head away from me. "I think you sit here and let yourself *rot*, and you're afraid to come home because you don't want the rest of us to see it—but the thing is, Elena, we do. We *feel* you dying from the inside out. I feel it, right here." I point at my chest. She refuses to look at me, jaw trembling as she stares at the wall. "We hear it in your voice, in the silence you leave when you don't answer our calls. We don't have to see it. We know.

"I can understand your fears, but you've got to try understanding mine too. Imagine if the roles were reversed, and you were in my shoes? Imagine if Leo was refusing to attend your wedding?"

I watch a tear roll down her cheek, and she bats it away, thinking I didn't see it.

I don't tell her about Leo's ultimatum, because I know it'd only make things worse. Elena's too damn stubborn to be swayed by something like that. She'd challenge him to give up on her and play into all of his fears. She's afraid those in her life expect the worst from her, and her defensive nature causes her to try to live up to those expectations when she feels cornered.

"You know if I had told you I was coming, you would've tried to talk me out of it. You would've found some excuse to keep me away, to avoid any conversation of you coming home. You know that, Lele." She still doesn't look at me. "I'll sit here until you're ready to talk, until you're ready to go and face whatever it is you're so afraid of. But I'm not leaving without you."

She looks at me now, angry tears glistening in her eyes.

"You'd do the same for me."

Her features soften just noticeably, and she gives me a shallow nod, her only glimpse of understanding. But she says nothing, leaning against the wall behind her bed and closing her eyes.

We sit in silence.

❧

"I don't do it on purpose." The words come out on a cracked whisper, startling me from my thoughts.

Thoughts about Dahlia, if I'm being honest. What she's doing. What she ate today. If she's missing me as much as I'm missing her. *Fuck*. I'm in deep.

I don't know how much time passed in silence, but I do know my ass is numb from sitting on my sister's floor. I look up at her, finding her on her side, head resting on her pillow as she faces me.

"Don't do what on purpose?" I ask.

"Avoid you guys. Avoiding coming home." She swallows. "I...I just feel so tired all the time, and sometimes, the thought of making small talk, or pretending I had a good day, or that I'm doing anything with my life is too much. I watch my phone ring with you, or Mom, or Leo, and I'm so fucking tired. I can't get myself to answer."

"I understand. We all understand," I respond softly. "You could always tell us that."

"You'd worry."

"We're already worried."

She sighs. "I've tried coming home. Last year for Mother's Day, I'd booked my flight and everything. I hailed a cab, got halfway to the airport, and then asked him to turn around. The thought of getting on the plane, spending all that time alone in the air, and then stepping foot back in California after so long..." She shakes her head, eyes glazing over with some faraway memory. "It felt too heavy. I couldn't bring myself to even try again."

Those words gut me, but I try not to let it show.

"I get it. This time, you won't be alone."

She looks so...numb. She refers to her feelings as heavy and tiring but can't seem to associate them with any emotion, like she doesn't know how to feel at all. She looks so small in her bed, surrounded by heaps of blankets, staring across the room but seeing nothing.

My mind reels backward as a sense of déjà vu floods me.

"Get out of bed, Elena. Please."

"She needs more time, Everett," my mother says, voice breaking with tears as she stands in the doorway.

My sister has been wasting away in the guest room of my apartment for two weeks now. She doesn't eat. I don't think she sleeps. Doesn't read or write. Certainly doesn't shower. She doesn't even speak. She stares at the wall, seeing nothing.

She didn't go to her apartment. Not the place she last spoke to him.

Not my parent's house—her childhood bedroom, the place she spent her whole life loving him.

She came to my house, somewhere safe, with as little association to Zach as possible. I welcomed her at first. I needed her. I let her wallow. Stare at the wall. Rot away if that's what she wanted. But when she didn't show up to the funeral, when she refused every meal I made for her, when she ignored my parents' calls—I hit my limit.

The only time I've seen any ounce of emotion from her is when August tried to visit. A rage I'd never seen her possess flashed across her face.

"Keep him the fuck away from me," *she'd said.*

Everyone told me to give her space. Give her time. She'd come around eventually.

It has been over two weeks since Zach's death, and as unfamiliar as we are with grief, I know this isn't fucking normal. She's not even in this room. She might as well be dead too. I feel her more deeply than they do, so I don't give a shit what my parents or my brother say.

She needs to get the fuck up.

"Elena, please. Take a shower. Go for a walk. Do something."

Dead eyes and silence are my only response.

"C'mon, Lena. For us," Leo murmurs from beside me, tears streaming down his face.

"Talk to me. Look at me." I grab her face, tilting her head to face me. Nothing. "Fucking do something, Elena!"

My fear and hopelessness hit their boiling point, rage spilling over. The smallest flash of recognition passes through her eyes, but it's gone an instant later.

On my knees next to her bed, I hold her limp hand. My face falls into the mattress, and for the first time since I was told my best friend died, I cry.

Because I think I lost my sister too.

I can't ever let her get back to that place, and the way she looks right now is hitting too fucking close.

"We shouldn't have let it go on this long, Lele," I say. "We hoped starting over somewhere new would heal you, but it's clear you're not healing at all. We should've been here for you more."

"I didn't want you to be," she whispers.

"I know." I nod. "And we should've realized it's not always about what you want; it's about what you need." I scoot across the floor until I'm sitting in front of her bed, and she has no choice but to look at me. "And you need to come home." I take her hand in mine. "You're not alone this time. I'll be with you. I'm here to help."

"What if I can't? What if I get in the cab, or get to the airport, and I can't do it?"

"Then we'll come back here and start again, as many times as you need. But I'm not going home without you."

She runs her fingers across the flowers tattooed on my hand.

"Plus, it'd be really unfair to leave Leo all alone out there with Mom and Dad. They're far too suffocating to be one-child kind of parents."

A soft laugh filters out her mouth, and I breathe easier at the sound of it.

"What about my stuff?"

I smile, feeling hope rise in my chest. "We'll pack tonight. I've got some guys coming by tomorrow morning who will get it shipped home for you."

"Tomorrow morning? How were you so sure I'd say yes that quickly?"

"Hope, Lele." I tap her nose, and she swats my hand away, hiding a smile. "You'll find it again soon too."

She gives me an eye roll that says she's unconvinced, but I'm not. We all let ourselves wither away the last few years, but as I've rediscovered what it means to live for something, I refuse to allow my sister to have any other outcome. Leo found healing in waves and in Darby. I found it in our businesses, in Dahlia and Lou. Elena needs to find her way back to words. She needs to write again and rediscover the one thing she was put on this earth to be: an author.

She may refuse to search for hope on her own, but Elena has always been stubborn. Sometimes, she just needs someone to push her out of the boxes she places herself in, and I've forgotten that I'm uniquely qualified to do just that.

She needs her home. Her family. She needs to fix whatever shit happened between herself and August. Once she finds that hope, I know she'll be okay.

Forty - Wildflower

Notes On My Sister's Car

I stand frozen at the kitchen window, watching some man I don't recognize lift my windshield wiper and slide a folded-up piece of paper beneath it.

I don't know why I don't chase after him—that's what my younger self would've done. I don't know why I don't yell for my sister, who's sitting ten feet away from me at the dining room table.

I don't feel fear. I don't feel alarmed or even surprised, though I should. I was so sure it was Tana and the parents from school fucking with me, but I don't know who this person is. I've never seen him at a function. I've never seen him anywhere.

I should feel anxiety crawling up my throat.

I've been getting stalked by someone who I now know is a stranger for months. Yet, I can't seem to find it in myself to care. I'm too numb. There is too much of it—too much to be afraid of, too much to think about. I don't have the energy to be afraid of this anymore, to even stop it.

"Hey, honeysuckle, have you seen my—" Leo's words halt as I hear him enter the kitchen. "Dahlia? Are you—" He stops short again as he steps up beside me. "Who is that?"

"I don't know." My tone is completely void of emotion.

"What is he doing?" His voice rises, concern edging his words.

"Leaving another note on my windshield."

Quicker than I can comprehend, Leo's darting through the dining room and throwing the front door open. "Leave the lights off," he says as my sister stands from the table, moving to follow him. "Stay inside!"

Darby freezes, head whipping to look at me with fear on her face. "What is going on?"

My eyes are dragged back to the window, where I watch Leo run down the front porch steps. The stranger sees him coming and turns to get away, but he has nothing on my brother-in-law.

It's completely dark outside. I was only able to catch the guy because I'd been grabbing a glass of water from the kitchen and left the lights off, giving me an illuminated view of the driveway.

My sister stands beside me, gasping as we watch Leo snatch the man by the back of his collar and throw him against the side of my car. He's pinned between Leo and the door as Leo says something, baring his teeth in the man's face.

That snaps something in me, and suddenly, I'm running through the kitchen and out the front door too. "Stay inside, Darby," I call.

"Oh, fuck off," she mutters, following me out.

I rush down the porch steps and close in on Leo, his voice ringing through the night. "I'm not going to ask you again. Why the fuck were you leaving notes on my sister's car?"

The guy is young; he can't be older than early twenties. Dark hair slicked back beneath a baseball cap, his eyes shut tightly as he winces while my brother-in-law yells in his face. "I...I was told to."

"By who?" Leo growls.

"Can you... You're choking me," he grits out. I realize Leo has his fingers twisted in the boy's collar, straining his neck.

"I don't give a fuck. Tell me, are you the piece of shit who has been leaving these notes behind the whole time?"

The kid clenches his teeth, nodding as he shrinks beneath Leo's towering presence.

Leo grips him tighter. "I'm going to ask one more time. Why?"

"I...I do odd jobs. I have an online posting. I'll pick up any kind of work," he stutters between heaving breaths. "Sometimes, it's landscaping or under-the-table construction. Sometimes, it's... deliverables." He gulps. "A few months ago, a man responded to my ad and asked to meet up in Pacific Shores... He–he told me he would wire me money if I messed with someone a little bit, someone who wronged him."

I hear my sister's sharp inhale of breath behind me, the sound matching the sensation of my stomach dropping to the ground beneath me.

The guy gulps. "He'd wire me money with a memo. I was to translate that memo onto a piece of paper and put it on this car." He nods behind him. "He...also made me fuck with the spark plug once so...so it wouldn't start."

I think back to the car trouble I had all those months ago, Everett's confusion as to why the spark plug on a car as new as mine was so worn down. I'd never thought much of it.

"What's his name?" Leo seethes.

The kid flinches. "Ja–Jackson. He never gave me a last name."

"What?" my sister gasps.

Leo's head whips to us, eyes wide and wild. "I'm going to fucking kill him, Darby. I'm going to fucking kill that—"

"It's not Jackson," I say. "There is no way."

My sister's ex-fiancé is no winner. That's for sure. He's definitely manipulative and conniving enough to do something like this, but I know he didn't. Not to me. I know in his head he thinks he was wronged by Leo and Darby when she skipped town on the day of their wedding, but he wouldn't fuck with me. He'd go after my sister directly, and in all reality, I don't think he cared enough about her to go to such lengths for revenge.

"It's Dad," I whisper. Looking at the stranger, I raise my chin. "What did this man look like? And when did you meet up with him?"

He chews his lip. "Last year. Late summer. August, maybe? September. Sometime around then." Leo's practically shaking with rage, but I see his grip loosen just slightly. Taking a deep breath, the kid continues, "He was older. Mid-fifties, I guess? Blond-ish. Brown eyes. Mean as fuck looking."

I let out a sarcastic snort. "That's our daddy."

My sister lets out a long, devastated, defeated sigh. Leo looks gutted at the sound of it. He lets go of his hold on the kid as it's made clear he's nothing but a pawn, another victim of our father's manipulation and mind games.

Stepping back to give him space, Leo reaches into his pocket and pulls out his wallet. Thrusting a wad of cash at the kid, he says, "Look. You don't accept any more of those *jobs* from *Jackson.* If he reaches out to you again, you come find me, and I'll pay you double whatever he does to tell me every detail."

He nods furiously. "I will. I'm..." Looking at me, he says, "I'm so sorry."

I dip my head in acknowledgment, and the kid turns to walk away. As he reaches the end of the driveway, a thought dawns on me. "The first note!" I call out. "I found it after a soccer game. How did you know where I was?"

"I came by early but noticed you walking out the door as I pulled up across the street. So, I just waited until you left and then followed your car." He slips his hands into his pockets and drops his head. "Swear I wasn't stalking you guys all the time. Only when he told me to. I...I needed the money."

I don't know how else to respond, so I turn on my heel and head back inside the house, thankful my daughter sleeps deeply enough that this incident likely didn't wake her.

"Dahlia," my sister calls behind me, and I know what's coming next.

I run up the staircase and sneak into my room to obtain the item I've been hiding in my bedside table for months now before making my way back downstairs where I know Darby and Leo will be waiting for me.

I reluctantly step into the kitchen to find the two of them leaning against the counter. Leo looks angry, but I know it's not aimed at me. His eyes soften with concern when they land on me. My sister's eyes are red with rage and the tears I know she won't allow herself to shed.

I silently slide the thumb drive in my hand across the counter until it glides to a stop in front of them. Both of them raise their heads, confusion on their faces.

"That's why," I whisper. "*That* is the reason for all of it."

"I think it's time you stop harboring whatever bullshit you've been keeping to yourself and tell us what the hell is going on," Leo says.

I nod, because my line has been drawn, and soliciting a stranger and telling them what kind of car I drive and where I live—where my daughter sleeps—is crossing it. My father thinks the only thing I've ever wanted is his acceptance, but he's dead wrong.

I want my child safe. Happy.

That need trumps all else, and he has called it into question too many times.

"That thumb drive contains files that compromise Dad and his entire company. Fraud. Embezzlement. Forged documents. Enough to put him away for quite some time. I found the information when I was still working for Andrews Development, and when I left town, I used it for blackmail so he wouldn't come after us." I swallow, looking directly at my sister. "So, he wouldn't come after you."

"Dahlia..."

I cut her off as I spill everything I've been hiding the last few months. The conversations with my father and his threats. The reason he told Jason I left. The reasons why I kept it from them and why I was trying to protect them.

As I speak, my sister's tears begin spilling down her cheeks. Leo wraps her in his arms, pressing a kiss to her forehead. Her trembling body instantly stills at his touch, settling whatever war is raging in her mind. Suddenly, I miss Everett.

He's on a flight back from New York right now, his sister with him. He has enough going on with bringing her home, and I can't imagine what emotions that's going to stir up in all of them, but it doesn't stop me from wishing he was here to hold me too.

"We have to do something," she says, more to Leo than to me. "He can't keep doing this to us. I don't know why he won't let us go and leave us alone."

"Do you think he'd stop if you gave him those files back?" Leo asks quietly.

"No." I shake my head with confidence. "He told me that if I gave it back, he'd leave me alone, and he'd get Jason off my tail too. He point blank told me that he'd never give up on Darby, though." I chew on my inner cheek. "He sees Darby as his property, a cherished item you stole. He saw me as something he never asked for but couldn't get rid of."

I honestly don't know which one of us has it worse.

"I hate him," my sister chokes through her tears.

I don't have it in me to cry over that man anymore, but I say, "Me too."

I hate seeing her broken, especially when she has been fighting so hard to find her happiness, when she's come so far. I can't stand seeing her spiral.

After rounding the counter, I pull her from Leo's arms. He lets her go as she turns to face me, face falling into my shoulder. "It's okay, Darby," I whisper. "We'll figure it out. But we can't have you crying like this a week before your wedding." I force a smile on my face. "We've got too much to get done, and crying all the time is gonna make you puffy."

She lets out a broken laugh, nodding against my chest.

"Let's get you down the aisle first, and we'll deal with the rest of this bullshit later."

I meet Leo's eyes over the top of her head. Looking as devastated as I feel, he sends me a silent nod.

Forty-One - Wicked

Got Pickles?

I rush through the front door, attempting to remain as quiet as I can but too on edge to care much. The house is dark and silent, as it should be in the middle of the night, but the text message I received from my brother on the flight back to California had me rushing to his house the moment we touched down.

I find my brother sitting on the couch in his living room with his face in his hands. He lifts his head when he hears me enter, a mix of exhaustion, devastation, and anger coating his features.

"Where's Dahlia?" I ask.

He silently stands and leads me down the hallway behind the kitchen, where I know his bedroom is located. Quietly, he creaks open the door, and we both peek our heads inside. Darby and Dahlia are in bed together, sleeping deeply, turned on their sides and facing each other.

All of my instincts go on alert at the sight of them.

Something happened.

"Lou?" I ask, panic rising in my chest.

"She's okay," Leo reassures me. "She's asleep in her own room."

Knowing I should let her sleep, my instincts betray my efforts as I step to the side of the bed she's sleeping on, brushing my lips across her temple. I need to feel the warmth of her skin—it has been too long, and I'm too worried to go without reassurance.

She stirs, turning to face me as her eyes slowly flutter open. She blinks rapidly, taking in her surroundings before realizing I'm standing in front of her. "Everett?" Her voice is groggy and sleep-mused, so I hush her, kissing her head again.

"I'm here, baby. I needed to make sure you were all right." I run my fingers through her hair. "You go back to sleep, Wildflower. I'll be here when you wake up, okay?"

She raises a hand, covering my fingers with her own. "You promise?"

I bend forward, pressing my lips to hers breathily, inhaling her coconut scent and warmth. "Yeah, baby. I promise."

She turns back over, inching closer to her sleeping sister as I back out of the room and shut the door behind me, following my brother into the kitchen.

"What the fuck happened?" I ask.

"You hungry?" he asks, opening the fridge.

Actually, I am, but there's no way I'm going to keep anything down until I understand what happened to Dahlia. "No."

He nods, shutting the fridge as I fall into a barstool across from him. "We caught the fucker leaving notes on her car."

"What?" I immediately stand back up.

"Calm down," Leo says, motioning for me to sit. "I took care of it. It won't happen again."

I nervously scratch my beard, taking a seat as Leo does the same across the island from me. "Who was it?"

"Random kid. He was paid by her father."

"And that's who has been behind it this entire time?"

My brother nods solemnly.

"Fuck." I rub my eyes, suddenly feeling bone tired. The last forty-eight hours have been a whirlwind of stress and anxiety. This was the last thing I expected to come home to, but when I saw the message from my brother that something happened to Dahlia, adrenaline rushed through me. I couldn't breathe or think or halt until I reached her.

"Is this guy a complete basket case or what?" I ask.

"She has been blackmailing him." Leo sighs.

"Who?"

"Dahlia," he confirms. "She has been blackmailing him with files that incriminate his company. This was his retaliation." He runs a hand down his face. "I don't understand his motivations—I'm not even sure he understands them. I guess he thought he could scare her into running back to Kansas?"

"Why the fuck would Dahlia blackmail him?" I seethe.

Unease funnels in my stomach at the thought of the secrets she's been keeping all this time. Why would she knowingly and willingly play with fire after she spent her entire fucking life being burned? I rub my chest, feeling the sensation there, the worry and dread and trepidation.

I swear to God, she's the most complicated, stubborn, reckless woman I've ever met. I feel so angry at her for putting herself at risk, and at the same time, I'm in utter awe, because I know whatever her reasoning is, she was doing it to protect her sister and her daughter.

Dahlia is complicated, stubborn, and reckless, but fuck—she's also selfless. She's protective and nurturing. She's the most incredible woman I've ever known.

"She drives me crazy," I find myself murmuring.

Leo lets out a laugh. "Yeah. They'll do that to you."

"I don't understand the logic behind it," he continues. "But at the time, I guess she felt it was the only thing that was going to keep him from coming after Darby and forcing her to go back to Kansas."

"Darby's a grown woman." I shake my head. "He can't force her to do anything."

Leo nods but adds, "Dahlia clearly learned to blackmail from somewhere. I mean, the guy is manipulative and controlling. He forced Darby back home once before, and I know it's something Dahlia feels a lot of guilt about. I think she was afraid of him succeeding again." My brother looks down at the counter, frowning. "She told us she owed us this, that it was her turn to protect Darby. She thinks it's her fault Darby went home all those years ago, her fault Darby lost..." Leo doesn't finish his sentence.

"Dahlia was not responsible for that," I snap. "That was an accident, and the aftermath of it was no one's fault but *his*."

"I agree with you," my brother shoots back. "Darby and I have never blamed Dahlia for a goddamn thing."

I nod, feeling sorry for assuming otherwise. My face falls into my hands. "This is fucked."

"Yeah," Leo agrees. "Darby broke down when she found out, and we agreed she doesn't need this kind of stress so close to the wedding. I told that kid to fuck off with his notes and come to me if he receives any more messages from their dad. In the meantime, we're going to get through the next few weeks and then figure out what to do."

"The only thing there is to do is hand those files over to authorities and put that piece of shit in prison."

"I know." My brother nods. "But that's not up to us. We need to let them figure that out on their own. That decision comes with a cost too."

I let out a long sigh. "Fuck."

Rounding the counter, Leo pats my back as he takes off toward the back door. "C'mon. I've got something for ya out here."

I follow him out of the house and into their detached garage. He flips on the light before unlocking a small box on the top shelf where he stores his surf gear. He turns to face me, smiling with a joint between his lips and a lighter in his free hand.

"Let's go take a walk."

"Are we bad boyfriends?" I ask, blowing out a puff of smoke.

Leo snatches the joint from my hand. "We left a note." Taking a hit, he adds, "Plus, we checked in, and all was well. We locked the door behind us. They'll be all right."

I nod. We reach the end of Oceanside Avenue, taking a right

down Pacific Street.

"They needed their sister tonight, and we needed our brother."

God, I remember why I don't smoke with him anymore. Leo gets annoyingly affectionate when he's high.

"How's Elena?" he asks, sounding suddenly solemn.

With all the chaos surrounding Dahlia and Darby, we hadn't had the chance to even address that our sister is finally home after three years. I didn't have the capacity to talk about it, I don't think, but the weed has my head feeling a little quieter and my body feeling a little lighter.

"She's okay, I think."

Leo nods. "She at your house?"

"Yeah. Mom and Dad waited up for us, so they were there with her when I left." I look at him, watching his throat work as he inhales another hit. I can tell he's thinking deeply. "You're going to go see her, right?"

He turns to me, eyes narrowed. "Of course."

"Good."

I turn left down an alley that separates Pacific and Strand, heading toward the house I know but never visit. "Where are we going?" Leo asks, catching up to me.

"August's."

I hear him halt behind me. "At one thirty in the morning?"

"You know he'll be up."

"Why?" he calls from behind me.

I turn around. "We've got to tell him she's back. He needs the heads up."

My brother sighs, taking one last hit before snuffing it out and placing it into his pocket. We finish the rest of the walk in silence, arriving at the two-story, craftsman-style home. I walk up the front porch steps with my brother on my heels before knocking lightly on the olive green door.

A minute goes by with no answer, but I can see a dim light on from the window next to the door that I know to be the living room. Leo walks right up to the window, cupping his hands around his mouth and shouting, "Auggie! Let's open up, brother."

"Shut the fuck up," I hiss. "He's got neighbors and shit."

My brother shoots me a dopey, stoned smile.

Finally, the door creaks open, and two green eyes assess us from the other side behind a pair of black-rimmed glasses. "What the hell is going on?" he whispers aggressively.

"We came to say hi," Leo says.

"I want a tattoo," I add, deciding suddenly.

"Are you guys drunk?"

"No, we're high." Leo chuckles.

August rolls his eyes, opening the door wider to allow us in. We follow him into the sunroom off the side of the house—the house his brother bought but never had the chance to move into before he died. Zach always planned on having August be his roommate, and after his death, he couldn't sell it, not when it was a home Zach loved so much and had been so excited to spend his life in. August has been here on his own ever since.

He utilizes the sunroom as an art studio, where a table sits in the corner with sketchbooks scrawled across it. In the other corner, he has a make-shift tattoo set-up, which rarely gets used now that he has his own shop.

"Why am I tattooing you in the middle of the night on a Thursday?" he asks, sorting through his equipment as I fall back into the leather chair.

Leo sprawls out next to us on the couch at the center of the room. He looks at me and raises a brow, as if to say: *this is all you.*

"Let me walk you through the design first, and we can talk while you're working."

August gives me a bemused expression, but he only shrugs before going back to the box he's sorting through. He pulls out his sketchbook, and I walk him through my idea. It's something I've had in the back of my mind for a while, but something about this night and all the chaos in my life has me wanting to pull the trigger on the idea.

Watching him effortlessly draw up a design far beyond anything I was capable of imagining in my head. After I approve the artwork, August sanitizes the spot on my chest where I want the tattoo, and I take a deep breath as the gun buzzes to life, dull burn and razor-sharp sting blasting through me.

I've gotten enough tattoos that I don't react much anymore, but that first prick is always a jolt. As I settle into the discomfort, August is focused on my skin, but he clears his throat expectantly.

"Well, I guess I'll just rip off the band-aid," I grit out. "Elena's home, and we thought you should know."

August freezes, body tensing for just a fraction of a second. I swear, I see a shiver roll down his spine, but whatever reaction he's having inside, he hides it quickly. I watch him swallow before he casually asks, "How long is she visiting?"

"She's not visiting. She's *home*." There is finality in my tone because like the conversation I had with my sister, I'm making it clear it's not temporary. She tried her hand in New York, and it did nothing for her. She's home for good, at least until she's healed enough to become a functioning human being again.

I booked her flight for her, and I made damn sure there was no return ticket.

"Oh," he says quietly. "Well...good. I'm glad."

"Are you?" I ask.

He stops, eyes rising to meet mine. "Of course I am."

"You two don't speak."

"Her choice. Not mine."

The tone in his voice seems to end the conversation there, and I glance at my brother, who watches us from his spot across the room. He shrugs at me, and I do the same back. It's clear whatever happened between the two of them is locked up tight, because when I brought the situation up to Elena, she shut it down the same way.

I guess we'll have to leave it up to them to resolve it on their own.

"You got, like, potato chips or something? I need to eat." Leo pats his stomach, getting up from the couch.

"I don't have much," August responds. "But I know you'll make yourself at home anyway, so feel free to scrounge around for whatever you can find."

"You got pickles?" I ask, realizing how hungry I am. Fuck, if a crisp dill pickle doesn't sound good right now.

"Yeah."

"Leo!" I shout after he's gone into the kitchen. "Pickles!"

"Pickles! Fuck yeah."

The next hour passes quickly as we make small talk. We discuss the coffee shop more, both August and Leo elated that Dahlia agreed to be part of it with us. August asks about the wedding, and Leo practically vibrates with excitement over it.

Like he has been waiting all his life to marry Darby.

Finally, after my entire body feels practically numb, August shuts off his equipment and rolls his chair back. "I've got the line work done, but you're going to have to come back next week for shading."

"Got it." I salute him.

"At the shop, though. I can't do it here."

"Why?" I ask as I hop off the bench and admire his work.

"I've got some realtors coming by throughout the week so I'm going to be having to hide all this away and keep the place clean."

I whip around just as Leo dives off the couch. "You're selling?" we ask at the same time.

"I'm just exploring my options," August says in a light-hearted tone, but the smile he gives us is strained. "The mortgage on this house was never intended to be paid with one income." He shrugs. "I've just...I've got to consider downsizing before I get to the point where I'm choosing between my business and my home."

"I can help—" Leo starts.

August holds up a hand, shaking his head. "Do not even start with that."

My brother sighs defeatedly, sinking back into the couch.

"How long do you have? Managing both?"

"I'm okay," August says reassuringly. "I'll make it through the summer just fine. You know how things die down in the winter. We all take a hit."

Leo and I nod in understanding, though none of us are at risk of choosing between our businesses or the roof over our heads.

"If it gets that bad, please consider letting us help you," Leo pleads.

"What about a roommate?" I ask.

August looks at me, tilting his head, as if he hasn't considered that before. His lips twitch up at the corner, almost imperceptibly. "Yeah. That could work."

Forty-Two - Wicked

I'm Their Fucking Endgame

I swing my key ring around my finger as I stroll into the parking lot of Lou's elementary school. A last-minute floral emergency caused a change in plans, and while Darby and Dahlia are at Honeysuckle finalizing arrangements for the wedding tomorrow, I offered to pick Lou up from school this afternoon so they could focus.

Lou doesn't know about the change and would be looking for her mom's Honda rather than my Jeep, so I figured I'd just wait for her in the lobby. I flip my sunglasses on top of my head as I walk inside and plop down in one of the chairs.

Tana sits at the reception desk on the other side of the glass, chatting with a tall, lanky man who has his back turned to me. "I'm so sorry you've been going through that," she says softly. "That's awful."

The guy shrugs. "All that matters is that I'm here now."

"I'm sure she'll be so happy to see you." Tana smiles.

I zone them out, pulling out my phone to check on Elena. I'm constantly afraid she's going to fucking bolt, that I'll come home one day, and she'll just be gone. She's been keeping to the house a lot, but she tells me she's back to writing, so I'm hopeful. If I'm not there to check on her, my parents step in. Leo, too. She hasn't met Dahlia or seen Darby yet, but I'm trying to give her time.

"So, I was actually hoping I could sneak her out a few minutes early. Wanted to take her down the boardwalk and get some ice cream. Ride the Ferris wheel."

"Well, Lucille's class has about fifteen minutes left until their final bell, but... Let me call down to her teacher and see if I can reach her."

"Great. Can you have her meet me—"

Her name rings through my skull, causing the hair on the back of my neck to stand up. "I'm sorry," I interrupt, standing from my chair. "Did you just say *Lucille*?"

There certainly could be another Lucille in this school, but the name isn't common enough for me to let that slide without asking a question.

I step up to Tana, watching her eyes go wide with recognition. "Oh, Everett." She clears her throat awkwardly. "I didn't see you come in."

"Hope that's not my kid you're talking about," I respond, not bothering to sound pleasant.

The man next to me turns sideways, giving me a bewildered expression. "No, we were talking about *my* kid. If you'll excuse us."

Tana's eyes dart between the two of us rapidly, and I'm about to back off, assuming I'm mistaken, and there is another student here with the same name, but the trepidation in Tana's expression has me on edge.

"Everett, does... Does Dahlia know you're here?"

"Yes?"

She glances at the other man, seeming unsure of what to do.

"Who are you?" I ask him.

"How do you know Dahlia?" he asks me.

I study his face. Long, narrow nose that's different from Dahlia's but matches her daughter's. Sandy blond hair with hints of red. And his green eyes. *Lou's* green eyes.

Knowing I should drag this fucker out of the building by his goddamn throat before Lou gets up here, I instead find myself turning to face the reception desk head-on, all my newfound rage directed at one person.

"Were you about to let her fucking leave with him?" I snarl

at Tana.

She gulps, cheeks going flush. "He's...he's her dad." She glances at Jason again. "He said Dahlia knew about it. I..."

"Did *Dahlia* call you and give permission? Do you see this man's name on the approved sign-out list given to you by Lou's legal fucking guardian?"

She tilts her head, sighing. "That's not entirely fair, Everett. You may not know the whole story. Dahlia wasn't allow—"

"I'm going to stop you right there, Tana, because *you* do not know the full story," I seethe. "Are you unaware that over half of all Amber Alerts reported are because the child was abducted by one of their parents? Have you had any sort of training on how dangerous it is to let some random person claiming to be related to a child into the school and tell them where that child is, what time they get out of class, and that you will allow them to leave the premises with the child? Are you telling me that you work here every day, and none of those thoughts has ever crossed your mind?"

She shakes her head rapidly. "I know that. I– He...He knew her name. He knew Dahlia. He wasn't some random person. He's... He's her dad."

"He has no rights!" I'm shouting now, body vibrating with anger. "Do you know why he asked you to have her meet him outside? Because Lou *does not know* him. He has not seen her in years. He legally has *no* claim to her."

Tana's mouth drops open, a look of horror flashing across her face.

"Are you so wrapped up in your petty bullshit? So desperate to think the absolute worst of this woman, you would put her *child* in that kind of danger?"

I'm trembling, my vision going hazy with panic and fury.

I need to know what the fuck that man is doing here, what he wants with my kid. I need to make sure he stays the fuck away from Dahlia too.

"Everett, I—"

Glancing around the lobby, I realize for the first time that he's nowhere to be found. "Fuck!" I run toward the front entrance of the school, shouting behind me, "Do not let Lou out of your fucking sight until I come back. Do you understand?"

Tana nods. "I'm so sorry."

"I'm not the person you need to apologize to," I mutter as I fly out the door.

I take a look around, catching him walking briskly with his hood up about twenty yards ahead of me. He makes a beeline toward the deserted back parking lot, but I'm chasing after him.

"Jason!" I call, catching up. "We weren't done with that conversation."

He halts, slowly turning to face me with his hands raised. "Look, man, I wasn't trying to cause any trouble, all right? I was just—"

"Bullshit," I growl, and before I can think twice, my fist is connecting with his jaw.

He grabs his face, stumbling backward, and I take the opportunity to snatch him by his collar, spinning him around and slamming him against a car. "Tell me what the fuck you're doing here."

"Fuck you," he spits. I cock my fist to hit him again, and he laughs. "Dude, you're doing the most for a woman who is not worth the effort. I'm telling you, she was ruined after she had that kid." He smiles, shrugging. "I know the pussy is good, but the woman attracts chaos. She ain't worth it."

My vision blurs, flooding red.

Suddenly, I've got Jason pressed into the pavement, my knee in his chest. I lean in with a dangerous calm, an effort when my instincts are screaming at me to strike and strike until there is nothing left of him at all. "I fucking dare you to say something else about her." Letting my face hover just over his, I say, "I don't ever want you coming near my girls again. I don't want their names leaving your mouth. I don't want their faces crossing your mind. I want you to fade from their memory entirely, until you're nothing but a name they can't remember. You do not deserve to know them. Do you understand?"

He sneers. "You can call her your girl, call her your kid, but she's still my daughter."

"Father is a title earned, not given, and you're both unworthy of it." He gives me a look of confusion as I tighten my hold on the collar of his sweatshirt. "Give me your phone."

"What?" he grits.

I slam his head against the ground. "Give me your fucking phone." He wrestles his hand into the front pocket of his jeans, pulling out a phone. "Find Dane Andrews in your contact list."

"I really don't think you want to—"

"Shut the fuck up."

Limbs trembling, face red with lack of oxygen where I hold my hand to his throat, kneeling on his chest, Jason slowly begins the call. It rings twice before a deep, male voice rasps, "Jason?"

"You piece of shit."

With utter calm, Dahlia's father responds, "Everett, I assume?"

"Yeah, and you're the sadistic psychopath who plotted to have your own grandchild *kidnapped*, I take it?"

"Is that what she led you to believe?" He chuckles. "I'm surprised to see you so...concerned, especially considering the last time I spoke with her, she called you her...what was it? *Flavor of the week*?"

I scoff, knowing Dahlia doesn't speak that way. He's so full of shit.

Jason shakes his head, barking a sarcastic laugh. "Man, you're nothing but a fuck buddy."

"I'm not a fuck buddy." I press my knee harder into his chest, sending him gasping for air. "I'm their fucking end game." Shifting my weight so my elbow falls into his throat, choking him even harder, I add, "So, listen here, you waste of oxygen: you come around my future wife or my kid again, I won't stop until they have to peel your flesh from the pavement."

I pull off him, standing up and taking a step back.

"That applies to you too," I spit into Jason's phone. "Jason here will be crawling back to Kansas with a black eye and a broken rib to show you just how serious I am."

He scrambles away from me, crawling back against the tire of a car, finally having the good sense to look afraid of me as he catches his breath.

I hear the calculated click on a tongue on the other end of the line. "This is the woman you want to make death threats for? Are you sure about that, boy? She's got a lot of daddy issues."

"Wouldn't worry about that, sir." I smile, watching Jason's eyes blow wide. "I fucked all those daddy issues right out of her pretty head." Knowing it'll twist the knife further, I add, "The only man she'll be calling daddy from now on is me."

I hang up the call, tossing the phone to the ground at Jason's feet.

"How'd you know he was involved?" Jason asks, looking up at me.

"You're not smart enough, nor do you have the motive, to show up here on your own and try to abduct a child."

"I warned her not to fuck with her dad."

"How much did he pay you?" I ask.

He's quiet for a moment, staring at his feet. "Look...yeah. At first, it was about the money. He paid me off a little here and there to call and fuck with Dahlia. He thought if I gave some notion that I was interested in being part of the kid's life, she'd come back to Kansas. I don't know." He shrugs. "But I drew the line at this. I didn't want to be involved. I didn't want to come out here. I tried to warn her, and she didn't listen." He shakes his head. "The man has connections. He has shit on me too. I didn't have a fucking choice." He looks at me, and I see a flash of sincerity in his eyes. "I never would've hurt Lucille. All I was going to do was take her to her grandparents. That's what he asked of me. Drive her back out there so the girls would follow."

I squat down so we're face-to-face. "Here's my friendly piece of advice: don't ever come back here, and don't ever bother my family again, or I will actually kill you. If I were you, I'd take your sweet time heading back to Kansas and do what you can to cut all connections to Dane Andrews, because I'm going to end him too."

I don't wait for his reaction. I don't wait for a response.

I stand straight, spinning on my heel and turning back toward the school to pick up my kid.

Forty-Three - Wildflower

Family That We Chose

"Baby, listen to me. I need you both to leave the flower shop right now and go home. Call my brother and have him meet us there."

"Everett." I sigh. "They delivered the *wrong* flowers. We're having to swap out everything at Honeysuckle with the fucked-up flowers we received from the vendor into make-shift arrangements for a wedding taking place in less than forty-eight hours. We'll probably be stuck in here until tomorrow morning."

My fingers are numb from plucking stems all goddamn day.

"Dahlia," Everett says with deadly calm. "It's an emergency. I just dropped Lou at my parents' house, and I'm heading to your place right now. You need to get Darby out of the flower shop and meet me there."

My breath gets lodged in my throat, a sickening feeling coiling in my stomach and snapping tight. "Is Lou okay?"

"Yes. She's with my mom. She's fine."

It loosens just slightly, but the urgency in Everett's tone has all my atoms on edge. "What's going on?"

"Meet me back at the house, okay?"

He hangs up before I have the chance to ask another question, so I place the roses in my hand back into the bucket of water I found them in and turn to my sister. "Everett said there is an emergency, and we need to head home now."

Darby turns to me, nostrils flaring with undiluted frustration. "I don't think Everett wants to talk to me about emergencies right now. If he has something he needs from us, I greatly invite him to come organize some goddamn flowers here."

"I know, Darbs." *Bridezilla has arrived.* "He seemed really concerned, though. He said we need to get out of here and go home, and that we need to get Leo too."

She groans, throwing her bouquet into a bucket. "Fine. But he is the one coming back here later and finishing these arrangements. I need a bath."

"All right," I say, placing my hand at her back and ushering her out the door. "We'll let him know."

We grab Leo from Heathen's and pile into Darby's Mustang, since I'd gone with her to work this morning, taking the week from work to help her with wedding prep. We're back at their house within ten minutes, but Everett's Jeep is already parked outside.

We all find ourselves huddled around the kitchen island, Everett pacing back and forth across the floor, wringing out his hands. His entire body appears to be trembling with tension.

"What's going on?" Leo asks.

Everett turns to face the three of us, jaw tight and eyes wild. He says nothing as he rounds the counter and closes the distance between him and me, grasping my face between his hands and kissing me roughly.

It's a desperate, urgent, needful kind of kiss, the kind that makes you feel like the other person has been drowning and you're their only source of oxygen.

"I'm so sorry, Dahlia," he whispers against my lips.

"Tell me what happened."

He closes his eyes, shuddering like he's in pain. "They tried to take her."

I step back, gripping his forearms and feeling my nails dig into his flesh as my veins flood with fear. "Who?" Panic rises in my chest, causing my vision to go blurry and my head to spin. "Everett, where is my daughter?"

"She's with my parents." He opens his eyes, keeping my face between his hands. "She's safe, I promise. They're taking care of her. I just.... We needed to talk." His gaze darts to our siblings. "All of us, and I wanted to keep her out of it."

"Who tried to take her, Everett?" My voice cracks, my entire body shaking with the sound.

"Jason," he says quietly. "Your dad."

All that apprehension floods from my veins, my body going taut with the knowledge. My knees buckle, and suddenly, he's the only thing holding me up. It feels like the room is crumbling around me, and all I want to do is go down with it.

"Oh, my God." I hear someone gasp behind me. I think it's my sister.

As the reality of the situation dawns on me, and my instincts finally kick in, I find myself spinning in Everett's arms and reaching for my car keys. He says my daughter is safe, but I don't trust a goddamn person on this planet, not when the man who made me, and the man who made her, are the most dangerous I've ever come across.

"I need to see her."

Everett lets me go immediately, and I run toward the front door.

"If you need to check on her, we can, Wildflower, but are you sure you want her to see you like this? I left her with my parents so we'd have time to sort through this and figure things out."

I pause, turning to face him. "She doesn't know what happened?"

He shakes his head. "No. I caught Jason before she got out of school. She has no idea he was there to begin with."

That has me halting, body falling against the dining room table. She doesn't know. He made sure she didn't have to witness the nightmare I put her in, the nightmare I've subjected all of us to. "She has no idea someone tried to kidnap her today?" My voice comes out a broken whisper.

"No, baby." I feel a warm, rough hand fall to the center of my back, dipping beneath the hem of my shirt to find my bare skin. "Can you guys give us a minute?" he asks from behind me. I hear the shuffling of feet and the slam of a door. "She thinks I picked her up from school because you were busy with the wedding. She thinks she's at my parent's house because Mom needs to hem her dress—which is true, and they're doing that as we speak. The only thing Lou knows is that she's loved and cared for. Those you left behind are of no thought to her," he whispers against my ear, planting a kiss on my shoulder.

Whatever dam was holding me together suddenly ruptures, my tears free-falling. Everett holds me together, wrapping his strong arms around my waist and securing me against him, the rhythm of his heart keeping me grounded.

"What did you say to him?" My tone is a wretched whimper.

"I told him to stay away from my future wife and my kid." He runs his palm down the backside of my head, cradling me into his chest. "That if he came near either of you again, I'd fucking kill him."

I spin around, tilting my face up so I can look at him, desperately searching for the dishonesty I'm accustomed to hearing, for the doubt, the joke. Amber eyes stare back at me with sincerity and fervor and love, so much love that I melt beneath them.

"Your kid?"

"Yes." He smiles, cupping my jaw and brushing his thumb across my cheek. "My kid. My woman. For as long as you both will have me."

I'm not sure where inside our bodies our souls are stored, but whatever location that may be seems to open now, giving itself over to him. My tears halt, and his steady hands wipe away the remnants beneath my eyes.

"Forever." I drop my head into his neck, savoring his warmth, his presence.

I feel his lips on the top of my head as he murmurs, "Okay. Forever it is, then."

Emilio slides a Vodka soda across the bar in front of me. "You remembered." I chuckle.

"You were pretty unforgettable, Dahlia." He winks, turning to my sister. "What can I get you, Darby?"

"Something strong." She sighs. "But also sweet."

He smiles. "I can whip you up something good. Don't worry."

Emilio makes Darby's drink and pours two beers from the tap before sliding those to Everett and Leo, who sit on either side of us.

The bar floods with bright light before dimming again, telling me that the front doors had opened and closed. I place a hand on my sister's leg, garnering her attention. "Are you sure you want to do this?"

Her eyes are sad, but she nods with confidence. "Yes. He went too far."

"He did," I agree.

"What's up, fuckers?" A vaguely familiar slim-framed, tall, Latino man slides into the seat beside Everett, and I assume he must be Ryan, Everett's sheriff friend. He nods at Emilio, who has a drink ready, setting it down in front of him. "You called?"

"Are you off the clock right now?" Leo asks.

He takes a slow sip of what appears to be whiskey. Swallowing, he sets the glass back down on the counter. "Officially so."

"Great. We need off-the-record advice," Everett adds.

Ryan frowns, looking annoyed but not surprised. "Did you break the law?"

"Not sure."

"Fuckers," he mutters.

The six of us lean in close while Emilio keeps other patrons at bay, and Everett and I break down our entire situation of the last months—the information I found on the company network when I worked for my father, the fact that I've been blackmailing him with it and that he used my daughter's father to try to kidnap her in an attempt to get back at me.

"Tana could definitely be fired," Ryan says after Everett explains to him how she nearly allowed Jason to leave school grounds with my child, all too easily believing whatever sob story he fed her about me restricting his relationship with Lou.

As much as I want to throttle her, I almost feel sorry for her. She must be bored and lonely to put so much thought into the reputations of people around her, to be so hung up on the lives of others. I hope she figures her shit out, and I hope she finds herself some real friends.

Friends like we have, because after Everett explained everything to Darby and Leo, it was clear that her wedding flowers were going to take a backseat tonight. So, Leo called Macie and asked her to help. She and Dom, plus their best friends, Carter and Penelope, dropped everything they were doing and made the two-hour trek south. The four of them are at Honeysuckle right now getting things ready for Saturday.

"I don't want to take responsibility for something like that," I say to Ryan. "I won't demand it, but I'll report it to the principal and let the school district investigate on their own. If it happened to me, there is a good chance she has done it before."

He nods. "As for the rest of it... You're definitely at risk, Dahlia. Not that I don't understand it, because I definitely do, but blackmail in and of itself is a felony, and holding onto documents like that without reporting them incriminates you as well."

"I know." I sigh, dropping my hands into my face.

Everett rubs my back reassuringly while my sister downs the rest of her drink, and Leo waves Emilio over to get her another.

"Are you some kind of mandatory reporter?" I ask. "Are you going to have to turn me in now that I've told you all of this?"

"Eh." Ryan takes another sip of his whiskey. "Crime happened in another state. Loophole."

"Is that really a loophole?" Darby asks.

Ryan smirks. "Eh."

Everett winks at me, his way of letting me know I'm safe.

"Do you have any other loopholes as to how we can get that piece of shit sent to prison without incriminating Dahlia in the process?"

Ryan nods, and we all huddle closer. "Does your dad have it in writing from you anywhere that you obtained this information months ago?"

"No." I shake my head. "We had one conversation in person in Kansas before I moved. I know my father does enough shady business that he doesn't keep cameras or recording devices at home. Plus, I caught him off guard, so he wouldn't have thought to set anything up beforehand."

"Good."

"But," I continue, "we did have a phone conversation back in December where I admitted to having the files then." I swallow. "I wouldn't put it past him to have recorded it."

"Were you here in California when this conversation was held?"

I nod.

"Two-party consent state. You're safe."

I hear Everett let out a breath at that.

"For argument's sake, is it possible that a thumb drive containing files from your father's business could've been mixed up with your personal belongings when you left your job at his company?"

"For argument's sake, it's not *impossible*," I respond, polishing off my drink.

"All right, and let's say those personal belongings got stashed away somewhere during your move from Kansas to California. You have your stuff in storage, right?"

"Right. I owned a home there, so I brought most of everything I have out here with me, but since I've been living with them"—I nod at my sister and Leo—"I had to get a storage unit for my stuff until I find a place of my own."

Everett's hand finds my thigh, squeezing lightly.

"So, you're saying it's possible that if you took a look through your storage unit—say you need to find something in there—you could potentially come across a thumb drive you don't recognize, take it home and stumble upon some incriminating documents?"

"I suppose that could happen, yes."

Ryan smiles. "Then I'd say, if you were to spontaneously come across something like that, it'd be your responsibility to turn it in to authorities right away."

"And if the incriminated individual claimed she had possession of the documents for an extended period of time and used them for blackmail?" Everett asks.

"His word against hers, and in my experience, criminals are not often believed. I imagine he and his legal team would be more focused on keeping him from receiving a life sentence."

An elephant of anxiety is lifted off my chest, and I take a deep breath, realizing for the first time that there may be a way out of this, a light at the end of the tunnel that my father has kept me locked inside my entire life.

Looking back, I know I should've taken those files and put this all to bed months ago. I could've saved us all a lot of heartbreak and fear, but at the time, I didn't have it in me. My dad was right; I'd secretly been pining for his approval all my life, and the thought of being on top—of finally having something over him—made me feel powerful where I had always felt weak.

The longer I held on, the harder it was to let go, to tell my sister.

Knowingly turning our father in—potentially sending him to prison—is a heavy weight in and of itself, but it's nothing in comparison to the fear that retched through me when I was told he tried to come for my child. If nothing else, she must be protected, and Darby and I agree on that. We need him out of our lives for her.

But maybe for the two of us as well. We deserve to move on, to heal, with the family we chose for ourselves. The family who chose us when our own never did.

"You know"—Leo snaps his fingers, gathering our attention—"I think I threw some decorations for the wedding in Dal's storage unit a few months ago. We're probably going to need to go get them."

Darby nods, face flushed with alcohol. "Yeah. I think you're right."

Ryan winks at them. "Well, I'll be at the wedding if you have anything you might need to...run past me."

They continue making small talk, hatching their plan. I notice Everett silently slide off his barstool and grab my hand, pulling me with him as he leads me toward the pool table at the back of the bar.

"You two better stay where I can see you!" Emilio shouts, sending a cluster of laughter our way.

"We're playing pool, asshole," Everett calls back, grabbing two cues and a rack off the wall. "Thought you could use some space to breathe, and you never did get the chance to show me your skills."

I hum, reaching up to kiss him on the cheek. "Well, I'm not faking them this time, so consider yourself warned."

He grabs my hips, spinning me around and pinning me between his body and the pool table. All the day's chaos, all the heartbreak weighing me down, dissipates at his touch. He's my life raft in a raging sea.

"We're not faking anything anymore, Wildflower."

Cupping the back of his neck, I pull his head down so his lips brush against mine. "We're real," I whisper against his mouth, feeling him smile. "Now, watch me really kick your ass."

Forty-Four – Wildflower

I Want To Dance With Them Anywhere

"I told you if you don't stop tearing up, I'm going to start slapping you," Macie says to my sister as she dabs at the corner of Darby's eyes with a tissue and demands she continue blinking.

"I'm sorry." Darby laughs. "You look so beautiful, Dal. That dress is incredible on you."

"Thank you." I smooth out the soft satin of my bridesmaid dress, fighting back my own tears. "Hopefully, you don't end up wearing it this time."

She snorts, rolling her eyes at me. Macie moves to the side, allowing me to zip up the back of Darby's gown and pin her veil into her hair. She looks stunning, and I can't stop thinking about what a contrast today is in comparison to her last wedding day.

She was beautiful then, but she was dead inside. Today, she's full of life, more than I've ever seen her, radiant and glowing and content. She's excited, practically vibrating with anticipation to run down that aisle to the love of her life rather than run away from it.

I also can't help but think back on how lonely she was at her last wedding a year ago. That bridal suite was full of people. Jackson's mother and sister. Darby's friends from work—though I'd use the term *friend* lightly. Our own mother, who wasn't particularly nurturing or supportive.

Today, there are only six of us.

Darby, Lou, and me, plus Monica, Macie, and Penelope. I know Darby was a little bummed that Elena refused to join us before the wedding. I haven't met her yet, but based on what I've heard, I think it's considered a win that she'll be showing up for the ceremony at all.

The makeup artist Macie hired just left, and we're putting the finishing touches on Darby's look as we drink champagne and laugh in her bedroom. Light music filters from surround-sound speakers across the entire house. There is more love and light in this space than there ever was in that traditional white church. People we've known less than a year are happier to be here than people we knew our whole lives back home.

Macie sways across the room in her tight, strapless red dress that makes her body look insane and sits down on the couch next to her best friend. Penelope is quieter, much more reserved. She doesn't demand attention the same way Macie does, but I've noticed that when she does speak up, she's witty and hilarious. Smart as hell, too.

Her auburn hair falls past her shoulders in thick waves, complementing the emerald color of the dress she's wearing. It's simple and silk, kind of like my dress. She doesn't need embellishments, because her features pull all the attention. She's striking, with her bright hair and deep green eyes, full lips, and thick eyelashes.

"Dahlia," Monica calls, pulling me from my thoughts. "Have you put any more thought into a name for the bakery yet?"

"Yeah, I have." I smile. "But I'm going to share it with Everett first before I tell anyone else."

I think Everett will especially love the idea I've come up with.

Monica smirks, opening her mouth to say more, when there is a knock on the bedroom door. "Can I come in?" a muffled voice I recognize as Carlos asks.

"Yeah!" We all respond at the same time.

He enters, looking dapper in a black tux. His salt-and-pepper hair is slicked back on the sides, and he's wearing a bow tie that matches the color of Monica's purple dress. "Amor," he whispers, bending down to press a kiss to her lips. She smiles back at him, squeezing his hand.

He lifts his head, and I watch his eyes go wide as he takes in the sight of my sister. Her dress is a perfect fit, cascading to the floor like liquid silk. Her honeysuckle-accented veil falls around her shoulders, draping her entire body in multicolored flowers.

But it's the undiluted happiness on her face that's most breathtaking of all.

"*Tan hermosa, preciosa,*" he gasps. "Let me look at you." He steps up to Darby, taking her hand as he spins her in a slow circle. She laughs as he lets out a low whistle.

He turns to me next, smiling just as brightly. "You look lovely, Dahlia. Absolutely beautiful."

"Thank you." I find myself grinning back at him.

"Would you ladies mind if I had a moment with the sisters alone?"

Monica stands from the couch, taking my daughter's hand. "Come on, you. Let's go get your dress on, yeah?" She winks at me, and I plant a soft kiss on Lou's forehead as she follows Monica out.

"We'll go check on the boys and make sure they're ready to go," Penelope says as she and Macie filter out the door.

Carlos shuts it behind them before taking a seat on the edge of Darby and Leo's bed. My sister and I sit next to each other on the couch across from him.

"I know you two have been through a lot, and for most of your life, you've felt abandoned and alone," he says softly.

My sister grabs my hand tightly, and I wonder if the emotion is thickening in her throat the same way it is mine.

"Traditionally, a bride would have her father walk her down the aisle, share a dance with him during the reception. He'd give a speech showcasing his pride and love." He clears his throat, letting out a rough laugh. "I know you don't have that today, and I don't know what kind of emotions that's stirring up inside you. Neither Monica nor I are looking to replace anyone in your lives or fill any kind of space you don't want us in."

My sister begins furiously dabbing at her eyes.

"It's okay," I whisper, removing her hands from her face. "We'll fix it."

"Sorry." Carlos winces. "I...I guess I just want you both to know how cherished you are. We are so grateful you found our boys. That we get to have you—and Lou"—he pauses, smiling at me—"in our lives." He blinks rapidly, as if attempting to fight off tears. "We always wanted a big family, a ton of kids. After Monica had some complications with the twins, she wasn't able to get pregnant again, and we accepted that for what it was. When Leo came to us, we didn't hesitate to make him ours. We thought... maybe it didn't work out all those years ago for a bigger reason. Maybe we were meant to have more kids. They just hadn't found us yet." His bottom lip trembles beneath his smile. "I believe that now more than ever. Now that we have you."

I didn't realize I had been crying, too, until I felt a tear spill over and run down my cheek. I've never been particularly interested in replacing my father figure before, never had much faith in the male species. Part of me still thinks I'm too far gone to ever accept that kind of relationship in my life, but at the very least, I know I have a deep love and care for the two people who I may someday call my in-laws. For the first time, I have faith that they're not lying to me when they tell me they love me too.

I trust them with my child, and I think every kid deserves a good pair of grandparents.

I never had that, never got to experience the kind of relationship with my grandmother that Darby had, and I never felt particularly close to my mother's parents. They're cold and distant, like she is.

But like everything else, Lou deserves better. I'm happy she has them.

Happy we all do.

Carlos stands from the bed at the same time Darby and I get up. He opens his arms to us, and we step into them. "I'd be honored if you saved me a dance tonight," he whispers.

"Of course," she whispers back, silent tears still streaming down her face. She pulls away, quietly thanking him as she squeezes his hand before heading into the bathroom to fix her makeup.

Carlos turns back to me as he reaches the door, flashing a knowing smile. "I hope you'll save a dance for me, too, when the time comes."

"Oh." I laugh. "I'm not sure I'm cut out for all of this."

"Save me a dance anyway, even if it's at the courthouse."

Tears sting my eyes, my throat thick as I swallow down my emotions. "Deal."

Wicked

"Darby's almost ready," Dahlia says from the top of the stairs. "She's in her room. I was just checking on Lou."

She descends in a light-green silk dress that clings to every curve of her beautiful body. It's simple, but she's not. She's exquisite.

There are flowers pinned in her hair, little white ones. Orange and pink, too.

Wildflowers, I think.

She smooths a hand down the fabric of her dress, deep blue eyes locking on mine. It's like the entire world stops spinning on its axis. It pauses at that look in her eyes, and I wonder if that pause is the Earth changing orbit, no longer moving around the sun, but around her instead.

My world. It's her.

"How do I look?" she asks quietly as she reaches me.

"Beyond comparison to anything in this plane of existence," I find myself whispering, more to me than to her.

Because I rack my brain for words, but they simply don't exist, not for the way she looks. Not for the way my chest cracks open at her smile, begging her to fill the gaps left behind.

Cigarettes After Sex filters softly through the house, intensifying the moment that much more.

Because she's a love song.

She's not words. She's music. She's harmony. Fucking peace.

"You look the way this song sounds."

Her breath hitches at that, eyes widening and mouth dropping open. I can tell she doesn't know how to respond, so I only hold my hand out. "Dance with me?"

She lifts her arm, hovering over her chest. A playful smile accents her lips. "Right here? At the bottom of the staircase?"

"Right here." Right now. Because I need to. *Because I need you.* "Please."

She laughs softly, twining her fingers with mine and letting me pull her in. I spin her, getting a glimpse of her phenomenal ass before I tug her against my chest and wrap my free arm around her waist. She rests her head on my shoulder, letting out a contented sigh as we sway in the entry of my brother's house.

He's spending some time with my dad before the ceremony, and I know Darby's in her room with Macie getting her hair and makeup touched up before we head outside. We only have a few minutes, but I couldn't help but steal a moment alone with Dahlia.

"Mom?" Lou's voice calls down from above us. "What are you guys doing?"

"Dancing." I chuckle.

Her little feet bound down the stairs, and I turn us so we're facing her.

"Next to the front door?" She gives me a bemused look, her *you're-a-weirdo* face that I've come to know all too well.

"Wherever we want. Next to the front door or in the grocery store. If I feel like dancing with my girls, I'm going to do exactly that, so you better get used to it."

She scrunches her nose at me like she's unimpressed. Dahlia laughs into my neck, the sound more beautiful than any melody floating around us.

I let go of Dahlia's hand, extending it to Lou. Keeping my

other arm tight around Dahlia's waist, I continue swaying side to side with her next to me. "C'mon, Luz. Take a spin for me and let me see your dress."

She rolls her eyes, but a small giggle escapes her lips as she takes my hand. I hold our arms above her head and twirl her around.

"*Mi lucecita.*" I laugh. "You look so beautiful."

When she's done spinning, she looks up at me with a face-splitting grin that sets my soul on fire. She wedges her way between me and Dahlia, and I rock my girls back and forth in the entryway.

I catch sight of my mother at the top of the stairs, who appears to have witnessed the entirety of the interaction. She's misty-eyed, smiling down at us. I toss her a wink, because while Dahlia and her daughter may not understand the true meaning behind my words, my mother does. She understands what it means when I say I want to dance with them anywhere.

I've finally found everything I've been searching for.

Forty-Five - Wildflower

You Deserve Everything, Dahlia.

"Looks like a rock-solid case. Tax fraud, felony embezzlement, and a fuck ton of forgery," Ryan says, stepping out of his car and meeting Everett and me in the driveway.

The low bass of music pounds beneath our feet, evidence of the raging party going on out back. Darby and Leo's reception is completely wild.

Everett and I took a trip to my storage unit earlier this morning, where I put together a box of Lou's old toys and dropped them at a donation center on our way home.

But as far as the police are concerned, I was grabbing table linens for the wedding and stumbled across an odd thumb drive I didn't recognize. After opening it up at home, I saw several concerning documents belonging to my father's business, and I thought it best to report them to Ryan and get his opinion.

Upon seeing the evidence, it was his duty to turn the files into the police.

"They're on their way to the local authorities in Crestwell, where the business is licensed. It'll take a few days to process, but I'm guessing official charges will be brought against him for at least tax fraud and felony embezzlement."

I let out a deep breath. "When do you expect the warrant will be issued?"

Ryan shrugs. "I expect it to happen very quickly."

Everett's arms tighten around my waist as I fall into him, letting out all the tension I'd been holding in. We head around the side of the house and enter the backyard. The reception rages on with lights, music, and dancing.

The ceremony was beautiful, taking place right at sunset on a crystal-clear day. The backyard was immaculately decorated, in white, green, and yellow florals, Darby and Leo saying their vows against the backdrop of the ocean.

My sister opted to walk herself down the aisle, but she only made it halfway before Leo ran out to meet her at the center of it, pulling her into his arms and kissing her before they even had the chance to say, "I do."

The reception is just as lovely. Everett and I both gave speeches. I opted for heartfelt, whereas he opted for funny, ending with a video of Leo doing a humiliating sandwich chain commercial several years ago, which is apparently the best way to embarrass him. Leo then spent the next several hours getting pleasantly drunk, my sister right along with him.

Now, they move around the dance floor to "Teenage Dream" by Katy Perry, an alarmingly fitting anthem for the two of them. Lou spins in circles with Carlos while Monica chats with August on the edge of the dance floor, smiling at her husband and my daughter.

Elena didn't stay long after dinner, claiming she was tired, though she did give Darby and Leo a surprisingly thoughtful wedding gift before she left.

I realize Everett and Ryan are chatting quietly next to me when Ryan pats him on the back and steps off the porch, heading toward the cake table. "Oh, and Dahlia"—he turns around—"is there any chance your mother could be involved in all of this?"

"I doubt it. He didn't think highly enough of women to let them be involved. Though, that's probably to my mother's benefit now."

Ryan nods. "They'll probably look into her anyway. Just so you know."

"Okay, thanks." I force a smile as he walks away.

"He's probably right." Everett wraps his arm around me, tugging me against his chest. "You could have Darby call her, though, if you don't feel up to it."

A sense of dread washes through me at the thought of talking to my mother. It's not the same kind of fear that comes with my dad, but the pain associated with her is still its own hurt. She was the first one to make me feel like I wasn't enough. Not pretty or thin enough. Not smart or accomplished enough. Not kind or poised or popular enough. She's the one who cared all too much what others thought, and other people always thought I stuck out like her sore thumb. Her black sheep. Her lost cause.

"No. She doesn't need that kind of pressure on her honeymoon." I step out of his arms, rising onto my toes to press a kiss to his cheek. "You go have fun. I'll be back in a minute."

"You're going to call her right now?" he asks.

"Might as well." I shrug. "I've still got some champagne in my system. Liquid courage and shit."

Everett lets out a laugh, shaking his head. "I can come with you."

"It's okay. You go," I urge. "I'll be right out. I promise."

"I love you, Dahlia." He takes my hand, brushing his lips across my knuckles. "No matter what your mother says to you in there, when you come back out, I'll be waiting, and I'll still love you. I'll still think you're the best thing that has ever happened to me."

My mind and heart and soul scream at me to say the words back to him, knowing I've never meant anything more. But they get lodged inside my throat, and all I'm capable of is offering him a smile, turning to head inside the house.

The music lowers to a dull roar as I shut the door behind me before running up to my bedroom and grabbing my phone off its charger. Scrolling through my contacts, I select my mother's name and press call. It's late here, even later in Kansas, which might be the reason why I pulled the trigger so soon, secretly hoping she won't answer but being able to say I tried to warn her.

She does pick up, though, on the third ring.

Her groggy voice echoes in my ear. "Dahlia?"

"Hey," I say lamely, unsure how to address her.

"Oh, my goodness," she gasps. I hear rustling on the other side of the line. "You're actually calling me. Is everything okay?"

"Not really," I mutter. "Um. Is Dad near you at all?"

"No. I–I'm, uh... Well, no. He's not here."

"Are you lying to me?" I find myself asking.

"No, Dahlia. I promise I'm not lying to you." For some reason, I believe her. I think I mostly believe her, because if my father had been in bed beside her when I called, he'd have already taken her phone to speak with me himself.

"Look, Darby and I thought it'd be best if we—"

"Today was the wedding," she interrupts.

"Yeah." I swallow. "She's still enjoying herself, which is why I'm the one calling."

"How was the ceremony?" my mom asks.

"Beautiful." I sigh, deciding to throw her a bone. "It was lovely. She looks stunning."

"I don't doubt it." It's almost as if I can hear her smile. "I'm sure you look stunning too."

I want to snort at that, but I choke it back.

"Is she happy?" my mother continues.

"She's very happy."

"And you... Are you happy?"

Chocolate brown eyes and steady, tattooed hands flash across my vision, bringing a smile to my face, one I know she can hear in my voice when I say, "I'm happy."

"Good," she breathes, sounding almost relieved. "Good. And Lucille?"

"Lou is doing well," I murmur.

"Thank goodness." She's quiet for a moment before she continues, "I...I want you to know that I heard what your father tried to do. I overheard him speaking to Jason about it yesterday morning. I–I would've called you if I had known beforehand. I would've tried to do something to stop him before he went that far." *That's a first.* I'm stunned by my mother's admission and the sound of her voice breaking. "I left him, Dahlia."

"What?" I crawl back onto my bed, covering my feet with blankets, as if it'll somehow protect me from what I've just heard.

"I'm in Indianapolis with my sister. I arrived yesterday evening." She sniffles. "I didn't tell him where I was going, but I have no doubt he'll figure it out soon enough. He's a little caught up in rage over your sister's wedding right now, so I imagine it'll take some time for him to recover from that. I'm hoping his fury toward me will take a backseat for a while."

"You left him?"

"Yeah." A soft sob rips from her throat. "He crossed the line. He's been crossing the line for years. I'm so sorry my line wasn't you, Dahlia. I'm sorry for that, and I know that nothing I ever do will make it up."

Tears stream down my face, and I do nothing to wipe them away, wishing she could see the way she's breaking me once again.

"My line should've been you, the same way yours has always been your daughter. It was my responsibility to teach you, but instead, you're the person I had to learn from, and I'm so sorry."

I don't know how to respond. I don't forgive her, and I'm not sure I can accept her apology either. I don't know if I have it in me, though it still feels like some inner child deep inside me is being embraced by her mother for the first time in her life.

"Dad has been doing a lot of shady, illegal shit, and I found out about it. I had proof, and I turned it over to authorities earlier tonight. A warrant should be issued for his arrest in the next few days," I find myself blurting out. "I hope they get him before he gets to you. Darby and I wanted to make sure you were aware this was coming."

"Thank you," she says quietly.

"You're welcome," I respond, unsure of what else could be said. "I... I've got to get going, get Lou to bed. Good—"

"Dahlia," she interrupts. "I... If you... If you ever need anything, if you ever want anything from me, I'm here." She sighs. "And thank you. For breaking the cycle. For saving them both."

I know she's referring to my sister and my daughter.

"I wish someone could've saved you," I whisper.

"I wish I could've saved you."

"I didn't want to be saved."

She chuckles. "No, I suppose you didn't, but it sounds like you were nonetheless." She's quiet before adding, "I hope he's good to you."

"Better than I deserve." My nose stings, and a knot of emotion forms at the center of my chest.

"You deserve everything, Dahlia."

Tears spill over again. Not sad or broken or angry tears, but ones of gratitude. Suddenly desperate to be back in his arms, I choke out, "Bye, Mom."

"Bye, Dahlia, darling."

I hang up, dropping my phone onto the sheets next to me. My head falls against my knees as I let out a lifetime of pent-up insecurity and loneliness.

I'm not healed, and I haven't forgiven her. I'm not ready to rebuild any kind of relationship with her, and I'm not sure I ever will be, but I think I finally received the one thing I needed more than the rest.

It wasn't my father's approval I was after all this time. It was hers.

I needed her to admit I was never the problem. I was never broken. She was the one who failed me. They both did. Her acknowledging that truth was the closure I thought I'd never have.

I give myself a few more minutes to cry it out before gathering my composure and heading back downstairs. The reception rages on as I make my way across the yard and find Monica and Carlos at one of the tables. They're watching Everett and Lou with amused smiles as he spins her around the dance floor on his toes.

"Darby and Leo have a car picking them up at eleven thirty

to take them to a hotel downtown, and they'll head to the airport tomorrow morning," Monica says as I fall into the seat next to her. They're honeymooning on some private island owned by a rich heiress friend of Leo's near the Maldives. "We're going to take Lou home with us for a sleepover so you two can have the house to yourselves."

"You don't have to do that," I say, leaning against her shoulder.

"Oh, but I already got Lou excited about it." She smiles down at me.

"Thank you," I whisper.

She responds by grabbing my hand where it rests on the table, and we go back to watching Everett and Lou dance together, my sister and her new husband laughing beside them.

It's then I realize everything I've ever needed is right here in front of me.

Forty-Six - Wicked

Light And All The Colors

"Hey! That's my wife!" Leo yells at me, the most elated grin I've ever seen on another human being plastered across his face as we follow Darby and Dahlia out to the front of the house.

Guests started heading home about an hour ago, and thank God for it, because this isn't the kind of send-off that calls for tossing rice.

Darby's stumbling down the porch steps, being held up only by her sister and laughing hysterically. Leo keeps pointing at her before screaming in everyone's face to remind them that she's his wife and telling her she *looks really cute for a baby giraffe.* Whatever the fuck that means.

I don't think either of them had a morsel of food all day, between pre-wedding jitters and a jam-packed reception, but they sure drank their fill of champagne.

"Oh, my God! A limo!" Darby squeals, taking off toward what is not a limo, but a town car Macie booked to drive them from the reception to the hotel.

Stumbling forward, Dahlia chases after her, holding her sister's elbow as she attempts to help Darby into the vehicle. As soon as the driver pulls the door open, Darby falls face-first onto the seat, crawling into the back. Dahlia groans, wiping a hand down her face before turning to look at me with a vexed expression. I help Leo down the rest of the entry, and he crawls into the back too.

"I don't think they're going to be consummating this thing tonight." I laugh quietly, kissing Dahlia on the cheek.

"We already did!" Darby pipes up from inside the car. "After the ceremony in the bathroom."

"Thanks for letting us know," Dahlia murmurs.

After he's settled, Leo pokes his head out and glares up at me. "Don't challenge me, brother. I'll consummate this thing right here and now." He hiccups, causing a bout of giggles from his wife beside him.

"Please don't," I mutter, slamming the door in his face.

Dahlia lets out an exasperated sigh as I turn to the driver. "Hampton Hotel downtown. Call the front desk when you arrive and let them know the reservation is for Leo Graham. They'll send someone out to make sure the two of them make it to their room," I say, slipping a fifty-dollar bill into his hand as I shake it.

He nods, rounding the driver side and taking off.

Dahlia and I walk back to the house hand-in-hand, meeting my parents at the front steps. My dad buckles Lou into the backseat of my parents' car, where she immediately fell asleep about ten minutes ago. Dahlia leans down, pressing a soft kiss to her head. "You don't have to take her; we can put her to bed upstairs."

Monica shakes her head. "You two take the night to yourselves. I've got plans for us tomorrow, anyway." She smiles down at Dahlia's daughter. "You guys can sleep in. You deserve it after all of"—she waves toward the car disappearing in the distance—"that."

Dahlia snorts. I press a kiss to the top of Lou's head, giving my dad a side hug before roping my mom into my arms. We say our goodbyes as they head out to their car. Guests are gone, and just a few event staff remain, taking down the reception. Most of the shit will stay overnight, and a team will come back tomorrow to complete the rest of the cleanup.

We enter the quiet, darkened house, locking the door behind us. Dahlia is silent as she leads us up the stairs into her bedroom.

Her dress shuffles with every sway of her perfect hips, the view of her body in front of me like a goddamn beacon.

It has been torture watching her move and dance and laugh in that fucking dress all day and not being able to touch her the way I truly want to.

It has been a rough week. Between the revelations of her father and my sister returning home, plus the last-minute wedding prep, we've had little time to spend together. I've seen her at work and around the house, but not being able to hold her and love her the way I need to, the way I do in the dark of night when it's just the two of us, has been excruciating.

As we reach her room, I shut the door behind us, and she spins to face me. Her blue eyes are on fire. She licks her full lips in a way that feels like an invitation, and on instinct, I find myself reaching out to grab her.

Wrapping an arm around her waist, I pull her against me but move behind her so she's at my front, and we're both facing the mirror on the back of her door. I brush her hair away from her shoulder, bringing my mouth to her collarbone.

"You look exquisite in this dress," I murmur, brushing the straps off her shoulders, feeling goosebumps rise across her flesh. "Breathtaking."

Her head falls back against my chest, eyes fluttering shut. "Thank y—"

"I'm going to take it off you now."

"Oh," she whimpers, eyes falling open to meet mine in the mirror, hooded and laced with lust. Her chest heaves, and I wonder if her heart is thrashing against her ribs the same way mine is.

Dahlia nods, and I bring my hand to the center of her back, taking hold of the zipper on her dress. My knuckles drag along her bare skin as I slowly pull it down, opening her body to me. The dress falls off her shoulders, and she lets it fall to the floor, pooling at her feet.

She's standing in front of me now in nothing but a strapless white bra and a pair of matching panties—the same set she was wearing on her birthday—and I twist the clasp on her bra, letting that fall to the floor too. Torturously slow, I run my hands down her sides, brushing my thumbs across each one of her nipples, eliciting a moan from her. Dipping my fingers into the waistband of her underwear, I tug them down to her mid-thighs, and she shimmies them the rest of the way off until they join her dress on the floor.

"Exquisite," I whisper, pressing my lips to her neck. "Breathtaking."

"Everett," she moans, lifting her arm to wrap her hand around my nape.

I run my hands up and down the length of her beautiful body, and she watches me do so in the mirror with utmost confidence—confidence she didn't have before. I know every day will look different, and some will be better than others, but I take pride in knowing that—at least right now—I might've helped her see the beauty in herself that has always been there, beauty she was blind to before I showed it to her.

She spins, smiling wickedly at me as she presses against my chest and sends me falling back onto the edge of her bed. "Your turn," she rasps, pulling at the buckle of my belt and making quick work of getting my slacks off my legs.

Once they're gone, she sends me moving backward on her bed until I'm sitting up against the headboard, and she straddles my hips. Her delicate fingers work away at the buttons of my dress shirt, popping them open one by one.

I know the moment she sees it as she tugs my shirt off my arms. She gasps, movements halting and hands flying to cover her mouth. Her eyes slowly drag from my chest to my face, growing wide as she takes in the tattoo August finished earlier this week. "Everett," she whispers, one hand slowly lowering to my chest, softly brushing across the ink there. "When did you—"

"The night I got back from New York. Leo and I went to see August while you and Darby were asleep. I'd been thinking about it for a long while before that, though." She shakes her head, tracing the dahlias that spread wide over my peck and up to my shoulder. "You're my compass, Wildflower," I repeat the words I said to her weeks ago. "You're where I find home."

Her bottom lip trembles, gaze meeting mine and glistening with emotion as she spreads her palm across the entire tattoo—right over my heart. It's a compass, needle pointing southwest, because that's the direction she was going when she came to find me. Nestled behind it are orange dahlias, a cluster of other wildflowers accented within them.

She tilts her head as she studies it further, a finger outlining the golden thread that wraps around the compass, weaving between the petals of the flowers. "What is this?" she asks.

"Our invisible string. Our thread of gold. Our light. *Nuestra luz*."

I watch her brows pinch together, watch the realization dawn on her. Dahlia's mouth drops open as she inhales sharply, and suddenly, tears are pouring from her bright eyes. I lean up, taking her face between my hands and kissing them away. Moving across her nose and cheeks, I make my way to her mouth and feather my lips against hers, moving softly.

"She's my light," I whisper. "And you're all my colors, Wildflower."

"Everett." She wraps her arms around my neck, kissing me harder. "You know that's permanent, right?" I feel her smile softly against my mouth.

"I love you permanently."

She pulls away, looking down at me with astonished eyes, brushing her hand along my jaw, as if she's checking to ensure I'm truly here. She doesn't respond, though. Instead, she surges forward, kissing me fervently.

I moan into her mouth, and she slips her tongue into mine. We're a clash of lips and breath and need. I knot my hands into her hair, and she runs her nails down my back. Our bodies flush together, but it's not enough. A primal urge to be closer—to be entwined—overcomes me, and I'm hardening beneath her legs, feeling her soft skin brush against my most sensitive area.

I let out a groan, and she returns it with a twin sound. “You’re mine.”

“Fuck,” I rasp. “Yes. Yours.”

She pulls away, lifting her hips and reaching between us. I hiss as her soft hand comes in contact with my cock, pumping me from base to tip. She licks her lips, pulling her bottom one between her teeth. Breathing hard, she whispers again, “You’re mine?”

“You own me, baby,” I grit out as she fists me once more. She swipes my head through her slit, so unbelievably wet. “Mind.” I grip my base as she removes her hand, keeping my cock in place. “Body,” I groan as she seats herself fully.

Her breath hitches as she adjusts to the fullness of having me inside her. She places her palms at the center of my chest, right over the tattoo at my heart. I grip her hips with both my hands and slowly lift her before dropping her back down.

We let out a simultaneous moan at the joining of our bodies.

“Soul,” I rasp, rocking her against me again. “I love you, Dahlia.”

Wildflower

“I love you, Dahlia.” His voice is rough and raw, eyes wild as he watches me ride him. Sensation soars through my body, sparks lighting along my skin as I move atop him, feeling him so deeply inside me that he may just be woven into the fabric of my being.

His name written across my soul.

I drop my face, pressing our foreheads together. Sharing breath, I watch his eyes flare with every meeting of our flesh. He tightens his hold on my hips, snaking a hand around my backside to grasp my ass and move me faster.

“Fuck me like you own me, Dahlia,” he whimpers into my mouth. “Because you do.”

I move quicker, and he lifts his hips to meet my thrusts,

the sound of our joining echoing through the silent space, only accented by our rapid breathing and whispered words. Pleasure coils in my center, growing taut and tight, heat building and begging to break.

"I love you," he repeats, lips moving against mine. "I love you so loud. I love you permanently." His mouth moves along my jaw. "I love you all the time." He peppers kisses along my neck, and I feel the sensation—our connection—from the place his mouth rests to the very tips of my toes and back up again. Stars dance behind my vision as I near that peak. "You're tattooed across my chest, etched into my bones," he whispers. "You've unraveled me, and..." His words have me spiraling toward release, my hips moving on their own accord, forcing us faster and harder and more powerful. "And...*fuck*. I love you. I love you."

Those words—his voice, and his hands, and his touch—have my climax ripping through me. My head falls back, baring my neck to him as he latches onto it. I cry out his name, feeling my body tighten and break atop him. My release floods from me, fireworks exploding in my mind and blurring my vision, my body clinging to him as I ride it out, feeling every piece of my soul fracture and piece itself back together.

"I love you, Everett." The words fly from my mouth on a moan.

Words I've rarely said before and never felt the way they do at this moment. They've been something I've always deemed impossible to say, but now, they come out effortlessly. I wonder if love has only ever felt unreachable because I was saving it all for him.

"Dahlia," he pants, eyes flying open. I feel him pulsate inside me, chest heaving as he looks at me with an infinity of emotion behind his amber eyes. "Say it again."

"I love you," I whisper, rolling my hips and kissing his jaw.

"Fuck." He thrusts up into me, cock twitching and sending a tremor through my core. "Baby, I'm going to—"

"Come inside me," I beg, grinding down onto him and

removing any semblance of space between our bodies. "Please, Everett. I need to feel you."

He grips my hips hard enough to bruise, eyes on mine. I watch his throat move as a moan tears through it, his cock swelling and pulsing once more before a soft groan leaves his lips. Warmth floods my body, filling me up with the final throb of his release.

Our chests press together, heartbeats pounding like twin drums. He holds my face, smiling up at me with deep, raw, all-consuming love in his gaze, and I can only hope I'm looking at him the same.

He wraps a hand around my neck, pulling me into him and kissing me hard. Grasping my waist with his other arm, he holds me tightly as he flips us over so I lay on my back. We both groan as he slowly pulls out, sitting on his knees in front of me with his gaze glued between my legs.

He licks his lips, brushing his hand across my leg to the apex of my thighs. I shiver at his touch as he dips a finger inside me, stuffing me back full of the release that began to leak out. "That's beautiful," he whispers, shaking his head. "Fuck. I love the look of that."

Butterflies erupt in my stomach, and I'm pounding with arousal once more.

"Do...do you want kids?" I find myself blurting.

His eyes snap to mine, and with the utmost seriousness, he asks, "Do you mean more kids?"

"Yeah," I respond breathlessly, my heart flying out of my chest. "More kids."

He nods, eyes dark and hazed with passion and fervor. "With you, yes." Swiping a finger through my center again and smearing his release between my legs, he asks, "Do you?"

"Yes," I say immediately. "I always have. I always wanted her to have siblings. I know at this point...she's so much older, it won't be like what I had with mine but...I'd like to give her someone."

Everett smiles, lying down beside me and wrapping me into his arms. My head falls into his chest, right over the tattoo he got for me. For us. Emotion pricks at my eyes again as I nuzzle against him, savoring his warmth.

"Then we'll give her someone. Multiple someones." His thumb moves in soothing circles along the bare skin of my shoulder, and he plants a kiss into my hair. "But you two will need to move in first, of course."

"What?" I gasp, lifting onto my elbow to look at him.

"Move in with me, Wildflower." He flashes me his wicked grin. "You keep talking about how you need to find a place, and I've got one. She'll have her own room, a backyard to play in." His eyes are pleading and hopeful, and he lifts his chin to brush his mouth along my jaw. "We know we're end game. We know we're a family. Don't make me go another goddamn night without having you in my bed. Please."

"How do you think Lou will feel about it?"

"I have a feeling she'll be elated. I have a feeling she'll ask us why it took so long." He laughs. "We can talk to her tomorrow, and if she shows the slightest ounce of hesitation, we can pump the brakes for a while, but I'm not too worried about it."

I look at him, seeing my whole world staring back at me. The easiest answer I've ever given falls from my lips when I say, "Yes. Let's do it."

Everett smiles, taking my face between his hands and pressing a kiss to my nose. "You love me?" he asks.

"I love you permanently," I whisper into the night.

"Permanently," he whispers back, kissing me again.

Forty-Seven – Wildflower

The Wicked Wildflower

"Wake up, Wildflower."

Warm, delicate, soft kisses trail down my neck, stirring me from sleep. I hum, turning into the source of that strong body and light voice.

There's a musical laugh before those lips find my head. "C'mon, baby."

"Why?" I groan into his chest, not yet ready to leave the bed.

I don't know what time it is, but I know we were up into the early hours of this morning, getting entirely lost in each other. I know we'll have to go pick up Lou soon and talk to her about moving in with Everett, and he's going to have to have a conversation with Elena about it, too, since she's staying with him indefinitely.

Not to mention, the aftermath of everything that went down with my father, and the fact that I haven't even begun to really process the conversation I had with my mom. We got a text from Ryan late last night after the reception, confirming that an expedited warrant had been issued due to the severity of his charges and the evidence against him—thanks to me. My father has likely already been taken in.

Highest priority on my list is to find both Darby and me a really good fucking therapist, because we've got some heavy shit to work through. But first, I just want to lie in bed with Everett for a few more minutes.

"Surf lessons, Dal."

"I told Lou not until school is out for the summer."

I feel his chest rumble beneath his laugh. "Not for Lou. For you."

I crack an eye open, glaring up at him. "Excuse me?"

"You once said you wished you could learn to surf." He's smiling down at me, obnoxiously chipper for this early in the day. "So, I'm going to teach you."

"I didn't mean it like that." I yawn, sitting up. "I meant it like if I was interested in surfing, I'd love to have the option to learn, but I'm too busy. So, if I was interested, which I'm not, I wouldn't even have the ability to take lessons, even though I don't want to."

He pops a brow. "Let's go. Everyone has to surf at least once in their life."

"Who made that rule?" I ask, watching him step out of bed, naked as the day he was born, and stretch. I'm fairly certain I have a Pavlovian response to this man's cock. He puts it in front of me, and I'm instantly salivating.

He smiles, watching my reaction to his body on display. "I think it's written into the constitution of California, so if you plan on staying here, you better get your ass up." A half hour later, we're standing in the sand at the base of the cove beneath the cliff. The sun is still rising behind us, painting the Pacific in soft blue as golden light glistening off the white caps. The sky above it expands endlessly in shades of lavender and fuchsia.

"I can't believe I get to live here," I find myself saying, the morning breeze brushing against my cheeks like a kiss, the rustling of palm leaves like music.

"I can't believe I get to keep you," Everett responds, eyes on me rather than the horizon. "If we stay to the left side of the cove, the cliffs create a barrier so the water is calmer. I'll take you out with me."

He holds one of Leo's surfboards in one arm, my hand in the other, leading me out to the waves. Once we're knee deep in the water, he beckons me to climb onto the board and straddle it with a leg dangling off either side. I watch it weave around my limbs as he pulls the board into deeper water, the shade of the ocean deepening the farther we go.

It's a calm, quiet morning, the board rocking comfortably beneath me in the current. Once we're past the break and Everett is about chest-deep, he stops. "Lean to the opposite side of me as I climb on, okay?"

I nod, and the board rocks, water rippling as he presses up onto it and throws one of his legs over the side. With the land at my back, Everett and I face each other, the sun shining across his beautiful face and setting his eyes on fire.

"So, this is surfing?" I ask.

"No, this is floating." He smirks as he shrugs. "But it's a good enough start."

I kick my feet back and forth beneath the water, the chill of it biting against my legs but not completely unbearable.

"This is everything I could've asked for, anyway." I smile, feeling nothing but peace and contentment in this moment.

We sit in comfortable silence for some time, listening to the sound of the waves around us, feeling the warmth of the rising sun and the whistling of the wind, when Everett asks, "Have you given any thought to a name for the coffee shop? We want to get started before summer."

"Yeah." I feel my lips quirk up at the corners. "I've thought of a name."

He raises his brows. "Well?"

"I was thinking of Wildflower," I say. Everett smiles, opening his mouth to respond, but I cut him off before he can. "But I decided it needed something more, something representative of the person who inspired me to take the leap."

He cocks his head.

I dip my head, feeling suddenly bashful. "The Wicked Wildflower... I thought that could be a good name."

That smile becomes a wide grin as he reaches around to grasp my neck and pull me into him. "I'm Wicked?"

I nod, feeling his lips against my nose.

"You're Wildflower?"

"So you say." I lift my chin so my mouth brushes against his.

His grin spreads against my lips. "The Wicked Wildflower. That's fucking perfect."

As he kisses me against the backdrop of the Pacific and beneath the early morning sunshine, I finally find a way to describe the feeling of being with him, in his arms, the sensation I've never been able to put a name to because I've never experienced it before.

Something inside my soul begins to bloom, like it finally found its destination, the spot to plant its roots. *Home.*

Epilogue – Wicked

All My Reasons to Breathe

One Year Later

"Wildflower!" I call out, stepping into the kitchen.

"Back here," she chimes. I move through the double doors to the back of the café, where I find her rolling dough. Hands are covered in flour, orange apron wrapped around her frame, hair pulled back into a bun. She lifts her head, smiling at me as she continues to work.

"Hi, babe." I kiss her quickly before stepping away, not wanting to compromise the food she's making.

I move to the corner of the room, pulling out a barstool. "Luz isn't here yet?"

Dahlia shakes her head. "No. Bus should be dropping her any minute, though."

When Lou started her last year of elementary school, we decided to allow her to take the bus home, since there is a stop just across the street from the boardwalk. I spend my mornings at the garage, managing Ramos Automotive, and moved back into my old office above Heathen's, where I work in the afternoons. That way, I can end my day with Dahlia at the bakery, and the three of us can go home together.

"You've got everything ready to go for next week?" I ask as we wait for our daughter.

"Yeah." She nods. "Elena's going to act as manager while we're gone, and Peggy will be here for the bakery."

Elena, by all appearances, is doing better since she began working at The Wicked Wildflower and she moved out of my house. I know she's not writing still, though. I think her inability to create stories continues to eat her alive, and I can only hope that, one day, she'll find it again.

Peggy is a pastry chef Dahlia hired to assist with bakery operations, and together, the two of them have masterminded several unique recipes that have people traveling from all around the region to get their hands on.

I'm the lucky bastard who gets my hands on Dahlia's goods as often as I want.

Dahlia has worked tirelessly the past year to get The Wicked Wildflower up and running, and it has become a smashing success—not without its early mornings, late nights, and a fuck ton of stress, though. That, paired with her father's sentencing earlier this year, which was hard on both Dahlia and Darby—especially in the final stage of Darby's pregnancy—meant Dahlia needed a break.

As a surprise, I spent the last several months secretly rebuilding an old school bus I bought off a friend, Tyler. I presented her with it last month and told her about my plan to take the summer off so she, Lou, and I could drive up and down the West Coast, exploring like she always imagined. It was tough to convince her to let the bakery go for two months, since this place has become like another child to her, but this summer may be our last chance to make it happen for a while.

Once she was finally swayed, we decided to take off when Lou finishes her school year next week, with plans to return early August, since that's Pacific Shores' busiest month of the year. I have no doubt that our businesses will be in the safest of hands with our family.

Once we return, our primary goal will be filling the final empty unit on the boardwalk, the one between The Wicked

Wildflower and August's tattoo parlor on the other end, with the hopes to have the boardwalk completely full by next summer.

"Mom?" Lou's sweet, soft voice floats through the kitchen as she swings open the doors.

"Hi, bug." She smiles. "How was school?"

"Good," she says, tossing her backpack onto the counter and sliding onto the stool beside me. "Hey, Everett."

"Hi, Luz." I plant a kiss on the top of her hair.

"Let me finish prepping for the morning crew, and then we can head home."

"Take your time, Wildflower." I wave her off, turning to our kid. "What'd you do today?"

I notice Lou looks a little bashful as she pulls her bag toward her. "I actually made you something," she says quietly.

"Made me something?" I ask dramatically. "How special am I?"

She smiles softly, digging through her bag. "We had a free craft day in art class since it's Friday, and I made bracelets. I know we already have a ton from the Taylor Swift concert, but I wanted to make one for you too."

"Did you make one for me?" Dahlia asks.

"No."

"Rude," she scoffs dramatically.

Lou rolls her eyes at her mom before glancing up at me shyly. "You know how I gave you like one hundred cool nicknames, and you said no to all of them?"

"Haven't found the right one yet." I shrug.

"Well..." She bites her lip, grabbing my wrist and laying it on the table in front of us. "My teacher was talking today about how Father's Day is coming up, and everyone was making little gifts for their dads..." She pulls something out of her bag, hesitantly slipping it onto my wrist. "I thought... Well, I thought maybe this nickname could work."

She looks up at me with uncertainty written in her eyes.

I glance down at the bracelet, a pattern of blue beads and

little orange flowers—a mixture of mine and Dahlia's favorite colors. In the middle of my wrist are three small letters: D-A-D.

I let out some kind of noise, though I'm not even sure what. My heart is so full, I feel like it's ripping right out of my chest. Emotion immediately pricks at my eyes, and my nose stings as I try and fail to hold it back. I swallow the lump in my throat, but my voice is thick as I say, "That's a good one, kid. I like that one a lot."

She smiles at me, so much hope in her gaze. "You do?"

I fold her against my chest, cradling her head. "Yeah." I inhale sharply as I'm overcome with that emotion, tears leaking down my cheeks. "I think that's the best thing anyone has ever called me."

I catch Dahlia across the kitchen looking at us with concern. Silently, because words are lost on me completely, I hold my wrist up so she can see the bracelet. She squints, face falling as she makes out the word scrawled in the center of it.

A hand flies to her mouth, quiet tears cascading down her cheeks too.

I extend my hand, beckoning her to me. She drops her rolling pin and rounds the counter, pressing her lips to her daughter's head and throwing her arms around us both.

I spent most of my life going through the motions, having no idea which direction I was headed. All I wanted was a purpose, one that made me feel like there was something worth working toward, something to live for.

I slide my hand down Dahlia's side, then spread my palm across her middle. With them in my arms, it's like I've found everything I've always needed and didn't realize I'd been searching for. It was right here, wrapped up in them.

All my reasons to breathe, my entire world.

My home.

Everett & Dahlia's Playlist

West Coast | Lana Del Rey
Rollercoaster | Bleachers
Glitch | Taylor Swift
Sparks | Coldplay
Young And Beautiful | Lana Del Rey
Delicate | Taylor Swift
Wild Heart | Bleachers
Rocket | Beyonce
Say Yes To Heaven | Lana Del Rey
Snow On The Beach | Taylor Swift
Wicked Games | The Weeknd
peace | Taylor Swift
Swim | Chase Atlantic
First Light | Hozier
invisible string | Taylor Swift
Wildflower | Thomas Day
My Home | Myles Smith
Endgame | Taylor Swift
Falling In Love | Cigarettes After Sex
Isimo | Bleachers
All I Need To Hear | The 1975

Acknowledgments

I don't even know where to start with this one, honestly. With every single book I write, my list of those to acknowledge for standing beside me continues to grow, and while my wrists are sore and my eyes are tired, I couldn't be more grateful to be spending these extra moments thanking those who support me so fiercely.

My husband, Bubs: There are so many things in life I'm grateful for, but number one on that list is undoubtedly the fact that I did not have to wait my whole life to love you. It's unbelievable to me that I was able to stumble upon you at sixteen and had the ability to hang on tight when everything else in life felt so fleeting. Being young and dumb with you was the time of my life, but I think I'm enjoying being old and boring with you even more. Thank you for showing me what love looks like, and for being patient with me when I have trouble loving myself. Thank you for showing me what it feels like to find home.

Jenna: You've hands down become the biggest champion for this book, and I don't know if I'd have gotten here without you. You're always the first person I bounce ideas off of, and the person I rely on when I need honesty, support, and to dump a twenty minute voice note. You treat my characters like their real people, and you love them as deeply as I do, and I don't have words to describe what it means to me to have you in my corner. You may be my content creator and my brand manager, and I may not make it through the day without you, but my favorite thing that you are to me is my friend.

Emily and Lexi: You both have been the biggest hand holders through the many, many, many mental breakdowns this book gave me. Emily, when you called me and jumped on the doc at eleven o'clock at night to help me research white collar crime and legal loopholes. Lexi, for so enthusiastically loving Everett and Dahlia (and Macie) and for helping keep the love of this book alive when I was doubting it. I love you and I don't know what I would do without you or the skin of a killer, bella.

My agent, Dani, and SBR Media: For helping this series reach places I never dreamed they could go.

The Page & Vine Team: For taking a chance on my little universe and bringing it to stores all over the world. You make me feel like the luckiest author alive.

The incredible indie bookstores and small businesses who have supported me and this series so loudly: Wildflower Fiction, Scribbles Bookshop, The Bubbly Bookshelf, Jadestone Creates, and Well Read Candle Co.

Luna Literary Management: You've taken so much pressure off my shoulders when it comes to the ARC process, and so many new readers have found this story because of you. I've had so much fun working with you!

My editor, Alexa: You make my books so much more beautiful than they could ever be without you, but you're so much more than an editor to me. You're quite literally the definition of the word Mother, but you're also a champion for my stories, and for me as an author. Thank you for always having my back, always looking out, and always making me feel like I belong

My beta team: Sarah, Jasmine, Melanie, Molli, and Taylor. Thank you for handling the early version of this story with grace, for your valuable feedback, and for being as feral over Everett as I am! This story wouldn't be what it is without you.

Ambar Cordova: Thank you for being a friend, vent, and critique partner, and for helping me perfect Everett's dirty little trilingual mouth.

My street team: I love you, my horny little gremlins. Thank you for your endless love and excitement over these figments of my imagination. You keep me going most days, and I couldn't be more thankful for your support.

Some of the mothers in my life that helped inspire this story: My mom, my mother-in-law, my best friend, Lauren, and my step-mom.

Also, Kes, Lilly, and Julie because I wouldn't be able to write sisterhood if I didn't have you.

About the Author

Sarah fell in love with reading as a child. She quickly learned that books can take her to all the places she always dreamed of going, and allow her to live endless lifetimes in the one that she was given.

Sarah believes that to be seen is to be loved, and that's why romance is such an important genre. She believes romance novels offer readers reflection and relatability, ultimately helping us understand ourselves, and the world around us, a little better. She prides herself on crafting healing, raw, and uplifting stories that explore the complexities of the human spirit through the guise of love.

Sarah was born in California and raised in Southern Oregon, and still considers herself to be a Pacific Northwest gal at heart; right down to being a coffee snob, collecting hydro flasks, adamantly believing in Sasquatch, and never having owned an umbrella.

She now resides in Arizona with her husband and their pup, Rue. When she's not writing, she's reading, and if she's not reading, she's probably out searching for a decent cup of coffee or binging Vanderpump Rules for the millionth time.

Connect with Sarah on social media: @sarahabaileyauthor

Sign up for her newsletter to be the first to know about updates and announcements: sarahabaileyauthor.com/newsletter

reckless
ROSES
A Pacific Shores Novel

SARAH A. BAILEY

Reckless Roses

COMING FALL 2025

For Augustus Hayes, first love was instantaneous. From the moment he found her scaling a tree in his yard, plucking purple flowers from its branches, August knew his heart belonged to Elena Ramos. Elena had the exact same experience; about August's older brother, Zach, that is. Deciding he'd rather have her as a friend than nothing at all, August ferments himself in Elena's friend zone, unable to let go of the hope that someday, she'll choose him.

Elena Ramos has always romanticized the world around her. Chalk it up to her writer's soul or her passion for romance novels, but she believes whole-heartedly in young love. Anyone can do it right the first time, if only they refuse to give up. At least, that's what she tells herself each time her on-again off-again relationship with Zach Hayes begins to feel more like a nightmare than a daydream. After nearly a decade, they call it quits for good, and her best friend steps in to fix her broken pieces. Only then does Elena realize how blind she's been to the person standing in front of her all this time.

Just as Elena and August decide to transform their friendship into something more, an unimaginable tragedy strikes them both. Will a lifetime of falling in love be enough to hold them together when their entire world falls apart?

vice &
VIOLET

A Pacific Shores Novel

SARAH A. BAILEY

Vice & Violet

COMING FALL 2025

Elena Ramos had always set a clear path for her future. She knew exactly what she wanted out of life, and was determined to find the kind of happily ever after she loved to write about. Until the most devastating of tragedies turned her entire world on its axis. Plagued with irreparable pain and guilt, the finality of this heartbreak feels impossible to recover from, sending Elena into a dark spiral she doesn't know how to escape.

Augustus Hayes considered himself a dreamer. Meaning, he forced himself into the contentment of dreaming up a reality that'd never be his. That is, until a door leading to the love affair of a lifetime opened, and he found himself grasping for the handle. But when the worst possible consequences for his choices came crashing down around him, he lost sight of everything he'd ever known.

There is only one person who can pull August and Elena from their respective depths of despair, but are their wounds too deep, and their secrets too dark for either of them to find the courage to be the other's light?

PAGE
&
VINE